storm glass

'We have a mission for you,' Zitora explained. She had twisted her honey-brown hair into a complex braid. The end of the braid reached her hips, but she fidgeted with it, twirling it around and through her fingers.

A mission from the Masters! I leaned forward.

'The Stormdancers' glass orbs have been shattering,' Master Jewelrose said.

'Oh.' I relaxed in my chair. Not a magical mission.

'Do you know how important these orbs are, child?' Master Bloodgood asked.

I remembered my lessons about the Stormdancer Clan. Their magicians—called Stormdancers—had the unique ability to siphon a storm's energy into an orb, taming the storm's killing winds and rain, and providing an energy source for the clan.

But why me? I was still learning. 'You need a master glass-maker. My father—'

'Time is of the essence, child.' Master Bloodgood's tone saddened. 'When an orb shatters, it kills a Stormdancer.'

Also by New York Times bestselling author
Maria V. Snyder

The Chronicles of Ixia

POISON STUDY
MAGIC STUDY
FIRE STUDY
STORM GLASS
SEA GLASS
SPY GLASS

The Insider series

INSIDE OUT
OUTSIDE IN

Avry of Kazan series

TOUCH OF POWER
SCENT OF MAGIC

www.miraink.co.uk

storm glass

MARIA V. SNYDER

Published in Great Britain 2011. This edition 2013.
MIRA Books, Eton House, 18-24 Paradise Road,
Richmond, Surrey, TW9 1SR

© Maria V. Snyder 2009

ISBN 978 1 848 45246 6

58-0913

MIRA Ink's policy is to use papers that are natural, renewable and recyclable products and made from wood grown in sustainable forests. The logging and manufacturing processes conform to the legal environmental regulations of the country of origin.

Printed and bound by
CPI Group (UK) Ltd, Croydon, CR0 4YY

THE TERRITORY OF IXIA

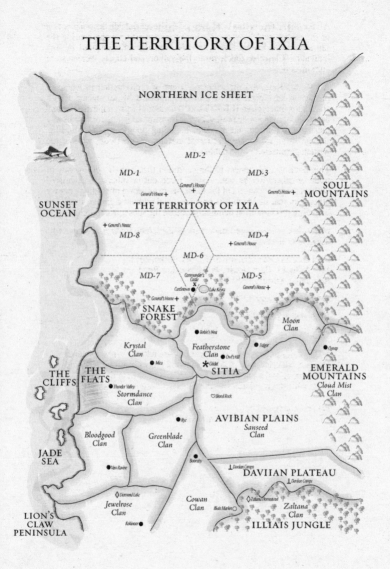

NORTHERN ICE SHEET

MD-2

MD-1

MD-3

SOUL
MOUNTAINS

General's House
General's House

THE TERRITORY OF IXIA

SUNSET
OCEAN

General's House

MD-8

MD-4

General's House

MD-6

MD-7

MD-5

Commander's
Castle
Castletown
Lake Keys
General's House

General's House

SNAKE
FOREST

Robin's Nest

Moon
Clan

Krystal
Clan

Featherstone
Clan
Owl's Hill
Fulgor

Cytop

Mica
Citidel
SITIA

THE
CLIFFS

THE
FLATS

Thunder Valley

EMERALD
MOUNTAINS
Cloud Mist
Clan

Stormdance
Clan

Blood Rock

AVIBIAN PLAINS
Sanseed
Clan

JADE
SEA

Bloodgood
Clan

Greenblade
Clan

Rye

Booruby

Davian Camps

DAVIIAN PLATEAU

Vine Ravine

Davian Camps

LION'S
CLAW
PENINSULA

Diamond Lake

Jewelrose
Clan

Cowan
Clan

Illiais Market
Zaltana Homestead

Zaltana
Clan

Kolinoor

ILLIAIS JUNGLE

To my sister, Karen Philips, for all the
advice, support and good times (BFF).
This book has a definite sister vibe!

THE HOT AIR pressed against my face as I entered the glass factory. The heat and the smell of burning coal surrounded me in a comforting embrace. I paused to breathe in the thick air. The roar of the kilns sounded as sweet as my mother's voice.

"Opal!" Aydan yelled above the noise. "Are you going to stand there all day? We have work to do." He gestured with a thin gnarled hand.

I hurried to join him. Working in the heat had turned his gray hair into a frizzy mop. Dirt streaked his hands. He grimaced in pain when he sat at his workbench, rubbing his lower back with a fist.

"You've been shoveling coal again," I admonished. He tried to look innocent, but before he could lie, I asked, "What happened to your apprentice?"

"Ran off once he figured out how hard it is to turn fire into ice." Aydan grunted.

"Well, I'm here now."

"You're late."

"Sorry, I had a...test." I sighed. Another frustrating, fruitless endeavor. Not only had I failed to light the fire, but I knocked over the candles, spilling hot wax all over my classmate Pazia's clothes and burning her skin. Her expensive silk tunic was ruined. She sneered in disdain when I offered to replace her shirt. Nothing new. Pazia's hostility spanned my entire four years at the Keep. Why would I expect my last year to be any different?

After starting my fifth year of lessons at the Magician's Keep, I had hoped to be able to do more with my magic. Pazia's abilities had grown so much since we sat next to each other during our very first session that the Master Magicians considered allowing her to take the Master-level test.

I'd learned about Sitia's history, politics, how to fight and about the uses for magic, but my ability to tap into the power source remained elusive. Doubts flared and the nagging feeling of being limited to one magical skill churned in my chest. And it didn't help my confidence when I overheard my fellow students calling me the One-Trick Wonder.

"Jealousy," Aydan had said when I told him about my nickname. "You saved Sitia."

I thought of the day—over four years ago—when I helped Liaison Yelena capture those evil souls. She had done all the work, I was merely a conduit. I tried to downplay my involvement, but Aydan remained stubborn.

"You're a hero and those children can't stand it."

Remembering his words made me smile. Calling fifteen to twenty-year-olds children was typical for Aydan, a proud curmudgeon.

He tapped my arm with a blowpipe. "Stop daydreaming and gather me a slug."

I grabbed the hollow rod and opened the oven. Intense light burst from the furnace as if a piece of the sun was trapped inside. I spun the end of the rod in the molten glass and twisted it up and out, removing taffylike ball before my eyebrows and eyelashes could be singed off again.

The cherry-red slug on the end of the iron pulsed as if alive. Aydan blew through the pipe then covered the hole. A small bubble appeared in the molten glass. Resting the pipe on the metal arms of his gaffer's bench, Aydan rolled the pipe back and forth, shaping the glass.

I helped him as he created an intricate vase with a twist at the bottom so the piece actually rested on its side yet could still hold water. In his hands, turning glass into art appeared to be an easy task. I loved the unique properties of molten glass which could be molded into such wonderful objects. We worked for hours, but the time flew.

When he finished his artwork, Aydan stood on creaky legs and said the words that were the reason I came to help him after my Keep classes. "Your turn."

He exchanged places with me and grabbed a hollow pipe. While he gathered a slug, I made sure all the metal tools lying on the bench were in their proper places. All I needed was my annoying younger brother telling me to hurry, and my patient older sister helping me to complete the feeling of being in my family's glass factory.

Sitting at the bench was home—familiar and comfortable. Here and here alone, I was in control. The possibilities endless and no one could tell me otherwise.

All thoughts fled when Aydan placed the pipe in front of me. Glass cooled quickly and I had no time to dwell on anything but shaping the molten ball. Using metal tweezers, I pulled and plucked. When the slug transformed into a recognizable image, I blew through the end of the pipe. The piece's core glowed as if lit by an inner fire.

My one magical trick—the ability to insert a thread of magic inside the glass statue. Only magicians could see the captured light.

Aydan whistled in appreciation of the finished piece. Technically his ability to light fires with magic made him a magician, but since he didn't possess any other talent he hadn't been invited to study at the Keep. I shouldn't have been invited, either. I could make my special glass animals at my home in Booruby.

"Damn, girl." Aydan slapped me on the back. "That's a dead-on copy of Master Jewelrose's red-tailed hawk! Did you make that for her?"

"Yes. She needed another piece." I never knew what I would create when I sat down at the gaffer's bench, but my time spent helping Master Jewelrose care for her hawk must have influenced me. The core glowed bright red and called to me with a song of longing. Each of my creations had a distinctive voice that sounded inside me. No one else could hear its call.

"See? That's another talent you have." He bustled about and placed the hawk into the annealing oven so it could cool slowly. "Magicians can now communicate over vast distances with these animals of yours."

"Only those who have the power of mental communication." Another skill I lacked, mind reading. For those who possessed the ability, they only needed to hold one of my animals and they could "talk" to each other through the magic trapped inside. I'd admit to feeling a measure of pride over their usefulness, but I would never brag about it. Not like Pazia, who flaunted everything she did.

"Pah! It's still one of the most important discoveries of recent years. Stop being so modest. Here—" he handed me a shovel "—put more coal in the kiln, I don't want the temperature to drop overnight."

End of pep talk. I scooped up the special white coal and added it to the fire under the kiln. Since Aydan sold his glass pieces as art, he only needed one—a small shop compared to my family's eight kilns.

When I finished, my garments clung to my sweaty skin and strands of my brown hair stuck to my face. Coal dust scratched my throat.

"Can you help me mix?" Aydan asked before I could leave.

"Only if you promise to hire a new apprentice tomorrow."

He grumbled and grouched, but agreed. We mixed sands from different parts of Sitia. A secret recipe developed generations ago. It would be combined with soda ash and lime before it could be melted into glass.

As I tried to trick Aydan into telling me where the pink-colored sand came from, a messenger from the Keep arrived. A first-year student, he wrinkled his nose at the heat.

"Opal Cowan?" he asked.

I nodded and he huffed. "Finally! I've been searching the Citadel for you. You're wanted back at the Keep."

"Why?"

"I don't know."

"Who wants me?"

He glowed with glee as if he were my younger brother delivering news of my impending punishment from our parents.

"The Master Magicians."

I had to be in big trouble. No other reason for the Masters to send for me. As I rushed after the messenger—an ambitious fellow to be running errands for the Masters in his first year, and who'd already decided I wasn't worth talking to—I thought of the mishap this morning with Pazia. She had wanted to get me expelled from my first day. Perhaps she finally succeeded.

We hurried through the Citadel's streets. Even after four years, the city's construction still amazed me. All the buildings had been built with white marble slabs streaked with green veins. If I was alone, I would have trailed my hands over the walls as I walked, daydreaming of creating a city made of glass.

Instead, I ran past the buildings as the brilliant color dulled with the darkening sky. The Keep's guards waved us through—another bad sign. We vaulted up the stairs two at a time to reach the administration building. Nestled in the northeast corner of the Citadel, the Keep's campus with its four imposing towers marked the boundaries. Inside, the buildings had been constructed from a variety of colored marble and hardwoods.

The administration's peach-and-yellow blocks used to soothe me, but not today. The messenger abandoned me at the entrance to the Masters' meeting room. Hot from my sprint, I wanted to remove my cloak, but it hid my sweat-stained shirt and work pants. I rubbed my face, trying to get the dirt off and pulled my long hair into a neat bun.

Before I knocked, another possible reason for my summons dawned. I had lingered too long at the glass factory and missed my evening riding lesson. In the last year of instruction at the Keep, the apprentice class learned about horse care and riding to prepare us for when we graduated to magician status. As magicians we would be required to travel around the lands of the eleven clans of Sitia to render aid where needed.

Perhaps the Stable Master had reported my absence

to the Masters. The image of facing the three magicians and the Stable Master together caused a chill to shake my bones. I turned away from the door, seeking escape. It opened.

"Do not hover about, child. You're not in trouble," First Magician Bain Bloodgood said. He gestured for me to follow him into the room.

With curly gray hair sticking out at odd intervals and a long blue robe, the old man's appearance didn't match his status as the most powerful magician in Sitia. In fact, Third Magician Irys Jewelrose's stern demeanor hinted at more power than Master Bloodgood's wrinkled face. And if someone passed Second Magician Zitora Cowan in the street, that person would not even think the young woman possessed enough talent to endure the Master-level test.

Sitting around an oval table, the three Masters stared at me. I quashed the desire to hide. After all, Master Bloodgood had said I wasn't in trouble.

"Sit down, child," First Magician said.

I perched on the edge of my seat. Zitora smiled at me and I relaxed a bit. We were both members of the Cowan clan, and she always made time from her busy schedule to talk to me. And, at twenty-five years old, she was only six years older than me.

I glanced around the room. Maps of Sitia and Ixia decorated the walls, and an oversize geographical map with its edges dropping off the sides covered the mahogany table.

"We have a mission for you," Zitora said. She had twisted her honey-brown hair into a complex braid. The end of the braid reached her hips, but she fidgeted with it, twirling it around and through her fingers.

A mission for the Masters! I leaned forward.

"The Stormdancers' glass orbs have been shattering," Master Jewelrose said.

"Oh." I relaxed in my chair. Not a magical mission.

"Do you know how important those orbs are, child?" Master Bloodgood asked.

I remembered my lessons about the Stormdance Clan. Their magicians—called Stormdancers—had the unique ability to siphon a storm's energy into an orb. The benefits were twofold: tame the storm's killing winds and rain, and provide an energy source for the clan's other industries. "Very important."

"And this is a critical time of the year. The cooling season is when the storms from the Jade Sea are most frequent and strong," Zitora said.

"But doesn't the clan have master glassmakers? Surely they can fix the problem?"

"The old glassmaker died, child. Those left behind were trained to make the orbs, but the glass is flawed. You need to help them find and correct the problem."

Why me? I was still learning. "You need to send a master glassmaker. My father—"

"Is in Booruby with all the other experts, but..." Master Jewelrose paused. "The problem might not be with the glass. Perhaps the old glassmaker used magic when he crafted the orbs. Perhaps magic similar to yours."

My heart melted as if thrown into a kiln. Events had become too hot too quick and the results could have cracks. I had worked with glass since I could remember, yet there was still so much to learn. "When...when do we leave?"

"Today," Zitora said.

My alarm must have been obvious.

"Time is of the essence, child." Master Bloodgood's tone saddened. "When an orb shatters, it kills a Stormdancer."

2

I GAPED AT Master Bloodgood. There weren't many Stormdancers born in the clan; to lose even one could threaten the western clans of Sitia. "How many?"

"Two have died. The first time an orb failed, the clan thought it was a fluke, after the second, they stopped dancing."

A fire of worry flared in my stomach. Just one full-strength storm could wipe out the four clans whose lands bordered the Jade Sea, leaving behind a wasteland. A huge responsibility. Problems with the glass I could probably handle, but with magic... No way.

"Go pack your saddlebags, child. You will leave as soon as you are ready. Zitora will go with you."

"And how many guards will accompany me this time?" She sighed.

The entire population of the Keep knew Zitora's displeasure over being accompanied by guards on her missions. Having only passed the Master-level test five years ago, most magicians still thought of her as an apprentice instead of the second-most-powerful magician. And with the horrible events that led to the death of Roze Featherstone, the former First Magician, the Councillors of Sitia were being overprotective of the three remaining Masters.

"Just the two of you this time," Master Jewelrose said with a smile. "You can move faster."

Zitora stood with a burst of energy. "We'll leave within the hour."

"Contact us if you need help. Opal, have you finished my new glass animal?"

"Yes. It's at Aydan's factory. I think you'll like this one."

"I love them all. It's a shame they lose their spark after a while." Master Jewelrose grew thoughtful. "But it makes sense. The magic inside is a certain quantity. Once used, it's gone."

"Job security for Opal." Master Bloodgood stroked the map in front of him. His gaze settled on me. "We have been searching for another magician to apprentice to you. No luck so far. The Council's been bugging us to share your wonderful glass...messengers."

Right now, I made them for the Masters and for magicians who were on assignment. At least one magician carried one of my glass animals in each town.

"It would be helpful if we could find another able to duplicate her skill." Master Jewelrose agreed.

My skill. Singular. The One-Trick Wonder. I should

be content with providing those messengers for the magicians. Content with my role in life. But I'd seen the wonders magic can do and I wanted more. Magic and glass had so much in common. Both were fluid. Both held endless potential to be shaped and used in various ways. I desired to gather the magic to me and spin it into a marvel.

"Let's go." Zitora strode toward the door and I hurried after her.

She paused when we reached the outside. Darkness blanketed the Keep's campus and the smell of burning wood tainted the air. The empty walkways reflected the weak moonlight. The other students were probably in their rooms, studying and preparing for tomorrow.

"We can get in a couple hours of travel tonight," Zitora said. "Go get a change of clothes and pack a few essential supplies. We'll buy food on the road. I'll meet you in the barn. You have a horse, right?"

"Yes, but I just started my lessons." Another worry.

"Which horse is yours?"

"A painted mare named Quartz."

"The Sandseed bred horse? How did you get so lucky?"

"Yelena was visiting the Keep when the new herd of horses arrived. She told the Stable Master to save Quartz for me."

Zitora laughed. "And Yelena is the only person the Stable Master listens to when it comes to horses. There are hidden perks when you save someone's life."

"But I didn't—"

She waved my protest away with her nimble fingers. It had been thoughtful of Yelena to choose a horse for me, but once the story about her involvement flew through the campus population like sand grains in the wind, I lost the few acquaintances I had to jealousy. Again.

Liaison Yelena was the true hero of Sitia and Ixia. If she talked to a student, the gossips mulled over the implications for weeks.

"Don't worry about not being an expert with a horse. Quartz will follow Sudi. All you need to do is stay in the saddle." She moved to leave, then stopped. "Opal, go visit the armory before you come to the barn."

"Why?"

"It's time to trade in your practice sais for real ones."

"Thirteen inches or fifteen inches?" Captain Marrok, the Keep's new Weapons Master asked with impatience, after I'd grabbed my supplies and cleaned up.

When I didn't respond, he yanked my right arm out and measured my forearm from wrist to elbow.

"Thirteen inches should work." He rummaged around the armory. Swords hung on the walls and spears glinted from racks. Arrows lined up like soldiers, and the odor of metallic sweat and leather filled the air.

I rubbed my forearm, massaging the thick muscles and tracing my burn scars with a finger. One benefit of working with glass, strong arms, but they limited my flexibility when fighting. By the end of my first year, the Weapons Master had decided that, even though I could heft and move a staff of wood like a pontil iron, I was too slow. He made the same assessment of me with a sword and a spear.

I found the sais by accident when I helped clean up after a practice session. They resembled strange short swords, but instead of a flat blade, the weapon's main shaft was thick—about half an inch wide near the hilt and a quarter of an inch at the tip—and rounded yet with eight flat sides. Octagonal, the Weapons Master had called it. Only the tip of the shaft was sharp. He was thrilled I had discovered them, claiming they were the perfect weapon for me as they needed arm strength and hand dexterity.

"Here, try these. If they're too heavy, I'll find you a lighter pair." The Weapons Master handed me two sais, one for each hand. The silver metal shone as if recently polished. The U-shaped guard pointed toward the tip of the weapon so the sais resembled a three-pronged pitchfork with a very long center tine.

I executed a few blocks and strikes to get the feel of the weapons.

"These are heavier than the practice ones," I said.

"Too heavy? I started to add weight to your practice pair, but the Masters are in a rush. That's always the way." He tsked.

"They're fine."

"Practice as often as you can. You might want to cut

bigger slits in your cloak so you can grab them quicker." He hurried over to a large chest in the corner of the armory. Lifting the lid, he sorted through the contents and removed a belt with two short scabbards. "Wear this when you carry them. Horses don't like to be poked with the pointy ends. Not good for your legs, neither."

I thanked him and ran toward the stables. The weight of the weapons hanging from my waist seemed heavier. Would I need to use them? Could I defend myself? This whole mission felt as if I'd been wrenched from a kiln before I could reach the perfect temperature.

In the stables, Zitora helped the Stable Master saddle Quartz. The Stable Master muttered and fussed to no one in particular as he yanked straps and adjusted the reins. In the weak lantern light, Quartz's reddish-brown areas appeared black and the white parts looked gray. She nickered at me in greeting and I stroked her nose. Her face was brown except for a white patch between her eyes.

Already saddled, Sudi, Zitora's roan-colored mare shuffled with impatience.

When the Stable Master handed me Quartz's reins, he said, "You're going to be sore tomorrow and in outright pain by the next day. Stop often to stretch your muscles and rest your back."

"There won't be time," Zitora said as she mounted Sudi.

"Why am I not surprised? Dashing off before she's properly trained is becoming standard procedure around here." The Stable Master shook his head and ranted under his breath. He ambled past the horse stalls, checking water buckets.

"Do you have a Barbasco yam?" Zitora asked. "That'll help with the pain."

"I don't need it. How bad can it be?"

It was bad. And not just regular bad. After three days, the pain was back-wrenching, legs-burning, mind-numbing bad.

Zitora set a killer pace. We only stopped for food, to rest and care for the horses, and to sleep a few hours. Not long enough to wring out the exhaustion soaked into my bones.

Memories of a similar trip threatened my sleep and nagged at me. The night Master Jewelrose had startled me from a deep slumber and hustled me onto her horse before I knew what was happening. I'd clung to her as we bolted for the Citadel. All I had known during that frantic five-day trip, was my sister needed me. Enough knowledge to ignore the pain.

I focused on the Stormdancers' troubles to distract myself. We had left the Citadel through the south gate, headed southwest for a day to reach the border of the Stormdance lands, then turned west. Zitora hoped to arrive at the coast in another three days.

At various times throughout the trip, my worries over the mission had flared, and doubts jabbed my thoughts. If magic was involved, I wouldn't be able to solve the problem and precious time would be wasted.

On the night of our fourth day, we stopped at a market in Thunder Valley. Zitora bought a Barbasco yam for me and managed to hand it over without any gloating. Impressive. My brother would have done an "I told you so" dance for weeks.

The market buzzed with activity. Vendors sold the usual fruits, vegetables and meats, but a strange shrub was heaped on a couple of tables. About three feet tall, the plant's leaves were hairy and separated into leaflets.

"That's indigo," Zitora said when I asked. "It's used to make ink, one of the Stormdance industries. They also make metal goods like those sais you carry."

And they harvested storms. Busy clan.

I chewed on the yam as we hurried through our shopping. I would have enjoyed lingering over the glasswares, but suppressed my disappointment. No sense complaining when exhaustion lined Zitora's heart-shaped face, reminding me this wasn't a pleasure trip. Perhaps we could stop on the way home.

After we secured our fresh supplies to the saddles, we mounted. I braced for the now-familiar jolt of protest from my abused muscles, but was surprised when none came. The yam worked fast.

Amusement lit her pale yellow eyes.

"Thanks for the yam, Zit...er...Master Cowan."

Her humor faded and I berated myself for my slip of the tongue. She had been adamant about the students calling her *Master* Cowan. We all knew her frustration caused by everyone's casual attitude toward her. But she was so sweet. When she noticed me and remembered details about my life, I wanted to confide in her and become her best friend.

She sighed. "Call me Zitora. I shouldn't expect respect if I haven't earned it."

"That's not it."

"What do you mean?"

Feeling as though I'd melted more glass than I could handle, I cast about for the right words. "You'll always be Zitora to the students. You're not...intimidating enough. You don't have the stern demeanor of Master Jewelrose or the walking textbook wisdom of Master Bloodgood. You can require us to call you Master, but we don't feel the title in our hearts." Her annoyance deepened toward anger, so I hurried on. "But you're... approachable. You're someone to confide in, to go to when in trouble. I think if all the Masters were unapproachable, the campus environment would be stilted. Uncomfortable."

When she didn't say anything, I added, "But that's my impression. I could be wrong." I needed to learn to keep my mouth shut. The One-Trick Wonder telling a Master Magician about how she was perceived was as ill-advised as the Masters sending me to the Stormdance Clan to fix their orbs.

Without a word, Zitora spurred Sudi into a gallop. See? She was too nice to chastise me. Master Jewelrose would have sent me to scrub the kitchen floors for a week.

But, when we finally stopped to sleep in the early-morning hours, and as I tried to get comfortable on the hard shale covering the ground, I thought her choice of a stop-over site could be in retaliation for my comment.

Zitora remained by our small fire, but noticed me squirming in my blankets. "It's all like this." She gestured to the ground. "From here on out."

"Like what?"

"Shale. Sheets and sheets of it. A few smooth places, others riddled with grooves or broken into gravel. All you'll see under your feet is an ugly gray until we reach the coast. It's called The Flats. No trees. A few bushes. Then... Well, The Cliffs before the sea are spectacular. Carved by wind and water, the piles of shale have been sculpted into beautiful shapes and bridges."

She returned to staring at the fire. "Go to sleep, Opal. You need the rest."

I was unable to keep my eyes open and too tired to question if she used magic on me.

For once, my overactive imagination and past memories didn't invade my dreams.

My sleep remained blissful until a sharp point pricked my throat, waking me. Alarmed, I stared at a sword's blade hovering mere inches from my chin. My gaze followed the long sharp weapon to its owner.

A person wearing a gray mask loomed over me.

3

"GET UP SLOWLY," the man ordered. "No sudden moves. And keep your hands where I can see them."

Hard to argue with an armed bandit. I sat and pushed my blankets off. The man stepped back as I stood. The tip of his sword dropped toward the ground, easing the iron vise of panic clamped around my heart. I released a shaky breath.

His shirt and pants were speckled with a variety of grays, black and white. His hood and mask matched the fabric of his clothes. Brilliant blue eyes stared back at me.

A laugh drew my attention to the right. Zitora was before three people who also wore gray camouflage. They pointed their swords at her. Interesting, she didn't look so sweet now. Red splotches spread on her cheeks. Anger or fear, I couldn't tell.

"This is it?" the man standing closest to Zitora

asked in amazement. "The Council sends two *students* to help the Stormdance Clan? This is too good to be true!" He cackled. "What are you...seniors? No. Don't tell me...you're a novice." He pointed his blade at me. "And you're a senior." The blade swung back to Zitora.

I had slept in my cloak and the weight of my sais underneath the garment pulled at my waist. She had insisted I stay armed at all times. Her sword rested on the ground nearby. I could reach through the slits in my cloak and draw my weapons.

I sought a signal from Zitora. Her pointed expression warned me to wait.

"What do you want?" Zitora asked.

"To stop you from helping the Stormdancers, but now I'm thinking of letting you go. You'll probably do more harm than good." The leader cackled again. His laugh grated on my nerves as if he gargled broken glass.

The man who woke me grabbed my hand. He showed my burn scars to the leader. "She is a glassmaker. We must stick to the plan." Blue Eyes released my arm.

"Aww. I can't kill two little girls," the leader said.

The word *kill* caused a hot flush of fear to race through me.

"This one's a magician," a woman said, gesturing at Zitora.

"Is she too strong for you?" the leader mocked.

The woman stiffened. "We have her firmly in our control." She glanced at the person next to her.

Through the haze of fear in my mind, I realized Zitora hadn't moved more than her mouth since I woke.

"And here we were all ready for a big fight," the leader said. "Brought the magicians, the muscle, the swordsman, expecting guards and Keep-trained magicians. Over*kill* for sure!" He laughed at his own joke.

Sweat rolled down my back at hearing *kill* again.

"Why do you want to stop us from helping the Stormdancers?" Zitora asked.

Anger reddened the leader's ears. "We want them to—"

"Shut up," Blue Eyes said. "The less said, the better. Finish the mission before we are discovered."

Perhaps the cackler wasn't the leader. An intelligent intensity radiated from Blue Eyes.

"We can take them along," suggested the woman. "Ransom them."

"No," I said with force. My vehement outburst surprised me as much as our attackers. I would rather die than be a kidnap victim again.

"Last chance to tell us why you're here," Zitora said. Authority laced her tone.

Snickers answered her. Only Blue Eyes considered her words. His grip tightened on his sword.

"The benefit of appearing so young is I'm constantly underestimated." Zitora raised her arms, warning me she would use her magic.

Breathing became difficult and fear stabbed my heart. Action would soon be needed. Could I fight or would I be too terrified to move?

This time the laughter didn't sound. The magician gestured with alarm.

"Now," Zitora ordered.

I yanked my sais from their holders as Blue Eyes lunged. With no time to think, I stepped in front of Zitora to protect her, blocking his sword. The ring of metal sounded as the strike vibrated through my arm.

He froze in place. The others rushed us, but when they reached Blue Eyes' side, they were immobilized, as well, coming no closer to us.

"That was fun." Strain vibrated in Zitora's words as sweat beaded on her forehead.

"What? It's over?" My body pumped with the need for action. I glanced between her and our attackers.

A tight grin flashed. "Perhaps being approachable isn't so bad."

"Do you have them all?" I asked.

"Yep, but now what?" She considered. "I can't hold them long."

To take control of four people's bodies required a great deal of skill and power. Zitora trembled with the effort. Her strength impressed me. I knew it shouldn't. She was Second Magician, after all. And Zitora's best ability was being able to wrap magic around a person, keeping them immobile. Yet seeing her in action enlightened me.

"Opal...fetch the darts." She huffed. "And vial...from my saddlebags."

I rushed to comply and soon returned with four darts and a small bottle.

"Dip them...do you know?"

"It's Curare." The words croaked out. I swallowed what felt like a lump of sand. Curare was a powerful drug. It paralyzed the muscles in a person's body for a full day and blocked the ability to use magic.

I shuddered, remembering when I had been forced to prick Yelena with the drug. My guilt flared, even though Yelena never blamed me, and she even admired the trick my kidnapper had used. I wish I could say the same for my Keep colleagues.

You can't let the past ruin your future, I chanted over in my mind. Yelena's words made perfect sense, yet I couldn't force my heart to believe them.

She gestured to the ambushers. I understood and treated each dart with the drug then jabbed each attacker in the arm. After waiting ten seconds, Zitora relaxed. She lowered her arms and the four bandits slumped to the ground.

Appearing as if her bones had melted, she dropped down to a sitting position. Her energy gone. I retrieved her water flask and a few baka leaves, handing them to her.

"Thanks." She chewed for a while, lost in thought.

The leaves revived her somewhat, but she remained sitting. Minutes passed. I fidgeted and wondered if I should put my weapons away.

Instead, I checked the horses and fed them. My hands trembled and I blamed the heavy feed bags for the shaking. Quartz rubbed her face on my arm in a comforting gesture.

Eventually Zitora joined me. She hunched over and moved as if afraid of falling. "We should go."

"What about them?" I asked.

She smiled. "And here they were, all prepared for a fight. No time to properly interrogate them." She rummaged in her saddlebags, uncovered the glass unicorn I had made for her and rested it in the palm of her hand.

The core glowed with an inner fire as it sang to me. The vibrations from its tune hummed deep within my soul. It brightened and quieted when Zitora stared at the unicorn, communicating with another magician. What did Master Bloodgood call them? Glass messengers? Interesting.

Finally she said, "Irys will contact the magician stationed in Thunder Valley. He'll inform the Stormdance's soldiers. They'll send a cleanup crew. Irys wasn't happy about the attack. She plans to personally interrogate them when they're in custody."

Considering they were going to kill us, they deserved to be interviewed by Master Jewelrose. The morning's events filtered through my mind and snagged on one question. "Zitora, why did you let them ambush us? You had to know they were coming. Right?"

A hint of mischievousness sparked in her tired eyes. "I knew. I wanted to see what they were after. My mind reading skills are limited. I knew they intended to accost us, but not why. And I can't hold them physically and examine them mentally. That's beyond my powers. Irys could do both, but probably not to all four." She considered. "A calculated risk, but it worked."

"No thanks to me," I murmured.

"Did another block that sword thrust? Funny, I didn't see him. Guess I was too busy using magic to notice."

"Sarcasm doesn't become you. You're ruining my image of you as the sweet Master."

"Good. Now go take the masks off and examine our attackers' faces."

"Why?"

"In case they escape. You'll be able to identify them."

"They could escape?" An alarming thought.

"Nothing's impossible, Opal. You should know that by now."

True. I thought about how Yelena had managed to escape after being paralyzed with Curare, a seemingly impossible situation. So why hadn't I been able to escape the same woman? Twelve days she held me, but I wasn't Yelena. Not as smart or as brave. By the end of my ordeal, I had been willing to do anything for Alea. Even pricking Yelena with Curare. Although I wondered, if faced with the same situation now, would I react the same? Did being older and wiser make me braver?

Painful memories threatened to overwhelm me. I bit my lip and focused on the task at hand, identifying our attackers. I pulled their masks off one by one revealing three men and one woman. I studied their features, committing them to memory, sculpting their profiles in my mind. I wondered if I could fashion glass statues to resemble people instead of animals. An interesting and appealing prospect that would have to wait until we returned home.

Blue Eyes stared at me with cold calculation. Long strands of black hair had sprung from his single braid. I stayed out of reach even though I knew he couldn't move. The drug only allowed a person to breathe, swallow and hear.

Clean shaven. No wrinkles lined his ginger-colored skin. I guessed he was in his early twenties. My attention kept returning to his diamond-shaped eyes fringed with thick lashes. I forced myself to search for distinctive features. He had a strong nose and an inch-long scar on his throat below his left ear.

When I returned to Zitora and the horses, my back stung as if Blue Eyes had the power to burn a hole right through my cloak and skin.

"Should we wait for the guards?" I asked Zitora when she mounted Sudi.

"No time. Don't worry, they're not going anywhere."

"What about predators?" A strange prickle crawled along my spine. It felt as if Blue Eyes' gaze had transformed into a spider clinging to the skin on my back, and that no matter how far I traveled, I wouldn't be able to lose the spider.

"If I loop a protective net around them, will you feel better?"

"Yes."

She guided her horse closer to the prone forms. Her brow creased and I guessed she pulled a thread of magic from the power source blanketing the world. Only magicians could tap into this power. When I worked with molten glass, I could draw magic from the source, but couldn't replicate the action without being in "glass mode."

I ignored the spike of envy. Zitora looped a protective strand around the paralyzed people and then connected it back to the power source so it remained in place. Or, at least, that was what she told me she had done. My awareness of magic was only through the glass. I couldn't see or touch or smell it.

The protection would guide an animal past the site without incident, but a human would break the net.

"What happens if one of the Stormdance Clan members stumbles on them? Or worse, if one of their colleagues is waiting for us to leave to help them?" I asked.

"No one lives on The Flats. And I can't sense anyone nearby. What is *really* worrying you?"

I couldn't pinpoint the reason for my unease.

"Perhaps you're still upset over the attack."

"Perhaps."

But as we rode away, the spider of doubt burrowed deep under my skin. If I chased my thoughts to the depths of my memories, I might match the anxious feeling to the incident over four years ago when I helped Yelena capture those malevolent souls. Match it to the fact that I heard their voices calling to me in my dreams from time to time.

Which is why I *wouldn't* contemplate those feelings—pure imagination on my part. I hoped.

4

I DISMISSED THE whole crazy notion of hearing the voices
of the dead and concentrated on keeping up with Zitora.
Galloping over the hard shale ground increased the
jolting through my body. I clung to Quartz's mane to
keep from bouncing off her saddle.

By the time we reached the coast the next morning, I
couldn't get off Quartz fast enough. We stopped where The
Flats transformed into The Cliffs—a sheer drop-off to the
sand below. The sea sparkled as if a million diamonds
floated on the surface. It spread before me in all its
glorious blue-green waters. White foam capped the waves
and fingers of rocks pointed to the horizon. The moist
breeze fanned me, smelling of salt.

Creeping to the edge, I glanced down and sank to my
knees. I had never been this high before. Five times the
height of the Master Magician's tower; I guessed the
distance spanned a hundred and fifty feet.

Zitora joined me.

"Where are the Stormdancers?" I asked. No life stirred on The Flats and only seabirds circled below. "I don't see any signs of them."

"Farther south. This is the only smooth part of The Cliffs." She pointed to the left. "And it's where the trail starts."

A narrow ledge of shale jutted from the edge of The Cliffs. A pregnant mare wouldn't fit on it. I eyed Quartz's middle. My leg would probably dangle over nothing.

"You're not afraid of heights are you?" Zitora asked.

"I guess I'm about to find out."

"We'll walk the horses down."

"Good idea."

"Just follow me and keep your eyes on Sudi." Zitora squeezed my shoulder.

During the first hour of our descent, I wasn't sure if I led Quartz down or if she guided me. My legs tended to freeze in place whenever I contemplated the thin ribbon of ground under my feet, and my breath came in short huffs whenever I caught sight of the rocks gleaming below.

The pungent scent of salt and fish dominated my senses. And the constant shushing of the waves filled my ears. Eventually, the soothing rise and fall of the water calmed my breathing, but the occasional harsh cry of a seagull would jolt a gasp from me.

Once we descended into the twisting network of the

wind-sculpted cliffs, my fears disappeared. The Storm-dance Clan had carved the trail through ripples of shale. Stunning wings of rock reached out to the sea and between these wings were caves and grooves.

Lower down on the cliff, the water added its own artistic touch, carving deep caverns and wearing away enough rock to leave bridges and chimneys behind.

According to Zitora, the Stormdancers lived in the caves closer to the sand. The higher ones were all empty. The lower ones had wood and cloth screens pulled across the entrances. Probably for privacy. When we finally arrived at the base of The Cliffs, the sun shone directly overhead—midafternoon. In a large cavern, we found a small group sitting around a fire.

Before going inside, I glanced up. This time, the sheer beauty and height of The Cliffs pressed down on me.

"Opal, give Quartz's reins to Tal, he'll take care of her," Zitora said.

A young man with skin the color of coal dust flashed me a shy smile. Tal led both horses along the sand.

"Where are they going?" I asked.

Another man had joined us. Around forty years old, he appeared to be about twenty years older than Tal. "We have temporary stables set up past the out-cropping." He pointed. The sun had tanned his skin to a warm brown and his short black hair was peppered with flecks of gold. "If a storm comes, we can move them into the higher caves for protection." He smiled, showing the reason for the wrinkles.

"I should go help unsaddle—"

"Don't worry. Tal will take care of them. We don't get many horses here, but Tal knows what to do. Come inside, we have much to discuss."

I followed Zitora and the man. With Tal gone, only four others waited by the fire. The man introduced us to them. Nodin and Varun were brothers and, along with their sister, Indra, the three of them made the special glass orbs. The fourth, Kade, was a Stormdancer.

By their solemn and dire expressions, they didn't appear happy to see us. The man—Raiden—was the camp manager.

"I sent the others back to the village," Raiden said. "No sense having everyone here if we can't dance. I hope you can help us out, Opal."

"I don't see how," Kade said. He threw a stick into the fire and stood. "She's younger than Tal." He stalked out.

The silence thickened until Raiden sighed. "Bad times, but we've been through worse. I sent for an expert and here you are. I trust the Council and Master Cowan." His round face and kind brown eyes radiated hope.

I knew I was supposed to respond with a comment about being the right person for the job, but I tended to agree with Kade. At least Raiden used Zitora's title.

"Tell us what's been happening," Zitora said.

Raiden explained about the orbs shattering. "...when the energy is captured inside, the Stormdancer seals the orb with a rubber stopper and we transport the orb to one of our factories. But with these new orbs, as soon as they are sealed the energy bursts through them, sending shards of glass out with killer speed. We lost two Stormdancers."

The three glassblowers seemed to sink down into themselves. Their guilt and pain piercing them as lethally as the glass debris had penetrated the Storm-dancers.

"What is different with these orbs?" Zitora asked.

"Nothing!" Roused from his misery, Nodin jumped to his feet. "We've been following Father's methods exactly. Same recipe. Same temperature. Same equipment."

"How do you make them?" she asked.

Nodin began a lecture on glassmaking. I stopped him after a few sentences.

"Better to show me exactly what your father did to make the orbs," I said.

They led me outside and up the trail.

"We make all the orbs before the two stormy seasons," Nodin explained.

Out in the sunlight, the tight curls of his short black hair shone. The three siblings all had the same color of hair. Indra had pulled her shoulder-length curls into a ponytail and Varun had twisted his longer hair into rows of braids tight against his head.

"We'll have to relight the fire," Varun said.

"You let it go out?" I asked in amazement. Getting the kiln heated to the proper temperature could take days.

"We finished the orbs for the cooling season storms," Indra snapped. "We were in the process of shutting it down until next year."

"Is there another kiln nearby?" I asked.

Varun barked out a short laugh. "No. Nothing is nearby. We bring all our supplies when we arrive for the storm season."

"We're wasting time." Indra glanced out to sea. Her brothers copied her. They seemed to be scenting the wind, judging the air. "Not much time left before the big storms hit. Our *expert* wants to see how we make the orbs. Let's get to work."

The kiln was housed in a large cave tucked behind a shale wall, protected from the wind and high water. A chimney had been drilled through the ceiling to vent the heat and smoke.

The glassmakers moved as one, reminding me of my family. While the brothers shoveled white coal, Indra gathered driftwood from a stack. Wood was easier to light than coal, but once a hot fire burned, more coal would be added.

Indra's little jab at me hurt, but I didn't want to stand there and do nothing. "Can I help?" I asked her.

I translated her grunt for assent. I collected wood. When we had a pile, the brothers made a lattice of branches. Nodin pulled out flint. Interesting how none of the three could light the fire with magic. I couldn't, either, but I had assumed a Stormdancer could. I glanced around. Kade wasn't in sight.

Zitora, though, hovered nearby with Raiden. She halted Nodin's efforts. With the smallest of frowns, she lit the branches. When she looked away, the fire died down to a respectable burn.

"Can you keep the fire hot?" I asked her.

"How long?"

"Long enough for the coals to ignite?"

She nodded and once again the flames intensified.

A purse of appreciation settled on Nodin's lips. "One benefit to having a Master Magician around."

"And she's good in a fight, too." I winked at her.

"Time to add the sand," Indra said.

The sand, soda ash and lime had been premixed and loaded onto a wheeled cart which had been parked in the back of the cave. Indra held a large metal bowl and a trowel. She paused before filling it. "How much?" she asked.

"Enough for two orbs," I said.

She scooped sand. I grabbed a fistful of the mixture and carried it into the sunlight. Once there, I let the grains fall through my fingers, inspecting them as they fell. Yellow and brown grains, large and coarse were mixed with small white grains. A number of red-tinted particles and a few black specks peppered the mix.

"Our family's secret recipe," Varun said as he joined me on the ledge.

I considered. "Forty percent local sand, forty percent from the Krystal Clan's sand quarry, fifteen percent from the Bloodgood Clan's red beach and five percent lava flakes."

He opened his mouth in astonishment. Closed it. Then stuttered, "That's...that's... There's no way... Who told you?" Suspicion tainted his voice.

"The mixture." He didn't brighten with understanding. I asked him, "What other glasswares do you manufacture?"

"None. Our sole job is to make the orbs and protect the recipe. Only my family and the lead Stormdancer know the percentages." He clutched my arm. "You're the first to figure it out. You can't tell *anyone.*"

"Don't worry." I gently pried his hands off. "I won't. I know how important it is. Growing up in a glass factory, my family made many different types of glasswares from drinking glasses to fancy bowls and custom vases. My father has hundreds of sand recipes for various colored glass, as well as glass with assorted qualities and clarities. Father delights in bringing home a new mix and making us guess the composition." I smiled at the memory. Most fathers brought presents home for their children. Mine brought sand. My smile grew wider as I realized how excited my sisters and I had been when Father's wagon was spotted in town, returning with a new batch of sand.

I brushed the sand from my fingers.

Varun gazed at me with frank curiosity. But before he could voice his question, Nodin joined us. "The coals are heating. We should have melt by dawn."

Zitora's magic had accelerated the process by a full day.

"Until then, let me show you the orbs we've made," Nodin said.

I followed him along the cliff trail to a small cave high above the beach. We crouched down to step inside.

"Another protected cave. The wind doesn't blow in here and the water never reaches this high."

I peered over the edge. "How high does the water get?"

Nodin grinned. "Depends on the storm. The stronger the wind, the higher the water."

He shuffled to the back of the cave and returned with a glass orb. He handed it to me. The sphere weighed as much as a healthy newborn baby. The orb had a small lip and opening, making the sphere resemble a fat coin purse.

"When the rubber stopper is inserted, it seals the energy inside," Nodin explained.

"How do you release the energy without hurting anybody?"

He picked up a stopper. "There is a hole that goes about halfway through. See?" He poked a finger up to his knuckle in the one end. "A glass tube is inserted in this end and, when in place, a small hole is made that goes all the way through the rubber. The energy flows through the tube and into the machinery."

I brought the orb closer to the sunlight and stroked the glass with my fingers. Smooth and translucent, the orb had a purple iridescent film on the outside as if it had been dipped in soap. As wide as the length of my forearm, it had no seams; the glass was blown into this shape. No bubbles or other flaws marked its surface.

It sat inert in my hands. No glow. No singing. No magic.

"Why glass?" I asked Nodin. "Why not metal or silver to contain the storm's energy?"

"Only glass will work. I don't know why." Sadness blanketed his face. "Now even the glass won't work."

"Do you have one of the old orbs?"

Nodin stared at me as if deciding what he should tell me. Finally he said, "Kade keeps one in his sleeping quarters." He scooted closer to the edge and hung his legs over. "It's one of the smaller orbs. And it's...full." He swung his feet and looked down at the beach.

"So if the orb breaks..."

"Exactly." Nodin spread his hands wide. "It would kill anyone standing or sleeping within ten feet."

"Why keep it?"

"Don't know. It's a suicide waiting to happen." He gestured to the sea. A single figure stood at the end of a rocky outcrop.

"Or it could be a strong desire for privacy."

Nodin laughed. "It does guarantee him his own cave."

We sat for a while in silence. Each contemplating our own thoughts.

"I'll need to examine Kade's orb," I said.

"You'll have to ask him."

"Me? I thought..."

His brown eyes sparked with glee. "Yes, you. I'm beginning to like you, Opal. But not *that* much." He grabbed the sphere and returned it to the back of the cave. "If you want to see Kade's orb before dark, you better hurry. Once the sun dips below the sea, it turns black fast."

I followed Nodin down to the beach. The sun hovered near the edge of the horizon, casting shadows along the water's rippled surface.

"Good luck." Nodin waved.

I wondered if Zitora should be the person to ask Kade about his orb. The Stormdancer didn't have a lot of confidence in me. I tended to agree with him, but I knew I would try to discover the problem. It was too important and I wouldn't feel right unless I made the effort.

The wind whipped hair into my eyes when I stepped out onto the black rocks. I pulled the leather tie from my messy ponytail and tried to recapture all the strands into a neater knot. Funny how I hadn't noticed the wind on the beach. Calling to Kade had proven futile. My shouts drowned by the sea's song.

I hadn't noticed how uneven and jagged the rocks were, either. Waves crashed into them, sending spray high into the air. Water soon coated my skin and soaked my clothes. The rocks became slicker with each wave. I was glad I wore my brown boots, even though they filled with water; their thick soles helped me navigate the slippery and rutted outcrop. At one point I climbed over a few sharp boulders, and at another I leaped over a gap. The tight knocking of my heart warned my body to turn around and go back to the beach, but I was determined. Stupid?

No. Determined. Until I reached a space too big to cross. Too big for me. Kade was three rocks farther out. Each separated by a large opening. Had he swam or jumped? It didn't matter. All that mattered was he heard my shout.

He spun around. And I wished I had waited on the beach. With an angry scowl, Kade moved. I would have marveled at his speed and grace as he flew over the gaps, except he aimed toward me.

An errant wave knocked into me and I grabbed a rough edge to keep from falling. Pain laced my palm and blood welled.

Kade stopped before spanning the space between our rocks. His mouth moved, but the wind snatched half of his words.

"...idiot...dangerous...go back!"

I understood his intent and turned to retrace my steps. The waves grew in size and frequency. They hunted me, attacking when I was vulnerable.

"Opal," shouted Kade.

I looked back in time to see a giant blue-green wall of water rushing toward me.

The roar of the wind and sea ceased the moment the monster wave engulfed me. For one heartbeat, my world filled with gurgling sounds and foamy green light. Then the force of the crashing water slammed me into an un-yielding object. The sea grabbed my limp body and tossed it about. Confusion dulled the pain until my forehead smacked into a jagged rock.

My vision clouded with blood and saltwater. Kade and the outcrop grew smaller as the sea sucked me into her liquid embrace.

5

I TRIED TO SWIM. But each wave pushed me under and my waterlogged pants and boots dragged me down. I managed a few panicked gulps of air before the salt-water closed my throat.

A sense of inevitability pervaded my body and I relaxed. The underwater half-light was a beautiful canvas for my memories. My sister Tula arrived to welcome me into the sky. I was surrounded by warmth and love.

She frowned at me. "Silly girl. Take a breath. You're surrounded by air."

I opened my mouth to argue and coughed out a lungful of water. My stomach heaved with the effort to expel the salty liquid. Once I regained my composure, I froze in amazement. I sat in the middle of a bubble of air. The blue-green walls appeared as solid as glass, but moved like water.

Eventually my bubble floated to the surface of the

sea. I bobbed in the waves, staying dry as land drew closer. Kade still stood on the rocks, but his eyes were closed and he held his arms straight out to the sides.

Once I reached the shallow water, my bubble popped. I splashed back into the cold sea. The waves pushed as I crawled from the water and collapsed onto the sand. Soon voices wormed through my water-filled ears. A crowd had gathered.

My sodden state was met with a mixture of emotions. Zitora was concerned and fluttered around me like a mother. The glassmakers smirked and tried to conceal their laughter. Raiden tsked and muttered under his breath about stupidity. Tal helped me to my feet and stayed beside me.

"What made you go out there?" Zitora asked.

"I wanted to talk to Kade. Nodin said I should go before dark."

A burst of chuckles escaped from the siblings. Raiden scowled at them. "Opal, you shouldn't have listened to him. He was fooling with you."

"I didn't know it would be so slick." I shivered. The weak sun floated on the sea, painting a bright ribbon of red light along the waterline.

"You three stop laughing." He scolded the glassmakers. "If Kade hadn't seen her, she would have drowned. Then no one would want to help us!"

They sobered in an instant.

"Sorry," Nodin muttered before they shuffled away to check on the kiln.

"Now you know to avoid climbing on the rocks." Zitora smoothed my hair from my face and wiped sand off my cheek. "You're bleeding."

Her finger traced a line of fire across my forehead. She repeated the gesture and the pain disappeared.

"You'll have a slight scar, but it could have been worse. You need to wash and change into dry clothes. There's a freshwater pond behind the stables. Let me *know* if you have any other injuries." Her eyes promised to question me further. Probably when we were alone. She left with Raiden to retrieve our saddlebags.

Tal lingered. He kicked the sand. He peered past my shoulder then back to me. "Before you talk to Kade about what was so important, make sure you thank him first."

I glanced behind me. Kade reached the beach with a light hop. He walked toward us. "Thank him?"

"For saving your life."

"Ahh… My bubble of air."

"A Stormdancer power." Bitterness warped Tal's words. He turned and hurried away.

I wanted to chase after Tal, especially when Kade drew closer, but I waited for him. Cold fingers of air stroked my wet body, raising goose bumps on my skin.

His wet tunic and pants clung to his muscular frame, but at least his angry scowl had turned into tired annoyance.

I braced for his lecture.

Instead he gave me a wry smile. "Don't know why I was

mad," he said. "I've fished out so many clan members I've lost count. And I'm sure you weren't warned to stay off the rocks. Not that it would change anything. No matter how many times you warn a person, he still has to climb out there just to see for himself."

He sighed and gazed out to the horizon. The sea had turned a slate gray.

"At least I won't have to fish you out tomorrow. I can save my energy for the storm."

"A storm's coming?"

"Yep. Nasty one, too. That's why the waves are so greedy."

He walked by, but I touched his arm. He jerked away as if stung.

"Thank you for fishing me out."

He nodded and continued past.

"There was a reason I wanted to talk to you," I said to his back.

He paused.

"I want to examine your orb."

His shoulders stiffened. "Why?"

"To compare it to the new orbs."

Kade made no reply as he strode away.

The simple state of being warm and dry felt wonderful. I wore tan-colored linen pants and a light orange tunic made of the same material. The nicest part of being a student at the Keep was being able to wear what we wanted on a daily basis. Formal occasions, though, either called for our official robes, or fancy dress.

In the main living cave, my brown leather boots steamed beside the campfire. I lounged as close to the heat as possible in a chair made of wood and canvas. The glassmakers, Tal, Raiden and Zitora ringed the fire, talking in low voices which echoed off the shale walls. Fish soup bubbled over the flames and my stomach growled loud enough for Zitora to pause and smile at me.

As we ate the tangy soup, Nodin and Indra discussed the kiln watch schedule and Zitora and Raiden talked about recent Council decisions. Each clan elected a member to represent them on the Sitian Council, which met at the Citadel. With the three Master Magicians, the Council consisted of fourteen members who decided on laws and policies for Sitia.

My father loved dissecting the Council's decisions, but I never had much interest. Even now when I could have learned more about the Stormdance Clan's internal policies, my mind wandered. Where was Kade? Didn't he need to eat?

I eventually dozed in my chair.

"Opal." Zitora woke me with a nudge. "Time for bed. Do you want to sleep down here near the fire or go to another cave?"

Confused, I glanced at Raiden.

"Some prefer their privacy. There are many places to sleep and a few have fire rings or coal stoves. Most of us just sleep here."

I was used to sharing a room. First with my sisters,

and then at the Keep. "Here's fine. This way you can wake me when it's my turn to watch the kiln's fire."

"You're not on the schedule," Nodin joked.

"I know. The three of you can shorten your shifts to two hours and I'll take the last shift."

Varun drew breath, but I said, "Don't argue with the *expert.*"

"I assume you mean an expert at glass and not at swimming?" Tal teased.

I remembered Kade's comments on the beach. "So, your superior attitude comes from having never been fished out?"

Indra laughed and flicked her long ponytail. "He's been fished out countless times."

Tal shot to his feet and scowled down at her.

"Now he's going to run outside and pout," Indra said. "You have to learn how to laugh at yourself, Tal."

"I'm going to sleep in the stables. The horses smell better than *you.*" Tal stalked from the cave.

Indra sighed. "I'm surrounded by boys," she grumped to herself. "I'm glad I have my own cave. I enjoy my privacy after dealing with these children all day. I'm going to bed." She made a dramatic exit.

We folded the chairs and stacked them against the back wall. Raiden handed me a cot and helped to set it up.

"We do have a few comforts," he said. "No sense sleeping on the cold hard ground."

Within seconds of getting comfortable, I fell asleep.

The wind whistled in my dreams as I ran from the waves. The sand sucked at my feet and hindered my movements before melting under me. I slogged through thick molten glass as a huge wave grew behind me. Riding on top of the wave was Blue Eyes. He beckoned to me. His voice echoed in my chest. "Finish the job."

I woke with a start. Nodin shook my shoulder. White ash clung to the ringlets in his hair.

"Must have been some nightmare," he said.

I shuddered. "You have no idea."

A haunted expression gripped him. "I know all about nightmares."

"I'm sorry, I didn't mean—"

"I know." He straightened. "It's your shift."

Nodin stole my cot as soon as I vacated it. He was probably asleep by the time I left the cave.

The cold drove out the last vestiges of sleep from my mind. I glanced at the sky. No stars. No moon. A heavy presence pushed down from above, adding to the moisture in the air. Probably clouds filled with rain, although I couldn't smell anything besides the salty air.

The sea moved like a living being. Its chest rose and fell; waves crashed and drew back as it breathed, the rough surf a testament to its displeasure.

Protected by the wind, the kiln's fire burned hot. I poked the sand mixture inside with a rod. It needed a few more hours to melt into the required consistency. I added a handful of coals to the fire.

Now what? I hiked down to the beach and checked on

the horses. Quartz nickered in greeting. The small stables had been constructed from bamboo stalks lashed together. The three stalls smelled clean and the walls protected the horses from the wind. Tal snored in an empty bay. His long arms hung off the edge of his cot.

I returned to the kiln's cave. The fire warmed me and its familiar roar masked the alien sounds from the sea. I squirmed into a comfortable position at the entrance and rested my back against the wall. The perfect spot to see both the sea and the kiln.

It wasn't long before a weak light diluted the black sky to a charcoal gray, which weakened into a drab gray. Clouds boiled on the horizon. The water underneath the sky churned the color of a two-day-old bruise. I stepped closer to the edge of the cave. Lightning snaked from the clouds followed by the rumble of thunder. It would be a bleak day. Depressed, I huddled in my cloak as I descended the trail and walked onto the beach, thinking to feed the horses their morning grain.

A spark of joy touched my soul. Startled, I looked around for Zitora. Had she uncovered her glass unicorn? Instead Kade strode toward me, holding a ball of fire.

As he drew closer, the song in my heart expanded. It buzzed along my skin, vibrated in my blood. He stopped and held out the sphere to me. His orb.

I grasped the ball. Energy sizzled and popped up my arms and down my spine. Light swirled inside, changing colors at an amazing speed. The sweet harmony of pure magic sang in my ears. Overwhelmed, I sank to the sand and cradled the orb in my lap.

Kade knelt next to me. "What's the matter?"

"It..." Words to describe it died in my throat.

"What?" he prompted.

"It calls...no, sings to me. Silly, I know."

"Not silly at all. It sings to me, too." His gaze met mine.

It was the first time I had a chance to see him in the daylight. His amber-colored eyes held flecks of gold. Even though he radiated the air of someone much older, he had to be close to Zitora's age. Straight hair fell to his shoulders, but the color reminded me of the sand from the Jewelrose Clan—a mixture of golds, browns and reds. Small droplets of mist clung to his long eyelashes, thin mustache and anchor-shaped goatee underneath his bottom lip.

"Full orbs sing to Stormdancers, but I've never heard it call to anyone else." Kade touched the orb. "Is it the energy inside or the glass that sings to you?"

I concentrated on the sphere, running my fingers along the surface. It was smaller than the one Nodin showed me. About eight inches wide it was the size of a cantaloupe. I ignored the swirling light and focused on the glass.

No marks. No flaws. Thick glass. Thicker than the empty spheres? No. Denser. The glass had absorbed the magic used to trap the storm's energy. The vibrations felt different, so I thought magic hadn't been used to form the glass.

"Have any of these orbs shattered?" I asked.

"A few over the years."

"Do you know why?"

"Young fools trying to stuff too much energy into one sphere. Or they can shatter when a Stormdancer loses control of the waves and wind around him." Chagrin tainted his voice. "In that case, the sphere is dashed to pieces on the rocks and if the Stormdancer is lucky, he'll be rescued before his head meets the same fate."

"Talking from experience?"

"Unfortunately. It's a hard skill to learn, keeping a bubble of calm around you while the storm rages."

"Kade! What are you doing?" Raiden's voice called. He and the others stopped about twenty feet from us.

Kade stood. "She wanted to see the orb."

"Are you crazy? What if she drops it? You both could be killed."

I gained my feet and scanned their faces. They truly didn't know. Not a clue among them. Even the glassmakers.

I dropped the orb.

6

THE ORB BOUNCED on the sand and rolled a few feet. Horrified cries filled the air until the onlookers realized the orb hadn't shattered.

Kade blanched, but he hadn't thrown his hands up in protection as Tal and Varun had done.

"Heck of a demonstration. Did you know it wouldn't break or are you just suicidal?" Kade asked with a touch of sarcasm.

"Glass is an amazing material. Versatile, malleable and very strong."

"But not indestructible."

"No. I wouldn't spike it on the hard ground, but no need to handle it like a delicate seashell."

"Point taken." Kade retrieved the orb.

"Nodin, can you get me one of your new orbs?"

"Sure." Nodin's voice sounded thin as if he had forgotten to breathe. He hurried away.

Zitora looked thoughtful and I wondered if she would reprimand me later. I wasn't quite sure what had come over me. Perhaps it was in response to their reaction.

Nodin returned with an empty sphere. I flung it hard to the sand. Again everyone flinched. This time the orb cracked into three large pieces. I picked up a shard and examined the inside of the glass.

I wiped the sand from my hands. "Is the melt ready?"

Varun nodded.

"Okay. Let's see how you make one of these."

The entire group hiked up to the kiln's cave to watch as the siblings worked in perfect unison. As the oldest, Indra sat at the gaffer's bench while Nodin gathered the molten glass on the end of a blowing pipe and placed it in the holders on the bench. Varun handed tools to his sister as she worked.

During the process, Indra blew through the pipe and the ball expanded. Moving with a practiced quickness, Indra shaped the sphere. After multiple reheatings and blowings, she increased the size. When she was satisfied with the roundness, she signaled Nodin. He gathered a small dollop of melt onto the end of a pontil iron, making a punty. Attaching the punty onto the end of the sphere, Indra then dipped her tweezers into the bucket and dripped water onto the end of the blowpipe.

Cracks webbed and, with a hard tap of the tweezers, the glass sphere cracked off the pipe and was now held by the pontil iron. Nodin inserted the sphere back into the kiln to soften the glass. Indra expanded the little hole left by cracking off the pipe, and formed the sphere's lip.

The piece was soon done and into the annealing oven. They did nothing wrong while crafting the piece. No actions that rendered it flawed. No magic, either.

"Make another one, but this time I want to blow into the pipe," I said.

When Indra nodded to me, I bent, pursed my lips and blew through the pipe. Power from the source and not air from my lungs flowed through me and into the orb. It didn't expand. The sphere stayed a fist-sized ball. Indra finished the piece and cracked it off into a heat resistant box.

"That didn't work," I said into the silence.

"But it glows," Kade said. "You drew power."

Except Zitora, everyone stared at my piece in confusion.

"Are you sure?" Nodin asked. "No offense, but it looks like a beginner's effort."

"I've trapped a thread of magic inside the ball," I explained. "Only magicians can see the glow."

"No." Tal tensed and scowled. "That can't be right. *I* can't see the glow."

"It's been tested," Zitora said. "And we've been using Opal's glass animals to evaluate potential students for the Keep. If they can see the glow, we know they possess magical power."

"No." A stubborn line formed along Tal's jaw. His eyes held fear.

"Tal." Raiden placed a hand on the young man's

shoulders. "You tried to call the wind with no success. You're past puberty—"

"No!" Tal shrugged Raiden's hand off. "My father... My sister..."

"Strong Stormdancers, I know. Stormdancing is a rare gift, be thankful your sister—"

"I have it, too. It's just...late. It's just like the stubble on my chin, I don't have enough power right now, but it'll come. I know." He left in a huff.

Raiden stared after him. We stood in an uncomfortable silence until an earsplitting crack of thunder announced the storm's impending arrival. Donning thick leather gloves, Nodin picked up my orb and placed it into the annealer. Indra and Varun reorganized their tools.

Another rumble sounded. "The horses?" I asked.

"I'll get them," Raiden said. "Go down to the third level. That's the storm cave where we keep all the necessary provisions."

Zitora hurried to help Raiden.

I turned to go when Kade stopped me. He handed me his orb. The energy within it intensified. It pulsed and quivered, sending shooting pains along my arms.

"Keep it safe," he said.

"Where are you going?"

"Out." He gestured to the sea.

"Why? You don't have an orb."

"I can still bleed off energy from the storm."

"To where?"

He huffed with impatience. "Into the rocks."

Before I could question him further, Kade said, "Ask Raiden, he'll explain it." He jogged down the trail.

The sea heaved and thrashed around the rocks all but obscuring them. Foamy spray whipped through the air. Yet wherever Kade stepped, the water smoothed and his hair stayed in place, not even bothered by a faint breeze.

Zitora's voice cut through the storm's rage, calling me. I rushed to catch up to her as she led Sudi into a low cave. Although the horse ducked her head, it was a tight fit. The top of the opening scraped along Sudi's back.

Once inside, the cavern's ceiling rose to twelve feet. The area was roomy, with horse stalls near the back and torches blazing along the walls. Cots and chairs had been set up, Zitora helped start a fire, and Raiden filled a pot with water.

"You shouldn't bring that in here," Raiden said, pointing at the orb in my hands.

"It would take a lot more than dropping it on the ground to break," I said.

"I know it takes a hard blow to shatter it, but I don't want my people to start being careless with them. Every Storm-dance Clan member knows to handle the orbs with the utmost care and I want to keep it that way. Would you want to risk losing a life?" When I didn't answer, he said, "There is a reason for the fear."

Chagrined, I said, "I hadn't thought about it that way."

"Next time, you might want to think before you act."

Chastised, I stared at the floor.

"There is a reason for everything, Opal. You might not be able to figure it out, and time might have made us all forget it, but the reason is there all the same." Raiden hung his pot over the fire. "Who's hungry for clam stew?"

Raiden gave everyone who said, "me" a bucket of clams to open. I carried the orb to a safe spot in the back, setting it down on a pile of blankets. My hands and arms were numb from holding it. I covered it with another blanket to muffle its song. Between the roar of the storm and the trill of the orb, I would soon have a headache.

I checked on Quartz before returning to the fire. She munched her hay, appearing to be unconcerned about the weather. I scratched behind her left ear and she groaned in contentment.

When I sat down, Raiden handed me a dull knife and a handful of clams. I wouldn't be allowed to partake in the meal without helping. I fumbled for a while, trying to pry open a shell. It didn't take me long to find a rhythm, discovering another use for my strong hands.

Tal arrived soaking wet and sullen. He popped open a few clams without looking or speaking to anyone. The rest just ignored him.

Conversation focused on the orbs. I had been reluctant to state my theories before seeing how the glass was made, but when I examined the new orb in the firelight I felt more confident.

"Something is wrong with the mix," I said, holding up my hand to stop the protest perched on Indra's lips. "The recipe is right, but the sand, soda ash or lime isn't."

"What's wrong with them?" Nodin asked.

"You could have gotten a bad batch."

"Not helping." Nodin tossed a clam into the pot.

"There is something in the mix that is causing the glass to be less dense. It can't absorb the energy from the storm."

"Which ingredient is deficient?" Indra asked.

"I don't know. I could take samples of each to my father. He would be able to find out."

"What do we do in the meantime?" Raiden asked. "The storms are only going to get worse."

"Kade is dancing now. Why can't you have all your Stormdancers bleeding off energy until we figure out what is wrong?"

Tal snorted with derision. "All he's doing is taking a small stick out of a big fire."

"It's dangerous. No other Stormdancer would do it. There's no *reason* for the risk." Raiden nodded at me as if we shared a private joke.

"The almighty Kade likes to show off," Tal grumbled. "Rub it in."

"He has his own reasons." Raiden stirred the stew.

After we had tossed the empty shells to the beach, Nodin asked about my magic. "Tell me again how it works."

Zitora and I explained about the two uses of my pieces.

"I can use this new one when my unicorn is spent," Zitora said.

"No." The word sprang from my throat before logic could be applied. "I want to keep it to...to compare it to...my other works." Weak explanation, I knew, but this orb hummed like Kade's sphere and I was reluctant to give it away.

"How is this different?" Nodin asked.

"It has a different...call."

"Call?" Nodin cocked an eyebrow, inviting enlightenment.

"Each of my glass pieces calls to me. I don't hear it like sound. I feel it." I tapped my chest. "Inside. Whenever one of my animals is close to me, I know which one it is and where it is even if I can't see it."

He whistled. "You could feel this *before* you fell into the water and hit your head on the rocks? Right?"

"Yes."

"Because it makes more sense the other way."

"Nodin," Raiden warned. "That's enough."

We ate our stew in relative silence. The keening of the wind echoed in the cavern and errant gusts fanned the flames. Soon a fine sea mist coated everything in the cave.

I didn't sleep well. My cot felt as if it bobbed on a wild sea and the wind infiltrated my dreams, moaning a name over and over in my mind. Laced with grief and loss, the wind's cry filled my heart with sadness.

The storm passed by daybreak. Kade arrived. Exhaustion lined his face and his clothes dripped with seawater.

"Fall in?" Tal asked with barely concealed spite.

If Kade noticed, he didn't show it. He nodded. "Lost my grip for a second and was blown into the water."

Raiden shot Kade a horrified look.

"Luckily I managed to construct a bubble and climb back onto the rocks." Kade squeezed the ends of his hair. Water rained to the floor.

"Luck had nothing to do with it," Raiden said. "Your powers have grown since—"

"Don't say it," Kade snapped.

Raiden frowned. "The storm almost killed you. You shouldn't dance anymore."

The Stormdancer lingered near the cave's entrance. He peered out to the sea. "You're right."

Raiden covered his surprise by turning away to concentrate on breakfast. I guessed Kade didn't agree with Raiden very often. Kade walked to the back of the cave to retrieve his orb. When the sphere was uncovered, I flinched with the sudden intensity of its song.

Tal narrowed his eyes at me. "Don't tell me *you* hear it."

When I didn't reply, he flew into a rage. "You can't possibly hear it. You're younger than me. And you're not even a member of our clan." He brushed past me, knocking me down.

"Raiden," Indra said.

"I know." The older man sighed. He helped me to my feet. "Sorry about that. Tal's getting worse. I'll send him home."

"Wait," Varun said. "He's having a hard time adjusting. Before Opal's device gave him proof, he still hoped he might develop magical powers. It'll take a while for him to accept it. I'll talk to him."

"Fine. But tell him one more outburst and I'm sending him home for good."

Varun agreed and followed Tal.

Raiden served the rest of us bowls of warm oatmeal. The thick mush had a fishy taste.

He laughed at my expression. "All our meals have fish in it. Cuts down on the amount of supplies we need."

"Speaking of supplies," Indra said. "What do we do about the glass ingredients?"

"Can you get a new batch?" Zitora asked.

"No. We stockpile the ingredients inland near Thunder Valley and bring only enough for each season. If one of the compounds is tainted, then the whole stockpile will be suspect," Indra explained.

"How about ordering in fresh supplies?"

The glassmaker shook her head. "We wouldn't get them in time. The special components in our mixture come from far away."

"We really need to know which one is causing the problem," Nodin said.

"Are the different components in separate stock-piles?" I asked.

"Yes. They're mixed right before we leave." He paced around the campfire, pulling at his tight curls. They sprang back as soon as he released one.

"Opal, you wanted to take samples to your father. Is there anyone else who is closer?" Zitora asked. "How about the Citadel's glassmaker?"

"Aydan only works with one type of glass. My father really is the best one to ask. He has an extensive laboratory and experiments with sand while the other glassmakers find a mix they like and stay with the same recipe forever."

"Can he come here?" Nodin stopped pacing. Hope touched his voice.

"He'll need his lab. If it was an obvious substance, I would have seen it."

"Is that why you ran them through your fingers?"

"Yes."

"How long will it take?" Kade joined us by the fire. He had wrapped his orb in the blanket and cradled the bundle.

"Seven days one way if the weather is good. Then it depends on Opal's father." Zitora looked at me.

"A day. Maybe two." I guessed.

"How long do you have before it's too late?" Zitora asked Raiden.

"The storms are forming every four days now. In another three weeks, they'll be coming every two days.

Without Stormdancers and orbs, this cavern will be underwater until the middle of the cold season."

"Let's say nine days from now we have an answer. We can communicate through Opal's glass animals and you can order a fresh batch."

Indra stood. "That could work. We'll need Opal back, though."

Surprised, I asked why.

"To test the ingredients before they're melted into glass. We can't guess that the new supplies are pure. Plus we couldn't tell the difference between the orbs. You'll know if they'll hold the storm's energy."

"But—"

Zitora cut me off. "What happens if it's one of your special ingredients that are tainted?"

"We don't dance," Kade said. "People die."

Kade's words weighed heavy on my mind as we prepared to leave The Cliffs. Varun and Kade would accompany Zitora and me to their stockpile near Thunder Valley and remain there until they heard from us.

I gave my little ball to the Stormdancer so he could try to communicate with Zitora through the glass. She was on the beach with her unicorn and we were in his tiny sleeping cave decorated with a cot, a chair and a desk. Piles of books lined the back wall. A small coal stove rested near the entrance, but not too close to the wood and cloth privacy screen. Kade had stored the orb—still covered with the blanket—under his cot.

After I had glanced around his cave, Kade shrugged. "It suits me. When I spend all day in the wild vastness of sea and storms, it's soothing to be surrounded by stone." Kade settled on the cot, sitting cross-legged and peered into the glass.

A heartbeat later, he yelped in surprise and fumbled the ball. I suppressed a giggle, but couldn't stop the smirk.

"I suppose the first time you heard a voice in your head you were unperturbed?" he asked in annoyance.

The smile dropped from my lips. "I don't have the magical ability to hear thoughts."

"I don't, either, but Zitora does. As long as you have magic, you should be able to hear her."

"I can't." I turned away before I could see his pity. The Masters could communicate with every magician in Sitia. Except me. Even people with only one trick could hear the Masters' call. Except me.

"Since the test was a success, I'd better go help Zitora saddle the horses." I ducked to leave.

"But you can hear the orb's call," Kade said to my back.

The orb's song pierced my heart. I jerked, turning around. Kade had uncovered the sphere.

"What does it say to you?" he asked.

I concentrated. The orb's song pulsed in time with the sea and hummed in tune with the wind. Among the melody moaned a name. The same name that haunted my dreams last night. "Kaya."

Kade froze in horror. He stared at me with such intensity I stepped back.

"My sister's name," he said as if every word pained him.

"You have a sister?"

"Had. She died. Killed by one of the flawed orbs."

7

GRIEF WELLED IN Kade's eyes. The obvious pain of his sister's death still ripping his insides like a broken knife. I remembered the weeks after my sister Tula had died. The pain would only dull with time.

"I'm so sorry," I said. "I know—"

"You know nothing." Kade spat the words out. "Please spare me the empty and banal responses of sympathy. They are meaningless."

I wanted to correct him, but from his reaction I knew he wasn't ready to hear it.

Kade grabbed my shoulders and dragged me close. "Did Raiden tell you her name? Hope that I would confess my woes to you?" He dug his fingers into my skin.

"No one told me. Let go. You're hurting me."

"Did Master Cowan pull the information from my head?"

I wished I had one of my sais so I could knock sense

into him. "She would never intrude on your private thoughts. The *orb* told me. Let go now!" I brought my arms up between his and swept them out to the side, breaking his hold on my shoulders.

He stumbled back and I pushed him farther away with my foot. He landed on his cot. At least I had paid attention in self-defense class. Another skill learned from my four years at the Keep. Yippee for me.

"Do you have water in your ears? What part of 'let go' didn't you understand?" I scolded, reverting into my really-annoyed-older-sister mode.

When anger flamed in Kade's eyes, I realized I dealt with a grown man and Stormdancer. He could probably order the wind to suck me out of the cave and drop me onto the beach far below. Big difference from fighting with my younger brother, Ahir, whose only talent was to pester me to distraction.

"Opal," Zitora called from below.

I glanced over the edge.

"We need to hurry. I want to reach The Flats by sunset."

My thoughts lingered on Kade and his orb as I helped Zitora saddle the horses and pack the bags. Varun and Kade arrived with full backpacks and I tied their sleeping rolls onto the saddles. Since they didn't have any horses, we would share mounts to Thunder Valley. I eyed Kade's pack with trepidation. He had taken his orb and its muted voice reached me even through the leather.

Soon the whole Stormdance team milled around, waiting to say goodbye.

Raiden gave us a few instructions. "If you're not back here in eighteen days, then don't bother. We're clearing out on day nineteen."

"If the storm pattern changes, don't hesitate to leave sooner. Just send me a message," Kade said.

"Will do." Raiden scanned the sky.

"We'll keep the kiln hot," Indra said.

After all the goodbyes and thank yous, we led the horses up The Cliffs. The ascent felt easier. Perhaps because I tended to look up instead of down.

We reached The Flats without any problems. As soon as we were rested, Zitora mounted Sudi. "Varun, you'll ride with me. Kade, you're with Opal."

When no one moved, Zitora ordered, "Let's go. I want to get in a few more miles before we stop for the night."

I don't know why I thought Zitora and I would share a mount, but it appeared the men had assumed the same thing. They glanced at each other. Varun shrugged. He shouldered his pack and swung up behind Zitora.

Quartz bumped my arm with her nose. If horses could laugh, I had the feeling she would be chuckling.

Kade grabbed Quartz's reins. "Should I?" he asked.

"No. She's my horse. I'll take them."

"Suit yourself."

I hopped into the saddle and Kade settled in behind me. It was a tight fit. I tried not to think about his legs pressed against mine, and about where my backside was nestled. Strong arms wrapped around my waist. I was suddenly glad he couldn't see my flushed face. His chest molded to my back and the orb's song grew louder. Its energy vibrated in my heart.

I urged Quartz into a gallop, hoping to distract myself from the hot tingle pulsing through my blood.

We aimed toward the setting sun and kept going once the light disappeared. Zitora slowed our pace, allowing the horses to find a good path in the darkness.

Kade had remained quiet, but I felt him draw a breath. "When I asked you what the orb says to you, I meant just general feelings like happy, sad or angry. Stormdancers hear the storm's personality in the orb. I wanted to see if it was the same for you." A pause. "You surprised me with your answer."

Was this an apology? I searched for a reply. "I didn't mean to upset you."

"I know that…now."

We rode for a while without saying anything. Finally, I asked, "Storms have personalities?"

"Yes. There're subtle differences in the storms. A few blow big and angry, others delight in their energy, some rage with malice, while others brood. Strange, I know."

"Not strange to me. It's similar to my glass animals. They all call to me in different ways. If I really thought about it, I could assign emotions to them like you do with the storms."

He huffed. "I never would have thought storms and glass could have something in common."

"But you put the storm's energy into glass."

"Before I met you, I thought glass was just a container. No personality. I didn't realize what could be done with it."

"What do you mean?"

A grunt of frustration. "It's like paint."

"Paint?"

"Yes, paint. I can dip a brush and smooth paint on a canvas, but all I end up with is a smear of paint. While another can use that same paint and create a masterpiece."

"I would hardly call my animals masterpieces."

"Can anyone else do it?"

"Not that I know of."

"Then they are truly unique and you should be proud of them."

I squirmed at the thought. I was proud of what they could do, but Tula's glass creations were crafted better. More life-like in detail and sought after by collectors, especially since there would be no more. A flare of grief burned in my throat. I swallowed it down and changed the subject.

"Why do you keep the orb?" I asked.

His grip on my waist tightened for a moment before he relaxed. "I was filling the orb when my sister died. Kaya worked on another outcrop two hundred feet away during a sullen storm. I knew the instant her orb shattered. By the time I reached her, she had lost too much blood."

I wanted to express my regret, but, after what had happened in his cave, I kept quiet.

"I keep the orb because it...comforts me. I don't expect you to understand, but it reminds me of Kaya. She could be sullen and moody, yet when she smiled, all was forgiven."

I understood all too well. Siblings fight. They hate each other and love each other, and there are times when one emotion is a heartbeat away from the other.

"Perhaps that's why the orb sings her name," I said.

"Perhaps." A long pause, then he whispered, "But I don't hear her name."

Zitora finally stopped when the moon reached its zenith. We made a fire from the driftwood we had packed. After sitting on the ground for a few minutes, I wished we had taken a couple chairs, too.

"We'll have to buy fresh supplies," Zitora said. "How far are your stockpiles from the market?"

"Not far. The market is an hour's ride east," Varun answered.

I thought about the location of their stockpiles. "How do you get the glass ingredients down to the beach?" I asked Varun. "Wagons won't fit on The Cliff's trail."

"There is another way to the beach. If you head northwest through the Krystal Clan's lands, there's a wide slope down to the coast. Then you go straight south to reach The Cliffs. It's the long way. When we're in a hurry, we take the loads over The Flats and lower them with ropes. An unpleasant task."

He launched into a story about losing a whole load of lime when a rope broke. "It looked like it snowed on The Cliffs" He chuckled. Then he added—with a touch of sourness—"Being the youngest, I was assigned the task of scraping lime off the rocks and picking out impurities before my father and sister could put it into the glass mix."

"Why make the orbs on-site? Why not make them in Thunder Valley and transport them to The Cliffs?" I asked. "It would be easier."

"I asked my father the same thing." Varun squirmed into a more comfortable position. "He quoted me three reasons. Tradition, secrecy and convenience in case more orbs are needed during the storm seasons. Although having to wait twelve hours for an orb seems long to me."

"Better than two days," Kade said. "And it could be the difference between life and death."

Varun and I talked for a while about glassmaking in general.

At one point, Varun shook his head. "I don't feel the same…enthusiasm you do about working with glass," he said. "To me, it's a job to get done so I can go do other things."

"You have time for other activities?" I asked.

"Sure. We work for four weeks making orbs, wait out each season just in case they need more, and then have the rest of the year to ourselves." Varun picked up a stick and poked the fire. "Usually we work other jobs." Poke. Sparks flew. "We don't get enough money from crafting orbs to live." He jabbed at the embers.

"You're well paid for a half a season of work," Kade said. His tone held a warning note.

Varun snorted, but said nothing.

Zitora broke the awkward silence with orders for everyone to get a few hours' rest.

"A few?" Varun asked.

"Seventeen days left," Zitora replied.

"What about setting a watch schedule?" I asked her.

"No need. I'll know if anyone comes close."

"Will you let them? I'd like a little notice if I'm going to wake up with a sword pointed at my throat again." I shivered at the memory.

"Again?" Kade asked.

Zitora filled him in about the ambush.

"Does Raiden know?"

"Yes."

"Isolated attack or can we expect more trouble?" Kade asked.

"We didn't have time to find out. I'm hoping Master Jewelrose has interrogated them before we arrive in Thunder Valley. Do you know anyone who wants to keep you from dancing?"

Kade's gaze grew distant. "The other clans have always complained about our using the storm's energy to fuel our factories, saying it gives us an unfair advantage in producing cheaper goods. The Krystal and Moon Clans have been most vocal. They've even offered to buy full orbs from us, but there are just enough orbs for our factories. And some years are leaner than others. It all depends on how many storms we get and how strong they are."

"Hopefully once we arrive at Thunder Valley, we'll find out who wanted to stop us from helping you," Zitora said.

"Then I'd better come to town with you," Kade said. "We'll drop Varun off at the stockpiles and I'll walk back."

"I get to babysit piles of sand while you're in town." Sarcasm dripped from Varun's voice. "How exciting."

Sleeping on the uneven shale ground proved difficult. I struggled to find a comfortable spot and managed only short snatches of sleep. And Kaya haunted my dreams. She beckoned to me, wanting my help, but I couldn't reach her. She was encased in glass.

A shrill sound pierced my mind and I bolted into a sitting position. Kade sat with his orb cradled in his lap, staring into its depths, lost in another world. Zitora and Varun appeared to be asleep. The fire had burned down into a few glowing embers.

"Kade?"

He jerked as if startled, but didn't look at me. "Go back to sleep."

"I can't."

Now he peered at me through the darkness. "Why not?"

"Your orb." I gestured. "Your sister. You need to cover it."

He returned his attention to the orb. "She was so stubborn. We had a couple of the old orbs left, but she insisted on using a new one despite the danger. Claimed Gian's death was his own fault. Said he had been too ambitious and caused the orb to shatter. Called the old orbs brittle."

I waited, sensing he had more to say.

"She was the strongest Stormdancer, and therefore in charge of us. She made the final decisions." He smiled at a memory. "She was a year younger than me, but she bossed me around since we were toddlers." He laughed. "My parents knew what they were doing when they named her. Kaya means 'my older little sister.'"

"And I thought that bossy quality was reserved for annoying younger brothers," I said. "Mine thinks he knows everything and will argue about it even when I prove him wrong." Funny how I could miss having him around.

"I would have liked to have a brother, but all I had was Kaya. Do you have any other siblings?"

"Two older sisters, but—"

"Do they all work with glass?"

"Yes."

"Do they have magical abilities?"

"So far, I'm the only one. Ahir has just reached puberty. The Keep magicians will test him when he visits me this year."

"Kaya and I could both call the wind," Kade said. "Very fortunate and very unusual, considering neither of my parents has that ability."

"Who is the strongest Stormdancer now?"

"I am. Although I shouldn't be. When Kaya died, my powers doubled."

Our early-morning conversation woke Zitora. She rubbed the sleep from her eyes. "Since you're awake," she said drily, "you can feed and saddle the horses."

I was happy to oblige. Another minute on the hard shale ground and I would have a stiff back. Not pleasant, considering I had run out of Barbasco yams.

Kade helped with the horses while Zitora roused Varun. In no time we were on horseback, eating a cold breakfast of beef jerky. Yesterday's awkwardness between Kade and me was gone, but my skin still tingled where our bodies touched.

Just past the edge of The Flats, we dropped Varun off at the stockpiles. Mounds of sand littered the clearing. Soda ash and lime had been heaped inside small buildings to protect them from the rain. A log building housed an office and modest living area. The building was used by the glassmakers before the season started to make sure the proper goods were delivered from the other clans.

We left Varun a few provisions and Kade promised to bring back more. I collected samples from each stockpile before we headed east.

We soon reached Thunder Valley. The main core of the city was only a few blocks long, about half the size of my hometown of Booruby. However, Thunder Valley wasn't the capital for the Stormdance Clan.

Kade explained the town grew around the market. "The market was located here so it would be equidistant from all the towns in our lands. It's also along the main north-south road."

People hustled through the streets. Most carried packages while others pulled wagons. The heavy scent of fresh bread floated in the air. The buildings, made of wood or stone or a combination of the two, leaned together in an odd collection of sizes and shapes.

We stopped at the town's square. Zitora pointed to an official-looking building that was three times as wide as its neighbors and had been constructed with large white stones. Iron bars covered the windows along the ground floor of the structure.

"I'll talk to the authorities about our ambushers. To save time, why don't you buy our supplies and I'll meet you at the market." She recited a list of items to purchase.

Kade slid off the saddle to join Zitora and I was left to take care of the horses. Without the Stormdancer behind me, the cool air on my back gave me a chill. I couldn't help feeling left out even though I knew Zitora was right. We shouldn't linger too long since we had another five days before we reached Booruby.

I found the market by following the scent of spiced

beef sizzling over an open flame. Tying the horses to a nearby hitching post, I wandered through the market's stalls. The open wooden stands had roofs tiled with shale shingles and all had bamboo shades to protect them from the wind and rain. On a clear day like this morning, the shades were rolled up and tied to the roof.

I bought a loaf of bread, a hunk of cow cheese and a handful of pork jerky. After I finished shopping, I packed the supplies in our saddlebags. With my chore done, I strolled through the market again. This time I purchased a spiced beef stick to eat for lunch and lingered to examine the glasswares for sale.

A stall filled with decorative pieces drew my attention. I stopped to appreciate the craftsmanship of a delicate vase. The clear glass had a swirl of green bubbles spiraling around the tall flute. Sometimes bubbles or seeds meant a mistake, but the effect was stunning. The vase didn't sing, but faint pops throbbed in my fingertips.

"Ten silvers for the vase," the stand owner said. She was an older woman with gray strands streaking her faded black hair. Her lined face looked as if she had weathered one too many storms.

"Did you make this?" I asked.

"No. Imported from Ixia."

"Ixia?" The few pieces I've seen from Ixia had all been thick and practical. No popping. She wanted to inflate the price.

"Nine silvers, but not a copper less." She waggled a slender finger.

"Do you know who made the vase?"

"I'm not telling you! You'll go right to the glassmaker, undercut my business. Eight and a half silvers. Final offer."

"Six," I countered.

"Seven."

"Deal."

The woman muttered under her breath as she wrapped the vase and snatched my money. I hoped to find the artist and the best way would be to show the vase around to see if anyone knew who made it.

The woman handed me the package. I could no longer feel the pops through the thick wrapping. Even so, I felt certain the glassmaker was in the market. I hurried toward the east side positive I would find him.

A column of gray smoke rising in the distance must be from a kiln, I decided. The hot smell of molten glass drew me on until I passed through the market and followed a narrow cobblestone street. Convinced I would find the artist working in one of these abandoned warehouses, I peered through all the windows.

One of the buildings had collapsed and covered the road, creating a dead end. When I reached the rubble, all signs of a kiln disappeared. And my conviction fled. The air smelled of excrement and garbage.

I turned to go back.

A man blocked my way.

He held a sword.

Blue Eyes.

BLUE EYES. But he should be incarcerated in the Thunder Valley jail with the other ambushers.

Yet there he stood. His blade poised for trouble.

I labored to keep my breathing steady. The collapsed building behind me prevented any chance to run away. In fact, the whole alley was quite deserted. A place I would normally avoid. I must have been tricked by magic. His sword was not his only weapon.

Setting my package out of the way, I pulled my sais from their sheaths, and slid my legs into a defensive position, turning my hips and feet to the right side so I made a thinner target.

I rested the sais' weight in the crook of each hand. My forefinger lay on the hilt, pointing toward the weighted knob at the top. The rest of my fingers curled around the U-shaped guard. The metal shaft of my weapons felt icy against my hot forearms.

He advanced. My heart slammed in my chest as fear shot through my body. Sais were not cutting weapons. They blocked swords and bow staffs and could—in the hands of an expert—trap and yank those weapons from an opponent's hands, but with a quick change in grip I could strike, knocking an attacker unconscious.

Five feet away from me he stopped. "Put your sais down," he said. "And I will not hurt you."

"No. Last time you wanted to finish the job, which included killing me and my companion."

"Your companion." His mouth twisted into a tight smile, but the humor failed to reach his cold eyes. "A Master Magician. A surprise that should not have been." He stepped another foot closer. "I do not want to kill you."

"Good to know." I glanced at his blade. Sharpness gleamed from the edges. His actions didn't match his words.

"Your life is precious to me now that I know who *you* are."

"You knew I was a glassmaker before."

"Yes, but not *The* Glass Magician."

"What?"

"You *will* come with me."

The desire to agree pressed on my shoulders and climbed up my throat. I bit my lip to keep the words trapped in my mouth. My muscles tensed with the need to obey, yet I resisted, knowing he used magic. He had caught me unaware before to trap me here, but now I was braced for his magical suggestions.

"No," I said, hoping his powers were weak. Controlling the mind and/or body was an advanced skill, requiring strong magic.

His brow furrowed and the compulsion to join him flared inside me with a painful intensity. An annoyed breath huffed from his lips. "Submit or I will hurt you." He snarled, showing his teeth.

I had done the willing victim routine before. Last time the order had been the go-with-Alea-or-my-sister-would-be-killed threat. My sister died anyway. Lesson learned. "No."

He moved. Jabbing his sword toward my arms, he lunged.

I yelped and blocked the blade, swinging my right sais down. With a flick of his wrist he looped his weapon out of reach. The tip snaked past my upper left arm, leaving behind a burning slash. Blood brimmed and spilled, soaking the sleeve of my tunic.

I was out of my league.

"Do you submit?"

"No."

He shrugged. In a blink, his sword thrust toward my neck. I flipped the sais into an X and deflected the blade up. The force of his blow throbbed through my wrists. The clang of metal echoed in the alley.

Blue Eyes pulled his sword back and tried another lunge. I pushed the weapon toward the ground, but again he flicked his wrist. A line of fire blazed on my right arm. Wonderful. Matching cuts.

He paused with his sword held in midair. My blood stained the tip.

I glanced past him. Didn't anyone hear the fight? Should I scream?

"Submit? You will have so many cuts on your arms and legs, you will faint from lack of blood."

"No."

"Suit yourself." He launched another flurry of attacks.

My breath puffed from the effort of defending myself. When he halted, blood soaked my upper thighs. The ground wobbled.

"You cannot beat me," Blue Eyes said. "And there is no one here to help you."

Not yet. I aimed my left sais at his temple. He blocked with ease and countered. This time he nicked both my shoulders.

A buzzing sounded in my ears as dizziness danced behind my eyes. "Okay." I gasped. "I can't...beat...you." I drew in two deep breaths, trying to steady myself. "But I can...*delay*...you." I sucked in a large gulp of air and yelled, "Master Cowan, over here."

Blue Eyes spun. I rushed him, knocked him over and sprinted past.

In my mind, it was a great plan. If he hadn't recovered so quickly, I would have made it out of the alley. Instead, he tripped me. I fell and rolled over in time to see Blue Eyes level his sword at my throat. I'd been here before.

"Submit."

No other alternative at this point. He wasn't going to kill me, but the overwhelming dread at being helpless and at his mercy made me wish he would. "All right."

Pleased, Blue Eyes stepped back and offered a hand. "Stand," he ordered as if commanding a pet. His sword remained pointed at the ground.

I ignored his help and summoned the energy to move. A high-pitched whistle sounded behind me before a wall of air slammed into us.

The force rolled me along the ground. Blue Eyes flew back and landed in the building's rubble. I rubbed the grit from my eyes in time to see Kade running toward me.

He yanked me to my feet. "Let's go," he said.

"My vase." I gestured to the package. It had been blown against the rubble pile. Probably broken, but I wanted it.

Kade huffed in annoyance. He sprinted over and grabbed it. Blue Eyes stirred. Kade hurried back and hustled me from the alley, only stopping when we reached the market.

I sank to the ground to catch my breath.

Kade knelt next to me. "Are you all right?"

"Dizzy."

"You're covered in blood." He pulled at my clothing, searching for injuries.

I slapped his hand away. "Arms. Legs. No others."

"Let's get you to a healer. Come on, before your attacker finds us."

"Why the hurry? Couldn't you just—" I waved my hand "—blow him over again?"

He gave me a dry smile. "The air is calm today. Happy. It required a lot of effort to convince it to blow. I doubt I can do it again."

Kade practically dragged me to the healer's house. We met Zitora on the way and she supported his decision to take me there, claiming her healing powers could only do so much.

The tall healer led us to a room which contained the equipment needed to tend to the sick—a bed and a table loaded with supplies. After I lay on the bed, Zitora peppered me with questions, which distracted me from the healer's ministrations. I had thought it hurt before he cleaned the cuts, but the wounds screamed with a new level of pain as the sharp sting of alcohol inflamed them.

I answered Zitora as best I could. I faded in and out of consciousness as the healer and Zitora worked on my injuries.

I woke. Lanterns blazed in the room and shadows waltzed along the stone walls. Worried I had wasted time, I sat up too fast and had to wait until the dizziness passed. Once the room stopped spinning, I found a clean set of my own clothes folded at the foot of the bed.

The cuts on my arms and legs throbbed. The injuries looked about two days old with ugly scabs forming, but they remained tender to the touch.

My abused muscles protested each movement as I dressed. I considered the discarded pile of bloodstained and tattered clothing. They were too ruined for even the

Keep's talented seamstress, so I left them there. I would have to order more of the long-sleeved tunics and linen pants that I preferred to wear. Good thing I had left my cloak with the horses.

Zitora and Kade waited in the front room of the house. Both had dark smudges under their eyes.

Exhaustion lined Zitora's face. "Feeling better?"

"Thanks to you...and Kade. How did you find me?" I asked the Stormdancer.

"I heard you yell for Master Cowan."

"We were supposed to meet at the horses. Why were you there?" I asked.

He exchanged a glance with Zitora. She nodded. "We were searching for you."

I waited.

Zitora sighed. "We met with the Stormdance officials. They arrested the group of ambushers we paralyzed, and despite keeping the magicians unconscious, they escaped the first chance they got. Since we knew the ambushers were free, we wanted to warn you. When we couldn't find you in the market, we broadened our search."

"How did they escape?" I asked.

"There was another magician. Since he didn't use his magic during the attack, I didn't pick up on it."

"Blue Eyes is a magician." I explained about being lured away from the market.

"He could be a one-trick. Makes sense since he couldn't force you to go with him when you knew about his magic." Zitora rubbed her eyes.

"Do the guards know who the members of the group are?" I asked.

"Not really," Zitora said. "After tending your wounds, I returned to talk to the administrator. Seems they are from the Krystal Clan. But we don't know whether they're sanctioned by the main government or a separate group. I've contacted Irys and she will detour to the Krystal Clan's capital to investigate."

"Irys?" Kade asked.

"Master Jewelrose. What about the other magicians?" I asked Zitora. "The woman and man. Are they Keep trained?"

"No. I've never seen them before."

Apprehension coiled in my stomach. "Warpers?"

Zitora shook her head. "No. There are no more Warpers. After General Cahil captured them all, they were executed."

I relaxed.

"I feel like I've come late to the party. What are Warpers?" Kade asked.

I almost groaned out loud. An explanation could take days to tell. "Have you heard of the Daviians?"

"The group of rogue Sandseed Clan members who formed their own clan on the Daviian Plateau?"

"Right. The Daviian magicians, who used to be Sandseed Story Weavers, were the Warpers. They used blood magic to enhance their powers and tried to take control of the Sitian Council."

"And control the Master Magicians," Zitora added

with a bitter tone. "They almost succeeded, too, because of Roze."

"Roze Featherstone," I added for Kade's benefit. "She was First Magician *and* the leader of the Daviian Clan."

"Yes, but Yelena Zaltana stopped them—that part I know. Could this be another group of rogue magicians?" Kade looked at Zitora.

"I don't know if they're organized as a group or are just a couple of dissatisfied magicians. Not all magicians in Sitia have to be Keep trained. You've learned how to control your power from other Stormdancers. Same with the Sandseed Story Weavers. The Masters can detect uncontrolled power and we find the person before they can flame out, which will kill the person and damage the power source. Once a magician has control of their power, the danger of a flameout is little to none."

Zitora stood and smoothed the wrinkles from her pants. "I wish I could stay and investigate more, but we need to go. And—" she smiled "—it seems I can't leave Opal alone without her getting into trouble."

Her words reminded me. "Did the city guards find Blue Eyes in the alley?"

Zitora sobered. "When we returned, he was gone. And they haven't found any trace of him."

My skin crawled with the feeling of being watched by Blue Eyes. I crossed my arms and rubbed my hands along my upper arms. The pain reminded me of how close I had come to being captured and of my inexperience with fighting. "All the more reason to practice with my sais."

"And more reason for me to ask around. See if I can discover any helpful information," Kade said. "I'm sure Varun will be fine for another day."

"Be careful," Zitora said. "He's armed."

"I'm a Stormdancer! Mere metal is nothing compared with the power of a storm." Kade made his voice boom and spread his arms wide. His eyes sparked with humor. "I. Am. Invincible."

"Until a happy wind blows," I said.

"Curse those sunny days."

"The bane of your existence."

"The scourge of society."

"The downfall of decency."

"And boring, too. Nothing like a good gale to put a spring in your step." Kade grinned.

It was the first real smile I'd seen from him. His stern demeanor disappeared; replaced by a carefree mischievousness. There was an inner fire in his soul. Muted by grief and loss, but there all the same.

"All right, that's enough," Zitora said. "Kade, send us a message if you learn anything."

"Yes, sir," he snapped and probably would have saluted if Zitora hadn't pushed him out the door.

Zitora and I raced to Booruby. She was determined to get there as quickly as possible without exhausting the horses. At different times during the five-day journey, I wished I were a horse, wished I was back at the Keep and even wished for a day of rain to slow our brutal pace.

The Barbasco yams only helped with aches and pains, not bone-deep fatigue.

On the afternoon of the fifth day, I caught sight of the brick smokestack from my family's glass factory. I cried out and urged Quartz faster through the busy streets of Booruby. Located on the far east side of the city, our buildings were the last ones before the Avibian Plains. Funny how I never considered the flat grasslands of the Plains to be so welcoming before.

The commotion from our arrival was loud enough to draw Ahir from the factory. I never thought I would be so happy to see my brother. I slid off Quartz in time to be knocked over by Ahir.

"Ugh…you're heavy. Do you have sand in your pockets?" I asked.

"You wish, *big* sister." Ahir helped me to my feet.

The top of my head reached his nose. He had grown at least six inches since I had visited during the hot season, towering over my own five-foot seven-inch height.

"Now you can't call me your *little* brother anymore." He smirked.

"Sure I can, Ahir. No matter how big and fat you get, you'll always have a *little* brain."

"You wish, snake spit," he countered.

"I know, fly breath."

"Opal, that's enough. We're on a time schedule," Zitora said in exasperation. "Ahir, where is your father?"

His eyes lit up. "Is Opal in trouble?"

Ahir ignored her annoyed frown, relishing the possibility that I might be in trouble.

"Ahir, you don't want to keep *Master* Cowan waiting," I said.

"Oh boy! You must be in *big* trouble." He rubbed his hands together. "He's in the factory, working with Mara."

Ahir trailed behind us like a dog hoping for treats. Zitora hesitated on the threshold of the building. The heat and roar from the eight kilns presented a physical force, but she pushed through. To me, the thick air and pulsing growl wrapped around me like a favorite blanket. Home.

My father worked at a gaffer's bench with my sister assisting him. His wide, adept hands pulled and plucked at the molten glass with ease. Hunching over his work, he didn't notice us. The familiar sight of his broad shoulders and strong back tugged at my bruised body. I wanted to hop into his embrace so he could make everything all right again.

Instead, I signaled to Mara. She paused in her duties and sent me a welcoming smile. Her perfectly shaped features and wide tawny-colored eyes attracted men to her like snakes to the heat. She had gotten Tula's and my share of beauty. With her long golden curls and curvy figure, she had the complete opposite of my, with my straight hair and athletic build. While all of us had brown eyes, hers were light and interesting; Tula's and mine were dark brown and ordinary.

Ahir's were almost black, which matched the color of his short moppy hair.

I let Mara know we would wait for Father outside. Ahir tried to come with us, but Mara snapped her fingers at him and pointed to another kiln. He hung his head and slouched back to work.

"It's an oven in there," Zitora exclaimed. "How do you stand it?"

I shrugged. "Growing up, I spent more time in the factory than the house. Probably the reason I hate the cold." I rubbed my arms. "It gets really hot when all eight kilns are fired. Eight is too many for my family to handle, so we hired a few locals, two uncles and a bunch of cousins to work the kilns. Shifts help with heat exhaustion. My father makes us take a break after each piece we make."

When my father came outside, his shoulders brushed the doorway. He squinted. In the sunlight, his resemblance to Ahir was unmistakable. Although only a few black strands remained in his short gray hair and Ahir still had a couple more inches to grow before catching up with Father's height.

"Opal." Father crushed me in a bear hug.

I suppressed a wince. Five days of hard riding had not been conducive to healing. My injuries remained tender to the touch. He released me.

"Father, I would like to introduce you to Master Cowan, Second Magician. Master Cowan, this is my father, Jaymes Cowan."

He shook her hand, and invited us inside the house for refreshments. Heat and the smell of molten glass radiated off his body.

Zitora declined. "It's an urgent matter. Is there a private place we can talk?"

He shot me a look of alarmed concern. A familiar situation. If I had been guilty of any misdeed, I would have burst into tears and confessed upon seeing his ire. I quickly shook my head lest he suspect me of being in trouble.

"We can talk in my lab," he said.

We followed him to a small one-story building tucked behind the factory. He led us into his laboratory, where he experimented with various sand mixtures and chemicals to produce glass of different colors and consistencies. Metal tables lined the room. Tools and various measuring equipment hung from neat rows of hooks, and stainless steel bowls had been stacked in precise piles.

The countertops gleamed in the light. Not a speck of errant sand marred the tables or crunched under a boot. Mother used to complain of Father's messy armoire, and would wonder out loud how he could keep his lab pristine, yet fail to hang up his clothes.

His reply had always been one word. Contamination. He didn't want any of his experiments being contaminated by spilled ingredients. It would throw off all his results, he claimed. Contamination also included children with sticky hands and dirty clothes, but his rules hadn't stopped Tula and me from sneaking in here on occasion. I remembered the one time we hid under his desk, shaking in fear of being discovered, which inevitably happened. Our punishment had been to clean his lab for a season. After that season, we never ventured in here again.

Father sat at his desk and gestured for us to sit in the two other chairs. "What's so important?"

Zitora explained about the Stormdance sand and fragile orbs. We placed the samples onto his desk.

"You think one of these ingredients is bad?" my father asked, staring at me. "How did you come to this conclusion?"

I told him about the old orbs and the differences I noticed. "The new orbs aren't as sturdy. Same thickness, just not as dense." I handed him a shard of Indra's orb.

He examined the glass and tapped it on his fingernails, listening to the clinking sound. "All right. I'll work on these. See what I can find." He sorted through his bowls. "Why don't you go into the house? Mother will be thrilled to see you both."

I stood. "Can I help?"

He looked at me in surprise. "It's better if I do it myself." He must have seen my disappointment, because he added, "Would you like to learn what I do here?"

"Yes." I had always wanted to know more about glass, but I knew he preferred to work alone.

"Okay. When we have time, I'll teach you."

"Really?" My turn to be surprised.

He smiled. "I've been waiting for one of my children to

show an interest. Ahir doesn't have the patience and Mara...
Mara is more interested in Leif than glass right now."

We shared a laugh. Even though Mara had been
pursued by every young man in the Cowan lands, only
Yelena's brother, Leif, had caught her attention. But
since he was a powerful magician and worked at the
Keep, they hardly had any time together. I wondered
if Aydan still needed an apprentice. Mara could move
to the Citadel and live near the Keep. She would be
closer to Leif. And to me.

My humor leaked away. Back at the Keep, I knew no
one missed me.

My mother worked in the kitchen. The delightful
smell of bread stew permeated the air. Following the
scent, I found my mother stirring a large pot. She
greeted me with a peck on the cheek.

"Mara told me you were here. What took you so long?
Your mother isn't important enough to say hello to?"

I rushed to apologize. "We had—"

"Urgent business with Jaymes," Zitora said.

Before she could lay on the guilt about not introduc-
ing her, I said, "Master Cowan, this is my mother,
Vyncenza."

My mother perked up at hearing Zitora's title and
launched into gracious host mode. "Opal, go get the
good dishes from the cupboard and set the table. Use
the fancy Jewelrose tablecloth, and make sure to put out
enough silverware." She clucked over my appearance.

"Better get washed first and put on decent clothes!" She shooed me from the kitchen.

Her offers of every liquid beverage to Zitora reached me as I ascended the stairs. My mother wouldn't be happy until the magician was seated with a drink and snack in hand.

The house had four bedrooms. Tula and I had shared a room. Only seven seasons apart in age, most who met us for the first time had thought we were twins. I entered the room. Tula's grief flag hung suspended over her bed and I wondered how long Mother would keep it there.

Zitora and Yelena had sewn the white silk banner. They decorated it with animal shapes surrounding a single blade of grass with a drop of dew hanging from the tip. Honeysuckles were sewn along the border of the flag. It was a representation of Tula's life and personality. A customary endeavor, making a flag for the deceased and flying it from the highest pole, to release the person's soul to the sky. Then the flag was used to cover the soul's most precious possessions in order to keep them from returning to earth to retrieve them. After a few years, most people removed the flag and gifted the items.

I had missed Tula's flag-raising ceremony while a prisoner of Alea. Sitting on her bed, I ran my hand over the quilt. Last time I had seen my sister, she was in the Keep's infirmary, recovering from being raped and tortured by Ferde Daviian. Alea—another one of those cursed Daviians—had promised Tula would live if I cooperated with her.

Curling up on Tula's bed, I shuddered as a fresh wave of grief crashed into me. Alea had taken me to the Daviian Plateau, pricked me with Curare and left me paralyzed and alone for hours in her tent. And then *he* came.

No. I would not think about him.

I concentrated on Tula. My ordeal was nothing compared to hers. When I had finally been freed, I learned Ferde strangled her to death and stole her soul. Two weeks gone before I even knew about it. Two weeks a captive for nothing. She died anyway.

"Opal, are you done? The table won't set itself," my mother's voice called.

I wiped tears from my cheeks as I hurried to wash and change. My thoughts turned to Kade's grief over his sister, and I remembered thinking about how time would dull his pain. Which was true, but I had forgotten about the occasional knife of grief that stabbed you without warning.

I was mortified during most of dinner. Ahir and my mother were intent on telling embarrassing stories about me to Zitora. The Magician seemed to enjoy them and laughed, but I wanted to hide under the table.

"…naked and soapy from a bath, Opal goes streaking toward the factory, intent on telling her father about her toy duck. Well…" Mother paused for maximum impact. "She crashes right into him and he spills a bowlful of sand on her head! I cleaned sand from every nook and cranny in her body. For months!"

I cut through the peals of laughter. "Do you think I should check on Father? Won't his dinner get cold?"

"Leave your father alone for now. You know how he gets when he's working in his lab. Dinner will keep."

I sighed. One avenue of escape thwarted.

Before my mother could launch into another humiliating story, I asked Zitora about her family.

Her humor faded. "I don't remember my parents. My older sister raised me. We are ten years apart."

Mara made sympathetic noises. "Sisters are great. I wish I saw mine more often." She gave me a pointed stare.

Perhaps I would tell her about Aydan's glass factory in the Citadel.

"Sometimes I wish mine would get lost," Ahir joked.

"Mine *is* lost," Zitora said in a quiet voice.

"What do you mean?" Mother asked.

"When the magicians came, they said I had strong magical powers and should be Keep trained. She escorted me to the Keep and left. I haven't seen or heard from her since."

Gasps of horror ringed the table. Zitora shook her head through the barrage of questions from my mother and sister, and waved away Ahir's apology.

"I searched for years," Zitora said. "Chased every possible lead, visited every infirmary in Sitia, and viewed every unidentified corpse. Either she doesn't want to be found or she's dead and buried." The Magician said the words with a flat tone as if she could no longer produce any emotions about her sister's fate. Or she had exhausted her emotions.

"Why wouldn't she want to be found?" Mother asked.

"Perhaps she wanted to start a new life," Mara said. She rose from her seat and cleared the table.

"Perhaps someone is holding her against her will." I suppressed a shudder; better to be dead and buried.

"Perhaps she was jealous of me. I don't know anymore. I've thought about it for the last ten years and nothing feels right." Zitora stood. Her chair scraped along the floor with a loud squeal. "Here." She grabbed the dirty plates from Mara. "I'll wash."

Mother jumped from her seat with amazing speed. "Oh, no you don't." She hurried after Zitora, disappearing into the kitchen.

Mara, Ahir and I looked at each other.

"Who do you think will win?" Mara asked. "A Master Magician or Mother?"

I considered. "If you could call washing dishes winning, I'd bet money on Mother."

"As much as it pains me to say this, I'd have to agree with Opal." Ahir wrinkled his nose in mock distaste.

Sure enough Zitora returned from the kitchen. "Your mother—"

"A force of nature. We know," Ahir said. "Come on, Mara, let's go help her while Opal entertains her guest."

My father woke me in the middle of the night. The bright glow from his lantern seared my eyes. Already awake, Zitora sat on the edge of her bed—my bed, actually. I had slept in Tula's bed under her flag.

His words finally sank into my sleep-fogged mind.

"...found the cause of the weak glass," he said. "Come."

I GRABBED MY cloak and hurried after my father. The sky glittered with stars and the half-moon cast a weak light over our compound. Father led Zitora and me to his lab.

Torches blazed and crackled. The air smelled of camphor and honey. Bowls filled with sand and water rested on the countertops along with opened jars and spilled ingredients. It was the first time I'd seen his lab messy.

"I had forgotten all about it," he said, picking up a small porcelain bowl. "Hoped never to see the cursed substance again." He thrust the container at Zitora.

Confused, she handed it to me. The contents appeared to be lime. I grabbed a pinch, and rubbed the white substance between my fingertips. Lime.

"Jaymes, what are you talking about?" she asked.

"What's wrong with the lime, Father?"

He drew in a deep breath and settled into his chair.

"Thirty years ago, well before the Commander's takeover of Ixia, we used to import sand and other glass compounds from the north. There were a number of glass factories in Booruby back then—twice as many as today—and competition was fierce." My father's gaze was unfocused as he stared into the past.

"I only had two kilns then, but my wares were different and I was new. Business boomed and I ordered another two kilns."

Zitora opened her mouth, but I placed my hand on her shoulder, warning her to keep quiet with a slight shake of my head. He would get to the point of his story eventually, interrupting or hurrying him would only prolong the tale. We sat in the other two chairs and listened.

"Unfortunately my rivals took exception to my newfound success and plotted ways to discredit me. They started what's now known as the Glass Wars. My factory was hit first. They contaminated my lime with Brittle Talc. It looks like lime, feels like lime, but if it gets into your molten mix, the talc affects the quality of your piece."

"Makes it less dense?" I asked.

"Exactly. Drove me crazy, wondering why my glass broke so easily. Almost drove me out of business, too. Soon only a few glass factories remained. We suspected sabotage, but had no proof. I discovered the contaminant by accident. While shoveling my lime into bags to sell to the farmers because I was desperate for money, I spilled a bucket of water onto the pile. The lime turned purple."

"Purple?" Zitora asked.

"Purple," my father repeated. "The water reacted to the Brittle Talc, changing color. We didn't know the name then, but when I made glass with lime that didn't turn purple, it didn't break. I was just happy to be back in business, but the other glassmakers who had been hit by the Brittle Talc decided to retaliate."

"The Glass Wars," I said, remembering my father's stories. "You never told us about the Brittle Talc before."

"I didn't want you to know about it. Eventually, the man responsible for bringing the talc to Booruby was caught and the factory owners who started the whole mess were arrested. The factories that had survived the war in one piece signed an agreement to work together. Only a few of us knew about the talc and we promised to keep it quiet. There hasn't been a problem—besides minor disagreements—since."

Father pulled the bowl from my hands and set it on his desk. "This is a sample of the lime you brought back from the Stormdance Clan." He tipped a glass of water into it. The lime turned purple.

"Could the talc get into the Stormdance lime by accident?" Zitora asked.

"Nope."

"Who knows about Brittle Talc?"

"Me, my brother and two other master glassmakers."

"Where does it come from?" I asked.

My father shot me a proud smile even though my question didn't show any great intelligence on my part. "Ixia."

Ixia. The northern country was named twice since I've been working with the Stormdancers. The old lady who sold me the glass vase at the Thunder Valley market also mentioned Ixia.

"We have a trade treaty with Ixia. All goods sent over the border either way are supposed to be recorded. Perhaps we can find out who is exporting Brittle Talc to Sitia. What is it made from?" Zitora asked.

"From the flowers of the Chudori plant. When dried, they can be crushed into a fine powder. The plant grows near the northern ice sheet and at the base of the Ixian Soul Mountains."

"In other words, in locations where no one lives." Zitora frowned.

"Where no one can witness the harvesting of the flowers." He swirled the contents of the bowl.

"What about the man who was caught for bringing Brittle Talc to Booruby?" I asked. "Was he from Ixia or Sitia? Did he mention anyone who helped him make the talc?"

"Back then you could cross the border to Ixia without papers or permission. He had the pale coloring of a northerner. He claimed he worked alone, but he wouldn't tell us anything more about himself or the talc."

"Is he still alive?"

"No. He was killed in prison by a glassmaker's son. The young man's father killed himself when his business was destroyed and the son managed to get arrested and thrown into the same prison. No one in Booruby grieved."

We sat for a while in silence. I mulled over the information my father had given us.

"Are any of the other glass ingredients from the Stormdancers tainted?" I asked.

Father gestured to the array of bowls. "Not that I could find, but there is always a chance it could be a substance I haven't seen before."

Zitora leaned closer to the desk. "How big of a chance?"

I answered for him. "Tiny. He's been working with glass for over thirty years."

"Opal, now don't go making me sound so smart. But I will say the Brittle Talc is the only substance I found that affects the density of the glass. If there was another problem with the orbs, then I would tell the Stormdancers to buy all new ingredients for their glass."

But all they needed to buy was clean lime. "So the spiked lime was sabotaged. Who would do it?" No one spoke for a moment. I listed suspects in my mind, including the Stormdancers and the glassmakers. "Do you think the ambushers had anything to do with the tainted lime?"

"It's possible. They planned to stop us from helping the Stormdancers. I would like to know who told them we were coming," Zitora said.

"What's next?" I asked her.

"I'll contact Kade and tell him to order clean lime. We can question the glassmakers who knew about Brittle Talc before we leave."

"I'll talk to my brother," my father said. "See if he heard anything."

While Zitora returned to the house to pack, I stayed and helped my father clean his lab. As he handed me bottles of chemicals to put away, he explained the purpose of each one.

"When you add this white sand to the mix, it helps reduce seeds in your glass," Father said.

His comment reminded me about the vase I had bought at Thunder Valley. It had many seeds or bubbles. When we finished, I ran to the house to retrieve my vase and met him in the kitchen.

"Missed dinner," he said between bites.

I unwrapped the package, hoping the glass was still in one piece. The vase had been well cushioned and survived being blown by Kade's wind.

My father held the piece up to the lantern light to examine it. The green bubbles refracted the light, casting splashes of color along the walls. "Interesting use of seeds."

"How does it feel?" I asked.

"Light yet sturdy. Smooth. Well crafted."

He misunderstood my question. I searched for the right words. "Do you feel any popping or throbbing through your...?" My words died in my mouth. His bewilderment told me all I needed to know.

"Throbbing? As in magic?"

A glimmer of hope. Perhaps he did know. "Yes."

"No. I never felt anything from glass. It feels like a cold piece of crystal in my hands."

I masked my disappointment.

"However, I recognize the craftsmanship and can tell you who made this."

"Who?" Perhaps another magician like me!

"Ulrick, Cesca's youngest son. Do you remember him?"

"Vaguely. Didn't you work with Cesca on a big project?"

"Yep. I had an order for a hundred jars I couldn't fill in time. She offered to help and we've worked together on a number of projects since then. In fact, she's one of the glassmakers who was around during the Glass Wars and knows about the Brittle Talc."

The coincidence seemed too easy, but it made sense. Cesca reminded me of my father. She was dedicated to her craft; she experimented with different recipes and tried new methods of glassmaking. Her children probably learned from her.

The only memory I have of Ulrick was his complete disregard for Ahir, Tula and me. He had followed Mara as if she held him on a leash.

Zitora came into the kitchen, dragging her saddlebag. My mother followed, carrying my bags.

"Mother," I admonished, rushing to relieve her of the heavy burden. "You should be in bed. Dawn's not for another hour."

"Who can sleep with all the ruckus?" she said. "Besides you're not leaving *my* house without something hot in your stomachs." She held a hand up. "I don't want to hear it. Opal, stir the fire to life and heat up the teakettle. Jaymes, take Master Cowan's bag and saddle the horses."

I laughed at Zitora's chagrin as we hurried to complete our assigned tasks. "You might as well sit down and enjoy the attention," I told her. "Next time you visit, you'll be considered a member of the family and she'll order you around, too."

A slight wistful tone crept into the Master Magician's voice. "I would like that very much."

With stomachs full of Mother's special sweet cakes, Zitora and I said our goodbyes to my family, and headed into the heart of Booruby. It was about an hour past dawn. The streets hummed with early-morning activity. Citizens bustled along the sidewalks as wagons rumbled over the cobblestones, making deliveries.

"Wicent's factory is down Morgan Street." I pointed to the curl of gray smoke hanging above a stone building. "Where do you want to meet?" Wicent was the other glassmaker who knew about Brittle Talc.

"The main road near the west side of Booruby. Stay in populated areas, Opal. We still don't know where Blue Eyes is or why he wants you."

"I'll be careful."

Zitora nodded and urged Sudi down Morgan Street. I stayed on the main road for a few blocks before turning left onto Glass Alley, so named for the numerous glass factories located here. I found Cesca's factory. The largest on the block, her building housed ten kilns. A store to sell her wares occupied the front section of the factory.

I tied Quartz to a hitching post and entered the crowded store. All the sales staff were busy, so I examined the goods. Plates and bowls with swirls of colored and clear glass lined the shelves along with matching wine goblets. Water pitchers and vases all had the same delicate twist of color. A few pieces showed the artistry of another hand, with thicker handles on the pitchers and heavy drops of color in the bowls.

In the corner, a few of Ulrick's pieces rested on a shelf. Covered with dust, the decanter and matching goblets were bumpy with bubbles. The glass resembled frozen sea foam. I stroked the decanter. Pulses of energy darted through my hand, numbing my fingers.

"Can I help you?" a woman's voice asked.

I removed my hand and looked up. A saleswoman waited with a polite smile and bored eyes.

"I need to speak with Cesca. It's important."

"I'm sure *you* think it's important." The woman eyed my travel clothes and sighed. "She's busy *working*." She put her hand on my elbow and guided me toward the door. "Send her a message, perhaps she'll agree to meet."

Before I knew it, I stood outside on the sidewalk. Quartz snorted in what sounded like amusement. I shot my horse a sour look. Peering through the window of the shop, I flinched. The rude saleswoman laughed with a customer. She pointed and everyone in the store turned to look at me. I moved from their sight. Not wanting to make a scene, I circled the building, searching for another entrance.

The storage sheds were located behind the factory. Workers pushing wheelbarrows moved between the shed and main building. I followed a man with a load of soda ash into the heat and roar of the factory. A sense of urgent production radiated from the workers. Serious expressions and quick motions kept them absorbed in their tasks. I spotted a few women bent over their work, but none resembled Cesca.

A hand touched my arm and I spun to deflect it, thinking about the rude saleswoman. A man stepped back with his hands out. I stopped and stared. The green in his eyes was so vivid it reminded me of lush grass lit by morning sunlight. Long black eyelashes outlined his eyes and matched his short dark hair. Even the smudges of dirt on his chiseled chin enhanced his features.

"...doing here?" He shouted over the din.

"I'm looking for Cesca. Do you know where she is?"

He peered at me with distrust. I hadn't realized Cesca was so famous.

"Why do you want to see her?"

"Tell her Jaymes's daughter, Opal, wishes to see her about an important matter."

"Mara's younger sister?" Interest flared in his gorgeous eyes.

Every man in Booruby knew and worshipped my sister. He looked close to her age of twenty-two, which probably meant they went to school together. I suppressed my annoyance. "Yes. And the matter is rather urgent."

"Follow me." He led me from the factory and into the cooler air. The man cut down an alley.

I hesitated on entering the quiet narrow street, remembering Zitora's orders to be careful. But I decided the need to talk to Cesca was more important.

He stopped midway and knocked on a door, ushering me into a large storeroom filled with glasswares, crates and packing material. In the far corner an elderly woman sat behind an immense desk. Her thin skin clung to her face, revealing the contours of her skull beneath.

"This had better be imperative, Ulrick, or I won't let you near my kilns for a season." Her voice barked surprisingly strong.

I glanced at Ulrick with interest. He was the popping glassmaker. Unaware of my appraisal, Ulrick introduced me to his mother and retreated to the other side of the room to allow us more privacy. I explained to her about the Stormdancers orbs and the Brittle Talc.

"Nasty," she said. "That horrid stuff almost ruined me. How can I help?"

I paused. Knowing I needed to choose my words with care, I gathered my thoughts. "Does anyone else know about the properties of Brittle Talc?"

"Yes. My children all know. We still check every shipment of lime for the contaminant."

"And you have...?"

"Five children, three boys and two girls. Two daughters-in-law, one son-in-law and six grandchildren." She beamed with pride. "They all work here, except the grandchildren and my daughter Gressa—she's in the Moon Clan's lands. All have been trained to work with glass. They make wonderful pieces. Well...most do." Cesca glanced at Ulrick.

He sorted goblets, rolled them in cotton sheets and placed them into a wooden crate. His movements precise and efficient; the strong muscles in his arms and body apparent to me even though he wore plain gray overalls.

Cesca's family created eight more suspects. I wouldn't have time to talk to them all. "Has anyone asked you about Brittle Talc?"

"Besides my family?"

"Yes."

"No."

"But someone within your family was interested?"

The woman shot me a scathing look. "I hope you're not implying one of my family members could be responsible for those brittle orbs."

I rushed to assure her. "Of course not. But they may have talked to a friend or colleague. We're just trying to find out who knows about the substance."

"Ulrick had asked for more information about it. He wanted to use it. The boy likes to craft flawed pieces," she said with a disdainful tone in her voice. "I told him if he ever brought Brittle Talc anywhere near Booruby, I would report him to the authorities. That is a criminal offence around here." She pounded on her desk with a bony fist. "He never mentioned it again. Smart move." Her pointed stare implied I should do the same.

Time to retreat. "Thank you for your time. If you think of anything else about this matter, could you please tell my father?"

She agreed, but, by her dismissive wave, I knew she wouldn't pursue the subject. As I threaded through the crates, I spotted another one of Ulrick's vases lying on the floor. I picked it up. The blue glass contained bubbles that had been stretched into long thin tubes. Marvelous. Tiny tremors rumbled in my fingers.

"Here," Ulrick said, holding out his hand. "I'll put that away."

"Did you make it?"

A guarded expression cloaked his emotions. "Yes."

"It's fantastic."

He rocked back in surprise. I stifled a laugh, remembering when Yelena had shocked me by being able to see the inner glow in my glass animals.

"But it's unconventional. The seeds…" He shrugged.

"The bubbles enhance the piece."

He gaped. I gave him the vase. When both of our hands touched the glass, it sang. A brief burst of surprised joy. If Ulrick heard the song, he didn't give any indication.

I decided to risk being ridiculed. "What I also like about this vase is its joyful tune."

Shock, fear and amazement flashed. He glanced at his mother, then grabbed my elbow, dragging me out to the alley.

"You heard it...sing?"

He hadn't let go of my elbow.

"Only when you and I both touched it. Otherwise I *feel* its song."

"Feel?" His fingers dug into my skin.

I pried his hand off. "Yes. It pops when I touch it."

"But...but..." He yanked at his hair. "No one else can hear it. Or feel it. I don't even know what it is."

"It's magic. Another magician should be able to feel the vibrations."

Sudden recognition lit his eyes. "You're the one who was invited to the Magician's Keep! You're the glass magician."

I flinched. He used the same title as Blue Eyes.

He held up his vase. "Does this make me a magician?"

Probably a One-Trick Wonder like me, but I wasn't going to say it aloud. "I don't know. I'm meeting with Master Cowan soon. Perhaps you should talk to her. Can you leave for a few hours?"

Ulrick frowned at the door to the warehouse. "No one will miss me."

"Sorry I was rather abrupt earlier," Ulrick said as we led Quartz through Booruby's crowded avenues. "I didn't recognize you. You've grown."

"So have you." I glanced at him before focusing on

the street. Quartz bumped my arm and I almost stumbled into him. "Watch it," I muttered to her.

"Excuse me?"

"Not you. Quartz."

Ulrick scanned the horse. His eyebrows cocked into an appreciative arc. "She's well-bred. Must be a Sandseed horse. I'm surprised there are any left."

The renegade Daviian Clan had decimated the Sandseed Clan, but a few members survived and started anew on the Avibian Plains. "Quartz is the first one to come to the Magician's Keep in four years."

"And she was given to you. You must be a powerful magician."

"I'm not powerful." I rushed to explain. "I helped a friend, who put in a good word for me about Quartz."

"Fortunate for you." His mouth twisted into a bitter frown. "Fortunate that you were invited to the Keep in the first place. That you get to travel with a Master Magician." He was quiet for a few paces. "I guess you don't feel lucky. You seem so casual about it all."

"Would you rather I flaunt it?"

"I would flaunt it."

But I didn't earn my position and, even if I did, I wouldn't take it for granted. At least, I hoped I wouldn't. "A combination of tragic circumstances led to the discovery of my talent. You might have the same power."

"I'm too old. Even my mother has given up on me." Anger laced his words.

"You're not too old. The Keep brought in Yelena Zaltana when she was twenty."

"Really?"

"Yes. And Master Bloodgood mentioned searching for another…glass magician. Perhaps you'll be one, too."

"Perhaps."

He didn't sound happy about the prospect. I studied his strong profile. Eventually, he turned to me. "I've learned not to hope. When I made my first bubble vase, it sang with happiness. I was so proud of my creation until my mother dashed it to pieces in the cullet barrel. She claimed it was flawed and I should try again. Nothing I made suited her, while my younger sister, Gressa's pieces thrilled her. Mother only let me display a vase in her shop to stop me from pestering her. She figured no one would purchase it, and its coating of dust would deter me from making more."

"But you've sold some. I bought one at the market in Thunder Valley."

"You did? Which one?"

I stopped Quartz and rummaged through my saddlebags. "The design caught my eye, but the popping sealed the sale." Holding up the little vase with its green bubbles, I smiled at Ulrick's surprise. "You just need to find the right customers."

Tucking the vase back into my bag, I grabbed Quartz's reins and headed west on Vine Street. The road emptied. Ulrick could now walk beside me without being jostled.

Maria V. Snyder

"Nelinda said she could sell my pieces," he said in amazement. "I didn't believe her."

"Well, she claimed the glassmaker lives in Ixia."

He laughed. It was a rich sound, heavy and deep. "Never trust a saleswoman. I guess an Ixian glassmaker gives them a more exotic appeal."

"They would sell well in the Citadel's market." I thought about Aydan and his kilns. Perhaps Ulrick could work with Aydan and me while he studied at the Keep.

Now I was hoping. I shook my head. After my last year of schooling, I would probably return to my parents' factory. I should be concentrating on the problem at hand and not daydreaming about the future. My thoughts led to the Stormdancers' orbs, and I remembered Cesca had said her children knew about the Brittle Talc.

"Do you use any special ingredients for your pieces?" I asked Ulrick.

"A few. I like to experiment with the mixture. I used vinegar once to see if I would get more bubbles in the glass." His gaze held a faraway look as he grinned in amusement. "I did get bubbles. More than I could handle. The vinegar reacted with the lime as soon as I added it. I cleaned the mess for days and I was banned from the mixture room for a season."

"What other compounds have you tried?"

He shot me a sly smile. "Fishing for information?"

"Just curious."

"My mother taught me to never trust a fellow glass-maker. What do you really want to know?"

I debated about what I should tell him. "Your mother mentioned you had an interest in Brittle Talc."

"So that's why you came to see her. Has someone spiked your family's lime?"

"No. It's regarding another matter."

He waited. The tight buildings of the city dwindled as we walked. A scattering of houses and factories trailed from Booruby like crumbs from a cookie. The acrid smells of the city faded into the moist aroma of manure and wood smoke.

"Never trust a fellow glassmaker. You said so yourself," I said.

"You think I used Brittle Talc to taint another's glass?" His voice rumbled low in warning.

It was possible. Instead, I said, "No. I just wondered why you were interested in the substance."

He stopped. "It's none of your business."

"But it is *my* business," Zitora said from behind us.

I jumped and Ulrick spun around. She sat on Sudi's back with her sword in hand.

"Who are you?" he demanded.

"That was my question, considering you're with *my* student."

I introduced the Master Magician to Ulrick. He had the good sense to relax his threatening stance, but he ruined any chance of getting on her good side with a comment about her youthful appearance. She scowled.

"Sorry, Master Cowan." He rushed to make amends. "You surprised me. I didn't hear you behind us."

"You weren't supposed to. Now answer Opal's question about the Brittle Talc."

"No."

Zitora glanced at me, questioning. I knew she wanted me to name him as a suspect, then she could have Master Jewelrose delve deeper into his private thoughts. But the breach in privacy would cause more harm than good. The magic in his glass pieces might be beneficial to us and it wouldn't help if he was resentful over the Master's intrusion.

"Is that why you brought me along?" Ulrick asked me. "To find out about Brittle Talc? Was all the talk about magic glass a ruse?" Anger pulsed from him. He was about six inches taller than me and he tried to intimidate me with his height.

It might have worked if Zitora hadn't been there. Hard to feel insecure with a Master-level magician on my side. I shouldn't be worried, but here I was, even with sais hanging from my belt, relying on Zitora's presence.

"I was serious about the magic." To prove my point, I removed his vase from my bags and handed it to Zitora. "Can you feel anything?"

She sheathed her sword, and examined the delicate piece. "No. It feels like a regular glass vase. Although, I do like the swirl of bubbles." She peered at the base. "What's this?"

Ulrick stepped closer. Zitora pointed to the bottom and he reached to steady the vase. When his fingers closed on the top, Zitora cried out and almost dropped it.

"It...hummed," she stammered.

"What did it sound like?" I asked.

"Contentment."

I pressed my fingertips to the vase in Ulrick's hand. A pleasant rumble rolled through my palm. When I pulled it from his grip the song died, but the vibrations remained. I brought it to the Master Magician. She touched the glass with me. Nothing. No song. No rumble. It only sang with Ulrick's touch.

Zitora motioned for Ulrick to grab the vase. Her lips settled into a contemplative purse as they both held the glass. She let go and dug into her pack, uncovering her glass unicorn. "Ulrick, what do you see?"

He stared at the animal, then shrugged. "A rather ugly creature."

"Anything special about it?"

"No."

Zitora and I exchanged a glance.

"Opal, you feel the magic without Ulrick's touch. Right?"

"Yes."

"We don't have time or the resources right now to investigate further. Ulrick, would you be willing to travel to the Keep and let Masters Bloodgood and Jewelrose test you?"

"Test me for magic?"

"Yes."

He brightened with interest. "How will they know I'm coming?"

"I'll send a message. Although, if you want to wait until Opal and I return to the Keep, that's fine."

"How long?"

"About fourteen to twenty days."

"Where are you going?"

"To finish our mission."

"Can I come with you?"

"No. We only have two horses and we're in a hurry. I already delayed here long enough."

Ulrick considered. "I'll meet you at the Keep in fifteen days. That should give me enough time to tie up any loose ends."

My thoughts returned to Ulrick as Zitora and I raced back to the Stormdance lands. He knew about Brittle Talc. Perhaps he had told one of the Krystal Clan members who had ambushed us. Although, anyone in his family could have passed along the information. We would have to investigate after we finished helping the Stormdancers.

Once again, Zitora set a hard pace, and soon my mind numbed with exhaustion. Thoughts reduced to the basic tasks of eating and staying in the saddle.

By the morning of the seventh day, we reached the coast. My bruised and stiff muscles turned my dismount from Quartz into an awkward tumble. The thought of being able to stretch out on one of the Stormdance cots propelled my feet down the tight trail of The Cliffs.

Kade met us at the halfway point. "The lime has been delivered. The kiln is ready to go. Indra has melted the ingredients." He hustled us along, handing Quartz off to Raiden in the storm cave.

There were a few new people in the cave, but I didn't have time to meet them before Kade pulled me outside. "We need orbs. Now." He pointed to the sea. "A deadly storm is coming."

"When?"

"Tonight."

10

I FOLLOWED KADE back up The Cliffs and to the kiln's cave high above. The need to hurry had given me a jolt of energy, and banished my aches from the long ride.

Along the horizon, greenish-black clouds, thick and menacing, blocked the sun's rays. Only a dim light escaped, creating twilight in midmorning. The still air hung heavy with potential as if waiting for a signal to blow. The quiet caused my skin to tighten.

No waves crashed against the rocky shore. The flat water resembled a sheet of glass. I stared at the sea, surprised by the conflicting images of an advancing storm over calm water.

"The beast is sucking energy from the water," Kade said. "Although far away, it's moving fast. But no waves means the real danger will come when the center of the storm passes overhead. The winds will shift toward us, pushing all that seawater into The Cliffs."

Kade escorted me into the cave where the glassmakers waited. "Which means, I need to be out there before the center hits. And I'll need orbs."

Sand and the other glass ingredients littered the floor of the cave. Indra sat at a gaffer's bench and her two brothers, Varun and Nodin held blowpipes ready to gather slugs for their sister.

"Come get me when they're ready. I need to conserve my energy." Kade left.

"Did you test the new batch of lime?" I asked Varun.

"No purple color and we already melted enough sand to make six orbs," Varun said.

"Our expert's here," Indra said with genuine pleasure. "Let's get to work." She ordered a slug and Nodin hurried to gather a molten ball of glass on the end of his blowpipe.

He placed the pipe on the bench's holders and passed tools to Indra as she shaped the slug into an orb.

In the tight cave, I tried to stay out of their way. I checked the ingredients piled on the floor. The soda ash and sands looked free of contaminates, but without testing them in a lab, there would still remain a lingering feeling of doubt. After all, someone had tried to sabotage the orbs before.

Indra made six orbs. Although they were similar in appearance and size, each orb held a distinctive shape. While they cooled, Nodin mixed more sand to melt and Varun regaled me with his adventures with the lime merchant.

"...he couldn't understand why we needed more lime, and he almost had heart failure when Kade dumped a bucket of water onto his stockpile." Varun chuckled. "The merchant threatened to cut off our supplies until Kade created a swirling wind. Sand flew everywhere. And the look on the guy's face when Kade speculated out loud about how much stock could be lost in a hard gale was comical. Our order was filled in record time."

"We almost lost the load over The Cliffs," Nodin said. "Where did you find that old rope?"

"Tal brought it up from the stables," Varun said.

"The boy probably didn't take the time to check it over. If the rope had broken two seconds sooner, Tal would have been squashed on the beach." Nodin slapped his palms together.

"Better he's killed by his own sloppy work, than someone else's. I, for one, would not miss him."

"Indra!" Varun scowled at his sister. "That's not nice."

"While you were getting the lime, he's been driving everyone crazy with his whining and moping and pouting. And it's gotten worse since the other Storm-dancers arrived."

"Other Stormdancers?" I asked Indra, remembering the new people in the storm cave.

"Raiden sent a message to them once Kade returned with the new lime. If these orbs work, they'll be needed to help harvest the energy from the storms."

Sour nervousness turned in my stomach. *If* they work.

Near midnight the orbs had cooled to room temperature. I inspected them in the lantern light. No flaws marred the surface and the glass felt solid in my hands.

But there was only one way to test them for brittleness. I flung one to the cave's floor.

The orb broke into multiple pieces with a blood-chilling crack. It hadn't shattered. A good sign. I examined the broken sections.

"Better?" Nodin asked. He hovered over my shoulder.

"Yes. Denser than the ones you made before."

"Strong enough to hold a storm?"

"It better," Raiden said from the entrance. "If we don't bleed energy from the monster brewing out there, we'll be sleeping with the fish tonight."

Raiden moved inside and Kade followed him, holding a torch.

"How many did you make?" Raiden asked.

Nodin glanced at the broken orb. "Five."

"Good enough. Kade can fill two and that will leave one each for Heli, Wick and Prin."

"No," Kade said.

Raiden frowned. "But we'll need all the orbs filled."

"I'm going alone. If the orbs are flawed, then we'll only lose one Stormdancer."

"Two orbs' worth of energy won't be enough to calm—"

"I'll bring all five with me."

"But—"

"I'm not risking the others. Here." Kade handed Raiden his torch. He pulled a netted bag from his pocket, and placed the orbs inside the sack. "You'd

134 *Maria V. Snyder*

better get down to the storm cave before it hits." He wrapped the handles of the bag over his shoulders. The weight of the orbs rested on his back.

The glass spheres resembled oversize seashells. They appeared fragile and inadequate to handle the storm's fury. Anxiety gnawed and chewed up my throat.

"At least stay on the beach," Raiden said. "With the amount of water being pushed toward us, you'd be ten feet under out on the rocks. You'll waste your energy keeping the water away from you. And…" The older man looked as if he wanted to say more.

"And if the orb kills me, you'll be able to recover my body?" Kade finished Raiden's sentence with a flippant tone.

Raiden pressed his lips together.

The Stormdancer sighed. "Sorry, Ray. But you always see the worst in a situation."

"Part of my job. Someone has to make sure you hotshots don't get yourselves killed. If only Kaya had listened."

He rested a hand on Raiden's shoulder. "You had a better chance of a storm listening to you than Kaya."

"When she was determined, that girl made a hurricane seem tame. I miss her."

"Me, too." Kade headed out.

"Kade, wait," I said.

He paused.

"What if—"

"Nothing I can do about it now." He continued down to the beach.

Raiden ushered me to the storm cave. He muttered under his breath about Kade's actions. The glassmakers would stay with the kiln and keep the fire hot. Their cave was high enough that even a rogue wave would not reach them, and the entrance was protected from the wind. Once the second batch of sand melted, they would make more orbs.

Out on the trail, the wind sucked at my body, tugging me toward the swirling mass of clouds. Flashes of lightning lit the sky, illuminating an agitated sea boiling under the tempest. With each flicker of light, waves jumped in size and advanced in leaps toward the shore.

Once we ducked inside, the entrance to the storm cave was blocked with sheets of bamboo rods lashed together. They were anchored to the cave walls.

"The curtains let the air in, and filter out the sea spray," Raiden explained. "Bamboo is flexible so they won't crack under the wind's pressure." He paused and sniffed the air. "Although this storm might tear them up. At least we have a few Stormdancers to keep the water out."

"How do you know what the storm will do?" I asked.

A wide grin spread. "Experience. Years and years of being out here during the storm season. I've learned to look for certain signs—the air smells different for each type of gale and the Stormdancers will let me know what to expect. They're connected to the storm's consciousness, and they're seldom wrong."

The fire and lanterns filled the large cavern with a

warm yellow light. Exhausted from our travels, Zitora slept on a cot next to Sudi's stall along the back wall. Tal pried open oyster shells over a cook pot. He scowled, but I couldn't tell if his ire was aimed at the oysters or at the others sitting around the fire.

Raiden introduced me to the three Stormdancers. Heli jumped to her feet and shook my hand with a big smile. With her skinny arms and short stature, she looked as if she was twelve years old, but she moved with confidence and grace. Wick grunted by way of a greeting. He hunched over the fire and complained of the cold, even though he wore a thick woolen sweater and sported a full beard.

Prin matched my height and age. She appraised me with her silver-colored eyes, giving me a tepid smile. "The glass expert?" she asked Raiden. When he nodded, her attention returned to me. "Are the orbs ready?"

"I think so," I said.

"Think?" She glanced at Raiden.

"Kade has them."

"Should we go down to the beach?"

"No. He doesn't want to endanger you. He'll fill the orbs."

"Can he do all five?" I asked.

Raiden considered. "Probably at least four. His power has grown immensely since Kaya died. Four or even three should be enough to tame this typhoon."

"Unless the storm takes a turn for the worse," Prin said.

"Do you think it will?" Raiden asked with alarm.

Prin peered past us as if scanning the wind. "It is un-settled. Angry and restless. It could blow harder—the sea is warm enough and with the cold air sinking down from The Flats, the potential is there."

"What happens if the storm intensifies?" I asked.

"Four orbs will not be enough, and we will be needed to help evacuate you and the horses to higher ground." Prin frowned.

"What about Kade?" I clasped my hands together to keep them still.

"It depends on where he is and how much energy he has," Raiden said. "We can't risk any Stormdancers. We've lost too many already."

His words reminded me of the brittle orbs. "How will you know if the new orbs work?"

"The storm will tell us," Prin snapped.

Raiden joined Tal and helped with dinner as Prin returned to her seat by the fire.

Heli had listened to our conversation and now she leaned close to me and whispered, "*He* won't take the risk, but *I* will."

I smiled my relief.

"Besides," she said a little louder. "It won't intensify. Those two see gloom and doom in every storm. Prin won't be happy until she's made everyone sick with worry."

"Everyone but you."

Heli's green eyes glowed with amusement. "I love storms. The raw wild power gives me a charge."

"I'll give you a charge," Raiden called. "Go fetch Kade's orb. If the storm gets worse, I don't want the damn thing to break."

"Aye, aye, Captain." Heli saluted and slipped through the bamboo curtains.

"What happens if it breaks?" I asked.

"It will release energy back into the storm. Not a good thing." Raiden placed the pot in the fire. Sparks flew into the air.

His comment reminded me of another question. "You said Kade's power had grown since Kaya's death. Is that typical for Stormdancers?"

"Not really. As Stormdancers age, they do become stronger and better at harvesting the storm's power. They learn by experience how much energy to expend on keeping calm around them. But Kade's powers doubled when Kaya died. It's unheard of and almost seems like her magic was transferred to him, which is impossible."

My thoughts lingered on the word *impossible*. Zitora had said nothing was impossible, and I believed her to a degree. But why wouldn't Kade's newfound strength be from Kaya? The Soulstealer, Ferde, had performed the Efe ritual to steal his victim's magic. The Daviian Warpers used blood magic and the Kirakawa ritual to increase their powers. Did a magician really need these rituals and blood to capture another's magic? Each method involved death. Perhaps Kaya's death released her magical energy and it was absorbed by Kade, making the impossible possible.

I wandered to the rear of the cavern to check on Quartz. She munched on grain, content despite the whistle of the wind. I stroked her long neck and fretted about what the horses would do when the full fury of the wind hit.

Quartz cocked her right ear back. She rubbed my sleeve with her muzzle as if comforting me. I jumped when thunder cracked, and stepped closer to Quartz.

Whenever a thunderstorm had raged over Booruby, my sisters and I would huddle together under the blankets of Mara's bed and scare ourselves by telling silly ghost stories. I hugged Quartz. After helping Yelena to imprison those souls in glass, I had learned ghosts were real. Those old stories didn't sound so silly now.

Yelena had said ghosts were lost souls. Being a Soulfinder, she gathered them to her and guided them either to the sky or the fire world.

Quartz huffed at me and I released her. Intelligence lit her brown eyes, and I wished I could communicate with her. Yelena also possessed the ability to mentally "talk" with horses. All I could do was trap magic in glass, which I couldn't even use. Worthless.

"Ow!" The side of my face stung where Quartz's tail had flicked me.

My horse snorted as if to say "snap out of it" before going back to eating her grain.

Heli returned with Kade's orb. The energy trapped inside pounded in my head with insistence. All the Stormdancers winced when Heli walked past the fire.

I showed her the pile of blankets near the horse stalls, and we covered the sphere.

The last of my energy faded as I sat with the others around the fire. They talked among themselves about past storms. After our late dinner of oyster stew, I arranged a cot near Quartz and fell into an exhausted sleep.

Unfortunately, my oblivion didn't last long. The keening of the wind and the roar of thunder kept intruding. The bamboo curtains clattered and waves pounded the shore. My head ached. Unable to return to sleep, I sat on my cot and looked around. Zitora, Raiden and Tal slept nearby. The Stormdancers dozed by the glowing embers of the fire. Heli sat cross-legged next to the bamboo curtains. Her arms were spread out to each side and her eyes were closed.

When I stood, she opened her eyes and winked at me. "Just keeping the wind from snuffing our fire. I hate eating a cold breakfast."

"Is the storm almost over?"

"No. It strengthened when it encountered the warm, shallow water, but slamming into The Cliffs knocked it off its stride." She cocked her head to one side. "That and Kade's efforts."

"The orbs worked?"

Heli grinned. "We felt the first orb fill after you fell asleep."

The tight grip of anxiety released me and giddiness replaced it. I would have whooped out loud if everyone was awake. "Do Indra and her brothers know? We should tell them."

"We'll have to wait until the storm passes. It's too dangerous to be outside."

"Even for you?"

"Yes. The safest way to dance is to be in position *before* the storm hits. It's easier to hold calm air around you than to tame the winds and create a bubble of calm from the maelstrom. In that case, you use all your strength just to make a buffer around you, and you don't have any left to harvest the storm's energy."

"What about your efforts now? Are they draining?"

"A little. All I'm doing is blocking the wind, keeping it from shredding the curtains. I'll wake Wick when I'm tired. He hates to be cold and will sacrifice sleep to keep the fire hot." She glanced with affection at the snoring Stormdancer. "His blanket fell off again. He's just like a little kid." Heli uncrossed her legs as if to stand.

I stopped her. "Stay there. I'll get it."

"Thanks." She settled, squirmed into a comfortable position and closed her eyes.

Part of Wick's blanket was trapped underneath his body. Not wanting to wake him, I tiptoed to the back and grabbed another one, and uncovered Kade's orb.

The ache in my head flared into a painful jab. The stinging spikes rapped against my skull as if impatient for my attention. I was about to recover the sphere, but paused. I'm not sure what guided my actions—curiosity perhaps—but I dropped the blanket and laid both hands on the orb.

An icy tingle permeated my fingers, turning them

numb as the sensation ripped up my arms and encompassed my body. My world spun as if I was caught in a whirlpool. The muscles and bones in my body stretched. I thinned and lost all sense of being rigid. A force sucked at my feet as dizziness and nausea flushed through me. I squeezed my eyes shut.

When the motion ceased, I opened my eyes. I stood in a round chamber. Purple, blue and silver swirled on the smooth walls. The glowing iridescent colors reminded me of soap bubbles. I wondered if I was inside one. Sand crunched under my boots when I walked over to the wall. The surface was glass. Past the translucent chamber, a storm raged.

A wind blew from nowhere, sweeping the sand off the floor. The granules piled together forming the shape of a woman. I gaped at the perfect construction, unable to believe what I saw.

I yelled when she grabbed my shoulders with her rough hands.

"Opal, help Kade," she said. Her voice grated. "He's weakening. The monster has grown and only three orbs are filled. The storm will take him."

She seemed familiar to me. "Who are—"

"Help him. Now!"

A ROUND OPENING appeared in the wall. The sand woman exploded into a whirling funnel. Pulled and spun by the strong currents, she disappeared, leaving me alone.

Darkness loomed past the opening. A flash of lightning revealed wet rocks. Another flash lit a figure. He slumped against The Cliffs, head bowed. Rain and sea spray bombarded him. Kade.

The storm's energy pulsed around him. The weight of exhaustion hung on his body. He turned toward me. A brief flicker illuminated the pain in his eyes.

The doorway moved. Dizziness blurred my vision. The air thickened as the storm's essence filled my chamber—orb!

I stood inside an orb. Logic rejected the conjecture because it was impossible, but my gut instinct had no problems accepting it. In fact, a part of me even knew I was in one of Kade's orbs on the beach and not in the cave.

The flow of energy slowed and eventually reversed. The sand woman had said Kade was weak and I had to help him. He couldn't fill the orb. But I possessed no magical skills of use. If he needed a glass dolphin, I could oblige him. Otherwise he was out of luck.

A wave crashed into Kade, knocking him down. My orb bobbed and spun, water gushed in. Just when I thought the orb would be sucked out to sea, Kade grabbed the lip. He tried again to funnel the storm's power.

He failed.

Panic and fear flared.

He would die.

Trapped inside an orb, my thoughts raced, but kept coming back to the fact that glass surrounded me. What did I do with glass? Come on, Opal. Think!

I drew in a deep breath and blew magic into the glass. Concentrating on the power in the air, I inhaled and exhaled. The orb filled with the storm's misty extract. It pushed me up as if a life raft inflated under my feet. My emotions linked with Kade's and his surprise matched my own.

The opening rushed toward me. A black stopper brushed my shoulder and I flew into the open air. A cascade of images spun around me. My body light and as indistinct as a fog, I floated into Kade.

"Opal?" He looked around. The sea beat at the beach, hammering against The Cliffs. The sand around his feet remained smooth; his bubble of calm restored, blocking the waves.

Picking up the last orb, he drew power and I blew my strength into him, giving him all my energy to finish the job.

"Opal...Opal...you...all right?"

The words hissed in my ears. Heli's nose hovered inches from mine. I sighed with relief, glad to be back in the cave even if I lay on the cold floor exhausted. "What happened?"

"I'm not sure. You left to get a blanket and next time I looked you were on the ground." She glanced at the pile of blankets. "I covered the orb. Raiden told us you can hear it. We really didn't believe him, but, by your reaction, I'd say the orb's cry overwhelmed you. They become really agitated during a storm. Although this monster stumbled when it hit land, and I think the danger is past."

Her explanation made sense. Better than believing I had been sucked inside the orb, had a conversation with a sand woman and assisted Kade with his work.

When Heli helped me to stand, grains of sand rained to the floor.

"Looks like you were on the beach," Heli said with amusement.

My legs wobbled.

Heli's grip on my arm tightened. "Perhaps you should lie down." She guided me over to my cot and steadied me until I sat. "Do you want a glass of water?"

I tried to say no, but my throat was raw. Swallowing,

I choked on the taste of salt and sand. Heli strode over to the water pitcher. I glanced around, hoping I didn't wake anyone.

Zitora was up on her elbow, watching me. "Care to tell me what *that* was all about?"

"That?"

"Don't play the simpleton. You know what I mean."

I knew. I liked Heli's explanation, overcome by the orb's song. Zitora wouldn't be satisfied, though. "Can I tell you later?" It was an effort to talk and my eyes kept drifting shut. Besides, I needed time to figure it out.

"All right, but…"

I stopped listening and lay on my cot, falling asleep in a heartbeat.

Light stabbed through my closed eyelids. I groaned and rolled over, blocking the annoyance. Eventually the sounds of people moving and talking with happy voices burrowed into my consciousness. A dry breeze fanned me. As much as I wanted to, I couldn't go back to sleep.

I pretended to be unconscious, needing time to go over last night's odd series of events. What would appease the Master Magician? Should I tell her I was sucked into an orb by a woman made of sand? Questions swirled in my mind. Unfortunately no answers formed from my stew of thoughts.

With reluctance, I peeked to see if anyone had noticed me. Kade slept on a cot next to mine. His tunic was stiff with dried seawater. Grains of sand clung to his chin. I reached out to smooth his hair, remembering our brief union, but jerked my hand back when he opened his eyes.

He stared at me and I knew the sand woman's name. When he frowned, it cemented my conviction. The sand woman was Kade's sister, Kaya. How or why, I hadn't a clue, but it explained why she looked so familiar.

Before he could speak, Zitora walked between us. "You're up. Good. Raiden and I would like to have a word with you and Kade."

Kade sat and looked around. "Where's Raiden?"

"Down on the beach, assessing damage."

We followed the Master Magician. Raiden directed Tal and Varun as they piled driftwood onto a wooden cart hitched to Sudi. When we drew closer, Tal muttered an oath.

"Excuse me?" Kade asked.

"Oh, sorry, I forgot to genuflect," Tal said. "The hero's here with his glassmaking sidekick. All hail the wonder that is Kade." He bowed with mock reverence.

"All right, Tal. I've had enough," Raiden said. "You can stop with the wood. I'm sending you home. Tell Soshe to send another helper to take your place."

"Fine by me." Tal flung his load to the ground. "There are far better uses for my talents." He strode away.

Raiden helped Varun finish loading. The glassmaker grabbed Sudi's reins and led her up the path. He watched as they climbed the steep slope. "I should have Soshe send a horse, too. Usually by this point in the season, the orbs are made and we don't need to haul supplies up to the kiln."

"Once Sudi is rested, we should return to the Keep," Zitora said. "But first I want an explanation about last night." She crossed her arms, waiting.

Raiden squinted at Kade in confusion. "I thought you said everything went well. You brought back five filled orbs."

"I found out five is too many for me," Kade said. His gaze sought mine. "I think I had help with the last two."

Everyone stared at me. I stammered for a moment, then told them a condensed version of my adventures inside the orb. I omitted the part about Kaya and about linking with Kade.

"An interesting development, but it makes sense," Zitora said almost to herself. "Opal can trap magic within glass and Kade uses magic to trap the storm's energy. The two actions are similar. Do you ever use two Storm-dancers to fill one orb?"

"All the time," Kade said. "Usually when we are training a new dancer."

"But both Stormdancers are together with the orb. We don't have one in the cave and the other on the beach. I don't think any dancer in our history could claim that skill." Raiden shrugged. "It must be a talent of Opal's. Either way, it worked out. We finally have orbs we can use and one safe Stormdancer. Now, if only the storm season lasts a little longer than usual, we can make up for lost time." Raiden rubbed his hands in anticipation and hurried away to make lunch.

"We can experiment more with your new skill at the Keep," Zitora said to me. "Since the problem with the orbs is fixed, there's no reason to stay." She left to organize our supplies.

But I wasn't ready to leave. I had made friends with the glassmakers. They accepted me for who I was. The thought of returning to the Magician's Keep and to the snide gossip of my fellow students formed a cold lump in my throat. And I was reluctant to leave Kade. He was the only person, besides Yelena, I had shared power with. I wanted to connect with him again, to feel the strength of a storm and to have control over the wind. Even though the power was vicarious, I still craved it.

He watched the sea, lost in his own thoughts. I turned to go.

"Opal?"

I paused.

"Why didn't you tell them about Kaya?"

"I thought she was a figment of my imagination."

"I thought she had come for me," Kade said in a quiet voice.

I moved closer to hear him.

"I was happy to go with her. Fly to the sky. I wanted…" Kade shook his head.

I knew what he desired. He wanted his sister. Missed her so much, he was willing to leave this world to be with her.

"You wouldn't understand."

I swallowed my reply.

After a while, he huffed with amusement. "Imagine my surprise when you flew from the orb."

Sudden annoyance tinged with anger flared in my chest. "Of course *you* would be surprised." The words erupted from my mouth of their own volition. "So wrapped up in your own problems, you can't even see the people around you. You're not the only person in this world to lose a sister." I strode away.

The emotions dissipated as fast as they had arrived. I regretted my outburst. Even I had been surprised by my ability with the orbs. Although, the more I thought about it, the logic became evident. It was just my one-trick power. Nothing new, except Kade's involvement, which was similar to when Yelena linked with me to trap those souls. I had shared her emotions, too.

Boots crunching on sand sounded behind me. A hand grabbed my elbow and spun me around. Kade.

"I'm sorry. You were right." He searched my face for a moment.

"Go on."

A flash of teeth. "I am being selfish, and I shouldn't have been surprised about your help last night. I should be grateful. You saved my life."

I dismissed the notion. "Kaya—"

"Wasn't the one that gave me her considerable strength."

"But she—"

"Told you I was in trouble? But you didn't have to exhaust yourself for my sake."

"Who wouldn't?"

He shook his head as if he pitied my naiveté. "You're too young—"

"Oh, for sand's sake! I'm almost twenty. Probably only a few years younger than you."

Kade considered as I fumed. "My mistake. I should have known the Master Magicians wouldn't send a first-year student. Plus you solved our problem."

"With the orbs?"

"Yes."

"I didn't solve it. My father did." Before he could comment, I walked away. The crux of my worry revealed. My first mission for the Masters and I had run home to my father for help, wasting precious time.

But Kade wouldn't let me go off in a huff. He caught up to me and matched my stride as I ascended the trail toward the cave.

"You wouldn't be mistaken for a younger woman if you had a little more self-confidence."

I stopped and he almost bumped into me. "What do you mean?"

"Examine your actions during the last two weeks. Is there another who could have done what you did?"

"My—"

"With both the glass orbs *and* with the magic?"

I cast about for an answer, but as the delay grew longer, Kade became smugger.

"You win. I'm the all-powerful glass magician. Happy now?"

"No. More." He waited.

"More?"

"Yes."

"The savior of the Stormdancers. The founder of long-distance communication." I clamped my mouth shut on another boast—the creator of the glass prisons—mentioning them would ruin the mood.

"Good. Now remember all those deeds the next time you're presented with a problem. Knowing what you can do will help you feel confident enough to tackle the next storm."

"Storm?" I asked.

"Sorry. I tend to compare everything to storms. People, life and problem solving."

I considered his philosophy. "What happens when you feel able to deal with a gale, yet, despite your best efforts, it still wreaks havoc?"

"Clean up the pieces, rebuild and continue as best as you can." The humor faded from his eyes. "Although a few things will be permanently destroyed."

That was the kicker. Some things were too precious to lose, and I was sure Kade referred to his sister. My thoughts turned to Tula. Was my sister completely gone?

"You're wrong," I said.

"How so?"

"At first, it feels as if she has vanished forever, and all

traces are destroyed. But later, when the pain of loss doesn't overwhelm all your other feelings, every time you think of her, or hear her voice in your head, or remember a happy time together, you realize she's still a part of you and will never be totally gone."

"Is this from experience?" Kade held himself tight as if afraid to move.

"Unfortunately." I told him about Tula, avoiding the horrible details of her death, but making it clear she had been taken from us.

"Then this fire burning inside me will extinguish?"

I assumed he referred to grief. "It'll die down in time. After all, storms do fizzle."

A brief smile touched Kade's lips. "Now you're using weather analogies. If you hang around here any longer, you'll be spouting storm lingo like a dancer."

I widened my eyes in mock horror. "Then I'd better go."

He laughed. And I marveled at the rich sound—a rare gem, considering all his sour looks and ill humor.

"You better hurry then." His laughter died, but his amusement remained. "Stay safe on your journey home. I won't be there to blow away your attackers." Kade grinned. "I must admit, knocking Blue Eyes over was the most fun I've had this season."

His shoulder brushed mine when he strode past. Energy sizzled down my arm, raising all the hairs as if the air around me was charged for a lightning strike. If Kade felt it, he showed no signs. He continued up the trail, bypassing the storm cave.

* * *

I arrived at the cavern in time to see Tal swing his pack over his shoulder, almost knocking Indra over with the motion.

"I'm ecstatic you're leaving, Tal," Indra said. "I think you'll be much happier harvesting indigo and mucking out stables."

"I don't really care what *you* think. You act like you're so special. How special can you be when you needed little Opal's help? She's proven there's no magic involved in your work. *Anyone* can make those orbs." Tal spun on Raiden. "Deliver your own message to Soshe, old man. I no longer work for you." Tal stomped out.

I hurried to get out of his way. He never looked back.

"Finally," Indra said.

She settled back in her chair between her brothers and next to the fire. Lines of weariness marked the three glassmakers' faces. Varun stared at the entrance with his lips pursed in contemplation. Raiden sat cross-legged on the floor, repairing a fishing net. The other Storm-dancers were absent.

"Where are Heli and the others?" I asked Raiden.

He gestured with a threaded needle. "Out searching for treasure. Big storms deposit all types of goodies on the beach. Heli has a huge collection of beautiful sea-shells." He broke the black twine with his teeth. "I would suggest you join them, but it looks like your boss is getting ready to go."

I glanced toward the back of the cave. Zitora saddled

Sudi. As I skirted the fire to go help her, Indra gestured to me.

"The new orbs worked. Are we good to go?" Indra asked.

"Yes. But you should keep watch over your ingredients until all the orbs are made. One of you should stay in the kiln's cave at all times."

"Surely, you don't think one of *our* clan members sabotaged the lime?" Nodin asked.

"There's no evidence to suggest it. But, then again, there's no evidence to disprove it, either. Tal—"

"Would never jeopardize a Stormdancer's life," Raiden said. "He's upset and disappointed, but I've known the boy since he was little. He's all bluster."

"He's no longer a little boy, and all he ever wanted to be was a Stormdancer. Opal made a valid point. Who wants to take the first shift?" Indra asked her brothers.

Varun volunteered. "Stop by and say goodbye on your way home." He left in a hurry.

I finally joined Zitora by the horse stalls. She had finished saddling Sudi. The contents of her bags littered the floor.

"We don't have much food. We'll stop at the market after we talk to the officials in Thunder Valley. I hope they have more information on Blue Eyes." She organized our remaining provisions and packed them as I hurried to prepare Quartz for the journey.

The Stormdancers returned from their scavenging in time for us to say farewell. Heli gave me a shiny pink-

and-white shell. The almost-flat fan shape was ridged and there was a tiny hole near the top.

"It's a scallop's shell. You can string in on a necklace and wear it if you want," Heli said.

"Don't you want to keep it for your collection?"

"It's for you. A small token of my thanks for helping with the orbs."

I clamped down on my desire to contradict her, remembering Kade's words.

My legs felt as if they were full of sand as we trudged up the trail to The Flats. I tried to convince myself my reluctance to leave was due to a dread over spending the night out in the open and sleeping on the uncomfortable ground. And not due to missing the company of a certain Stormdancer.

We arrived at Thunder Valley the next afternoon. Tired and sore from a night of restless sleep, I followed Zitora into the town's administration building. Even through my fog of fatigue, I noted the elaborate candelabra on the mantel in the lobby. The candleholder's teardrop pattern made with red crystal was a trademark of my uncle's. I remembered how proud and excited he had been when he was asked to make the piece. It was an honor to be chosen to decorate a government building.

Zitora led me into the security offices located in the west wing of the first floor. She warned me that since the escape of the ambushers the local guards were outright hostile to anyone with magic abilities.

We entered an open common area strewn with desks. Guards either worked at their desks or stood in groups. Our arrival caused a bit of a stir and one man approached us.

"Can I help you?" he asked Zitora.

"Yes. Is Captain Loris in his office?"

"No. He's on patrol. I'm Lieutenant Coll. Perhaps I can help you…"

"Master Cowan."

He jerked and stared at me. Three other guards moved closer and spread between us and the door. Everyone's attention pressed on my skin.

"When will the Captain be back?" Zitora asked.

But the Lieutenant ignored her question. He kept his focus on me. "Is she traveling with you, Master Cowan?"

"Why do you want to know?" The firm authority in her voice caused the man to switch his attention back to her.

"I apologize, Master Cowan, but I need to know her identity."

"Why?"

The question was weighted. I recognized the signs. If the man had any intelligence or any sensitivity to magic, he would rush to answer her question before she forced it from him with her magic.

"She matches the description of a wanted criminal."

Zitora's posture relaxed a bit. "She's not a criminal. Her name is Opal Cowan. She's an apprentice at the Magician's Keep."

Coll nodded to the men behind us. I thought they

would return to their desks. Instead, two of them grabbed my arms.

"Hey," I said.

"Explain, now," Zitora ordered Lieutenant Coll.

"Opal Cowan is under arrest."

12

"WHAT'S THE CHARGE?" Zitora demanded.

Silence filled the entire room. All of the officers in the security department's common area watched us. My two guards kept a firm hold on my arms. The third man searched me for weapons, removing my sais.

Twelve armed men against one Master Magician. Her power was considerable and she had disarmed four, including two magicians. But twelve? The odds weren't in our favor.

"Robbery," Lieutenant Coll said. "After your visit sixteen days ago, a woman reported a young girl named Opal stole a glass vase from her market stand."

"I bought it for seven silvers," I said.

"The stand owner said you returned later and snatched a second vase. The woman has two witnesses."

One of the guards handed Zitora a sheet of parchment. "Here's her arrest warrant, Master Cowan."

She frowned at the warrant. I craned my neck but couldn't read the neat printing.

Lieutenant Coll recited a statement about my arrest and rights. His words wouldn't take root in my stunned brain, until he said, "Escort her downstairs. Cell three."

No one moved.

I looked at Zitora. "I didn't steal anything."

"I know. It's an obvious misunderstanding. Release her into my custody, Lieutenant, and we'll settle this matter."

"I'm not authorized. You'll have to submit a request to Captain Loris."

"As Second Magician of Sitia, *I* have the authority. Release her."

Coll blanched, and his right hand hovered near the hilt of his sword. But he pulled it together. "I'm sorry, but I can't unless I receive an order from my direct supervisor."

I hated to admit I was impressed by the Lieutenant, standing his ground when faced with an angry Master Magician.

The tension in the room increased. If Zitora tried forcing Coll to release me, the officers would have to decide who to support. From the array of determined stances, I guessed they would help Coll.

With a huff of annoyance, Zitora relaxed. "Opal, don't worry about anything. I'll have you out before dinner."

"But—" The two guards holding my arms pulled me from the room, cutting off my protest.

In no time, I was led down a flight of steps, through a massive metal door, along a drafty corridor lined with cells on both sides and pushed into a small room. The door closed with a clang, raising goose bumps on my flesh and the loud rasp of the lock hit me like a punch to my stomach.

I marveled at how fast my life had changed. One moment making a stop for food and supplies, the next locked in a prison. Should the turn in events surprise me? If I reviewed my history, I could list many other upsets. But would the anticipation of ambushes and kidnappings make life easier? Probably the opposite—constant paranoia would be a strain. Caution mixed with the quick ability to adapt and respond would be a good combination. If only I possessed those qualities.

None of my thoughts helped me with my current predicament, but I had faith in Zitora and in the knowledge of my innocence.

At least the cell appeared to be clean. Iron bars formed the wall and door facing the hallway, and the rest of the room was constructed with stone. Weak sunlight shone through a small rectangular-shaped window located high on the back wall. Thin bars striped the opening.

A narrow bed was anchored to the floor. A thin straw-filled mattress rested on top of it. If I stood on the end of the bed, I could see outside. I peered out, but the limited view of an empty alley didn't provide any entertainment.

I sat cross-legged on the mattress. This wasn't so bad. No odors. The slop pot was clean, and tucked behind a short privacy screen bolted to the wall. No sign of rats.

I wouldn't be here long. This was bearable. I tried to convince myself this was just an inconvenience despite the tightness ringing my chest. Despite the desire to pace the cell and yell for the guards to let me out. Or should I scream for them? Those doors to the prison were rather thick. Airtight. Spots swirled in my vision. A crushing weight pressed on my lungs.

Drawing in a couple of deep breaths helped relieve the tension. This was tolerable. Much better than being confined in a stuffy tent, unable to move.

Memories of my two-week ordeal with Alea flooded my mind. Almost five years ago, but I still could recall the long periods of boredom, lying there on the floor all day with my muscles paralyzed. Alea had always arrived at sunset and before the Curare's effects had completely faded.

Once the drug wore off, feeling returned to my body. The first few nights, she gave me food and water, and let me stretch my legs. She pricked me with a thorn dipped in Curare when she left in the evening, robbing me of movement again.

I was lulled into a sense of routine. My fears weakened each day, and I looked forward to her arrival. It didn't last long.

On the fourth night she brought a man with her. He wore a red mask and dark glasses. Alea didn't bother to introduce us.

She said to me, "He will be in charge of you until the night of the exchange." She turned to him. "The girl *must* listen to our instructions. Make sure she knows exactly what will happen to her if she disobeys."

He nodded.

"Good. Meet me at Blood Rock on the night of the full moon. Bring her with you."

Alea left the tent. The fabric flap snapped shut with an ominous slap as if she wiped her hands of me. Finally able to move, I sat. He reached for me.

The crash of a door and strident voices interrupted my morbid reverie—thank fate. I recognized Zitora's voice.

"...to talk to her, Captain. You can't deny me entry."

A man's voice replied. "I'm not denying you, I just want you to wait until we can conduct a proper interrogation."

The word *interrogation* sent a cold jolt of fear through me. I moved closer to the bars, waiting for my visitors.

Zitora strode into view first. She had pulled her long honey-colored hair into a severe bun. Her annoyed demeanor radiating an impressive authority. If she had packed her magician's robes, I bet she would have worn them to add to her strong presence.

An older man wearing a navy uniform followed her. Two gold bars glinted from the collar of his shirt and his belt bulged with weapons. He scowled at me.

"Can I go now?" I asked, trying and failing to keep the hope from my voice.

"Not yet. Opal, what's this?" Zitora held up a glass

vase. Made to hold a single flower, it was long and thin. Small bubbles decorated the rim and base of the vase.

I hesitated. Everyone knew what it was. What did Zitora really want me to say? I stuck my hand through the bars. "Can I see it?"

"No," the Captain said.

Zitora gave me the vase. The Captain muttered, but stopped when the Master Magician shot him a look.

The glass popped with magic. "This is one of Ulrick's pieces. Did you purchase it from the woman in the market?"

"No. Captain Loris found it in your saddlebags. It's the stolen vase. Care to explain?"

I stared at her until full comprehension of her words managed to bypass my surprise. "My saddlebags? Are you sure?"

"I witnessed the search." She kept her tone neutral.

"It wasn't there when we left the Stormdancers. Someone must have planted it in my bag." I put my arms out to the side. "Go ahead. Scan my mind."

"She's telling the truth," Zitora reported to the Captain.

"No offense, Master Cowan, but you're biased. She's your student and traveling companion. You're young—"

"Captain." She growled with frustration. Her hands bunched into fists; her body poised to punch the man. But she paused, and made a visible effort to relax. Her arms dropped down and she laced her fingers together.

"Fine. Summon another magician. One who can sense the truth."

"Now you're thinking. I'll send a message. The magician should be here in two days."

"Two days!" My cry echoed in the stone cell.

"This isn't the Citadel. Thunder Valley is a small town. We only have a healer. And we're lucky to have him." The Captain peered at me with suspicion. "I believe you met him. He cleaned up your sword cuts."

"I already explained about the man who attacked Opal," Zitora said.

"The magician you didn't warn us about? Who escaped from our prison? You're saying he stayed in the area, risking capture just so he could attack Opal?"

"And Stormdancer Kade," I said.

"So you say."

Zitora leveled a dangerous stare at the Captain. "Are you calling *me* a liar?"

The Captain refused to back down. "No. But magic is involved with this situation, which makes all memories, information and people suspect."

He was either brave, intelligent or ignorant of the amount of power Zitora could wield with ease. Probably a combination of all three. But at least he agreed to let us have a private conversation, moving away from us.

"I'm sorry, Opal. I have to go through the channels and make nice with the local authorities. They have hard evidence against you—I know." She held up a hand, stopping my denial. "The Captain's right, there is magic in

play, and I intend to get to the bottom of this misunderstanding."

"Could one of the other Masters help you with
your investigation?"

Zitora smiled ruefully. "I contacted Irys. She told
me—with malicious glee I'm sure—that I'm to resolve this
situation on my own. Seems she thinks this a good opportunity for me to practice my diplomacy."

I glanced around the darkening cell. Even though I
was upset and disappointed, I tried to make the best of
it. I didn't have a choice, but no sense upsetting Zitora.
"I have complete confidence in you. And two days is
nothing."

My bravado lasted until she left. I huddled on my cot,
wrapped in my cloak, hoping a guard would light the
lanterns in the corridor.

Zitora had brought me a few comfort items from my
saddlebags. I hadn't even noticed the bundle when she
first arrived. Either that or I had noticed, but denied its
implication.

Two days. Two days wasn't so bad. The kilns reached
the perfect temperature in two days. My brother would
finally apologize to me two days after hurting my
feelings. Mother roasted her succulent pork for two
days before she would let us eat the juicy meat. Two days
was…two days of being a suspected criminal, locked in
a drafty cell.

I fell asleep on the cot, waking only to the sound of a
metal tray being slid under the door. Dinner. I gnawed

on the stale bread, drank the tepid water and ate all of the thick soup.

The lanterns had been lit. Shadows, thin and black, vibrated on the stone wall opposite my cot. Shutters outside my window had been closed and bolted. With nothing else to do, I watched the flames dance inside the glass lanterns until the guard extinguished them, leaving me in darkness. I tried to sleep, hoping to spend as much time as possible in the oblivion of my dreams.

A click of a bolt and a gush of cold air woke me. Crouched next to my window was a figure. The person gestured. I stood on the bed for a better look.

Zitora sawed through one of the bars with a thin metal thread. The cord glittered in the pale moonlight. I figured she was a dream, until the unmistakable high-pitched rubbing sound of the diamond string reached me. With a pop, Zitora moved to the bottom of the bar.

"Watch for guards," she said.

I hopped to the floor and positioned myself near the cell's door, keeping alert for any signs. After enduring the nerve-racking, blood-numbing slide of the diamond string for an hour, I marveled that the guards, let alone the entire town hadn't come over to investigate.

"Let's go," Zitora said.

"But—"

She shushed me. "Later. Pass me your cloak."

I did as ordered.

"Give me your hand."

Surprisingly strong, Zitora helped me through the narrow opening. Once I stood in the alley, she handed me my cloak and a rucksack. "Put these on and follow me." She slung a bag over her shoulder.

I tied the garment under my chin, glad of the warmth. The heavy pack dragged on my shoulders, and liquid sloshed inside. Probably water skins, but I wondered where our original packs were. "I thought you were playing nice with the locals."

"Changed my mind."

We ghosted through the sleeping town, staying in the shadows as much as possible. The half-moon's position in the sky indicated four hours remained until dawn. I asked Zitora about the horses, when we headed out of town.

"Too hard to hide," she said.

I puzzled over her reply. With her magic, surely hiding two horses wouldn't be any trouble.

We continued on the road, traveling north toward the Krystal Clan lands. The indigo plantations thinned, replaced with a smattering of pine forests. I tried to question Zitora on why she rescued me and where we were going, but only received clipped and vague answers.

When dawn brightened the eastern sky, we encoun-tered a few fellow travelers on the road. Zitora turned into one of the clusters of pine trees. Pushing my way through the fragrant branches, I tried to keep up with her.

"Why are we in here?" I asked.

"Too many people. We'll hide until dark."

We reached a sandy clearing.

"Breakfast." Zitora dropped her bag and rummaged through the contents.

I joined her in the open area and sat on the ground with relief. My legs ached from the hours of walking. Fire burned from my blistered shoulders. We split a few hunks of cheese and an apple. During the meal, Zitora kept glancing into the surrounding forest as if expecting someone to burst from the trees.

"Do you sense something?" I asked.

"No."

I studied her. Her emotions were hard to decipher. Each interaction with Zitora seemed off. She acted distant and our student-teacher relationship was gone. Now she gave orders without explanation. Perhaps she was angry with me for causing so much trouble.

The sun cleared the treetops, warming the clearing. Tired from our flight, I considered napping.

Zitora stood and wiped the sand from her clothes. "I'll check the surrounding area."

Confused about why she wouldn't just use her magic, I stared at her back. When she strode out of sight, I caught a glimpse of her shadow.

My heart locked. The black shape following her heels was not Zitora's shadow. It was the shadow of a man with a sword hanging from his belt.

13

MY FIRST IMPULSE was to deny what my eyes had seen. In the quick glance I had of Zitora's shadow, I couldn't have discerned a man's shape or a sword. Could I?

But it made perfect sense. Zitora had acted strange since freeing me last night. Even the rescue was out of character. She had been determined to prove me innocent.

I cursed myself for my incredible stupidity. If I was killed, it would be a good thing, preventing my idiocy from being passed on to my children. My self-recriminations wouldn't help me now, so I ceased them and concentrated on what to do next.

Who was the shadow man? Blue Eyes? He wanted me for an unknown reason—unknown to me. Disguising himself as Zitora and tricking me into going with him was plausible. As a magician, he possessed the skill.

Scanning the surrounding pine trees, I searched for

signs of his return. What should I do? Run? Hide? Yell for help? All three? In order or in a different order? My thoughts spun in place, failing to produce an answer.

Gut instinct urged me to run. Logic argued for hiding, but I dismissed the idea, knowing he would find me with his magic. We were away from the road, doubtful anyone would hear me if I screamed.

Another option presented itself, and every inch of me wanted to reject the notion. I could play along and find out what he wanted. That was the logical plan.

Taking in a few lungfuls of air, I settled my spinning thoughts. If I intended to pretend everything was normal, I needed to act calm.

Of course, as soon as he returned, a wedge of fear lodged under my heart. I hoped the terror hadn't spread to my face. Concentrating on Zitora's image, I tried to ignore the mismatched shadow and pretended the Master Magician was with me.

"Find anyone?" I asked.

"No, but there's a trail through the forest. Let's go."

I regained my feet and brushed the sand off my pants. "Where are we going?"

"North to the Krystal Clan lands."

"Then back to the Citadel and the Keep?"

"Eventually." He wouldn't meet my gaze. "Let's go." Blue Eyes led the way through the pine trees.

Thick branches whacked me in the chest, but soon we broke through the dense cluster and traveled along a thin path. Conversation was kept to a bare minimum just as before. This time, though, I was glad for the quiet.

We stopped for a quick lunch. Fatigue dogged my steps and I lagged behind. Eventually, he decided to find a spot to sleep.

Worried about what the imposter would do while I slept, I fought to stay awake. I tried to think of a few questions to ferret out information about our destination or about his plans, but my overworked mind refused. Sleep won.

My round house of glass shook. It rocked in the wind and threatened to break. Cracks appeared, carving a spiderweb pattern along the smooth walls.

"Opal, wake up." A man's voice hissed in my ear.

My glass world shattered. I jerked awake before the jagged shards could pierce my heart.

Yanking me to my feet, the Zitora impersonator said, "We need to go."

The cold night air, the quick pace and the knowledge of who I traveled with blasted the tired fog from my mind. I kept an eye out for any sign of our destination, but we pushed through thick stands of pines and crossed empty stretches of black-streaked sandy soil.

By morning, I knew we had crossed into Krystal lands. Glints of quartz sparked from the white sand. The open areas widened. Stone and sand quarries dotted the horizon.

I searched the surrounding area for people or houses,

but found none. We had traveled far from the main roads. Panic simmered below my ribs. Once he revealed his true identity, I would no longer have the upper hand.

Unfortunately, I wasn't smart enough to use my advantage. My mind couldn't produce a plan. Even if I had my sais, I knew Blue Eyes' skill with the sword would reduce me to a bloody mess. I hoped we would see a few Krystal Clan members so I could enlist help.

After traveling all day, we rested for a few hours before setting out again. We encountered no one. When I finally spotted a wooden barn-shaped building the next morning, hope bloomed. No animals roamed, and the renovations to the structure implied its new use could be a house or workshop. Smoke billowing from the large stone chimney meant at least one person was inside.

In fact, four people waited within. I recognized three of their faces. They stood among glassmaking machinery. The warm, kiln-humming comfort contrasted with the cold, heart-drumming fear of understanding. A moment of disorientation swept over me.

Tal leaned on a post in the center of the room. His smirk matched the superior cock of his hips. The two others were the ambushers. I expected the leader to start cackling as he had on the day they had tried to stop Zitora and me from reaching the Stormdancers. The woman magician seemed pleased with my reaction. The man sitting on the glassmaker's bench was unfamiliar to me.

I glanced at the Zitora imposter, expecting to see Blue

Eyes with a smug smile. But it wasn't him. Standing next to me was the other magician.

"I love a surprise. Don't you?" he asked, pulling the backpack from my shoulders.

"And I love it when a plan is executed without trouble," the leader said. He hustled over and linked his arm around mine. "Come in, come in." Pulling me away from the door and from any chance of escape, he made a swooping gesture with his free arm. "We've been waiting for you."

My advantage was at an end.

"Let me give you a tour," the leader said.

With his arm still tight around mine, he showed me the kiln, the glory hole and all the other equipment needed to make glass. Bowls, vases and a few glass balls littered the work space. My mind registered the information, but couldn't produce any intelligent thoughts beyond my terror.

The leader escorted me through a door behind the kiln and brought me into a long thin room studded with bunks.

"Our sleeping quarters, but look!" He opened a door at the back. "Your own room."

A single cot had been wedged into the narrow space. No windows and the formidable door locks were on the outside.

He pointed at my cloak. "Why don't you leave that here for now." He released my arm long enough for me to toss the garment on the bed.

Reclaiming my elbow, he walked me to the opposite side of their quarters and through another door, entering into a kitchen with a table and chairs. The place also had a couch along the side wall.

He whisked me back to the main room. The others looked at me as if expecting me to say or do something. "Who—"

"I've forgotten my manners." The leader tsked. "Let me introduce you. My name is Sir." He pointed to the man who had led me here. "His name is Tricky. She's Crafty. Our glassmaker's name is Ash."

The ambushers all shared grins with each other, and I knew their names were pseudonyms. Sir gestured to Tal. "I believe you already met him."

I studied Tal. He was obviously in league with these people. Logic followed and I guessed he had been the one to sabotage the lime with Brittle Talc.

"I know him," I said. "His name is Traitor."

Tal purpled with rage. He moved toward me with the intent to harm clear in his body language.

Tricky blocked his path. Tall and muscular, the magician was the strongest-looking person of the group. I marveled at his skill in convincing me he was the diminutive Zitora. Even criminals possessed more magic than I did. Wonderful.

"After. Wait until after," the magician told Tal.

His ominous comment reminded me there was no sense in lamenting over my deficiencies when my situation was…well, I wasn't quite sure. Perhaps I should draw out the "pleasantries," and give the real Zitora more time to reach me. She had to be searching for me. I hoped. I would even welcome the arrival of Captain Loris and Lieutenant Coll.

"Where is your other companion? The magician with the blue eyes?" I asked.

Sir frowned. "Devlen was hired for his skills with the sword. We expected you and your magician friend to have a cadre of soldiers with you." Sir paused.

Blue Eyes' name was Devlen. Which clan did he belong to?

Before I could ask, Sir continued. "Devlen surprised us when he used his magic. I haven't seen him since we escaped." A murderous glint flared in Sir's eyes. "That was a disaster. But the plan is coming together now. Much nicer than the original."

Finally, my frozen thoughts thawed as the shock dissipated, allowing fear to flow into the empty places. What part of the plan was I in? "Why—"

"Are you here? I'd thought you'd never ask." Sir's cackle increased my unease. He was enjoying himself. "You're going to help us make orbs."

"And if I don't?" I dreaded the answer.

"You will." Sir's voice held confidence. "Do you want the painful details? Or vague threats? Or perhaps you would rather be surprised?" His grip on my arm tightened.

I should have run. When I had discovered the trick about Zitora, I should have bolted. Wrong decision.

Again. I should have known better. But there was no comfort in should-haves. None.

I asked another question instead of answering Sir. "Why do you want to make orbs?"

"That's not your concern," Sir said.

"Why do you need me? You have Tal and Ash; surely they know how to make the orbs."

"We need you to mix the sand. The Stormdance glass-makers keep the percentages of the sand ingredients a secret. Job security, I suppose." Sir shrugged.

"I don't know the percentages."

Sir released my arm and spun, slamming his fist into my solar plexus. I doubled over as the air in my lungs exploded from my mouth. Pain radiated. I knelt on one knee, keeping my bent position and tried not to gasp for air. Unfortunately, I had experienced this sensation before when sparring with my sais at the Keep. When I could breathe without pain, I straightened.

"Don't lie to me," Sir said.

"I overheard Varun telling his brother you figured out the recipe of their precious sand," Tal said.

Sir accepted my silence as agreement to Tal's statement. I had estimated the percentages, but Varun hadn't said how close I had been to the actual numbers. Even a small difference in the mix could affect the quality of the orb. I wasn't about to tell Sir. He might decide my usefulness was over. Tricky's comment about "after" was a more powerful threat than Sir's sucker punch.

"Now that the introductions are over, why don't we

get started?" Sir grabbed my wrist and led me over to a
line of four barrels.

While Tal pried the lids off, Ash brought an array of
bowls and a spade.

"Tell Ash what the proper percentages are," Sir instructed.

Secret recipes were secret for a reason. My father had
taught us never to divulge his special recipes. They were
our pride and our livelihood. What Sir wanted went
against twenty years of habit. "No."

Without warning, Tricky slapped me. The force sent
me reeling back as pain stung my cheek. Sir pulled me
forward. Tricky kicked me in the chest. This time Sir let
me fall. My impact with the floor was a mere nuisance
compared to the sharp pains emanating from my ribs.
Each time I gasped for breath, fire flared.

Tricky placed his right boot on my throat and leaned,
closing my windpipe. Panic overrode all other emotions
and I clawed at his leg.

"Enough," Sir said.

The pressure lifted and I gulped in lungfuls of air.

"What are the percentages?"

When I regained my composure enough to sit up, I
said, "One hundred percent sand."

"Magic this time, Tricky. Be creative."

A half smile quirked before the amusement in his eyes
died, replaced by an icy gleam.

I scooted away from him; hoping distance would lessen
the magical attack. A black beetle, the size of a thumbprint

crawled over my knuckles. I yanked my hand from the floor when I spotted a couple more beetles scurrying toward me.

A light tread ran down my pants. Four more of the bugs crisscrossed my legs. Pricks of movement climbed my back. In no time, beetles coated my body.

I yelped and swatted, but they clung with tenacious determination. They started to bite. Tearing holes in my clothes, they soon reached skin. A fiery pain burned with each bite. Blood welled and a beetle would drink, while his partner chewed hunks of my flesh. Two gnawed into my stomach, disappearing from my sight.

They were eating me alive. Horrified, I writhed on the floor trying to dislodge them, my motions frantic. I didn't want to die.

One of the beetles ate through my cheek; I felt its hard body on my teeth before it clamped down on my tongue. The hot tang of blood filled my mouth.

"Do you want it to stop?" Sir's voice asked.

Choking on beetles and blood, I tried to say yes, but a gurgle was all I could manage.

The attack stopped. No bugs. No pain besides my aching ribs and burning throat. My clothes were intact. I rubbed my hands over my skin just to make sure it wasn't pockmarked with gaping wounds. My fingers slid over smooth skin.

Sir helped me to stand on trembling legs. "The percentages?"

I hesitated.

"If your sand mixture doesn't match the sample Tal brought from the Stormdancers, Tricky'll make sure you do better with your second try."

The threat pulsed in my heart with a familiar ache. The controlling fear. To do as instructed because the alternative was unbearable.

"Tricky—"

"No. Give me a minute. I can't think." Was keeping silent about the Stormdance recipe worth the anguish? The beetle attack replayed in my mind as a shudder of revulsion ripped through my body. I wasn't strong enough before; what made me believe I could endure this time?

I pushed the horror of the beetles from my mind. I needed to concentrate, to become a glassmaker.

Wrong numbers would cause my sand to look different. Even though they had a sample, they still needed me. A small portion wasn't an accurate representation of the entire batch. During the Glass Wars, competing glassmakers tried to steal buckets of their rival's sand to deduce the ingredients. It hadn't worked. The coarser, heavier components tend to settle to the bottom of the pile.

Sir yanked on my arm, twisting my elbow. "We're waiting."

He released my wrist. I rubbed my left shoulder while I examined the contents of the barrels.

The lava flakes and red Bloodgood sand were easy to identify. I dipped my hand into one of the remaining barrels. White Krystal sand flowed through my fingers, powdery and light.

The second barrel contained sand from the Storm-dancer's beach. The coarse yellow and brown grains rasped when they poured from my palm. This, along with the Krystal sand made up eighty percent of the recipe. I would have to keep the red sand and lava flake numbers the same, but I could fudge the others.

In fact, the heavier granules would settle to the bottom of a stockpile over time, leaving the lighter particulates near the top. If Tal had been in a hurry when he stole the sample, he would have scooped from the top.

I pointed to the Krystal barrel. "Fifty percent."

Ash filled one of his bigger bowls with the contents and handed it to Sir. He carried it over to another table.

"Thirty percent from this one."

Ash used a smaller bowl this time.

"Fifteen percent for the red sand and five percent lava flakes."

The glassmaker filled his two remaining bowls. Sir and Tal helped him carry them over to the mixing table. Using a scale, Ash weighed each bowl and adjusted the contents to meet a certain weight.

Again a sense of disorientation swept over me. The effect of seeing a scene from my childhood acted out by people who wanted to harm me. My father had taught me how to use the scale to calculate the right weight of sand for a certain mixture before I learned how to read.

Once satisfied with the weights, Ash dumped all the bowls into a drum mixer. Inside the drum were metal fins. He secured the hatch and spun the drum using a handle, mixing the ingredients with a quick efficiency.

After he emptied the contents into another container, Ash compared the mix with Tal's sample. A new surge of terror swept over me. I willed myself to stay calm and suppressed the desire to swallow the hard knot in my throat.

"Looks the same," Ash said.

The tight band around my neck eased. I drew in a quiet breath as the tension in the room dissipated.

"Can I go now?" I asked.

Sir snorted as if I had made a joke. "You're our guest. We would be remiss in our duties if we didn't feed you and let you rest. Besides we need to make certain the sand melts overnight and the orbs are made properly. And I'm sure Ash will appreciate your expert help tomorrow."

With an arm around my shoulder, he guided me toward the kitchen. Crafty served me a meal of beef jerky and a glass of water before Sir escorted me to my room.

When the lock snapped shut, I almost laughed out loud. I promised myself this would never happen again. But here I was. Again.

I lied.

And the knowledge that I would give them the right percentages if my duplicity was discovered ate through my heart as efficiently as one of Tricky's beetles.

Not only a liar, but a coward, as well.

* * *

I used my cloak as a blanket and managed to get a few hours of sleep before my door was unlocked. Bright morning sunlight spilled into the narrow room.

"Time to work," Tricky said.

He followed me and kept watch as I helped Ash arrange the tools near his bench. The glassmaker had tied his hair back. The smoky color of his eyes matched his hair and could be the reason for his nickname. Powerful muscles sculpted his arms from a lifetime of working with molten glass.

"Empty the annealing oven," Ash instructed. "The items inside should be done."

I pulled open the hatch. The oven slowly cooled the pieces to room temperature to avoid cracking the glass. Removing a glass ball from one of the metal racks, I paused. Sir and his group had tried to make orbs before. The ball appeared to be an early attempt.

"That batch wasn't quite right," Ash said. "We thought we had matched the formula, but the elasticity of the glass wouldn't let the orbs get any bigger without breaking."

The weight and thickness of the orb was wrong, but yet the glass under my hands felt familiar. The odd desire to fill the orb with magic pulled at my heart. I dismissed the impulse. I couldn't put magic into a glass piece I hadn't made. Or could I?

The memory of a sand woman and my connection with Kade floated in my mind. I had blown magic into Indra's glass orb, but with Kade's help.

I set the pieces on a nearby table already laden with past attempts. Sir arrived to watch, but Crafty and Tal remained in the other room.

"Gather a slug," Ash ordered.

Taken aback, I blinked at him for a second. He was letting me collect the molten glass. I moved to obey before he could reconsider. An idea formed in my mind. A chance to escape. I thought of a hundred reasons why it wouldn't work before I could plan. The biggest reason loomed next to me. Tricky.

Reaching for the blowpipe, I focused on the task at hand. I noted the craftsmanship of the kiln. The iron hatch was tight, but swung up with ease. Bright yellow light carried by waves of searing heat pulsed from the opening. I squinted into the glow, wishing I had my goggles.

I inserted the larger end of the pipe into the mouth of the kiln, letting the metal heat. Hot glass wouldn't stick to cold metal. The feel of the pipe in my hands and the habitual actions of warming the end calmed my mind and body. Doubts and worries disappeared, and the real possibility of never having another decent opportunity for escape dominated my thoughts. At least I should try.

Dipping the pipe into the molten glass, I spun it. The motion gathered the slug as if I had twirled a stick in a bowl of taffy. I kept the pipe turning so the slug wouldn't drip when I removed it from the kiln.

Once clear of the kiln, I ceased spinning the pipe. The glowing slug sagged.

"Keep it going," Ash yelled. "You're supposed to be an expert."

A small drop splattered on the wooden floor.

"Hey!" Ash leaped to his feet. He grabbed a metal scraper from his row of tools and tossed it to Tricky. "Clean it up before the floor catches fire."

But I wanted the room to burn. When Tricky bent to clean the smoking globule, I swung the pipe.

14

THE END OF the blowpipe connected with Tricky's temple. It wasn't a hard blow, but getting molten glass on his head was worse than being knocked unconscious. Along with Tricky's shrieks, an acrid smell of burning hair and flesh filled the room.

I moved fast. The commotion would alert the others. Sir grasped the hilt of his sword. I rammed him in the stomach with the hot end of the pipe. His shirt caught on fire. Flesh sizzled. He yelped and hopped back.

Ash was on his feet, reaching for me. I brandished the pipe and he backed away. A woman's voice hollered. No time left. Wiping the rest of the slug onto the floor-boards, I sprinted for a window. An odd instinct pulled at me and I grabbed one of the glass balls from the table.

Cries and shouts followed me as I ran. Smoke fogged the room. I broke the windowpane with the blowpipe and cleared the jagged edges before diving through.

Hitting the ground with an audible thud, I gasped for breath. At least the sandy soil softened the impact. But I wasn't free yet. I staggered to my feet and raced to a nearby copse of pine trees. Once there, I paused in amazement, I still held the glass ball and blowpipe.

Logic insisted I leave the ball there—I would need two hands to defend myself. But the little orb wanted to come, so I cradled it in the crook of my arm.

Bushy green branches thwacked me as I maneuvered through the forest. I increased my speed when the trees thinned. A rustling noise sounded behind me. I glanced back. Nothing. The sound increased.

I stopped, listening. Surrounded by the pitter-patter of movement, I scanned the forest. A brown melon-sized shape dropped from a tree branch. Suddenly the trees around me were filled with these shapes. They rained down to the ground and advanced toward me. Spiders.

Panicked, I searched for a clear path. None.

Magic, my logical mind told me. Illusions. Keep moving. Get out of the magician's range.

My body refused to heed the advice. The glass orb in my hand began to vibrate. Momentarily distracted from the encroaching spiders, I peered at the ball. Ordinary. No flaws or bubbles. No humming of power, yet I sensed potential. As if it waited for me.

I closed my eyes, blocking the vision of a mass of spiders mere feet away. Having nothing to lose, I concentrated on the glass in my hands. I imagined myself working with this piece and reaching a critical point in the process.

Summoning my energy, I channeled magic into the glass ball. A clink sounded. I peeked at the orb in my hands; a tiny brown glass spider was inside. Without thought, I continued. The clatter of the orb filling with spiders rang in my ears. The creatures on the ground disappeared one by one. When the clearing emptied, I held the orb up to the sunlight.

It was full.

The rest of the day passed by in a blur. I kept moving, and alternated running with walking. With no idea where I was or where I was going. I just went, hoping I would find something—a house, a business, people—anything that could help me.

I may have escaped Sir, but with no food, water, money or warm cloak, my troubles were far from over. All I had was a blowpipe and a heavy glass orb loaded with spiders. Spurring me on was my fear of being recaptured, which switched at times to the paranoid belief that one of Sir's group tracked me.

When the sun set, the air cooled fast. The prospect of spending the night outdoors seemed certain. I debated the merits of continuing my journey or finding a place to sleep. My body decided when I tripped over an exposed root and used my remaining energy to stand.

I found a group of pine trees and broke off a handful of branches with my pipe. Not easy considering the lack of a sharp edge. Under one of the bigger trees, I scooped out the sandy soil, making a shallow depression. Wedged below the tree, I used the branches as a blanket.

The thought of predators kept me awake for a while. Before falling asleep, I allowed myself one satisfied smile. I was free.

A cold wetness pressed against my temple. Snuffing sounds tickled my ear. Groggy, I swiped at the annoyance and tried to turn over. But the annoyer persisted and whined.

"Go away," I said to the dog before I realized the implication.

Scrambling from under the tree, I studied the yellow canine. She ran circles around me, wanting to play. Her short coat gleamed in the morning sunlight and her clear brown eyes were alight. Happy. Healthy. Well cared for. Not a stray. Or at least not a recent stray.

I searched for the dog's owner. The dog followed me, but tended to get distracted by various smells and objects.

"Home?" I asked the young dog, hoping she would lead me there.

No luck. She spotted a rabbit and dashed off. Her stocky body wasn't built for speed, though, and she soon loped back.

My stomach grumbled and I wished the dog had caught the rabbit. I mused over the possibility of making an animal trap, but decided to keep walking. The dog stayed with me.

After a couple of minutes, she paused and cocked her head to the side. She spun around and darted through the trees. I followed as fast as I could. Hearing a voice call out, I aimed for the source.

"There you are!"

I froze. Sir had found me. I waited for the inevitable rush, but none came.

"Where have you been?" the same voice asked, but with a playful tone.

Relaxing with relief, I realized the man was the dog's owner. Just past the next tree, an older man petted the yellow dog. She rushed to me with her tail wagging. Excited to see me, she danced around as if I'd been gone for years instead of minutes.

"I see you found a friend," the man said. He scanned my bedraggled clothes covered with pine needles. "Child, you're a long way from anywhere. Do you need help?"

"Yes, sir."

He led me to his farm, and introduced me to his wife, Judi. She immediately brought me inside. Only when I was fed and settled with a mug of hot tea in my hands did the couple ask questions. I hesitated. They lived close to Sir's workshop. What if they knew about him and were helping him?

The kindness and concern on both their faces didn't appear to be faked. I could invent a story of getting lost just in case. But what if Sir and Tricky tracked me here after I left? These people should know about the potential danger. I sighed. Being mistrustful and suspicious was hard work, and opposite of my nature. In the end, I told them a brief version of what had happened.

Horrified gasps followed my story. Judi bustled about the kitchen as if needing action.

The man named Riks reclined in his chair with his dog sleeping at his feet. A thoughtful frown pressed his lips together. "Thought I saw smoke. I'd better take you into Mica to talk to the guards."

The half-day trip to Mica, the long process of explaining about my kidnapping to the Mican authorities and the wait for the town's magician to arrive mixed together into one exhausting day. Riks offered to lead a few soldiers back to his farm and point them in the direction of Sir's glass shop, since I had no idea where I had escaped from.

Finally the town's Captain led me to a small guest room and I collapsed on the bed.

After all was said and done, Zitora confirmed my story through the town's magician, who used one of my glass messengers to speak with the Master. I felt a brief welling of pride to be responsible for increasing the speed of messages, which caused me to smile, thinking about Kade's pep talk on confidence.

Although a wonderful invention, there were difficulties involved with my animals. Setting up a Sitia-wide network and choosing who should be allowed to communicate what type of information had become a problem. The Sitian Council still debated the issue.

Currently, I made them for the Keep's magicians stationed throughout Sitia.

Through the magician, Zitora instructed me to return to Thunder Valley. My arrest warrant had been voided—the two witnesses and the stand owner had been paid by Sir to lie, and the stolen vase had been planted in my saddlebags—yet the authorities still needed to complete the proper protocols for my official release.

Zitora requested an armed escort for me, so I had to wait until the soldiers returned from their mission with Riks.

They arrived the next day, reporting the discovery of the charred remains of Sir's building. The kiln survived the fire, but little else. There was no sign of Sir or his gang.

No other problems occurred during the two-day trip south. I arrived at the administration building and waded through what seemed like a mountain of paperwork. By the time I finished, the sun had set and Zitora wanted to wait until morning to leave for the Keep.

I followed Zitora to the inn where she'd been staying since my disappearance.

"My room has two beds, you can share with me," she said.

We sat at an empty table in the busy common room and ordered dinner. My stomach growled. I hadn't eaten since breakfast.

Questions filled Zitora's eyes. We hadn't had time to discuss the details of my kidnapping. But before she could voice any, Kade arrived.

Strands of his golden-brown hair had sprung from a leather tie, and his clothes were torn and wrinkled. His frown deepened when he spotted us. Zitora and I exchanged surprised glances as he strode toward us. This time of the year was the height of the storm season.

"Kade, what—" Zitora started.

"Are you all right? What's going on?" he demanded, staring at me.

I stuttered, appealing to Zitora.

"I told you she was fine," she said.

"But little else." He rolled my small orb onto the table. "I can't use this to contact you. It only works when you're sending to me." Yanking a chair out, he dropped down, crossing his arms. "I want more details. Now."

I waited for her to bristle, to give him the cold Master Magician stare of affront.

Although she stiffened with displeasure, she kept her comments about his behavior to herself. "I told you to wait. I haven't discussed all the details with Opal yet."

"You haven't?" Outrage filled his voice. "Why not? *My* dancers could be in danger. I can't just *wait* for your information."

Ice crystals could have formed in the air around Zitora. "Opal's been through a difficult time." Her voice sliced with the sharpness of a sword's blade. "Since she kept the Stormdancer's orb recipe a secret despite being physically harmed, I would think you'd be a little more patient regarding this matter."

If I were to describe his reaction in storm terms, I'd say the hurricane just fizzled into a light mist. I tried to suppress my smile when he sought my forgiveness.

"Now that you're here, you might as well stay and hear the information firsthand. Opal?"

Reluctance knotted around my throat. "What do you want to know?"

"Everything from the beginning."

"But you already know—"

She held up a hand. "Doesn't matter. Go on."

Despite her orders, I didn't tell them everything. The incident with the spiders and the fact I had followed Tricky while well aware of his illusion, I planned to tell Zitora in private. The story sounded more heroic without those details. Was I trying to impress Kade?

"Odd," Zitora said after I finished. "This group of rogues wants to make orbs, but they don't have the power to harvest energy from a storm. I wonder what they're planning to do with them."

"Tal was with them. Maybe he told them he can fill the orbs," I guessed.

Kade had listened to my tale in stony silence. "I hope Sir doesn't kill Tal when he discovers the boy has no powers. *I'd* like to do the honors."

By his intent demeanor, I had no doubt he meant it.

"Justice will be served, not revenge." Zitora frowned as she contemplated. "What *would* Sir do once he finds out Tal has no power?"

I mulled over her question. The memory of being eaten alive by beetles came to mind. Tal would suffer, and I couldn't produce any sympathy for him. "If they're planning to harvest storms, then they would have to find another Stormdancer."

"Impossible," Kade said.

Zitora and I shared a smile.

"Nothing's impossible," I said, repeating Zitora's advice to me at the start of this whole mess.

"*My* Stormdancers wouldn't work for Sir."

"Are you sure?" Zitora asked.

Kade refused to back down.

"Sir could coerce or bribe a Stormdancer to work for him." I squirmed in my chair, thinking how easy it had been for Sir to force me to help him. If he had discovered my deception with the sand recipe and punished me again, I knew I would have given him the right numbers.

"A valid point," she agreed.

My thoughts turned to Tricky. Sir had two magicians working for him, could there be others?

"Could they have their own Stormdancers?" I asked.

"No," Kade said.

Zitora shot him an annoyed frown. "If a Master Magician can be corrupted, I've no doubt a Stormdancer can be, too. If you have nothing helpful to add, then be quiet." When she seemed satisfied, she asked me, "What did you mean about the Stormdancers?"

"You said before that not all magicians are Keep trained. Does the Stormdancer power only manifest in the Stormdance Clan members?" I paused, glancing at Kade.

"As far as we know," he said with a stiff tone.

"Then what if one of the clan married a Krystal Clan member? Say they live in Mica and raised a family. Could one of their offspring have the ability to capture a storm's energy?"

"Possible. But who would teach the child?" Kade leaned forward, finally getting into the spirit of the discussion.

I turned my thoughts back to the problem. "There could be a Stormdancer with a grudge."

Kade made a sound, but kept silent.

"Go on," Zitora urged.

"A rogue who decided to leave and start his own group of dancers. But he can't make the orbs so he hires Sir to help him get the recipe. No." I shook my head. "Sir wanted to stop us from helping the Stormdancers with their orbs. Why would the rogue sabotage their orbs?" Wheels turned in my head as I followed the logic. "To make them give up the recipe!"

"Why would the Stormdancers tell the rogue the recipe?" Kade asked.

"They wouldn't, but the glassmakers would. Their orbs are shattering and killing people. They're desperate to make them right. Sir shows up with an offer they can't refuse. Tell him the recipe in exchange for the reason their orbs are so brittle. Except we're called to help and ruin the rogue's plans. He sets Sir on us and when that doesn't work, he captures me."

"A possible scenario," Zitora said.

"It's pure conjecture," Kade said.

"It's an exercise in logic, thinking past the facts. The Masters and I do it all the time. Opal speculated a possible reason for Sir's actions by making an assumption. The rogue. Now, let's assume it's not a rogue dancer but an owner of a factory who wants the orb's energy to power his equipment. There is a lot of jealousy over the orbs. The other clans believe the Stormdance Clan should share."

Before Kade could defend his clan's actions, Zitora launched into another round of questions. I struggled to produce possible answers to how and why a factory owner would try to procure Stormdance orbs.

When fatigue slowed my responses, we stopped for the night. Zitora headed to our room, but I needed to retrieve a few things from my saddlebags.

Kade followed me to the stables outside. "You should never be alone. Sir and his gang are still at large. And don't forget about Blue Eyes."

"I found out his name is Devlen, and I won't forget about him." I shuddered, remembering his possessive hunger. "At least your Stormdancers are safe."

I found Quartz's stall and hunted through my bags, turning my back on Kade to hide my spider-filled orb. I was so engrossed in my task, Kade's quiet voice surprised me.

"I didn't travel all this way just because I was concerned for my Stormdancers," he said.

Afraid to meet his gaze, I kept sorting through my bag

even though I no longer remembered what I had been searching for. "You didn't?"

"No. I..."

I waited.

"I...wanted to ask you about your sister Tula." His voice changed back into his normal tone.

Closing my bags, I wondered what he had really wanted to say. I stood and faced him. "What about her?"

"How long did it take before you could think of her without..." He tapped his chest.

"The burning pain?"

"Yes."

"Two to three years. But don't go by me. Everyone grieves in different ways. For some, it could take longer or shorter. I do know it never disappears. An ember still smolders inside me. Most days, I don't notice it, but, out of the blue, it'll flare to life."

The air around me pressed against my skin as if charged with magic. I stepped closer to Kade, seeking to connect with him, ease his pain.

He jerked back, and the energy dissipated. "Then I should avoid getting burned again."

I masked my disappointment as he escorted me to my room. His distant demeanor returned and he remained business-like and brisk.

"Please inform me if there're any new developments with Sir and Blue...Devlen. Have a safe journey home."

"You, too."

He nodded and left before Zitora opened the door.

* * *

Since there was nothing more to do in Thunder Valley, Zitora and I set out for the Citadel the next morning. Even though she acted normal and knew information only Zitora knew, I still checked her shadow on occasion. Each time the black shape matched her figure, I released a breath I hadn't known I held.

Helping the Stormdancers had gotten me into more trouble than I cared for. I convinced myself that staying far away would be for the best. I stroked Quartz's neck, content to leave Thunder Valley behind. The sunshine warmed my new cloak and the cool air held a crisp scent of earthy pine. For once, I looked forward to returning to the Magician's Keep.

The day passed without incident. When the light faded to gray, Zitora scanned the surrounding area, and decided to make camp off the main east-west road, which led straight to the Citadel. An abandoned quarry was on the other side, and a thin wood occupied our side.

"Gather wood for a fire, and I'll take care of the horses," she said.

I picked up enough dead branches from the edge of the wood to get a fire started, but would need more for the rest of the night. Before searching deeper into the forest, I hesitated. Reluctance pulled. Every time I had been alone, something bad happened.

Determined not to let my fears rule me, I pushed through the underbrush and collected a few bigger logs.

Every sound caused my heart to jump and sweat dampened my shirt, but I persisted until my arms were full.

Zitora lit the fire and cooked us a pot of beef stew. The yellow glow from the flames cast shadows along the ground and in the woods. Multiple times I sought the familiar black shape behind Zitora as if I was a child checking the presence of my mother.

I wondered if Yelena's time as the Commander's food taster made her instinctively test each meal for poisons before she ate or if she avoided hugging people because they might prick her with Curare. Thinking back to the first time I had seen Yelena after I had tricked her, I remembered being so happy to see her I hugged her without thought. She hadn't recoiled. In fact, she hugged me back.

Her advice about not letting the past ruin the future proved impossible to follow. How could I stop checking Zitora's shadow? Wasn't I supposed to learn from my past mistakes? How did Yelena do it? How could she relax by a fire without worrying about a Fire Warper jumping from the flames and burning her?

Magic, of course. She was a powerful Soulfinder. If a person approached her with Curare, she would sense the intention and counter with ease. In my case, I don't think an attacker would wait while I fired up the kiln and gathered a ball of hot glass.

Zitora retrieved our bedrolls from the saddles. I stared at the flickering flames, wishing I could do more with my magic.

"What's this?" Zitora asked. Instead of our rolls, she held the spider-filled glass orb.

"One of the orbs Ash made. I grabbed it when I escaped."

She arched an eyebrow, but remained quiet.

The silence drove the story from me. I told her about Tricky's magical attacks, and how I countered the second one. "I really haven't had the time to wonder where the glass spiders came from. Filling the orb with magic, I can understand. But for the magic to convert into actual glass is beyond my ability to explain."

"Or mine," Zitora said. "Magical illusions are really just visions in your mind. A magician will send you images that cause your body to have a physical reaction, like feeling the beetles' bite and eat your flesh. Once the magician stops, the vision disappears and so does the magic. I've never heard of a magician able to turn magic into an object. Perhaps Bain would know more."

She tipped the ball and shook one of the spiders into her palm. "Are these the creatures that attacked you?" She handed me the piece.

Spider-shaped and fingernail-sized, the clear glass encased a single brown spider. The glass felt thin and brittle as if I could crush it between my fingers. "Yes, but they were bigger." My skin crawled with imaginary legs. I resisted the urge to swipe my arms.

"Why didn't you tell me about this sooner?"

I searched for the right words, but no matter how I phrased it, it would sound strange. "The spiders want to stay with me."

"They do?"

"Yes, and I was afraid the authorities would confiscate them. And we really haven't had time to discuss it yet."

"So you *planned* to tell me?"

"Of course."

Her dubious expression turned into a smile. She shook a handful of spiders from the orb. "There must be hundreds of them." Concentrating on the ones in her palm, Zitora hunched over them. "There's magic inside, but I can't use it to communicate or to do anything else. Perhaps you funneled Tricky's magic into the orb and trapped it."

I considered. If I could do it again, I would have a potential defense against a magical attack. Many questions circled my mind. Would I need to use the exact same type of orb? Or could I use any glass container?

"Very interesting." She poured them back into the ball. "I can't wait to get back to the Keep and try a few experiments."

"Experiments?"

"Yes. Don't you want to explore this new power?"

"I do, but I'll have classes." And tests to fail. Classmates to injure.

Zitora waved her hand. "Your curriculum so far has been geared for a standard magician. Since Yelena's arrival, we have realized that not all students match the standard. When we get back, I want to change your focus."

"You can do that?"

"Of course. Especially since you'll be my student."

I blinked.

"Don't look so surprised," she said. "Your powers have always intrigued me and I think it's about time I mentor a student. Although—" Zitora frowned "—since you've been ambushed, attacked, incarcerated and kidnapped while in my company, perhaps you'll want another teacher."

I rushed to assure her of my honor in being chosen.

She gave me a rueful smile. "My first mission without guards and I made a mess of it. The Sitian Council will never let me go alone again."

At least she didn't run home to her father. My first mission wasn't a success, either. I thought about Kade's instructions to be confident when I left the coast. Despite my boast of being an all-powerful glass magician, now I could think of another who might have done the same thing with the glass orbs and magic. Ulrick.

I counted how many days it has been since we left him in Booruby. Twenty days. My body ached as if seasons had passed.

But my mood lightened. Twenty days meant Ulrick should be waiting for us at the Keep. A potential friend and a potential colleague. I could be working closely with Zitora and Ulrick. My desire to return to the Keep increased threefold.

The sight of the white marble walls surrounding the Citadel made me whoop with joy. After three days on the road, I was more than ready for a warm bath, a hot meal and a soft bed.

Zitora shared my enthusiasm and we raced our horses to the Citadel's west gate. The guards at the entrance gestured for us to slow down, but otherwise waved us through. We maneuvered around the crowded streets and were soon inside the Magician's Keep located in the northeast quadrant of the Citadel.

At the stables, I rubbed down Quartz and fed her a bucket of grain. The other horses had whinnied greetings when we arrived. The Stable Master inspected her from tip to tail and declared her healthy. She sucked down two milk oats from his palm. Most of the horses in the stable would do just about anything for a couple of the Stable Master's special treats.

I returned to my quarters in the apprentice wing. Even though my residence consisted of two small rooms—a bedroom and sitting area—I had them all to myself. After sharing a room with my sisters, being crammed into the Keep's barracks for three years and one year living with four others in the seniors' quarters, I had my very own space.

Dust coated the furniture and a musty odor floated in the cold air. I had been gone for a total of thirty-six days, over half the cooling season. I threw my pack and sais onto the table. Assembling a bunch of kindling, I started a fire to warm the room while I hurried to the bathhouse to bathe.

Ordered to report to the Masters' meeting room right

after breakfast tomorrow, I had the rest of the evening to myself. I decided to grab a late dinner. On my way to the dining room, I passed many of my fellow students. No one stopped to ask where I had been. No one called hello. A few scowled and a couple of girls sniggered after I walked past. The usual reaction.

I wondered how the other students would feel once the news of my apprenticeship to Zitora leaked out. I imaged their stunned and jealous faces. Even better would be when they saw Ulrick by my side, as I gave him a tour of the campus. His gorgeous green eyes staring at me with rapt attention.

My little fantasy lasted until I entered the dining hall. Ulrick sat at the head of a large table filled with students. The group of mostly girls laughed and flirted with him. He was the center of their attention.

Only here a few days at most, Ulrick had managed to do what I couldn't accomplish in four years.

My appetite gone, I fled the hall.

15

I KNEW I shouldn't care Ulrick had already made friends. Most of my life had been lived in my sister Mara's shadow. She had all the friends and attention from every young man in the Cowan lands. I had Tula.

When Tula had been alive, I didn't need anyone else. We were inseparable. Until the night Ferde stole her. She'd sent me to bed early. I was supposed to help her keep the kilns hot, but I was sick with a fever. She dragged me to bed, tucked me in, and the next morning she had been gone.

Dark memories threatened to push up from the depths of my mind. I squashed them down. No reason to suffer the heart-shredding guilt again. No relief in playing the "I should have" game.

I glanced around my empty living area as I crossed to my bedroom. The glass owl Tula had made for me on my fourteenth birthday rested on my nightstand. The statue fit neatly in the palm of my hand. I examined the exquisite detail of each feather and the perfect shape of the talons. She had a finer hand with the molten glass. The tweezers in her expert fingers would blur in motion, resulting in a lifelike animal.

My hopes of finding a true friend like Tula at the Keep hadn't lasted long. With my involvement in imprisoning the Fire Warper and his partners, the other students either were jealous of my "fame" or afraid. And my propensity for classroom accidents didn't help my popularity.

Our classes were small—three to five students and an instructor. I remembered a session with Professor Greenblade, learning the history of Rodknee Bloodgood, the first magician to use magic to move objects. After the lecture, I had been paired with Pazia to recreate Rodknee's original experiment. Pazia had no trouble moving the lead weight off the table and high into the air with her magic. All my efforts resulted in nothing. I couldn't move the weight past the mark on the table, let alone off the surface. When the professor leaned on the table to check his mark, it collapsed under him.

Professor Greenblade laughed it off and continued his lesson, but Pazia and the others had spread rumors that I was a jinx to all magicians.

A knock pulled me from my musings. Going into the other room, I peered through the window. Ulrick.

Surprised, I opened the door.

"I thought I saw you in the dining hall," he said. "Welcome back."

I sputtered for a moment before words formed. "Come in." Moving back, I berated myself for my bumbling. If Ulrick noticed, he didn't say anything.

He walked around the room. On the left side, there was a couch in front of the hearth. Table and chairs occupied the right side, and a desk rested along the back wall and next to my bedroom door.

"This is nice. They have me in the guest quarters for now, but if they see any potential I might get a more permanent spot." Ulrick peeked into my bedroom.

"How long have you been here?"

"Two days. I already met with Master Bloodgood, but he thought we should wait for you and Master Cowan before doing more formal testing." He scanned the papers on my desk, and fiddled with my quill.

"I saw you already made friends." I tried to keep my voice even as if commenting on the weather.

He shrugged. "The kids are sweet and they've been very helpful in showing me the Keep." Moving over to my table, he picked up one of my sais. He hefted the weapon and jabbed the air with the shaft.

"You're bored."

He stopped in midsweep. "Is it that obvious?"

"You're fighting an invisible opponent."

Ulrick laughed and set the sais back down. "I was on the road for six days and here for two. I'm used to working in the factory every day. I need..." He made a vague gesture with his hands.

"I know what you need."

"You do?"

"Yes. I need it, too. Follow me."

"Where've you been?" Aydan demanded. Never one to waste time on pleasantries, he went straight to the point.

I smiled at the old glassmaker. "I've been on a mission for the Masters."

"Mission?" He glanced at Ulrick.

I introduced him to Aydan. "Another glass magician?"

"Maybe," Ulrick amended before shaking Aydan's hand.

The glassmaker snorted. "Another with confidence problems. At least Opal admits she's a magician." He handed me a blowpipe. "Gather me a slug."

I scanned the small shop. No signs of an assistant. Raising an eyebrow, I looked at Aydan.

"I can't find anybody good. They're all lazy. All whine about the heat and noise."

I exchanged a smile with Ulrick. We were probably the only two people in the Citadel who would seek out the glass shop for comfort. "Perhaps you need to hire someone from Booruby."

"Pah. I don't have the time. Besides, I can do it myself."

Why did men get so stubborn when they grew older? I sighed. "If I find you an assistant from Booruby, will you let them stay?"

He gave me a grudging nod. My thoughts turned to my sister, Mara. If she came here to work with Aydan, she would be closer to her beau, Leif. And to me. Selfish, I knew, but I would send her a message.

"Good. In the meantime, I'll help you." I hefted the iron rod.

Ulrick pulled the pipe from my hands. "*We'll* help."

Aydan chuckled. "Now we're talking. Gather me a two-inch slug, boy." He settled on his bench and arranged his tools. "Opal, make me a domed punty and tell me about this mission."

The two of us worked together as Aydan crafted a variety of vases and bowls. I filled them in on what I had been doing for the Stormdancers, skipping a few details. Uncertain about my ability to channel another magician's magic into glass, I decided not to divulge my role in helping Kade or mention the spider incident. I also failed to tell them about Devlen's attack in Thunder Valley, although I didn't know why.

At one point Ulrick interrupted. "They made a glass studio out of wood? That's idiotic."

"It's cheaper and faster to build," Aydan said.

"And it worked to my advantage." I continued the story of my escape.

"Damn. All that equipment burned." The glassmaker clucked his tongue.

Ulrick, though, appeared horrified. "How can you say that when Opal could have been killed?"

"She's here, ain't she? Shovel more coal into the kiln, will ya."

Muttering under his breath, Ulrick grabbed a shovel. When Aydan finished his last bowl, he stood and stretched his arms and back. "There's some melt left, refill it when you're done." Without another word, he left the workshop, heading next door to his home.

Ulrick stopped shoveling. "What is it with older glass-makers? They order you around and go off without a thank-you or goodbye. My mother's the same way."

"When you have a limited time left to live, would you want to waste it on small talk?" My brush with disaster had caused me to realize again how precious life was. Interesting how after Alea had released me over four years ago, I had felt the same way, intending to enjoy every free moment of life. Yet I had lapsed back into a daily routine, wishing my time away.

Ulrick looked at me. Strands of black hair clung to his sweaty forehead. The urge to wipe the dirt off his strong chin pulsed in my chest. I wished I could render his pro-portioned features in glass so I could stare at him without blushing, and I reconsidered sending the note about Aydan to my sister. Ulrick certainly wouldn't be paying at-tention to me if Mara was here.

I squirmed under his continued scrutiny. "Aydan mentioned melt. Would you like to work the glass?"

"Could you show me how to make animal shapes? My

mother always thought it was a waste of time." He shrugged. "No money in it. But I'd like to learn."

We worked together and, with my guidance, he made a swan. The piece didn't resemble a first effort. Ulrick's skills with the glass were impressive.

With the second animal, I gathered the molten glass onto the end of a blowpipe. When he finished shaping the legs and tail of a pig, I instructed him to blow through the pipe. The creature's body expanded as it should. Although well crafted, the pig didn't glow with magic. I didn't mention the lack of power. What worked for me didn't have to work for him, but my curiosity about how he inserted the magic into his pieces grew.

"Can you make one of your vases? One that sings?" I asked.

"No. I need a special sand mix. It's your turn. I'd like to see you work your magic."

Remembering his failure to see the inner glow in Zitora's unicorn, I said, "You probably won't be able to see it."

"Maybe I just need to be here. What are you going to make?"

"I don't know."

He huffed. "You sound just like my sister. How can you *not* know?"

I shrugged.

"I have to have the image of my finished piece firmly in mind before I sit down at the bench. Otherwise I end up with a cold slug of glass."

When I couldn't provide the exact reason my method worked for me, he gathered the last of the melt. All distractions disappeared as I focused on rolling the pipe and shaping the glass. My mind open to the slight nuances in the glass, I used my tweezers and tugged until a shape formed. Then I blew magic into the piece. The core glowed as if on fire.

"I thought you said your speciality was animals," Ulrick said.

"It is." I considered the finished sculpture. Technically it was a living thing, but I had never made a seashell before. It twisted around a center point like a conch shell. "Interesting."

"Crazy," he teased. "Crack it off. I'll put it next to mine in the annealing oven to cool."

"Do you see the inner light?"

He hesitated for a heartbeat. "No."

"So to you this is…"

"A lump of dull glass shaped like a shell. Sorry. Perhaps you should stick to animals."

I waited to see if he would remember seeing Zitora's unicorn. He frowned but didn't mention it. I said the words for him. "Or perhaps not."

"I didn't say—"

"Don't worry about it. My ego can handle it."

"I know my ego wouldn't. Otherwise I would have agreed with my mother and found another occupation instead of trying to prove her wrong."

We cleaned up the work area and filled the kilns with

Aydan's special sand. Ulrick added enough coal to keep the fire hot for most of the night. Aydan would need to check on it overnight. By then, the sand mixture should melt and be ready in the morning.

When we finished, we headed toward the Keep. The lanterns along the main Citadel road cast a yellow softness on the hard marble walls of the buildings. Our footsteps echoed through the deserted street. I marveled over how much time had passed while Ulrick and I had worked.

Nighttime fears and apprehensions crawled along my skin. I checked Ulrick's shadow, sighing with relief to see the shape matched my companion's broad shoulders. I wondered if he knew how to defend himself. Like an idiot, I had left my sais back in my rooms. The need to protect myself still wasn't instinctive in spite of my recent kidnapping. I had assumed Ulrick's company was all I needed to stay safe.

"Why is seeing the inner glow so important?" Ulrick asked.

I explained about the magic trapped inside.

"If I can't see it, then I'm not a magician."

"I wouldn't jump to conclusions. The Masters are just realizing there are a number of unusual magical abilities. If it hadn't been for Yelena, my magic never would have been discovered and I wouldn't be here."

Ulrick looked at me in surprise. "You know Yelena Zaltana?"

"Yes." I waited.

"What's she like? Is she as powerful as the rumors say? As beautiful?"

I suppressed my annoyance. At least he wasn't pumping me for information about my sister, and he hadn't heard about my involvement with trapping the evil souls. I confirmed the rumors and told Ulrick a few details, including her commitment to Valek, the Ixian Chief of Intelligence.

"The most hated man in Sitia in love with the hero of Sitia. Wow. I'd bet the story of how they met would be fascinating."

"It is." Before he could ask for more information, I changed the subject. We discussed the best way to explore his magic glass until we reached the Keep.

The gates were locked, and the guards suspicious until I explained who we were. We didn't see anyone walking around the Keep's campus, but Ulrick insisted on escorting me to my quarters.

"You really don't need—" I started.

"Nonsense. After what happened, you should have a battalion of guards with you at all times."

"A battalion? Six-hundred men?"

"All right. A platoon then, and not a single soldier less." He acted stern.

"I'm insulted, now. Only thirty men? I'm worth a cohort at least."

He considered. "I don't know. You're the only glass magician that we know of, but I've seen the shell you made, and—"

"Watch it."

"You're right. One-hundred men at least, although I'd be happier with two cohorts." He opened my door for me and gestured me inside.

As I passed him, he placed a hand on my shoulder. I paused.

"I'll go and order that battalion. We shouldn't skimp on safety."

The intensity of his concern sent a wave of warmth through me. We had been joking around. Hadn't we?

I couldn't think of a proper response, so I thanked him for taking me home. He nodded and left, closing the door behind him.

In my sitting room, I poked the dying embers of the fire into flames, adding wood until the hearth blazed with light and heat. The crisp air felt empty. And I longed to be... Be where?

Be home with my family? The familiar homesick ache didn't fill my heart. And the thought of going back to helping my father in the factory was unappealing.

Be at the coast with Kade? Tempting, except for the fact Kade grieved for his sister and kept himself at a distance. Plus the Stormdancers had no real need for my skills.

Be with Ulrick? I would enjoy getting to know him better. My skin still felt warm where he had touched me. But I might have read more into the gesture than he had intended. He probably viewed me as a younger sister who held no talent for shaping glass.

I guessed I would have to be content with my current situation. The thought of working with Zitora raised my spirits. Perhaps my last year at the Keep wouldn't be as lonely as the first four.

Tired from only a few hours of sleep, I dragged my body out of bed the next morning. After breakfast, I hustled to the Masters' meeting room in the Keep's administration building.

All three Masters sat at a conference table. They argued without anger. I hesitated in the doorway until Zitora waved me in and pointed to an empty seat.

Maps of the Moon Clan's lands covered the surface. Black lines marked the Ixian border.

"...Valek isn't involved," Master Jewelrose said.

"But that's his calling card," Zitora said.

"Was. Just because a black statue was found in Councillor Moon's house doesn't mean she's been targeted for assassination." Irys Jewelrose flipped through a file of papers. "The Councillor's sister desires the position. It is probably an attempt to scare the Councillor into retiring. We've seen this type of power struggle within the clans before."

"But what about the report of illegal border crossings into Moon lands?" Zitora asked. "We can't send Ixian refugees back to Ixia."

Good point. Before Commander Ambrose agreed to a trade treaty and created a dialogue between Ixia and Sitia, Ixian refugees were granted protection. But now it has become a diplomatic problem between the two countries. The Commander wanted to be informed about any deserters, but he hadn't been willing to let them live in Sitia. As far as I knew, an agreement still hadn't been reached, and the Council claimed ignorance over how many have crossed since the treaty.

"A mess," Master Bloodgood said. "Irys, send a message to Liaison Yelena. See if she will accompany you to the Moon lands. Best if we get this settled quickly. We need to step up our negotiations with the Commander, and finalize the refugee issue."

Irys collected her files and stood. "I'll leave as soon as possible." She paused next to me. "Good work with those Stormdancer orbs. I knew we sent the right person." She winked at me before leaving the room.

"I agree," Bain Bloodgood said. "Councillor Stormdance wanted me to express his thanks. You have impressed us with your knowledge and your escape from harm."

"And she made a few important discoveries," Zitora added.

"Indeed. I will leave you to discuss your plans." Bain's gray eyes sparkled with delight at the prospect of learning.

When the door closed behind Bain, Zitora rolled the maps and returned them to the iron rack. She spread a clean sheet of parchment in front of her. Picking up a stick of charcoal, she said, "First thing we should do is to construct a glass workshop in the Keep."

"Truly?"

"Yes. We should have built one years ago. You've supplied us with your glass messengers all these years and I never stopped to think how inconvenient it was for you to go to the Citadel. You should have requested your own shop."

"I didn't mind. I learned a lot from Aydan." Plus he always listened to my problems and frustrations.

"We now have Ulrick and all those interesting abilities of yours to experiment with. And the need for your magic animals has increased. The Council would love to set up a network of messengers all over Sitia, which means you'll need to make more and you'll need to access the equipment without working around Aydan's schedule." She flourished the charcoal. "I need a list of supplies and specifications."

Zitora wrote down the items needed to build a workshop and I roughed out the design and layout of the shop on another sheet.

"I'll find a location and hire a building crew," Zitora said. "You can buy the necessary supplies and equipment. Ulrick can help you. It'll give him something to do until the shop is ready for you both to use." She signed the bottom of the list. "Bring this list and all the invoices to the Keep's accountant to pay the bills. Make sure you're not cheated. You might want to enlist the services of the market's Helper's Guild. I hear Fisk can point you to the best merchants in the Citadel."

"I'll have to travel to Booruby for a few of these supplies."

"You're in charge." She handed me the paper. "Go where you need to."

"But what about my apprentice classes and studies?"

Her eyebrows spiked up in impish delight. "Besides daily self-defense, weapon and equestrian practice, this *is* your studies."

As I hurried from the Masters' meeting room, I thought about the classes I no longer had to attend. Would I miss the sessions with the Professors and my fellow apprentices? Every school day for the last four years, I had two morning classes followed by lunch. The afternoon activities included weapons and self-defense training with the Master of Arms, and an extra-long history class. Learning Sitian history spanned the entire five-year program. My evenings had been spent studying and practicing the day's lessons.

My emotions flipped from relief—no more frustration over what I couldn't do with my magic and no more accidents—to disappointment—no more hope that another aspect of my power would reveal itself.

However, the job of purchasing supplies and equipment for a glass workshop thrilled me. This task I could do. No worries, hesitation or doubts. A welcome change of pace.

Leaving the administration building, I searched for Ulrick. The weak midmorning sunshine tried to warm the air, but we were over halfway through the cooling season, and soon the dreary dampness of the cold season would dominate. First morning classes had ended. Students filled the campus pathways. Clustered in groups or hurrying to another building, they had a half-hour break before the start of the second sessions.

Intent on finding Ulrick, I sailed past the others not bothering to note their moods. I found him outside the guest quarters surrounded by a gaggle of senior girls. Hanging back, I waited for the group to disperse, but Ulrick spotted me. He excused himself and joined me.

"What's the plan for today?" he asked with a smile.

I filled him in on the details of my meeting with Zitora. Even with students walking past and calling out hellos, he gave me his full attention. Although my sense of importance died when Pazia Cloud Mist bumped into me.

"Sorry," she said with a tone implying she was anything but.

A fellow apprentice, Pazia's powers were impressive enough to cause speculation on whether or not she possessed Master-level magic. Knowing her, I didn't doubt she would demand the Master-level test. She had taken an instant dislike of me the moment we met at the beginning of our first year. And she always seemed to be a witness to my most disastrous efforts, including my latest goof of burning her with hot wax.

"I know I didn't interrupt anything vital," Pazia said. "Ulrick, do you need me to rescue you from the One-Trick Wonder?"

"Excuse me?" He looked at her in confusion.

Normally, I would ignore her snide remarks, but not

this time. "You did interrupt us. I suggest you get to class before you're cited for tardiness."

Anger flared in her olive-colored eyes. "You're going to be late, too. Especially if I set your clothes on fire."

A valid threat. Pazia was known for her temper. I should have backed down and kept my mouth shut, but I didn't. Perhaps the sais around my waist gave me a feeling of empowerment.

I laughed. "Set fire to my clothes? How first year. Pazia, you really should be *setting* an example for the younger students not *fires*. But if you must show Ulrick how petty you can be..." I held my arms out with a weary patience. "Go ahead."

16

INSTEAD OF IGNITING my shirt, Pazia pressed her lips together in annoyance. "You're not worth my time." Turning her back on me, she rushed away.

"You called her bluff," Ulrick said.

"She'll make me regret it."

"How?"

"By spreading lies and ugly rumors about me to her friends."

"Why would you care?"

I paused. Why *would* I care? It wouldn't change anything.

"She's a student, one of many," he said. "*You* work with a Master Magician. Liaison Yelena is *your* friend."

Ulrick's comment sounded logical, but just because I knew and worked with respected magicians didn't mean I deserved the same honor. I had to earn my place. Unfortunately with my limited magical abilities, all I'd earned from my classmates was contempt. And a few of them, like Pazia, even thought I had betrayed Sitia by pricking Yelena with Curare.

"Let's get started with this list," I said. "We should order the kiln supplies first."

"Is there a brick merchant in the Citadel?"

The Citadel had been built with marble, so I doubted there were many brick factories nearby. "Probably not, but I know who to ask."

"It's about time," Aydan said. The glassmaker had put us to work as soon as we entered his shop. "They should have built you a kiln years ago."

Ulrick pulled the cooled pieces from the annealing oven. He inspected my seashell. "I agree. Your magic glass is important to the magicians. You should have demanded your own shop."

I was just glad to be a student at the Keep. The thought of requesting special treatment seemed alien. Plus, coming to Aydan's had always been a good excuse to get away from my classmates. Not wanting to explain to Ulrick, I asked, "Would you demand kiln time from your mother to work on your pieces?"

He considered. "No. I see your point."

"And I see two people standing around doing nothing," Aydan said. "Ulrick, add coal to the kiln. Opal, gather me a slug."

We hastened to obey. When the glassmaker had finished his work for the day, he wrote a list of all his suppliers. "Don't forget you promised to find me a helper."

Since a trip to Booruby was required for us to finish our project, I planned to talk to Mara about coming to the Citadel. In the meantime, Ulrick and I agreed to help Aydan in the mornings. The glassmaker would find a temporary assistant for the rest of the day.

"Don't you have classes?" Ulrick asked as we left Aydan's shop and headed toward the market.

"Not anymore." A brief pang touched my heart, but when I considered working with Ulrick all day, the empty feeling filled with... What? Happiness? A sense of purpose? Excitement? Perhaps a bit of all three.

Located in the center of the Citadel, the large open market contained a variety of goods and services for sale. Unlike my hometown of Booruby, where stores were scattered throughout the city, the market had representatives from every business within the Citadel.

Even Aydan had a stand he shared with five other merchants. One day a week, it was his turn to sell his glasswares at the stand and take orders from customers. It made shopping easy. The biggest problem was the sheer size of the market. Certain vendors were hard to find in the bustle of shoppers.

Ulrick and I cut down a small alley and entered the market. He paused as the roar of voices and spicy smells crashed into us. But he adapted fast.

Pulling Aydan's list from my hands, he scanned the paper. "Bricks and large equipment will have to wait until the trip to Booruby. For now, we should tackle the smaller items. Let's find the blacksmith and order the irons, pipes and the hardware for the gaffer's bench. Then we'll talk to a woodworker about building the bench and cracking-off box." He glanced around the crowded market. "It might take us a while to find anyone."

"We should hire a member of the Helper's Guild," I said. Seeing his confusion, I explained how Yelena had inadvertently started the guild by paying a young beggar boy to help her navigate the market. "He expanded on the idea. With his friends and family's help, they were soon earning a living by providing services from haggling with vendors to carrying and delivering packages."

"We don't need to waste the money. With a little extra work, we can do it ourselves."

"You risk being cheated or hiring an unskilled craftsman. The Helper's Guild knows all the best merchants."

"I'm *sure* they do. I wonder what percentage they get *paid* by the best merchants. Twenty percent of the amount of business they bring in?"

Ulrick's cynicism surprised me. I never would have thought the guild would be dishonest. And why not? Just as there were deceitful merchants, there could be corrupt guild members. Zitora warned me to be careful and not get cheated.

"You're too nice, Opal. One day, someone is going to take advantage of you. Best to let me handle all the negotiations with suppliers. Come on."

He strode into the heart of the market, but I didn't follow him. Letting Ulrick make the decisions and be responsible for the outcome was an easy way to dodge my responsibility. But Zitora assigned me with this task. If I could escape from a group of rogues, I could handle ordering equipment for a glass studio. I grew up in a glass factory. I knew every inch, every procedure and every tool. The same could be said of Ulrick. A tinge of doubt touched my mind. I suppressed it with sudden—foolish?—determination.

I hovered on the edge of the market, creasing my forehead with uncertainty. As expected, a young girl appeared by my side.

"Lovely Lady, can I help you?" she asked.

Fresh faced with hopeful kindness radiating from her brown eyes, it was hard to believe this ten-year-old member of the Helper's Guild could be capable of deceiving me. But the possibility stained my thoughts.

"I want to hire Fisk," I said.

She shook her head. "He is very busy. Clients hire him *weeks* in advance. I've been working here for years. I can get you the best prices. Fisk trained me himself."

Her adult words contrasted with her youthful appearance. Keeping a smile from reaching my lips, I assured her that I wasn't worried about her skills. In fact, it was hard for me not to hire her on the spot. I collected my resolve and pushed past my reluctance. "My friend, Liaison Yelena Zaltana, told me to hire him."

"Lovely Yelena is your friend?" She peered at me with suspicion. "What is your name?"

When I told her, she instructed me to wait and disappeared into the crowd.

Shoppers ebbed and flowed. Ulrick returned, looking for me. A scowl etched on his face.

"Why didn't you follow me?" he demanded.

My voice locked for an instant, and I wondered if his ire was from concern or annoyance. I reached for the list clutched in Ulrick's fist. Tugging at the paper, I met his gaze. "You're helping *me* with this project. I'm hiring a guild member. Wait." I held up a hand. "You're right to be cautious, so I'm insuring we get the best and most trusted member."

Ulrick released the paper, but his scowl deepened. "You shouldn't be alone."

"The market is filled with people."

"Doesn't matter. In fact, it's easier to disappear in a crowd."

The girl returned with a young man.

"I hope I'm not interrupting anything," Fisk said.

He had grown since I last saw him. An inch taller than me, his lean frame was all arms and legs. But intelligence and confidence radiated from his movements. Only fourteen years old, Fisk was the founder and leader of the Helper's Guild.

"Thanks for coming," I said. "I need your expertise."

"One condition," he said with a smile.

"Besides your payment?"

"Of course. *That* goes without saying."

"What's your condition?"

"That you deliver a message to Yelena for me."

It seemed a simple request. One he could do on his own. "She's on a mission." I hedged.

"I know. But my message is too important to wait until she comes back from Moon lands. And you have the needed connections to get the information sent via those wonderful glass messengers of yours."

Understanding dawned. "You know about them?"

"Of course." He winked.

"I'll try to send her a message." Another thought occurred. "How did you know Yelena was going to the Moon Clan?"

A mischievous grin spread. "To quote my mother, 'I see all, hear all and know all.'"

Ulrick huffed in disbelief. He crossed his arms, attempting to intimidate the youth. But Fisk had grown up on the streets. His neat appearance and fine quality tunic and pants gave him the look of a pampered teen, but the cold calculation in his eyes as he studied Ulrick revealed his hard childhood.

"Obviously, you're new to the Keep," Fisk said. He turned to me. "A glassmaker from Booruby. Can he make magic glass?"

"That's none of your business," Ulrick said.

"We don't know yet," I said.

Ulrick shot me a betrayed look.

"Then there's hope he may be of use." Fisk gestured

to the young girl. She had stood beside him without uttering a word. "Jayella, help my client this afternoon. Madam Uriy wants to buy a pearl necklace for her grand-daughter. Do not spend more than two golds. Anything above that price is robbery. Try to get one gold and ten silvers. That's a fair price."

She nodded and disappeared into the crowded market with a lithe grace.

"My best apprentice," Fisk said. "She uses her sincerity and innocence to get her way when haggling for prices. In another five years, she'll have merchants tripping over themselves to make her happy." He seemed to relish the prospect.

"It's deceitful," Ulrick said. "Using a young girl to coerce the merchants. She should be in school."

"She should," Fisk agreed. "Of course, if she was in school, she would starve to death. Her parents abandoned her when she was four. No money for food or school clothes, survival was her only choice. And it isn't deceitful. Greedy merchants prey on the unwary. We make sure they charge an honest profit."

"For a price." Ulrick's posture was tight with tension.

"Exactly! Our clients are well aware of the cost of our services up front. And no one is forcing them to hire us." Fisk smiled as if he and Ulrick had come to an agreement. "Now, Lovely Opal, what can I do for you today?"

I showed him my list of supplies. He wrinkled his forehead in concentration for a moment.

"I know a woodworker from Owl's Hill. He's new, but does fine work and the best part is he's still hungry for clients. His prices are reasonable. And he's fast. Come on."

Fisk led us through the market. His popularity evident by the number of people who called his name and waved. Various members of the guild would appear by his side for advice before scampering off on unknown missions. He guided us to the woodworker, and then to a black-smith. In one afternoon, we had commissioned several pieces of equipment. More progress than even I expected.

Ulrick stayed sullen. Pouting or annoyed or suspicious, I couldn't tell. I paid Fisk for his time, arranging to meet the following afternoon.

"We'll finish your list tomorrow," Fisk said. He slipped a folded paper into my hand.

I placed the note into my cloak's pocket, remembering my promise to send a message to Yelena for Fisk. If Ulrick saw the motion, he didn't mention it.

On our way back to the Keep, I said, "Once we order all the items, we can leave for Booruby. Did you bring a horse with you?"

"No."

"The Stable Master probably has a few extra horses. Do you know how to ride?"

"Yes. But it doesn't matter," he said in a rush. "I'm not going to Booruby with you."

"Why not?"

"You don't need me." He increased his pace.

I hurried after him. "Look, if this is about Fisk—"

"It's not. You were right about him. It's just…" He stopped in midstride. "I told my family I was never coming back to Booruby again."

"Why would you say that?"

Ulrick raked a hand through his short hair. "I was angry. My mother insisted I was on a fool's errand. She predicted the Masters would send me home soon after I arrived. She griped about having to find a temporary worker. I lost my temper. Told her to hire a permanent employee because no matter what the Masters said, I wasn't coming back."

I tried to put myself in his place. My family had always supported me. They had made a fuss over my glass animals even though they couldn't see the glow. No doubt my life would have gone in a different direction if they hadn't encouraged me.

"That's a hard promise to keep," I said. "If you become a glass magician, you might be sent to Booruby for a mission."

Surprise flashed. "I hadn't considered that possibility. I guess I'm trying to keep from getting my hopes up, but returning to my hometown on a mission for a Master Magician would be different than returning a failure."

Hadn't I worried about the same thing? I understood his dilemma. "You don't need to come with me. My father will be happy to help." And here I was, running home to him again. But my list was bound to have a few essential items missing, and I would need a second opinion. Since my father had constructed eight kilns, he was the best person to consult.

Uncertainty lingered in my stomach. What about Sir and his gang? Or Blue Eyes? They hadn't been caught. I was safe in the Keep. Or was I?

I glanced at Ulrick's long shadow cast by the sinking sun. Tricky had convinced me he was Master Cowan. He could easily sneak inside. And I would be fair game on the road to Booruby. I wrapped my fingers around the handles of my sais. Searching the area near me, I looked for Tricky's shadow. An armed escort to Booruby wouldn't be enough against the magician. Perhaps Zitora would want to come along.

We continued toward the Keep. I jumped at every noise.

"Opal, what's wrong?" Ulrick asked.

"Just my overactive imagination." Although I wondered where the line was between caution and paranoia. I hated the feeling of unsettled worry creeping along my spine, and the burning conviction of Tricky watching me, waiting for a moment to attack. I promised myself Ulrick's warning about being taken advantage of wouldn't come to pass. But those promises were difficult to keep, and I had been exploited before. Alea used me as a weapon. I shivered and forced the horrid memory from my mind.

Ulrick must have sensed my distress. "Did you see Sir or Tricky?"

"No." Thank fate.

"You should really stay inside the Keep. It's safer."

"I know, but I won't hide. I'll take precautions and be vigilant," I vowed.

He kept quiet for a few blocks. "I can't tell you what to do. But I'm pretty good with a sword. I'll make sure to have it with me when we're together." He linked his arm in mine, pulling me closer to him.

The warmth of his body and the heat of his touch traveled along my skin. All unpleasant thoughts leaked away as I enjoyed his solid presence.

All too soon, we arrived at the Keep. Despite being dinnertime, Zitora still worked in her room in the administration building. Here she presented her public face, and her bare office lacked the softness of her tower home. A few sterile paintings of bridges hung on the walls, parchment and ink littered her desk and a handful of lonely books leaned against each other on the single shelf. Two empty chairs faced her desk.

We settled in the seats, reporting the day's progress and my plans to travel to Booruby for the remaining supplies.

"Very good," she said. "I'll see who we can get to escort you south."

Disappointment dragged on my shoulders. "Can you come? My mother's apple cobbler is worth the trip."

"Tempting, but I can't leave right now. There's too much going on."

Her comment reminded me about this morning's discussion on the Moon Clan and Fisk's note. I pulled the paper from the pocket of my cloak. "I have a message for Yelena from Fisk."

Zitora turned to Ulrick. "Go and have dinner before the dining hall closes."

"What about Opal?" he asked.

"She has a riding lesson with the Stable Master."

"She shouldn't be alone."

"She's perfectly safe inside the Keep."

"Are you sure?"

"Of course. We assigned an extra magician at the gate."

I listened to them argue over my safety as if I wasn't in the room. With so many magicians around, I knew I only had to scream and help would be mere steps away. My confidence in this plan lasted until I remembered Alea had entered the Keep without trouble. And we had left without any problems.

Before I could fret, I applied logic to her ease in my kidnapping. She had Ferde's help, who, at the time, had Master-level magical power. Alea also had my full cooperation.

Ulrick and Zitora arrived at an agreement, although I didn't know the exact details. He said he would meet me later at the stables, and left. Once he was gone, Zitora took Fisk's note and read it. She frowned. Not good news.

"Do you know what it says?" she asked.

"No."

"Fisk knows who to trust." She tapped a finger on her desk, lost in thought.

Dismissed, I headed to the stables. Stable Master greeted me with his usual gruffness. Quartz was saddled and ready to ride. She bumped her head against my chest, looking for sweets.

"After," I whispered in her ear. "I'll steal a couple of milk oats for you."

"Mount up," Stable Master ordered.

He put me and Quartz through the paces. We made figure eights until I was dizzy. Quartz trotted and galloped around the training ring, following his shouted orders faster than I could direct her. I cursed my luck in getting Stable Master for my teacher as my legs and back twinged with pain. All those days of hard riding still didn't prepare me for an hour's worth of jumping small obstacles. Next session, I would bring a Barbasco yam.

"That'll do for now," he said. "You've improved. But you still have a long way to go. Clean your tack and give her a good rubdown."

I muffled a groan when my feet hit the ground. Grooming Quartz was enjoyable, but cleaning the stiff leather tack with a rag and saddle soap was a nightmare.

By the time I finished my chores, the stables were empty of students. I led Quartz into her stall, checked her water bucket and fed her the promised milk oats.

Ulrick arrived to escort me to my rooms. My annoyance over his wrong assumption that he could defend against a magician better than me faded when he smiled. His concern was unexpected and nice. No one else in the Keep had worried about me before. I enjoyed his company. And there remained the chance he might link his arm in mine again.

My thoughts flicked to Kade. I had shared his mind. The Stormdancer saved my life twice; I still owed him one. But he was wrapped in his own stormy world. A world where I didn't belong. While I fit right into Ulrick's world.

In a bold move, I linked my arm in his. He pulled me close and I could have happily walked for days with him by my side.

Too soon, we stopped at the bathhouse so I could wash off the grimy horsehair clinging to my sweaty skin. He escorted me to my quarters and even checked inside for intruders.

"See you tomorrow," he said. "Lock your door."

"Yes, sir." I saluted.

"Opal, this is serious. You could be hurt or worse."

"I know *that*. It's just easier sometimes not to think too much about it, or I'll never leave my rooms."

"Good plan. Never leave your rooms without me."

"Now who's joking?" I teased, but his seriousness failed to diminish.

"I'll wait outside until I hear your lock click. Good night." He left, but, as promised, he stood with his arms crossed just past the threshold.

I closed the door. As I turned the bolt on the lock, I couldn't suppress a slice of worry. His overprotectiveness might infringe on my freedom to come and go as I pleased—one of the best perks in being an apprentice. But my emotions flipped. It could also be a sign of his wanting to become more than friends—an appealing prospect.

Three solid days were spent assisting Aydan and teaching his new assistant, Leda, how to handle the hot glass in the mornings. Once I'd let Fisk know Aydan sought a helper, Leda had arrived the next day.

Quick to learn, the young woman, much to Aydan's annoyance, beamed as she worked. Her demeanor remained placid despite his bursts of ill humor. Calluses lined her fingers and palms. Leda was no stranger to physical labor. I should have talked to Fisk sooner.

I suppressed a grin. Aydan would have a difficult time chasing Leda away, and he might even enjoy her company in time. When we were confident she could handle the glassmaker's demands, Ulrick and I left the workshop to spend the afternoon talking with suppliers.

Ulrick and I had ordered all the glass equipment we could from the Citadel's craftsmen. The next step would require a trip to Booruby to purchase a kiln.

Ulrick had been my constant companion these past days. I already missed him and I hadn't even finished packing. My saddlebags bulged with supplies and with the small orb I had taken from Sir and his group. I wanted to show my father the glass spiders. Zitora had been too busy for us to discuss the strange magical incident further, and I wanted to wait until the glass shop at the Keep was finished to experiment with magic. It seemed safer.

I packed the spiders in a leather bag and left the orb empty just in case I was ambushed on my way home, hoping I would be able to defend myself.

Zitora promised to assign an escort for me, but couldn't say who it would be. At dawn the next morning, I arrived at the stables. Unease over the trip rippled in my stomach until I spotted my companion. Leif.

He adjusted the straps on Rusalka's saddle. "How's my favorite glass wizard this morning?" he asked.

I laughed. He said the same thing to me every time I saw him. Quartz poked her head out of her stall and I hurried to get her ready for travel.

"What did Zitora bribe you with to babysit me?" I asked.

It was his turn to chuckle. "I volunteered once I heard *where* you're going."

"You're just using me to get to my sister."

"Of course. Otherwise I would hate you—you get way too much attention around here. And you know me, I..."

"Like to be in the middle of things, getting in the way," I teased.

He pretended to be hurt. "Perhaps I should let one of those boring guards accompany you."

"As long as he is handsome. I hear Mara is rather lonely."

He gave me a rueful grin. "Touché."

I threaded my new sheath through Quartz's saddle. While traveling on horseback, I would save time by having my sais on each side of the saddle instead of fumbling for them through my cloak. The need for the weapons dampened my playful mood.

"Did Zitora tell you why I needed a companion?" I asked Leif.

He mounted Rusalka and nodded.

"There could be five of them trying to get to me."

"I hope I'll sense them before we stumble into an ambush, and I've learned a few things from Valek." His hand rested on the hilt of his sword. A machete also hung from his belt. "And a few magical defenses from Yelena."

Yelena's name reminded me of the discussion the Masters had about the Moon Clan's troubles. "Why aren't you with your sister?"

"Politics." He said the word as if it tasted rancid. "I've had my fill. Besides, she has plenty of help. Master Jewelrose is with her and I'm sure Valek will appear if she gets into trouble." He huffed in amusement. "*When* she gets into trouble. Actually I'm looking forward to the trip. It'll be like a vacation for me."

"Leif, those men could—"

"Don't worry. The road to Booruby hugs the western border of the Avibian Plains. If we're outnumbered, we can detour into the plains. No shame in outrunning the bad guys."

"Outrunning?"

"Have you taken Quartz into the plains yet?"

"No."

Leif grinned. "Then you're in for a treat. These Sandseed-bred horses fly like the wind in the plains."

Our first day on the road passed without incident. With only a few weeks left of the cooling season, the temperatures hovered near freezing during the day and dropped at night. Since Booruby was five days south of the Citadel, it would be a little warmer.

There weren't many towns along the main road. Farm fields dominated the landscape to the west and the plains stretched to the east.

We stopped for the night in a roadside shelter. A crude wooden building with bare bunks, a fireplace and a large, fenced pen for the horses, it could house up to twenty people. Six fellow travelers were already inside. A fire blazed in the hearth. Lanterns were also lit outside the building to light the way for any late-night travelers.

Leif cooked our dinner, while I tended the horses. As we ate, Leif reminisced over the various meals he had eaten at my house.

"Do you think your mother will tell me the recipe for her bread pudding?" he asked.

"I'm beginning to wonder if your interest in Mara is just for my mother's cooking."

He faked being insulted, then said, "Oh no, I love Mara's cooking, too."

I swatted him on the shoulder.

After we settled in our bunks, I listened to the quiet

murmur of the others, the popping of the fire and the rustling of horses, straining to hear any sounds out of the ordinary. I touched my sais, checking they were within reach. "Leif?"

"Hmm?"

"Should we take turns keeping watch?"

"No. Rusalka will whinny if someone approaches the shelter."

"What if you don't hear it?"

"There's no sleeping through that racket. And if I don't come out to see what the matter is, she'll break the door down trying to come inside."

"What if the person is disguised by magic?"

"Magic fools the eyes, not the nose. She'll smell a...wrongness. I'll smell it, too. It's hard to explain." He paused. "Opal, go to sleep. You're safe here."

"Thank you for coming with me."

"Anytime."

Leif was right about Rusalka. The high-pitched and loud neighing woke everyone in the shelter. Leif bolted from his bunk with his sword in one hand and his machete in the other. I followed, holding my sais.

The outside lanterns cast a weak yellow light. My relief at seeing the cause of the trouble didn't last long. A pack of wild dogs surrounded the horses. Low growls emanated from bared teeth as they circled Quartz and Rusalka. From time to time, one would brave the horses' hooves and dash in to bite a leg.

Maria V. Snyder

Leif shouted and waved his sword, but there were a dozen black dogs. They were smart enough to stay out of range of his weapons. Too smart, in fact. The dogs widened their circle to include Leif, moving as if one intelligence directed them.

"Open the gate so the horses can get out," Leif called.

I rushed to comply. When the way was clear, he told the horses to go to the plains where they could outdistance the dogs. A good plan, except Rusalka wasn't going to leave without Leif.

The other travelers joined me by the fence.

"Rocks," one man yelled.

We scurried around, finding and throwing rocks at the dogs. My aim was horrible, so I passed my rocks to the man.

Eventually, we drove the dogs off. Two lay dead, kicked and killed by the horses. Leif checked the horses for injuries, while I dragged the dogs' bodies out of the enclosure. The man helped and the others kept watch, still clutching their rocks.

I knelt beside one dog. Its clean coat was free of fleas. I checked the other. Well fed. These weren't wild dogs. I reviewed their behavior during the attack. Yelena could communicate with horses. If the pack's owner was a magician, perhaps he directed the dogs' actions. He might try again.

Leif joined me. Besides a few cuts, the horses were fine.

"Guess we should have scheduled a watch," Leif said. "I didn't think we needed to protect the horses."

The man who had helped us frowned. "We never had a problem with dogs before," he said. "I'll talk to the locals, get a hunt organized or maybe set up a few traps with poisoned bait."

I kept my suspicions to myself. We thanked the man and his friends. They filed back inside.

"Go back to sleep," Leif said. "I'll take the first watch."

The attack bothered me. "Do you think the dogs were sent as a distraction?"

"It's possible. I thought I smelled magic. But why didn't they take advantage of the situation?"

"The horses didn't panic. Besides Rusalka's horrible squealing, they were calm. And she woke everyone. Perhaps the magician didn't want to try anything with six other witnesses around."

"Good point. We'll just have to be more vigilant."

I thought I would never get back to sleep after all the excitement, but I did. Leif woke me two hours before dawn.

"It's been quiet. But stay close to the horses," he said.

"What if the dogs come back or..." I couldn't say Tricky's name out loud.

"Tell Rusalka to cry, and she'll wake everyone again."

"Magical attack?"

"Same thing, but if you can't talk, the horses are sensitive to magic and she'll let me know. Sandseed horses are very protective. Keep them between you and an attacker and I'll be there in no time." Leif yawned.

I checked the enclosure. The horses leaned together, sleeping. Scanning the road and surroundings, I paced.

Jittery anxiety pulsed through my veins. I didn't like feeling as if danger stalked me. Nothing I could do about it, which added to my conviction of not being in control. My hands twitched for a punty iron with a slug of molten glass on the end—a formidable weapon.

Instead, I pulled my sais. Flicking the blades out and in, I practiced offensive strikes and defensive moves. The activity warmed me and I removed my cloak. Before I knew it, the dark sky paled, announcing dawn's imminent arrival.

I fed the horses a bucket of grain and checked their water buckets. Satisfied all was well, I slipped through the gate and fumbled with the latch, muttering under my breath over the complex catch.

Without warning, an arm snaked around my neck. "Cry!" I yelled as the arm locked tight, pressing against my windpipe.

RUSALKA'S LOUD SQUEAL pierced the air. The pressure on my neck eased a bit. I shifted my hips to the left and rammed my right elbow into the man holding me. Then I stomped on his foot. He yelped and released me. I spun and stopped.

"Ulrick! What are you doing here?"

He rubbed his stomach, glaring. "Changed my mind." He huffed. "Thought you might—hey!"

The tip of Leif's sword jabbed Ulrick's arm. "Step away from her," he ordered. Although he was shorter than Ulrick by a good foot, Leif's fierce countenance and powerful build made an impression. Ulrick hurried to comply.

I waved Leif off. "It's okay. I know him." Rounding on Ulrick, I demanded, "Why did you attack me?"

"To prove a point."

I waited.

"You were out here all by yourself. An easy target...or so I thought." He looked behind me. The others had come outside. Woken by Rusalka's warning, they clutched stones. "Still, if I had a dagger, I could have stabbed you before you said a word."

"Do the horses know him?" Leif asked.

Quartz did; Ulrick had been at the stables with me many times. "Yes. Why?"

"He wouldn't have gotten close to you if he was a stranger. The horses would have warned you." Leif studied Ulrick. "Didn't think I could protect Opal?"

"I didn't know who was with her. I just thought one more person couldn't hurt and I wanted to help with ordering the kiln."

I introduced him to Leif.

Ulrick's surprise turned contemplative. "The Soulfinder's brother?"

Leif huffed in annoyance. "Yep, that's me—The Soulfinder's Brother. Opal forgot to use my *new* name. I'm sure if he knew I was The Soulfinder's Brother, he wouldn't have worried about you. After all, Leif Zaltana isn't anybody of consequence." He kept muttering as he returned to the shelter to make breakfast.

"Is he truly angry at me, or just being sarcastic?" Ulrick asked.

"Probably both."

"Great."

"He'll get over it. It's hard having a famous sibling, and being judged by others based on that relationship.

I grew up being Mara's Younger Sister. No one knew my name. In fact, when we met in your mother's factory—"

Ulrick groaned. "I immediately associated you with Mara. I'm sorry. I should know better—my mother and sister are famous. No matter what the rest of my siblings and I crafted with glass, it was always compared with our mother's. I'll apologize to Leif."

"Good idea. Now what about your promise never to return to Booruby?"

"I'm still not visiting my family, but I wanted to help. There's nothing more to do and Aydan is quite content with his new assistant."

I looked around. "How did you get here? Do you have a horse?"

He ducked his head, and stuttered with guilt and chagrin. "I...uh...borrowed a horse from the Keep's stables."

"Borrowed?"

"He was one of the extras who hadn't been claimed by a student. I left a note for Stable Master."

"A note!"

"It was late; I didn't want to wake him." The excuse was weak.

I laughed. "Didn't want to face him is more like it."

"That, too."

"So where is he?"

"I tied him to a bush over that rise." Ulrick pointed down the road. "I figured you stopped here, but I wanted to check your defenses before bringing him here. I'd better go get him."

When Ulrick led the horse over the rise, I almost fainted. The all-black stallion had an unmistakable white moon on his forehead—Moonlight.

"There's a reason no one claimed Moonlight," I said, as Ulrick removed the saddle.

"Perfect name. He's quick and intelligent. A Sandseed breed, I believe." He patted the horse's neck.

"Don't you want to know why?"

"I'm afraid of the answer." His flippant response lacked conviction.

"You should be."

"Come on, get it over with. You're dying to tell me— I can see in your eyes. You want revenge for my mock attack."

"I'm not *that* vindictive."

"Now you're scaring me."

"Good. Because Moonlight was going to be a gift to Commander Ambrose of Ixia. Our relationship with Ixia has improved thanks to Liaison Yelena, and the Sitian Council wanted to make a gesture of goodwill."

All color faded from Ulrick's cheeks. "I'm in..."

"Deep shit?"

"Yes."

Ulrick failed to follow my suggestion to return the horse as soon as possible. He insisted on accompanying us to Booruby. Leif's cold shoulder toward Ulrick melted when he apologized. Also, Ulrick's ability to make travel rations flavorful won him Leif's good approval.

After traveling all day, we stopped and made camp along the road.

"We made such a racket last night," Leif said, "it's best we avoid the shelters."

Cornstalk stubble lined the harvested field and worked well as kindling. We sat around the campfire and talked about sisters. Ulrick had two, one older and one younger than him. I grew up with two older sisters, and Leif had Yelena, who was kidnapped when she was six years old and returned home five years ago after a fourteen-year absence.

"She made up for the lost time," Leif said. "We blew through all those years of sibling rivalry in two seasons." He laughed. "Probably a good thing she wasn't with me when I was growing up. I never would have lived to see age twenty. Since she's been back, I've been bait to an amorous necklace snake, kept under house arrest in the Commander's castle, squeezed through a tunnel too small for me and paralyzed with Curare! And do you know what the kicker is?"

"She's still dragging you along on missions and endangering your life?" I guessed.

"That, too. But *she's* the one who gets all the attention. I was at the Warper Battle and helped defeat the Daviian Vermin, but does anyone remember that? No! They remember Yelena diving into the fire, sacrificing herself to defeat the Fire Warper."

"You have to admit, that was pretty big," Ulrick said.

Leif grumbled halfheartedly. "Well, I have a scar." He showed us a four-inch healed slash along his forearm.

"We know the significant role you played in the battle," I said. "Don't forget you've already caught one person's attention and admiration. And she's a hard one to impress."

"True." Leif beamed. "Only three more days until I see her again."

Ulrick ahhed in understanding as he made the connection. "Mara."

I waited for his jealousy or for a longing and wistful look. My sister had not only been gifted with beauty, but she was a sweetheart, too. Kindness, concern for others and intelligence, she had it all.

His demeanor remained pleasant. "Lucky man. Every guy in Booruby has a crush on her."

"Including you?" I asked, unable to stop myself.

"I was in school with her, but she had no interest in any of us." He considered. "I probably did have a crush for her back then, but not now." Ulrick watched me.

"Good," Leif said into the lengthening silence. "Cause I'd hate to sic my sister on you. She's a better fighter than me."

We laughed.

"And I bet she lets you know it, too," Ulrick said. Then his smile faded. "My younger sister crafts magnificent sculptures from glass. Sitian Councillors were commissioning pieces from Gressa before she was fifteen.

She has her own shop in Moon Clan lands now. But it was hard to be proud of her when she flaunted it every chance she got. Especially when my own pieces fell far short of our mother's expectations."

"I understand that feeling. My glass animals looked crude in comparison to my sister Tula's. She had a finer hand."

"But look at you now." Ulrick gestured. "Tula's animals might be sought by collectors, and Mara sought for her beauty, but you're a famous glass magician. Your name is said after Yelena's when people discuss the Warper Battle, no offense, Leif."

"None taken," Leif said.

"Opal, your animals provide a service to all of Sitia. You're important." Ulrick raked a hand through his hair. "When my younger sister was born, she was the baby of the family. Everyone doted on her and I was ignored unless I managed to annoy one of my siblings or my parents." His lips formed a rueful smile. "At least I was good at being a pest."

I rubbed my neck, thinking of his surprise attack. "You're still good," I teased.

He cried out in mock indignation and pushed me gently on the shoulder.

"Don't knock the power of a pest," Leif said. "Persistence and stubbornness can be useful in many situations."

"Opal, why didn't you send me a message? Two guests! What will I feed them?"

"Mother," I said, trying to suppress my irritation. We had just arrived from five days on the road and I was saddle sore and tired. "You always have enough food to feed half of Booruby. They don't need any special meals."

My mother fussed about the kitchen, muttering over her supplies. "Go upstairs and move Mara's things to your room. We can use her room for Leif and this... Ulrick, is it? Cesca's son?" Mother shot me a questioning glance.

I nodded.

"Why doesn't he stay with his family?"

"They had a disagreement over his decision to come to the Citadel," I said.

"And he's been working with you at the Magician's Keep?" Her eyebrows hovered at midforehead.

I sighed at the unspoken question. "Yes. He's a *colleague*. We're building a glass shop for the Keep."

"He's a nice-looking boy from a reputable family." She scanned my rumpled travel clothes. "Perhaps Mara could lend you one of her pretty dresses for dinner tonight."

Ignoring the implication, I climbed the steps to arrange the rooms and stopped in shock at the threshold. Tula's grief flag was gone. The shelf above her bed was empty. Her glass animals and various treasures gone. I held on to the doorjamb, feeling light-headed. Footsteps sounded behind me, and I swallowed the emotional rock lodged in my throat.

"I forgot to tell you," my mother said. "We decided it was time. I saved Tula's fox for you. I know how much you liked it." She pointed to my bed stand.

I picked it up—all that was left of my sister. "It's been almost five years. Why now?"

"Both you and Mara are older now. You will be graduating this year. I'm hoping Leif will become a member of our family and perhaps you—"

"Mother," I warned.

"Well, I can hope, can't I? Besides every time you visit you have a *friend* with you, so we needed a guest room." She sighed. "It was time to stop clutching the old days and embrace the new. And I'm hoping one day this house will be filled with grandchildren." She held up a hand. "Don't 'mother' me. I'll say what I want when I want. Now get moving, I'm sure the boys will want to get washed up before dinner."

I replaced the fox on my table. My mother had a point about Tula's flag and, while we may embrace the new, we won't ever forget.

"...Opal decided to try to use a bellows to pump air into the molten glass. She made a huge bubble. It was so thin it cooled too fast and burst. Looked like snow," Mother said.

The dinner table erupted with laughter and I wished to disappear. Why couldn't they pick on Mara or my brother, Ahir? Because their mistakes weren't as funny and they didn't try everything they could imagine to put a bubble into glass and produce disastrous results. They just had to blow air into the pipe. Jealous? Who me?

Ulrick was enjoying himself so I tried to keep my sense of humor. At least my family paid attention to me. It would be worse to sit here while everyone ignored me. I suffered through the stories and didn't die of embarrassment. When dinner was over, I helped clean up and then escaped outside, needing a moment alone.

I sucked in the crisp night air. A half-moon hovered in the sky, casting a mist of light. I scanned the grounds around my home. A cat stalked a field mouse behind the glass factory, but otherwise all was quiet.

I hadn't told my parents about Sir and Tricky's abduction. But since the night of the wild dog attack, no other incidents had happened on the road. I felt safe here. The kitchen door opened. Leif and Mara headed toward the factory, hand in hand. I checked on the horses, and pulled a few things I would need from my saddlebags.

"There you are," my father said. "Let's go to my lab and go over your supply list. I told Ulrick to meet us there."

He waited while I dug the small orb and a few glass spiders from my bag. I wanted to show them to him.

"Nice young man, your Ulrick," Father said as we headed toward his lab.

"He's not mine. We're colleagues." I tried to keep the exasperation from my voice.

"Don't get all huffy at me." He aimed a stern stare.

I regressed into a ten-year-old being scolded. "Sorry, Father."

"As I was saying, Ulrick is quick and intelligent. I like him."

It was the same description Ulrick had used for Moonlight. I suppressed a giggle, thinking about other descriptors like strong and loyal, which could be applied to both men and horses.

"He comes from a good family," Father said.

A purebred, I thought.

"He has a very different style with the glass."

Unique markings.

"It's a shame Cesca didn't encourage his experiments."

Rejected by his mother.

"But I've told him he could use our factory anytime."

Joined a new herd.

When we entered my father's lab and Ulrick greeted me with genuine affection, I felt bad about my comparisons. Deep down I knew why I did it and why I kept telling my family Ulrick and I were colleagues. Because I didn't want to hope. Didn't want to imagine there was more between us than building a glass shop for the Keep. Avoiding the pain of rejection, I tried to rationalize. Or was my distancing due to a certain Stormdancer? Talk about slim hope. Kade had probably distanced himself from our connection. I should do the same. He would soon forget about me.

My father sat behind his desk and the three of us reviewed the supply list for the kiln. Beside each item, he wrote the name of a supplier Ulrick and I should visit in the morning. We discussed the specifications of the kiln and who to order the white coal from.

"A good day's work and you should have it all ordered," my father said. "Just make sure Gid doesn't charge you more than three silvers for a load of coal."

Satisfied we were done, I placed the orb and three glass spiders on my father's desk. "What do you think?"

He picked up the orb and examined it close to the lantern light. "Is this one of the Stormdance orbs?"

"No. It was made by another," I said. When he raised an eyebrow, I continued, "Someone named Ash. He might be from the Krystal Clan."

"Never heard of him. Hmm. Functional and a little misshapen, otherwise sturdy." He gave the orb to Ulrick and picked up one of the spiders. "It looks like a real spider. Who made these?"

Time for a little creative explaining. "I did…in a way."

Twin confused expressions peered at me. I steeled myself and launched into how I channeled Tricky's attack into the glass orb. "One reason for the decision to build the Keep's glass shop, so we can experiment with this ability."

"So these are magical spiders inside here?" my father asked. "Do they glow like your other animals?"

"No glow, and Master Cowan couldn't use the magic inside."

"Are you going to tell me why this magician attacked you?"

"As long as you don't tell Mother."

Father considered. "Unless there is a need to tell her, I won't say anything."

I explained about Sir's group and their desire to duplicate the Stormdancers' orbs.

Before he could reply, a muted shout reached us through the windows. The door flew open and Leif stood in the threshold. His eyes filled with horror.

"Mara," he panted. "Bit by a snake. Come. Help."

18

Leif bolted to the factory. Ulrick, my father and I scrambled to our feet. Mara had been bitten and had mere minutes to live. In my rush to leave, I knocked the glass spiders to the floor, and crushed one under my boot.

By the time I arrived, Mara was in Leif's arms. Sweat dripped from her forehead and her body shook. A decapitated fer de lance snake and a bloody machete lay next to her.

My father cursed. He knelt beside her leg. The bleeding punctures were above her ankle. The venom coursed through her leg. Shock froze all other emotions as I watched my sister die.

"Ahir ran for the healer. I tied a tourniquet under her knee. But that won't save her," Leif cried.

Suck the venom out, I thought and moved toward her. Father yelped. A large brown spider scrambled onto Mara's foot and bent over her wound. He drew his arm back to swat it away.

"No," I yelled instinctively. "Let it alone."

The spider stabbed its mouth into the bite. Its body grew like a water skin being filled. When it finished sucking, the spider vanished. Blood splashed on the floor.

"The poison's gone," I said.

"How do you know?" Leif asked with a voice laced with pain.

Everyone stared at me. "The spider told me."

Without hesitation, without question, Leif untied the leather strap on Mara's leg; my father covered the bite and rubbed her calf to improve the flow of clean blood back to her foot. Leif cradled her in his arms, and she was enduring Mother's worried attentions in the kitchen in no time. I loved my family. Only they would take the magical spider's appearance and rescue in stride. Questions would arise later, but, for now, they were focused on the happy result.

Ulrick remained in the factory, disposing of the dead snake and hunting for more.

"Mara, you should know better," Father admonished. "Cold night and hot kilns draw the snakes into the factory. What were you doing?"

She glanced at Leif, who had his arm around her shoulders. "I was...preoccupied."

"Doing what?" he demanded.

Kissing Leif, I guessed. As her cheeks turned pink, Mara silently appealed to Mother.

"Jaymes," Mother said, "you left the lanterns burning in your lab. Are you planning to do more work tonight?"

Deftly distracted, my father returned to his lab. I followed. About halfway to the building, I stopped. My emotions melted and drenched me. Relief—Mara didn't die. Surprise—she was saved by a spider. Shock—a spider who magically disappeared. Fear—it resembled one of Tricky's spiders.

By the time I joined my father, he had his magnifying glass in hand, inspecting one of my glass spiders. "Just what I thought. It's the same spider only smaller. Care to tell me what's going on?"

"I would if I could." I grabbed a dustpan and brush, sweeping up the crushed glass from the floor. "I stepped on one. Maybe I released the illusion?"

"That spider was no illusion. Are you sure you weren't attacked by real spiders?"

I thought back. The beetles Tricky had used first were illusions. Or, as Zitora had explained, figments of my imagination planted by Tricky, which is why I had felt pain. His second strike hadn't touched me. I channeled his magic before the spiders reached me, trapping his power. However, the creatures called to *me* in the glass, as if I had pulled the magic.

I collapsed into a chair. "I'm not sure of anything right now."

"Only one way to find out."

"Wait—"

Father tried to snap one of my glass spiders in half.

He dropped it to the floor, stomping on it. Nothing. "These things are indestructible."

"Here." I reached for it, remembering how brittle they felt in my hands. Sure enough, I broke one in half.

A whoosh of air, a huff and a flash and one brown-colored spider stood in the middle of my father's desk. Its body as big as two of my father's fists put together and eight thin legs spread out close to the edge.

I jumped to my feet, wanting to back away.

"Relax."

The creature remained in place as if waiting. The door opened behind me and even the night breeze didn't disturb the spider.

"Ulrick, don't come any closer," Father ordered. "Opal, what did you do after you stepped on the glass?"

I replayed the series of panicked events in my mind. "I ran to Mara. Stood there like a complete simpleton. And…" I closed my eyes for a moment. "And my next thought was the need to suck the venom from Mara. But the spider came and…"

"Did your bidding," Father said.

"A big leap in logic," Ulrick said from the doorway.

"Easy to find out. Opal, tell the spider to climb to the ceiling."

"With my thoughts or my voice?"

"We can try both. How many glass spiders do you have?"

I shuddered. "Hundreds." Drawing in a deep breath and feeling a little silly, I ordered the spider to climb.

It leaped to the wall and scurried to the ceiling. When it arrived, it disappeared. For the first time ever, magic responded to my wishes. A strange sensation swept over me and I felt weightless. I dropped into a chair and clutched the armrests to keep from fainting.

"Hmm. Once and done," my father mused. "I wonder if the first spider would have followed you around until you gave it an order. Only one—"

"Way to find out," Ulrick said. "I'll fetch more spiders. Where are they?"

I told him, then snapped the remaining one. This time I ordered the spider with my mind. The results were the same.

A couple hours after midnight, my father was finally satisfied with our experiments. The spiders were indeed real to the touch. They had sharp teeth and they would perform a task then vanish. They would listen only to me. I guessed when I had transformed Tricky's magic into spiders I had become the owner. Although Tricky might be able to direct the spiders, too. And, since the only way to find out would involve him, I wasn't going to confirm the possibility.

All those history classes I had taken never mentioned the ability to transform magic into a physical object. And it wasn't static. It moved, obeyed commands and disappeared. Did the magic dissipate when the spider finished its job? Or did the power return to Tricky?

My sluggish thoughts swirled in my head as if my mind had melted. No answers formed, just an endless loop of speculation. I dragged my exhausted body to my room. Leif dozed in a chair next to my sister's bed. Mara slept so still, I had to watch the rise and fall of her chest before I could relax. Leif roused. He drew me out into the hallway.

"What's been going on? I smelled magic."

As quick and succinct as possible, I explained about the spiders.

"That's amazing! You have a whole army of helpers. You don't have to feed them or care for them. The possibilities are endless!"

Only Leif would think of food. I was too tired to share his enthusiasm. "Leif, go to bed. I'm here now if Mara needs anything."

He gnawed his lip. "Are you sure?"

"Of course, she's my sister."

He hugged me. "Thanks, Opal. You saved her life."

"Inadvertently."

"Doesn't matter how. She lives. *That* matters."

By the time I woke, the morning was almost gone. My family and Ulrick sat around the dining room table, eating a late breakfast. Mara remained pale and Leif hovered over her. Questions about the lifesaving spider shot from everyone's lips as soon as they spotted me. Father enlightened them about my spiders, and I asked them to please keep the information quiet.

"Why?" Ulrick asked. "If it were me, I'd want everybody to know what I could do."

"But I don't know if I can duplicate the magic and get the same results. Best to wait until we have discovered everything about it."

Ulrick remained unconvinced.

"It's a logical strategy," Leif said. "One that could save her life."

"How?" Ulrick asked.

Leif glanced at my mother before speaking. "If, for example, someone was after Opal. If the person knows what she can do with her magic, they would have a way to counter it. If no one knows about her skill with the glass spiders, then she will be able to surprise them *if* she's attacked."

"Good point," Ulrick said.

"No. It's an *excellent* point. Those who brag and boast might cause problems, but they're easy to counter. It's the quiet ones who are deadly."

I considered Leif's words as Ulrick and I visited the equipment suppliers Father suggested. My instinct to keep a few magical incidents quiet had been correct. Although, I realized I shouldn't rely on my instincts as much. Working with Zitora, I'd been unwillingly involved with criminals. Thinking my actions through and approaching a situation with a strategy in mind would be prudent.

Over the next two days, Ulrick and I had ordered all the necessary supplies. We prepared to leave the following morning. Mara would be coming with us. Leif didn't want to leave her behind, and once the Keep's glass workshop was operational, there would be plenty for her to do. My mother was thrilled. I could see by the glint in her eyes, she viewed Mara's move as the next step toward grandchildren.

Mara rode with Leif on Rusalka. The trip to the Citadel would be a day longer because of the added weight on the horse. My emotions wavered from happiness at having my sister nearby to dread. Before this trip to Booruby, I kept meaning to send a message to Mara about Aydan's need for an assistant, but I never did. Since Leda turned into such an accomplished helper, the problem was solved.

I squirmed in my saddle as understanding revealed my childish jealousies. My reluctance had two main reasons. The Keep was my domain and I was unwilling to share it with her. And I didn't want to be Mara's Little Sister again.

On the road for six days, Ulrick studied her as fellow male travelers tried to flirt, and as everyone, even the women, tripped over themselves to accommodate her. It was hard to get angry at her. She didn't seek the attention; she shooed away Leif's efforts to do everything for her.

We arrived at the Magician's Keep without trouble. Mara was given a guest room. The equipment we had ordered before leaving had been delivered in our absence. Construction on the workshop had begun. The new building, built with marble blocks, was located in the northeast corner of the Keep between the pasture and Zitora's tower.

As predicted, the Stable Master was livid over Ulrick's horse theft. "...had to beg—do you hear me, boy?—*beg* Councillor Sandseed to send me another right away. How could he trust me with a new one, when I lost the other!"

"I did you a favor," Ulrick said.

His reply rendered the Stable Master speechless. A sight I've never seen. Impressive. And scary.

"Moonlight is a fantastic horse. Too good for the Commander. You should save him for a special student or future Master Magician or even for yourself." Ulrick's matter-of-fact tone didn't waver despite the flaming red color spreading on the Stable Master's cheeks. "I'll come exercise him for you until you find a rider." And with a jaunty wave goodbye, Ulrick swept out of the barn.

I hustled to catch up. There was no way I wanted to be anywhere near the Stable Master when he finally exploded.

I reported the whole spider incident to Zitora and she was most anxious for me and Ulrick to start experimenting with magic and glass.

"I'll ask Master Bloodgood if he knows about another magician in history who could transform magic into a useful object," she said. "Meanwhile, you should hire Mara to help you in the glass shop. There's lots of work to be done."

"Hire?"

"Yes. Offer her room and board plus a weekly wage—the accountant should know how much. You'll need a manager to keep track of supplies and work schedules while you and Ulrick concentrate on learning about your powers."

I knew all along what we would use the shop for, but when Zitora talked about managers and schedules, the reality of the situation hit me. It wouldn't be a hobby, but serious research. Results would be expected, and I could no longer look to another to lead the way. Perhaps we should hire Aydan as a consultant.

Squashing my fears into a hard lump that sank to the pit of my stomach, I asked, "Should we pay Ulrick, too?"

"No. We'll grant him student status and a stipend until you determine the extent of his magical abilities. Then we'll decide how to proceed."

As I returned to the glass shop, I thought there wasn't much difference between being a student and a worker. Mara would be given a small apartment in the staff quarters and Ulrick would be assigned a room in the apprentice wing. The stipend was smaller than wages, but not by much. Ulrick should be happy with the new arrangements. He would no longer be a guest, but a member of the Keep.

It didn't take long for Ulrick, Mara and I to settle into a pleasant routine. And a funny thing happened while Mara worked with us. The population of the Keep would introduce Mara as Opal's sister to others, and she never batted an eye. She even boasted with pride over being my sister. I berated myself for my previous misgivings and pettiness. In those few days, Mara showed me how I should have behaved.

And even though there had been no sign of Sir or Tricky or blue-eyed Devlen for a month, Ulrick accompanied me everywhere.

On the first day of the cold season, I received a message from Zitora to come to her office. Alone. I told Ulrick I would meet him at the glass shop after the meeting.

"I'll just wait outside her office, so you can do your secret magician stuff with Master Cowan," Ulrick said. He tried to keep his tone light, but his voice held a sharp edge.

"It's not secret magician stuff."

"Then what is it?"

"I don't know."

"My point."

Ulrick escorted me to Zitora's office. He leaned on the wall next to the entrance. She waved me in, then stared at the door. It swung shut.

A split second of jealousy pricked me. "Handy."

"Lazy. It's been a long night." She leaned back in her chair, rubbing her eyes. She wore the same clothes as yesterday. "You'll need to let Ulrick and Mara work on the shop without you for a few days."

"Why?"

"Remember the conversation the Masters had about the Moon Clan?"

"Vaguely." It had been close to three weeks ago and so much had happened since then.

"We've discovered there's more going on with the

Moon Clan than the illegal border crossings and a possible assassination attempt on Councillor Moon. There's a whole faction who want Councillor Moon to step down and the faction's leader to take her place. Rumors of a civil war have reached us and now—" Zitora waved a scroll in the air "—now I have a report saying this group is selling illegal Ixian goods in the Citadel to raise money for weapons."

"Bold."

"Not necessarily. There's always been a black market for certain Ixian goods—swords, tea, linen, spices. When we had no political relationship with Ixia, the officials at the Citadel turned a blind eye to the sales of Ixian merchandise. Once we negotiated a trade treaty with them, all the 'contraband' became readily available. It was no longer a problem."

"What are they selling now?" I asked.

"Diamonds."

The gemstones were a hot commodity in Sitia. Many riches were mined from the Emerald Mountains, but, so far, no diamonds have been found.

"The Commander keeps a tight control on the sale of his diamonds to Sitia, so there must be a new mine," Zitora said.

"With diamonds being sold on the black market, there'll be all sorts of problems."

"Correct. What kind of trouble?"

"Another lesson?" I asked.

"I can't pass up an opportunity to teach. You're my

first student and I endeavor to be a good mentor." She rolled her hand in the air urging me to continue.

"All right. The black market diamonds will be cheaper, so buyers will go to them instead of the legitimate sellers. Word of diminishing sales will get back to the Commander, and he'll want to know why. If the Sitian Council doesn't stop the illegal sales, it could strain our relationship with Ixia. Plus, the money is going to the Moon Clan to pay for a potential coup."

Each clan decided how they chose their Councillor. A few clans held elections, others followed family lines and the rest had committees who made the decision. The Moon Clan used a matriarchal system. It was understood the Councillor's daughter would be the next Council member, but birth order didn't always match the best candidate for the job. On occasion, sisters fighting for the position have been recorded in their history.

"There's more," Zitora said.

I thought about the people buying the diamonds. "Bigger chance for deceit. With more diamonds available from various sources, the buyers could be conned into purchasing glass."

"Can you tell the difference?"

"I don't know. I've never touched a diamond before."

"I have one for you to examine."

"Why?"

"Fisk needs someone he can trust to help him find the black market diamond sellers' source."

"Why would he care?"

No answer from the Master Magician.

Putting myself in Fisk's place, I tried to see the situation from his point of view. "His customers are getting conned, which brings suspicion on the Helper's Guild. And having the Citadel's guards arrest all the sellers wouldn't stop the source from going to another town to sell his diamonds. And the arrests would upset the legitimate people in the market. Fisk could lose business." I considered for a moment. "Better to have everything resolved without the general population knowing about it."

"Right. So we find the source and trace the *new* diamonds back to their point of origin before we arrest anyone."

Her serious tone and emphasis on the word new caused my heart to squeeze a warning. This was no longer a hypothetical discussion. "Who will trace the source?"

"We have a magician in mind to act as our buyer, but she'll need an expert with her so she doesn't follow the wrong trail and end up with glass. Fisk trusts you. So does Yelena. She agreed with this plan."

"I... But..."

"You'll have the perfect cover." When I didn't respond, she continued. "Diamonds enhance magical powers. You need many large stones together to increase the magic, so it wouldn't be out of the ordinary for a rich magician to buy a bunch of diamonds."

A sense of having been maneuvered into a corner

washed over me. I wanted to be part of the Keep's network of magicians. Wasn't this exactly what I would be asked to do when I finished my training? I could say no, but I would probably never be considered for another mission. However, my mission for the Storm-dancers had bordered on a disaster, and still wasn't resolved.

"What about Sir and Tricky?" I asked. "They haven't been found yet."

"The magician you'll be working with is strong enough to handle them."

Last question. "Who's the magician?"

"Pazia Cloud Mist."

19

I GROANED. Pazia detested me as much as I disliked her. It would be difficult to become a team and convince a black market diamond seller to reveal his source.

"What's the problem?" Zitora asked.

"She thinks I'm worthless. A One-Trick Wonder," I blurted.

"You're not..." She paused. "Hearing it from me won't change your perceptions. If you want to *believe* you're a One-Trick Wonder, fine by me. Just don't say it to me *ever* again. Understand?"

Stunned by her order, I drew in a breath before replying. "Yes, sir."

"Good." Zitora leaned forward in her chair. "You're an adult now, Opal. In order to be successful with this mission, you'll have to overcome your differences with Pazia. She's a strong magician. Maybe a Master. I'm certain she will behave in a professional manner toward you, especially since you're going to pretend you're best friends when you meet the diamond sellers today."

"Today?" Why did troublesome events have to happen so fast? Why couldn't I digest the information first, and then spring into action?

"This afternoon you're to meet with Fisk and Pazia at the Unity Fountain. Do you know where it is?"

"Yes."

"Once there, Fisk'll take you to a place to change and be briefed before he leads you to the seller. Do you have any questions?"

"Change into what?"

"Expensive clothes and obnoxious jewels. You're supposed to be rich, too."

"How will I tell if the diamonds are fake?"

Zitora opened her desk drawer and removed a small box. She handed it to me. "Open it."

I lifted the red velvet-covered lid. Inside a diamond the size of my fingernail sparkled. Clear as glass, yet the light played deep within the stone, obscuring the red velvet behind it. I marveled at the reflections jumping from the many facets on the diamond.

"You can touch it." Amusement colored her voice.

I pinched the diamond between my thumb and forefinger. Cold stabbed my finger pads and a brief image of snow-covered mountains filled my mind. Then heat seared my hand as the mental image transformed into burning mountains. A mere second later, the gem cooled to body temperature, and a slight vibration hummed against my skin.

My tongue stuck to dry teeth. I swallowed, and the hard motion scratched my throat. "Do you feel a...flash when you touch it?" I asked.

"Flash?"

"Feel cold through your fingers and get a mental image?"

"No. If I charged it with magic, I could feel the potential, but right now, it's inert." She studied me. "Does the flash mean you'll be able to tell the difference?"

"Yes." I closed the lid.

"Any other questions?" Zitora placed her hand on my shoulder. Her comforting gesture reminded me of Ulrick.

"What should I tell Ulrick?"

"Nothing about the diamonds. The fewer people who know, the better."

"He's not going to like the idea," I said. Even though there was plenty for him to do in the glass shop. Equipment and supplies were being delivered every day. Soon the shop would be ready to use.

"You're just going to have to convince him." She smirked. "Good luck with that. He has an overdeveloped stubborn streak and has decided to be your protector. Ditching him will be your hardest task today."

"Thanks." I couldn't keep the sarcasm from my voice.

Unaffected, Zitora's smile grew wider. "He's rather handsome when he's mad. All those tight muscles, and those sparks of anger shooting from his captivating eyes."

"Really? I hadn't noticed." A wave of heat flushed. I blamed the sensation on a lingering effect of the diamond and not on the mental image of Ulrick's strong arms wrapping around me.

She laughed, knowing I lied.

I tried not to blush when I left Zitora's office and spotted Ulrick waiting. He fell into step beside me as we headed toward the glass shop.

"What did she say?" he asked, once we were away from the administration building.

I decided to stick to the truth as much as possible. "She's sending me on another mission."

"And?"

"I'm going to be busy this afternoon, so you'll have to work without me. And don't worry," I rushed to add, "I'll be with a very powerful magician."

"Can you tell me what the mission is?"

"Sorry, no."

"I was right. Secret magician stuff."

"You were right, but the way you say it..."

"Flippant? Irreverent?" he asked.

"Like it's a big joke, something to sneer at."

He increased his stride, staring straight ahead. I hurried to keep up.

Just when I thought the subject of my mission had dropped, Ulrick said, "I'm jealous. I want to be involved." He swept his arm through the air, indicating the people around us. "I want to be a magician helping

Sitia. Making your assignment a joke is so I won't feel..."
His hands flicked as he gathered his thoughts as if they
were molten glass. "So I won't feel left out. Growing up,
I was always left out. The six-year age gap between me
and my older brother was too big and, since my glassmaking skills were limited, I was excluded from many
family activities." He drew in a deep breath. "I shouldn't
vent my frustration on you. At least allow me to escort
you to the meeting site."

His story echoed my years at the Keep as the odd
woman out. Sympathizing with Ulrick, I agreed.

It was too early for my rendezvous with Fisk so we
wandered through the Citadel, stopping on occasion so
I could explain the significance of a statue or fountain
we discovered. Surrounded by the white marble wall, the
interior of the rectangular Citadel had six districts, each
with its own personality. The Keep occupied the entire
northeast district.

With the market in the center position between two
areas, the north and south districts mirrored each other.
Comprised mostly of businesses, warehouses and factories, the buildings and streets arched around the
market and radiated out like rings around a bull's eye.
A confusing grid of narrow streets and dead ends could
be found in the northwest and southwest residential
districts. The labyrinth was a direct result of accommodating the Citadel's growing population.

The southeast district contained a number of admin-
istrative buildings and Council Hall, as well as the posh

residencies of the Councillors. The Unity Fountain was also located in the southeast. By the time we arrived, Fisk was already there. He waited with his apprentice Jayella.

Ulrick ignored the others to admire the fountain. Surrounded by waterspouts, an immense dark green sphere with holes rested on a pedestal. The jade sphere had been mined from the Emerald Mountains as a solid block. Inside the sphere were ten other spheres; each one smaller than the next. If the carving was sawed in half, the cross section would resemble a tree's growth rings. All the layers had been carved from the one stone—through the holes and from the outside in.

"Unbelievable," Ulrick said. "I've learned about this. Each sphere represents one of the Sitian clans, but it's more impressive than I imagined. The craftsmanship to carve this…"

"Five years of hard work," Fisk said. "A celebration of the clans uniting." He cocked his head to the side, considering. "Interesting. If one of the spheres inside would crack, the others would hold it together." Fisk met my gaze, and I wondered if there was a hidden meaning in his words.

"We need to keep our appointment," Fisk said to Ulrick.

"Keep Opal safe," he ordered, frowning. "Your business will suffer if rumors about a client being harmed in your care surfaced."

The friendly softness in Fisk's demeanor hardened. "Are you threatening me?"

No answer.

"You know nothing about my business or about me. Do you?"

Again no answer, just a stubborn set to Ulrick's jaw.

"In that case, your insult was inadvertent and due to ignorance. Opal, when you have time, please educate this *man* about loyalty and honor. Come." He turned and strode from the fountain's plaza.

I sensed Ulrick's molten anger, but couldn't mollify him now. I hurried after Fisk. He led me down an unremarkable side street. About halfway, he turned into a narrow alley. The alley's sole purpose appeared to be providing a shortcut to the next street, but Fisk disappeared. When I reached the same spot, I found a tight alcove. To a casual observer, it looked like a dead end. But near the back was a small door. We had to walk down a few steps and bend over to get inside the building.

"Guild headquarters. We don't like too many people to know where we are. Although—" he moved around the large room, lighting lanterns "—now that we're getting older, we'll need to get a bigger door."

As the light illuminated the room, I noticed several desks, a chalkboard and maps hanging from the walls. A detailed layout of the market spanned an entire wall. Letters and a few easy mathematics problems were written on the chalkboard.

Fisk noticed my interest. "We teach the younger members how to read and do simple math. Also about money. What items cost and how to make change.

Speaking of change, you need to get dressed. I have clothes laid out in the back room." He pointed to the far wall.

"What about Pazia? Wasn't she supposed—"

The headquarters' door opened. Pazia stepped through and closed it behind her. "Supposed to meet you at the fountain?"

"Did you read my thoughts?" I demanded.

"I had to make sure there were no surprises in here. And no, I wasn't planning on meeting you at the fountain. I know my way here. This isn't the first time *I've* worked with Fisk on a mission for the Masters."

Her dig touched the weak spot in my heart, being deemed unworthy to participate in important missions. But not anymore. I found a measure of comfort in my present situation, amazing given the circumstances.

"Why aren't you dressed yet?" She sighed dramatically. "Bad enough I have to work with you. The least you could do is be ready on time." Shrugging off her cloak, she flung it onto one of the desks. The material of Pazia's clothes had been woven with an expensive linen-and-silk blended thread. Her tailor's efforts enhanced her slim waist and petite stature. She pulled her long golden hair up and clamped it in place with a jeweled clip.

I headed toward the back room, but her next words stopped me in midstride.

"Fisk, are you sure we need her? I grew up in the mines. I can spot a fake ruby at twenty paces. She can't be trusted."

"*I* trust her. Besides, rubies are not diamonds. And it would be suspicious for you to be alone. Rich ladies always go shopping in pairs."

I tuned out her irritated reply as I entered the back room. On a small cot lay a beautiful indigo-colored blouse and black skirt made from the same material as Pazia's clothes. I fingered the lace trim on the skirt. Fisk had even provided a pair of high-heeled shoes and an assortment of jewelry and hair clips.

Dressing as fast as possible, I squeezed a sapphire ring onto my finger, and covered my wrists with a distracting array of ruby-encrusted bracelets. The other gemstones throbbed when I touched them, but nowhere near the intensity of the diamond. I left my hair down. Just wearing the luxurious clothes and gemstones helped me to assume my role as Pazia's friend. Of course her sneer of contempt quickly drove those feelings away when I joined them in the main room.

She huffed and pointed to a seat. "Sit."

When I hesitated, she said, "*I'm* a professional, unlike you. I won't hurt you."

I ignored her reference to the burning incident and sat. She combed my hair and twisted a section into a knot at the back of my head.

"Clip," she ordered.

I handed her one and she secured the knot.

"We are going to meet a number of diamond merchants. Fisk will introduce us, but won't come with us to negotiate. As a rule, the Helper's Guild avoids the black market. Since I'm a very good customer, he'll bend the rules for me." She pulled the rest of my hair back. "Clip." When she finished, she examined the rest of my clothing. "Move the ring to your right hand, third finger if possible, and all the bracelets go on your left arm."

As I complied, she continued her lecture. "I'll do all the talking. Your role is to let me know which diamonds are real by simply agreeing with me. I'll ask your opinion on a certain stone and you'll either like it or not. If you don't like it, I'll know it's a fake. Understand?"

"Yes."

"Good. Try not to do or say anything to jeopardize our mission. I'm not as *resourceful* as Liaison Yelena."

Another jab. Instead of bracing for the rest of the insinuation Pazia made whenever Yelena's name was mentioned and ignoring it, I decided to beat her to the comment. "You're right. You aren't as powerful or as smart as Yelena. I never would have betrayed *you* the way I did the Soulfinder. *You* would have been dead in a heartbeat."

"Then you admit it!" Her eyes lit with triumph despite my insult.

I shrugged, pretending nonchalance. "Facts are facts, Pazia. And it's no big deal. If Yelena had felt so deceived, it's doubtful she would still be my friend." I turned away from her, not bothering to note her reaction. As I retrieved my cloak from the back room, I marveled over my bold comments. Did I believe them? I knew the truth of my actions and what had led me to them, and realized my guilt lay not in what I had done, but why I had done it. A step in the right direction? I hoped.

"That ratty thing won't do." Pazia eyed my cloak, appearing to be unaffected by my outburst.

"It's all I have." Plus my sais were nestled inside the lining, within easy reach.

She removed a jeweled peacock brooch from her cloak. Sapphires and emeralds decorated the feathers of the bird. Pazia pinned it onto my garment. "There. If anyone notices what's under that beauty, we'll joke you wear the cloak for sentimental reasons. Blushing would help. And don't cover your clothes."

I followed Pazia and Fisk from the Guild headquarters to the market. The black market sellers weren't so bold to have stands, but their agents roamed the area, seeking customers. Fisk approached one man. Dressed as a farmer and acting as if he was in town for a shopping trip, the man regarded Fisk with surprise.

He scanned Pazia and me with suspicion. She kept her look of bored impatience. Quite an accomplishment and, knowing I couldn't match her, I settled for appearing nonthreatening.

Too low for me to hear, Fisk and the agent talked for a moment and the conversation ended with a defeated shrug from Fisk, as if giving in.

The man eventually agreed and led us to a thin building one street away from the market. The four-story structure was wedged between a warehouse and a shoe factory. He opened the door into a receiving room, introduced us to another man inside and left.

"What can I do for you?" the new man asked us. He wore a well-made linen tunic cinched with a gold mesh belt. His brown pants complemented the tunic's light sand color. A large emerald ring on his pinkie finger glinted in the sunlight.

"I want to see your diamonds," Pazia demanded, stepping forward. "The bigger the better."

"Why?"

"Does it matter?" She jingled a bulging leather pouch.

He flashed his teeth in delight. "No. Follow me."

Toward the back of the building was a showroom without windows. Lanterns blazed, illuminating the glass cases filled with jewelry. I scanned the items. Bracelets, rings and necklaces sparkled with every color stone from precious to semiprecious. No diamonds.

The seller draped a black velvet cloth over the cases, disappeared behind the counter and retrieved a silk bag. He shook out an array of large diamonds, then arranged them on the velvet with tweezers.

"These are the biggest I have right now. But if you need a particular size, I can always order more." He picked up a thumb-sized round stone and turned it so the candlelight would reflect off the facets.

Pazia seemed dazzled by the gem. She reached for it, but the man drew it back.

"Ten golds. That's two golds cheaper than what you'd

pay in jewelers' circle. I'll even give you a companion stone—" he pointed to a pea-sized diamond "—for free." He launched into a hard sell.

Pazia shook her head, but eventually just interrupted him. "I'm not buying anything unless I can look at it closer."

He placed the stone on the cloth near her. When she touched it, he frowned.

"Pretty." She held it up to the light then handed it to me.

The man scowled, but she ignored him.

"What do you think?" she asked me.

I hefted the stone. While it scattered the light in a pleasing way, it didn't flash. Glass. I placed it back on the counter and touched the others. The same.

"Pretty but ordinary," I said. "You need a diamond with more pizazz."

"I can order anything you want," the seller offered.

"No thank you. I was hoping to find something today." Pazia was quick to leave despite the man's insistence.

Out in the street, I drew in a breath of fresh air. "Now what?"

"We find Fisk and another seller."

The afternoon hours sped past in a blur. The showrooms all seemed identical; the sellers all had similar smooth personalities. Prices and incentives remained constant. And they all offered us glass. Exceptional glass of top quality that I haven't seen before, but glass all the same. Not a real diamond to be found.

As the sun sank into the horizon, we entered the last shop. This time a man and woman teamed up to make the sale. The woman was effusive with her compliments to Pazia.

"Look how the diamond pendant lights up your gorgeous eyes," the saleswoman said, holding a mirror for Pazia to see her reflection. "Why the green just comes alive doesn't it?"

Pazia beamed, getting sucked in. The diamonds were all mounted in jewelry. The woman slid a huge marquise-cut stone onto Pazia's right index finger.

"The ring will highlight your elegant hands. No one will be able to stop staring at you."

Before the saleswoman could put any more jewelry on Pazia, I bent to examine the ring.

"I don't like this setting," I said. "Do you have any loose stones?"

The woman glanced at the man behind the counter. He withdrew a tray full of diamonds of various sizes and shapes. I touched each one with a finger, but again every one was beautifully cut and polished glass, which caused me to wonder who manufactured them. Without the magic flash, I would have been hard-pressed to call these fakes.

"I don't like any of them," I said.

Pazia pouted with disappointment.

The woman ramped up her sales pitch, disagreeing with me. "Look at her." She pointed to me. "You probably picked out your friend's clothes only to have her ruin your efforts with that tacky cloak. You, my dear, are a ray of sunlight who deserves to be glowing with diamonds. Don't let her jealousy stop you. People will always be jealous of you. If you have it—flaunt it!"

The saleswoman was skilled. She had pegged Pazia's personality and would soon have a sale.

"It's getting late," I said. "Your *mentor* at the Keep will be concerned. Why don't you think it over and we can come back tomorrow."

"Excellent idea," the woman said. "I just hope you get here before Councillor Jewelrose's wife tomorrow. She's been eyeing that ring, and her birthday is today. The Councillor is so sweet. He always gives her gold to buy her own presents. She's my most loyal customer." She tsked, removing the ring from Pazia's finger. "But I'm sure I'll be able to find you something..."

A worried crease formed on Pazia's forehead. I pulled on her arm, guiding her to the door. I waved with my other hand. "Thanks for the offer."

The door opened before we reached it. Two men entered. They blocked our way. Swords hung from weapon belts. Apprehension slid down my spine, lumping in my guts.

"Your friend isn't ready to leave," the man on the left said with a slight lisp. His bottom lip had been cut. Blood-soaked threads from the stitches protruded from the wound.

"Yes, she is." I nudged Pazia with an elbow. "Her mentor is waiting for her. You don't want to make us late. Her mentor has *powerful* friends." Come on, Pazia, I thought, say something, do something.

Bloody Lip stepped closer. "I'm sure her mentor will understand about the...delay. Our girl spent so much time helping you, I'm sure you don't want to be rude by rushing off. In fact, we have a whole other room filled with...surprises. Bex, why don't you show this lady—" he stabbed a finger in my direction "—the back room while her friend completes her purchase."

Bex reached for me. I dropped all pretenses and yanked my sais from my cloak. Ramming the weapons' knobs into the man's solar plexus, I shouted, "Pazia, help me."

The man gasped, but recovered fast. They both pulled their swords. The saleswoman brandished a knife. I remained close to the men, deflecting their blades toward the ground. Pazia stood immobile.

"Fire," I yelled.

Finally she moved. Small flames erupted on the men's shirts. The woman squealed. Chaos manifested into four pairs of flailing limbs, swatting at the growing fire on their clothes. The motion reminded me of the flesh-eating beetles Tricky had used to attack me. Suppressing a shudder, I grabbed Pazia's hand and hauled her from the room.

I didn't let go of her until we reached the market. We paused to catch our breath and I put my sais away.

Pazia's flushed cheeks and the wild glint in her eyes meant either fear or excitement.

Fisk appeared at our side. "What happened?"

"They tried to use strong-arm tactics." I tucked a few loose strands of hair behind my ear.

"Not good. Did they have the required items?"

"No. Except for Bloody Lip and Bex, they were just like the rest."

Fisk considered. "I'll spread the word to my clients about the fake diamonds, but the seller who used the swordsmen will be out of business by tomorrow."

"I thought you didn't work with black market dealers."

"I don't. But I'll make sure they know about Bloody Lip and Bex. The other dealers don't want customers to be afraid to buy from the black market. It's bad for business. I've no doubt when the others are aware of the situation, it will be taken care of in record time."

I mulled over the implications and decided I wouldn't be upset to know Bloody Lip and Bex were run out of town. My thoughts then turned to the lack of real diamonds.

"Do you think the rogue Moon Clan faction is funding their activities by selling these fake stones?" I asked Fisk.

"Must be. We've run out of dealers to contact."

"They looked so real," Pazia said. "I almost..." She sighed.

"Someone is manufacturing them. Should we try and trace them back to the source?" I wondered if I could produce such high-quality glass. It would be an interesting challenge.

"I can take you back to one of the dealers you met with today," Fisk said. "Perhaps he'll tell you his source."

"Let's talk to Zitora first. See if she has any ideas." I pulled my cloak tighter as an icy wind blew through the market, causing the lanterns along the street to pulse. A hint of moisture clung to the air with the promise of rain.

We agreed to meet tomorrow afternoon.

"Keep the clothes for now," Fisk said, gesturing to my disguise. "And walk straight back to the Keep. The gossip is that two student magicians are looking to buy diamonds to enhance their magic. Play it up, so when you start asking for a big quantity of large diamonds no one is surprised."

Pazia and I headed toward the Keep. She had been subdued since we escaped from Bloody Lip. A few people walked along the quiet Citadel streets. I wondered how Ulrick's day had gone.

About a block before the Keep's entrance, two men stepped from the shadows and approached us.

20

PAZIA GASPED AS the men drew closer, but I reached for my sais, wrapping my hands around the hilts. The motion helped steady my frantic heartbeat.

"Magic, remember?" I whispered to Pazia. "You're powerful."

"I've heard you two are looking for sparkles," the man on the left said. He wore the plain gray coverall of a factory worker. Tools hung from his belt. Any one of them could be used as a weapon. His companion also wore coveralls, although the larger man's were covered with dark stains. Blood or grease, it was hard to discern in the lantern light.

I waited for Pazia to speak. When the silence lengthened to uncomfortable, I said, "We're looking for *real* sparkles. If you don't have anything good, we're not interested in doing business."

The man nodded. "Thought so. Watched you go to

all those others. You're looking for magical sparkles. Question is, can you afford it?"

"My family owns the Vasko mine," Pazia said.

I tried not to show my surprise. After all, I was supposed to be her friend. But the Vasko mine was famous for the quantity and quality of rubies, making the owners the richest people in Sitia. And she just took one hell of a risk, telling two strangers about her family connections.

"Care to see our wares then?" he asked, grinning.

Remembering our run-in with Bloody Lip, I asked, "Where?"

"Right here." He glanced at the big man. "Egg?"

Egg removed a pouch from his pocket and handed it to his friend, who opened it and poured diamonds into his palm. The four diamonds caught the light and held it. About the size of a teaspoon, they were the largest stones we'd seen all day.

"May I?" I asked.

He nodded. I picked up one of the diamonds and almost dropped it. The stone flashed cold, stinging my mind with a vision of an icy plain. Cold burned through my fingers then settled into a steady vibration. I had the same reaction with the other three, and I hurried to return them to him.

The salesman had been watching me. There was frank interest in his light brown eyes.

"What do you think?" he asked.

"They're adequate, but we're going to need bigger stones. The larger the better."

"Big?" he asked with an incredulous tone.

"If you can't supply them, perhaps we could negotiate with your supplier?" When he just stared at me, I added, "We'll pay you a finder's fee, of course."

"But, you're students…"

"Come on, Pazia, he's wasting our time." I pulled on her arm, but the man hurried to block our path.

"Pazia Cloud Mist?" he asked as if afraid of the answer.

She gave him a cold stare. "I told you my family owned the Vasko mine."

Color leaked from the man's face.

She studied him with an intense alertness. Kidnapping and ransoming Pazia would bring in more money than selling a few diamonds, provided they could capture her. Curare would work, but it was near impossible to find.

"Can you help us or not? I have a riding lesson." I gestured with impatience.

"I'll hook you up, but we get twenty percent of the purchase price as our fee."

"Ten percent," I countered.

"Eighteen."

"Twelve."

"Sixteen, or it's not even worth our time."

"Fifteen."

He sighed. "Agreed. Let's go then." He started walking down the street. Away from the Keep.

"Go where?" I asked.

"To our supplier."

We followed him back the way we had come. I wondered if one of the black market dealers had tried to sell us fakes first and we didn't give them enough time to bring out the real stones. I kept alert for any signs of Bloody Lip and Bex.

We approached the alley where the black market dealers had their showrooms, but instead of leading us to one of them, the man knocked on the back door of another building.

The building's front was on Jewelers' Circle.

A person opened the door and the man explained our reason for being there. We were taken to a small room. Lanterns on a single table blazed. Black velvet covered the top.

A woman entered. I caught a glimpse of the room beyond her before she shut the door, confirming my suspicions we were in one of the legitimate jewelry stores.

The woman's hair had been pulled into a complex knot behind her head. She scowled at the two salesmen. "Why did you bring them here?" she demanded.

"They wanted to purchase big stones. But we still get our fifteen percent."

"If they can pay," she said, giving us a pointed stare.

"I don't think the daughter of Vasko Cloud Mist will have any trouble with payment." The man grinned with a greedy glint in his eyes. "We'll leave you girls to work out the details." He left with Egg right behind him.

The woman perked up at hearing Pazia's name, but she eyed my clothing, clearly not impressed with my display of wealth. "Let me guess. You're two seniors from the Keep and you want to buy a few diamonds to help increase your magic." She sighed. "I'll sell you all you want, but let me warn you. The extra boost of power won't help you to be assigned a cushy job when you graduate from the Keep."

I waited for Pazia to start, but again felt compelled to fill the lengthening silence. "We're not interested in landing good assignments. We're interested in obtaining diamonds of a specific size and quality."

"Why?"

"Does it matter?"

She considered. "No. Tell me what you want and I'll find it for you."

"No. I have to see what is available. I can't quantify our needs with numbers, but with feelings." I waited for the inevitable disbelief.

But her posture softened and she grew wistful. "I understand. I've been a jeweler all my life and there are certain gems that just…speak to me."

Unable to stifle my curiosity, I asked, "Why are you selling black market diamonds then?"

"The Commander of Ixia gives us so few stones I can't meet the demands of my customers. When I was offered a chance to bring in more, I jumped. If not, I would have lost business."

"Do the other jewelers sell them, too?"

"I don't know for sure, but I suspect they do."

"Does the Helper's Guild know?"

"We've been doing business decades longer than the Guild. If you need a Guild member to help you shop, then you're not a loyal customer and not worth risking discovery." She narrowed her eyes at me. "You're asking a lot of questions."

"You're not the only one taking a risk. For all I know you could be working with the Sitian authorities."

"The same could be said of you." The saleswoman regarded me as if she were assessing the quality of a gemstone. "What's your name?"

"Opal Cowan." I couldn't think of any reason to lie and any hesitation would increase her suspicion.

She cocked her head to the side. "The glass magician. No wonder you spotted the fakes." She gestured to Pazia. "This is what you're doing now? Making sure your friend doesn't get conned? I thought the Master Magicians would have something better for you to do."

"I'm still in school."

The saleswoman nodded as if she understood. "All right. My supplier is delivering stones in the next couple of days. I'll ask him about your request and we'll see what we can do for you. Stop back in four days. Come to the rear door before the lamplighters get to the lanterns in the alley."

"Thank you…?" I stopped, realizing I didn't know her name.

"Elita Jewelrose."

Elita escorted us to the back entrance of her store. In the alley we heard the click of multiple locks. Pazia and I walked to the Keep. The hour had grown late. Only a few people hustled along the empty streets. For a while the silence hung heavy between us.

A few blocks from the Keep, Pazia said in a churlish tone, "You can *try* to tell everyone I was surprised by the men who attacked us, and I was completely sucked in by the saleswoman. But no one will believe you." She was right.

I laughed. "You can pretend all you want, but without me you would be wearing a gaudy piece of glass on your finger. *I* know it and *you* know it. I don't need to tell anyone else."

"You don't have anyone to tell anyway. You think you're so much better than the rest of us—we're not worth your time."

I stopped. "Hold on. *You're* the one who thinks she's so powerful and special."

"No. I don't think. I know. I *am* more powerful than all my classmates and teachers. But I treat everyone equally. *I've* made friends."

"Equally? What a laugh. You've been nasty to me since the first day!"

"That's because you thought you were too good for us. All *you* did was help the Soulfinder imprison the Warpers and you were lavished with special attention. And for what?" Pazia rounded on me. "One deed. One trick. No other talents and you just admitted to being a betrayer.

You don't deserve to be a student at the Keep. You've been given a free ride. And you didn't even have the decency to be humble about your good fortune. No. You expected it and expected everyone to fawn over you. Well, I wasn't going to do it." With a grunt of disgust, Pazia strode up the street.

I hurried after her. My thoughts swirled in my mind. I didn't act as if I deserved special treatment. What did she expect me to do? Leave the Keep? She slowed and I almost ran into her.

"Seems you have someone fooled by your noble routine." Pazia pointed to a dark shape.

A person waited by the Keep's gates. As we came closer, his features and agitation grew clearer. I steeled myself for the unavoidable lecture.

Ulrick shot Pazia a sharp look. "You trust *her* to keep you safe?"

Agitated by Pazia's accusations, I clamped down on a sarcastic reply. "I'm here aren't I? Why are you here?" I immediately regretted my harsh tone when he looked at me as if I had slapped him.

"It's late. I was concerned when you didn't return for dinner. Guess I shouldn't have bothered." He turned on his heel and stormed into the Keep.

Pazia smirked. "You're going to drive him away, too, and prove my point about you."

Her comment was one too many. My emotions knotted and I could no longer think straight. "Shut up, Pazia. You think you have me all figured out. You have no

idea. Let's just keep focused on the task at hand." I
headed for the administration building and didn't
bother to note if she followed me or not.

Zitora waited in her office. Two lanterns burned on her
desk.

She sprang from her seat the moment she saw us.
"Why have you been gone so long?"

We alternated in telling her about our day. Pazia
reported our findings in a factual manner, omitting the
reason for Bex and Bloody Lip's attack.

"So all the black market diamonds are fakes? Interesting and surprising," Zitora said. "Any guesses as to why?"

"Elita mentioned having to keep up with her client's
demands," I said. "Perhaps the illegal diamond seller is
working both sides of the street. Sell real stones to the
jewelers who can tell the difference and sell fakes to the
black market dealers who can't."

"A good scam," Pazia agreed. "One that would pull
in a ton of money."

"But do all the legitimate jewelers sell these illegal
stones?" Zitora asked.

Her comment reminded me about Elita's agent. He
and Egg knew we were searching for real diamonds.
"Elita knows about the fakes. We don't have any information about the other jewelers."

"Then we should find out." Zitora settled into her
chair. "You and Pazia keep your appointment with Elita.
We'll set up a watch on Elita's back door to see if we can
spot her diamond supplier."

A good plan. Yet I felt we had overlooked something vital. I reviewed the events of the day, searching for loopholes. "Fisk."

Zitora glanced up from her desk. "Fisk?"

"We told him the black market diamonds are fakes. He planned to spread the word."

"Which might scare away the supplier," Pazia said.

"Go. Find Fisk. Make sure he keeps quiet," Zitora ordered.

"Now?" Pazia glanced at the darkness pressed against the window.

"Yes."

We hurried from Zitora's office.

"Take off your jewelry," Pazia said. "This time we don't want to attract attention."

"Do you know where Fisk is?" I pulled the ruby bracelets from my arm, unpinned the brooch and shoved them into my pocket. My hair clips followed.

"He lives above the Guild's headquarters with his family. Come on, I have an early class tomorrow."

We arrived at Fisk's place without incident. Fortunately he was home and joined us in the Guild's common room. We explained what happened with Elita.

"She's well respected. It's hard to believe she's selling contraband," Fisk said.

"Have you heard any rumors about the other jewelers?" I asked.

"No. But I'll make a few discreet inquiries."

"Have you told anyone about the fakes?" Pazia asked.

"Not yet. I'll wait until we have identified the supplier." Fisk stiffened and held a hand up for silence.

The door to the alley opened and a small figure slipped inside. Appearing to be around six years old, the boy signaled Fisk with a series of hand and arm gestures.

"Thanks," Fisk said. He flipped a silver coin to the boy. The child snatched it from midair and disappeared in the same furtive manner as he had arrived.

"You were followed." He frowned at Pazia as if waiting for an explanation.

"I was in a hurry." She seemed unconcerned.

Unlike me. I was very concerned. "Do you know who?"

"A man. A little taller and muscular than average, according to Tweet."

My mind raced over potential attackers. Blue Eyes, Tricky, Sir, Tal, it was quite a list. Worry gnawed on my guts, chewing holes.

"You learned all that from a child named Tweet?" Pazia asked.

Fisk gave her an icy stare. "Tweet is the only sound the boy can make since his mother cut out his tongue for crying too loud. She actually did him a favor by abandoning him on the street. Even without parents, the boy understands better than *you* the importance of keeping the location of our headquarters a secret."

"Fine. We'll corner this man and find out why he followed us." She made to leave.

"Can't you just read his thoughts?" I asked.

She shooed away my question. "Too many people around."

"He's waiting at the end of the alley. Not far at all," Fisk said.

Pazia's annoyance turned to anger. "My ability to read minds is very limited. Happy now? Are you going to help us trap him or not?"

In the end, Pazia and I left the headquarters and headed toward the Keep. Fisk would wait a couple minutes and then recruit a few Guild members to set up an ambush near the Six Heathers Inn.

My legs wanted to run as fast as my heartbeat. Keeping my gait steady was an exercise in willpower. An itchy burning sensation bored into my back right between my shoulder blades, pushing me toward panic. I kept a sharp eye out for magical spiders and beetles.

The Six Heathers Inn appeared deserted. No lights in the windows and not a sound escaped from inside. The beginning of the cold season wasn't a popular time for visitors to the Citadel, but, even at this late hour, I expected to see a few customers.

A shrill tweet split the air when we rounded a comer. Sounds of a scuffle ensued. We raced back to the noise. Five gangly children sat on top of a man. His indignant cries of protest died in his throat when he spotted me.

"Kade?"

21

"ARE YOU GOING to call off your dogs or do I have to conjure a gale?" Kade asked.

"It's okay. He's a friend," I said to the children sitting on top of the Stormdancer. They didn't move.

Fisk appeared beside me. "Friend? Following someone at night isn't friend-like behavior."

"I feel an extremely annoyed thunderstorm nearby," Kade warned. "Actually, I'm the one annoyed. The thunderstorm could go either way."

Lightning flashed and thunder cracked. "I'm sure he has a good reason for being here," I said. My ears rang from the clap.

Fisk nodded and the children slid off Kade, disappearing into an alley.

Kade stood and brushed the dirt from his brown pants. He wore a short tan-colored cape and had a leather backpack slung over his left shoulder. A few dead leaves clung to his shoulder-length hair, which appeared black in the semidarkness.

"You do have a good reason, don't you?" I asked.

He scowled. "Considering two of our glassmakers have been murdered and the other is missing, I thought I would find you and give you fair warning you might be next."

I gaped as numbing fear flushed through my body. "Who…?"

"Indra and Nodin…pushed from the cave…we found them on the beach." He squeezed his eyes shut for a moment as if blocking an image. "Varun is nowhere to be found. Either his body washed away with the tide or he's been kidnapped."

"When did this happen?"

"End of the storm season—about a week ago. I really wish I could have used your glass orb to message Master Cowan."

"What—"

"We can discuss it with Master Cowan in private." Kade glanced at Pazia and Fisk. "I was just leaving the stables, when I spotted you crossing through the gate. I didn't want to interrupt your evening with your friend, so I followed you to keep you safe." He scanned the surrounding buildings with a rueful grin. All was dark, and a low rumble of thunder sounded in the distance. "Laid low by five street kids, though. I'm not much of a protector."

"You would have used the storm to escape," I said. Seeing Fisk and Pazia's confusion, I introduced Kade to them.

Fisk's eyes held a question.

"This changes nothing," I said to him. "We'll keep our appointment with Elita in four days."

"Good. See you then." Fisk walked away.

Pazia didn't hesitate to take Kade's arm and lead him toward the Keep. She chatted with him, asking questions about being a Stormdancer. I followed a step behind. My thoughts churned as my emotions seesawed from apprehension to grief. Questions without answers plagued me and I hustled Kade and Pazia along, hoping to get him alone.

Once inside the Keep, Pazia wanted to go with us to Zitora's office.

"You have an early class tomorrow," I reminded her. "This is just glass stuff. Boring to you, I'm sure."

She said a warm good-night to Kade, shot me a frozen glare and headed to her rooms.

"I take it she's not a good friend," he said.

We climbed the stairs to the administration building.

"We're working together on another project." Foreboding silence settled on me as I escorted Kade to Zitora's office.

As expected, a strip of lantern light glowed under the door. Zitora's surprise at seeing Kade was quickly replaced by concern.

"What happened?" she asked.

He repeated his news.

"Are you sure Indra and Nodin were murdered?" she asked. "You knew they might be in danger, didn't you have extra security?"

"We did. Two guards, both knocked unconscious. And there's no doubt they were killed. If they fell, they would have landed closer to the base of The Cliffs. And we think they were unconscious when they were thrown from the cave and hit the beach." Kade rubbed his leg. "It was late at night, and no one heard the 'fall scream.' It's a distinctive shriek of fear that abruptly stops. It's not a sound any Stormdancer can sleep through or ever forget." He drew in a deep breath. "The next morning, we found their bodies and a few drops of blood and scuff marks on the floor of the cave. No signs of Varun."

His explanation left one question in my mind. "Why them and not me?"

"The glassmakers were the only three besides you who knew the recipe. I'm guessing the Traitor Tal and his friends targeted Indra and her brothers after their attempt to coerce it from you didn't work. Once they had the sand percentages, they would have only needed one glassmaker to help them craft orbs. The others…"

Thrown away. I shuddered at the image of Tricky threatening Indra's life if her brothers didn't tell him the recipe. They were a loving family and would have obliged in a heartbeat. Varun probably volunteered to go with Sir's group. I understood all too well the desire to sacrifice for another family member. Did he know the sacrifice was for nothing? Did he feel the hot knife of grief ripping his body to shreds when he realized nobody was saved? Not if they wanted his cooperation. He would learn the truth later. If he lived.

My mind filled with what I had done to keep Tula safe. What I had promised to make the man stop.

"Opal, snap out of it," Zitora said.

"Sorry." I pulled my thoughts to the problem at hand.

"As we speculated before, the group wants to either put the Stormdancers out of business or use the orbs to bribe us." Kade paused as if deciding how much information to share with us. "The glassmakers have always kept the orb's exact recipe to themselves. As the strongest Stormdancer, my sister knew it and I planned to ask Indra... Well, you know how crazy this season has been. But if we can't make orbs, then we would be at the mercy of those that could."

"I can teach your clan members the recipe," I said.

"Exactly! And that's why you're still in danger and why I'm here to warn you. I'm sure Sir wouldn't hesitate to eliminate you so the Stormdancers have no other recourse."

My heart flipped. "Then I should tell you both the orb recipe. It's forty—"

"Write it down. Tell Master Cowan," Kade said. "I don't want to know it just yet."

I searched his face. Grim determination pulled the corners of his mouth taut. His amber eyes darkened as if a storm brewed.

"You're planning to go after them?" I asked.

"Yes."

"But what about teaching the new glassmakers?"

"It's the cold season. While the storms are mild in

comparison to the cooling season, the water is high and rough. It's safer to stay away from the coast until the warming season. Then you can come and help a new crew. If you would?"

"Of course."

"Do you know where Sir's group is?" Zitora asked him.

"No. They haven't been seen since Opal burned down their workshop. But we know they're not in Stormdance territory or the Krystal Clan's land."

"You still have nine more territories to search plus the Citadel." Zitora considered. "I could help you, but I'm embroiled in another problem. Perhaps you could wait?"

"No, I'll start. If you can join me when you have time, I would be most grateful."

"Sand suppliers," I blurted.

"What?" Kade asked.

"Sir's group would need to order the orb's ingredients from suppliers. There aren't many requests for lava flakes and Bloodgood's red sand. You could talk to the suppliers, see if a purchase was made and where it was delivered."

"Opal, you're a genius!" Kade grabbed me in a quick hug.

At his touch, a connection between us sparked with an intense heat. He stepped away in surprise. The memory of when we linked through the orbs rose in my mind.

If Zitora noticed our sudden awkwardness, she didn't mention it. Instead, she said, "That's an excellent idea. Opal, can you give Kade a list of suppliers?"

"Yes. I can even introduce him to the merchants who have stands in the Citadel's market. I'll send a message to my father. He can check with the suppliers in Booruby."

"Great. Kade, you can stay at the Keep as long as you want. Let me know if you need anything."

"How about a bodyguard for Opal?" he asked.

Zitora smiled. "She already has one. Opal, please escort Kade to the guest quarters, and show him where the dining hall is located."

As we left the administration building, Kade asked me about the bodyguard. "Was she talking about Pazia or Fisk?"

"Neither." I glanced around the darkened courtyard. Lamps lit the paths winding around the classroom studios and student barracks. The guest quarters were housed in two separate structures behind administration, kitty-corner to the back of the Keep's main building.

My rooms were in the southern tip of the east apprentice wing, close to both the guest lodgings and dining hall.

I spotted Ulrick lurking in the shadows. He followed us as we walked along the path.

The Stormdancer stiffened and raised his head as if scenting the wind. "Someone is behind us."

"I know. It's my bodyguard." It seemed silly for Ulrick to skulk about. I called to him, inviting him to join us.

By Ulrick's cold demeanor, I knew he was still upset with me. Yet the man did watch out for me; I would have to apologize to him later. I introduced him to Kade and had to stifle a laugh as the two men sized each other up.

They were complete opposites. Looking even more broad-shouldered next to Kade's lean physique, Ulrick's perfect features lacked the calm confidence in Kade's tanned face.

"A Stormdancer?" Ulrick asked. "Shouldn't you be dancing in the storm?" A legitimate question, but Ulrick's tone implied a sneering disregard.

"The season is over. I have other business to attend to," Kade said without emotion.

"What kind of business?"

Kade glanced at me. His annoyance barely concealed.

"He knows about Sir and Tricky," I said.

"Then perhaps *you* should fill him in on the new developments."

"What developments," Ulrick asked.

"Later," I said as we arrived at the east guest quarters. I talked to the night manager. There was a suite empty. The manager offered to escort Kade to his rooms.

Another questioning look and I assured Kade I would be fine. Ulrick hovered next to me in a protective stance.

"Rest," I said to the Stormdancer. "I'll meet you after breakfast and show you the market."

Kade nodded, following the manager. Instead of going to his own rooms, Ulrick trailed me to mine.

"Don't you mean *we'll* take him to the market?" he asked.

Remembering my harsh words earlier and his efforts to keep me safe, I ignored his snide tone. "Of course."

"What did he mean by new developments?"

I mulled over potential responses as we entered my apartment. Already overprotective, Ulrick wouldn't leave me alone for a second if he knew Sir had murdered the glassmakers. Watering down Kade's conviction that Sir's group was involved, I explained about Indra and Nodin's death and how they may have been killed.

My attempts to lessen the threat failed to work. Ulrick stood in the middle of my living room and declared he would sleep on the couch.

"Tomorrow I'll request an armed guard to stay with you until those men are caught."

I opened my mouth to protest, but paused. There had been a time when I would have welcomed an armed guard by my side, when I would have reveled in Ulrick's attention and concern for my welfare. Yet, I was irritated by his assumption that I couldn't take care of myself. I escaped Tricky before, I could do it again.

Could I? Doubt flared, but I reviewed the skills I'd learned since my last encounter with them. I still needed to explore a few more abilities and discover how to repeat the magic of trapping those spiders.

Perhaps I wouldn't be able to escape, but I had enough knowledge to avoid getting kidnapped in the first place. I hoped.

"Ulrick, I understand your worry and I appreciate your efforts. I'm really sorry I snapped at you earlier. I think I know why I was angry at you. You assumed I couldn't protect myself—wait." I held a hand up to stop his words. "I *am* capable of defending myself. And I *am* being cautious, but I don't think we need an armed guard following us around all day."

He considered my words. "This is the first time you've seemed confident about Sir and Tricky. Is it because that Stormdancer is here? Think he could better defend you with his magical powers?"

I suppressed my desire to throttle him. "You missed the point completely! You're acting…" The word stuck in my throat.

He didn't hesitate to say it. "Jealous?" When I nodded, he continued, "Now *you're* missing the point. It isn't jealousy. It's fear."

"Fear?" Not the emotion I expected.

"Yes. Fear. I'm afraid you'll be hurt or killed. I'm afraid I won't be able to protect you. I'm afraid I'll lose you to another man."

22

I NEEDED TO sit down. I'd heard other people talk about having to sit down when shocked by an event or revelation and I had dismissed the notion as pure exaggeration. Little did I realize the actual physical weakness. It felt as if my bones had dissolved and my muscles could no longer support my weight.

"I tried to remain the friend." Ulrick prowled around the room as he talked. "Remain the colleague you introduced to your family. The partner who was concerned about your safety. You kept me at arm's length and I thought I would be content with our friendship." He stopped and skewered me with an intent stare. "But I can't do it anymore. Not when I saw you with that Storm-dancer. I want more than friendship."

No sound escaped my throat. My body froze as my mind whirled, sorting through all the unexpected information.

"Opal, what's wrong?" Ulrick grabbed my arm. "You're swaying. Sit down before you fall down." He guided me to the couch. "Guess that's the last thing you wanted to hear right now. You've made it clear to me you're not interested."

When I sank into the cushions, I pulled Ulrick down beside me. His green eyes filled with alarm.

"You weren't the only one afraid," I said. "I kept a distance on purpose." I paused, thinking of Pazia's comments, how she accused me of acting better than everyone. "I was afraid, too. Afraid of rejection. Afraid of…" My thoughts shied away from the fear lurking deep within my soul where I had shoved it over four years ago.

Ulrick put an arm around my shoulders and drew me close. "Tell me what else you're afraid of, so I can fix it."

I wished it was that easy. "Afraid of my reaction to your…ah…attentions. Another man…"

"Raped you?" The muscles in his arm tensed, but he waited.

"No." I closed my eyes, not wanting to see his expression. "Tortured. Threatened." The words burned my mouth. "I haven't told anyone about it."

"Why not?"

Ashamed, embarrassed and humiliated. I had been so cowed into submission, so eager to make him stop the pain; I would have done anything for him. "It's…difficult." I sucked in a breath, trying to keep the storm of emotions from overwhelming me.

"Was this when you were kidnapped?"

"Yes. Did someone tell you?"

"Mara mentioned it and a few of the students. But they all said a woman held you."

"She had a partner." Revulsion ripped through my body.

"Was he caught?"

"No, but he had to have been killed during the Warper Battle. He was a strong Warper and he wanted to use me for a ritual, but Alea wouldn't let him. She needed me to trick…"

"Yelena," Ulrick finished. "I heard."

"And the worst part was…I was glad to do it." There I said it. Shouldn't I feel better? "I wanted to get away from him. I had no qualms about pricking Yelena with Curare." I waited for the admonishment about putting myself before another. Or he would offer empty words of comfort, telling me how it all worked out in the end. I kept my eyes shut tight, bracing for his reaction.

"Living with your decision must be hard. Nothing I or anyone can say will give you any peace. You must reconcile your actions in your heart. In the meantime, we'll take it slow."

His hand stroked my cheek. I opened my eyes. He leaned closer and our lips met. A tender kiss, short and sweet.

He smiled. "A good first gather."

I laughed at the glassmaking reference. Ulrick did spend the night on my couch, and I lay in my bed marveling over the turn of events. Thoughts of Kade also lingered. When we touched there had been that spark, yet he never indicated he wanted more. Ulrick and I had so much in common and his desire was evident. I touched my lips, remembering the kiss.

After breakfast the next morning, Ulrick and I found Kade sitting on a bench outside the dining hall. A small child giggled as the Stormdancer created a tiny whirlwind. Dead leaves and dried grass swirled around the girl. She held her arms out and let the air flow through her chubby fingers.

Pure delight shone in the girl's eyes. Eventually her mother came looking for her and Kade let the whirlwind dissipate. The child had wandered away from the kitchen. She was so unrepentant and defiant, I guessed this wasn't the first time she explored on her own, nor would it be the last. Her mother would have her hands full until the child was old enough for school.

A half smile lingered on Kade's lips as we strolled to the market.

"The girl will have quite a story to tell her friends," I said to him.

"Why?"

"Since I've been here, a Stormdancer has never visited the Keep, and usually the students and magicians are too busy to entertain the staff's children."

"That's a pity. Adults are so jaded when it comes to magic. Nothing compares to seeing a child's wonder and delight over simple tricks. Makes me appreciate my skills and reminds me not to take them for granted."

When we arrived at the market, Kade and I talked to the sand merchants while Ulrick kept watch. Fisk appeared to see if I needed anything, and he led us to two more dealers I didn't know about.

The morning progressed with little success. None of the suppliers had filled an order for lava flakes in the past year. Kade would need to visit the merchants in Mica and Fulgor.

As we navigated the crowded square, a blacksmith hailed Ulrick. The jacks we'd ordered for the glass shop were ready. Kade and I waited outside while Ulrick inspected the tools.

"You both are happier today," Kade said. "Did you settle your differences?" He kept his tone neutral.

"We did." I studied him, looking for any sign he may be unhappy. Any indication that his reasons for coming to the Keep included seeing me.

"Good. You're well matched." His demeanor remained impartial.

Again I remembered Pazia's criticism. Perhaps I had been the one to keep my distance from him. I took a chance. "We do have a lot in common. Same hometown. Same enjoyment from working with glass. But he lacks a certain... spark."

Surprise touched Kade's eyes for a moment before he resumed his bland manner. "Sparks are similar to lightning strikes and are harmful if you get too close. Also the problem with thunderstorms, they move with the wind and have other...ah...obligations. It's best for you to bask in the steady sunshine."

It was as I suspected all along. No interest in me other than dealing with the current problem. Even though I could rationally explain to myself how it was for the best, I couldn't stop the brief stab of pain deep inside me.

When Ulrick returned, we walked to the Keep's entrance. Kade wanted to talk to me in private. Ulrick scowled.

"Don't worry," Kade said. "On the off chance Tricky is lying in wait in the Citadel, I'll be able to brew a strong gale. The weather is unsettled today."

Apprehension and reluctance filled Ulrick's eyes, but he left to deliver the tools to the almost-finished glass shop.

"I'll catch up with you there," I called.

He waved.

Kade was bemused. "He's protective, a good quality in a bodyguard, but he needs to learn how to trust."

"He just met you," I said.

"I meant you. Trust you. You managed to escape Sir and Tricky without harm, so you do know how to take care of yourself."

We sauntered through the southeast quadrant of the Citadel. The cold air kept most people indoors, and there were few citizens on the streets.

"You followed me last night, trying to protect me," I countered.

"True. But you didn't know about Indra and Nodin then. Now that you know, I expect you to take extra precautions."

"Is this what you wanted to talk to me about?"

"No. I had a chance to speak with Master Cowan this morning. She explained a few more details of your escape from Tricky. She wanted to know if I've heard of any Stormdancers who could pull another's magic into an orb."

"Have you?"

"No. But I wondered when you helped me with the storm, why didn't my magic transform into glass raindrops?"

I thought back and reviewed the series of events. "Perhaps it didn't happen because you were pulling in a real substance, while Tricky's spiders were illusion."

"A possibility. Once this mess with Varun and the orbs is settled, I'll see about assigning one of my Stormdancers to help you with your experiments."

Another jab of disappointment pierced me. I berated myself, thinking of Ulrick.

"The reason I wanted to speak to you alone is..." Kade hesitated. It was the first time I'd seen him uncertain. "I have a favor to ask."

Intrigued and a little uneasy, I encouraged him to continue.

"It's about my orb. I didn't want to leave it with another Stormdancer, yet I don't want to carry it with me on this mission. It could be used as a weapon in the wrong hands. Will you keep it for me?"

"Of course, but why didn't you give it to Raiden?"

Kade fiddled with the sleeve of his cape. "Raiden

would send it off to be used to fuel one of our factories. We're short of orbs this year and he threatened to stop indulging me in my 'maudlin behavior.' The orbs are vital to the Stormdance economy, but I'm not ready to part with it just yet. And I knew *you* would understand why."

The orb was his last physical connection to his sister, Kaya.

"Is that why you asked me? Because I've lost a sister, too?"

"No. Because I trust you."

As we talked, Kade and I had wandered into the main section of the Citadel. Although a few people still shopped, most of the market stands were closed for the day. Twilight cast a pall on the marble walls. Strident voices pulled my attention to an alley on my right. Two men engaged in a verbal argument.

Kade and I were about to walk past when the snick of a switchblade reached us. I shared a look with Kade and he strode down the alley without hesitation. I followed.

"Excuse me," he called. "I'm in need of directions. Can one of you gentlemen tell me where the Council Hall is?"

The smaller man tried to step away from his companion, but the other grabbed his shirt. "Go ask someone else. We're busy," he said.

The voice sounded familiar. I peered at the bigger man. In the weak light, the raw gash on his lower lip oozed black. Bloody Lip. My hands grasped the handles of my sais.

"Sir, do you need help?" Kade asked.

"This man is trying—"

"Shut up," Bloody Lip growled. He raised his knife. "Leave now and I won't hurt you."

"We could say the same thing," Kade replied.

A wind gust blew through the alley, sweeping trash into the air. I pulled my sais and held them in the ready position.

Bloody Lip met my gaze and pushed the man down, turning all his attention to us. "I know you. You're that student who cost me my job." His other hand moved and with another snick he brandished a second knife. "You won't surprise me this time."

He advanced. Another gust flowed around us. It whistled and slammed into Bloody Lip, but the air around us remained calm. He kept his feet as the litter in the alley shot past. The victim huddled low to the ground.

A banging noise sounded behind me and I turned in time to avoid a couple of barrels rolled by the wind. They hit the edge of a cobblestone and launched into the air, connecting with Bloody Lip. He tumbled to the ground, cursing as a knife skittered out of his hand.

The wind stopped and Bloody Lip crawled to his feet and ran away. Kade helped the victim to stand.

"Thank fate you came along. That man was trying to rob me," he said. His voice quavered with a shaky indignation.

"Do you want us to escort you to the Citadel guards to report him?" I asked.

He flinched and attempted a smile. "No. No time. I have a delivery to make. Can you accompany me to the store? It's not far."

"Sure," Kade said. He moved aside to let the man lead.

"My name's Chun. Who do I have the pleasure of thanking for rescuing me?"

We introduced ourselves. Chun chatted about nothing in particular and once again thanked us when we reached his destination.

The storefront was unremarkable, but I recognized the place as belonging to one of the many black market dealers Pazia and I had visited. Chun's reluctance to talk to the authorities was now understandable. His delivery was probably of black market goods.

We left and headed back toward the Keep. Two blocks away I made the connection.

Stopping in midstride, I said, "Chun entered Bloody Lip's place." I explained about Bex and Bloody Lip's attempt to strong-arm me and Pazia into buying fake diamonds.

"Do you think Chun and he worked together?" Kade asked.

"No. Bloody Lip mentioned getting fired." I thought it through. "Let's go back and see where he goes."

We found a small alcove near the store and waited. My attention tended to wander. The air between me and Kade felt as if a mini thunderstorm brewed within the narrow gap. A sudden desire to grasp Kade's arm and share his energy swelled in my heart. I stifled it with difficulty.

Chun finally exited after the lamplighters had finished lighting the street. An errant gust had blown the lamp near us out. From Kade's grin, I knew it wasn't a coincidence.

Before Chun could move away, the door swung open and a man stuck his head out.

"I forgot about the midseason festival," he said. "Bring us ten more crystals. The tourists will snatch them up. Everyone loves a bargain."

They shared a chuckle, and I wondered if the crystals he mentioned were the fake diamonds.

Keeping a half-block distance back from Chun, we followed him to the Citadel's north gate. He stopped at the public paddock nearby. Each of the Citadel's entrances had a place where you could stable your horse or store a wagon. A convenience for those who only came for the day. The paddocks were run by the government and every large town in Sitia had one.

Chun hitched a dilapidated wagon to a brown horse. Spokes were missing from the wheels and the broken back gate was tied to the sides with knotted and frayed ropes.

"If he's selling the fakes, he certainly isn't putting his money into transportation," Kade said. "Then again, what better way to avoid robbers on the roads."

"Zitora didn't seem as concerned with the fakes, but we should know who is producing them."

We watched as Chun spurred the horse and drove through the north gate. Once he was out of sight, we questioned the paddock manager.

"Comes in twice a season," he said, checking a ledger. "Nice guy. I know he's a member of the Moon Clan because he told me about the troubles they were having with bandits and how he was unhappy with their Councillor."

"Do you know why he comes?" I asked.

"Deliveries, I think." The man shrugged. "Must be small because the wagon's always empty. He pays his bill on time and never leaves anything behind. Wish I could say the same for everyone."

I thanked him and we left his office.

"I bet he's supplying the black market with the fake diamonds," I said. "I wish I could follow the wagon."

"I can," Kade said.

"What about Varun?"

"There are sand suppliers in Moon lands."

"And the lava flakes are shipped down from the Emerald Mountains."

"Then I can interview the suppliers for clues to Sir's whereabouts and follow Chun."

A moment of regret consumed me. I had hoped he would stay a few more days, but it made sense for him to go. "What about your pack?" I asked.

"Keep it for me. I only have a change of clothes and my orb. I can buy what I need on the road."

Kade rented a horse from the paddock manager. I wrote him a list of sand suppliers in Moon and Cloud

Mist lands. To avoid traveling in the Avibian Plains, he would have to come back this way to reach the rest of the clans.

"I should be able to follow Chun. I'll send word if I learn anything," Kade said.

"Use the glass messengers. Every large town has a magician with one of them. Just tell him you have an important message for Master Cowan and he should deliver the information right away."

"I could always threaten him with a hailstorm." Eagerness laced his tone.

"That could land you in jail."

"Not for long."

I laughed at his boast. "Can wind unlock iron bars?"

"No, but metal gets very brittle when it's cold."

"And you know this from experience?"

"Let's just say I have a stormy past."

I groaned at the pun as he swung up on the horse.

Kade paused before leaving. His playfulness gone. "Be careful."

"You, too."

Back at the Keep, I wrapped Kade's orb in a blanket and stored it under my bed. Over the course of the next few days, I would be overcome with the need to unwrap the orb and sit with it in my lap. The magic trapped within the glass sphere pulsed through my body as I listened to its song and watched the swirls of color inside. At night, even through the thick covering, I heard the orb calling Kaya's name.

I missed Kade, yet I was enjoying Ulrick's company. My dual emotions unsettled me until I realized those mixed feelings occurred all the time. I longed for my family, but was glad for Mara's presence. I even wished for Aydan's company, missing his gruff commands and kind gestures. My missing Kade was all part of being his friend. Nothing wrong with it. No hidden meanings in it at all.

Equipment for our glass shop arrived. Ulrick, Mara and I assembled and installed the various pieces. My excitement grew as we planned the first set of experiments and recruited helpers from the Keep's students.

"Just need the kiln and we'll be good to go," Ulrick said.

We snuggled on the couch in my quarters. A fire roared in the hearth. The white coals from Gid had been delivered, and I was testing how long the coals would burn so I could determine how often the kilns would need to be fed. Once the kiln reached the correct temperature to melt the sand, the best course of action was to always keep it hot.

"I've managed to convince Seften to help us next week," I said. "His magical illusions are very good."

"You're hoping to duplicate what you did with the spiders?"

"Yes."

"What is he going to send after you? Snow cats would be useful or necklace snakes. No one would bother you if you had a snow cat following you."

I laughed. "I think we'll start with something a little smaller."

* * *

The day of meeting with the jeweler arrived. I joined Pazia in Zitora's office.

"We've been watching the store, and have followed a few people," Zitora said. "We think we know who Elita's main supplier is, but we'll know for sure today. I want you to arrange to buy all his diamonds over ten carats."

"All?" I swallowed. The cost would be unbelievable. Even Pazia paled.

"Yes. All."

"Why?" I asked.

"So he knows you're serious buyers. And when you ask him for more, he won't hesitate to go straight to his source."

"Why don't you just arrest him and extract the information from his mind?" I knew there were a few powerful mind-reading magicians at the Keep.

"As soon as he's arrested, word will spread and the source will disappear. Also only Third Magician Irys is legally allowed to obtain information that way, and she's still in Moon lands." Zitora handed Pazia a large money bag. "Make sure the diamonds you buy are real then return to the Keep. I've assigned another magician to follow the supplier."

With no need to disguise ourselves, Pazia and I set off for the meeting. Ulrick hadn't been happy about staying behind at the Keep.

"She's no friend of yours," he had said. "If you get into trouble, she's going to protect herself first."

Good thing the conversation had been interrupted by the arrival of the kiln from Booruby. Distracted, he had skipped his lecture on safety, settling for a promise from me to be extra careful.

My thoughts centered on trust as we hurried to Elita's store. She had said to arrive before the lamplighters lit the back alley. The troop of lighters was already out on the streets, shimmying up the posts with their flaming sticks.

The door opened after our first tap. Hustled inside, we entered the same room as before. Elita waited with a man of average height and weight, although I would never forget him. His pure white hair was buzzed close to his head and was in stark contrast to his midnight skin. Elita introduced him as Mr. Lune.

Six diamonds sparkled on the velvet-covered table. They ranged in size from a thumbnail to a cherry. We all hunched over them as if they possessed a magical attraction.

"May I?" I gestured to the stones.

"Certainly. They're as genuine as the mountains they were mined from," Mr. Lune said.

"The Emerald Mountains?" Pazia asked.

"Nice try, sweetheart. I'm not stupid enough to tell Vasko's daughter where I found my diamonds."

I picked up the smallest one. It was a round stone with the bottom cut to a point. Numbing cold soaked into my skin where the diamond rested on my palm. My mind's eye filled with a frozen and flat wasteland.

As I checked the others, my bones ached with cold. The snowy vision stayed and a few wooden structures came into focus. The wood, peeling and gray, appeared weathered by many storms. The buildings leaned as if constructed during a strong wind. Piles of snow decorated their roofs and icicles hung from the windows.

The gems were authentic. I signaled Pazia with a discreet gesture.

"How much?" Pazia asked Mr. Lune.

"For which one?"

"For all."

Shock and then gleeful greed blazed on Mr. Lune's dark face before he smoothed his expression into mild interest. His first amount was so ridiculously high, even Elita couldn't suppress a huff of amusement.

Pazia handled the brisk negotiations. Feeling had returned to my palm and I wanted to see what would happen if I touched all six diamonds at once. I laid my hand over the gems on the velvet. Ice pierced my skin and spread throughout my body, driving the heat out. Once again the white expanse formed in my mind. This time I concentrated on the structures, searching for any clue to their location.

Gray smoke billowed from a chimney rising above the only stone building. Footprints tracked between doorways. Another set of tracks ringed one small shack. These resembled snow cat paw prints, which ended in a scuffed mess stained pink.

Unable to endure the icy grip on my body, I pulled my hand away from the diamonds. I glimpsed a deep pit before the vision melted.

Rubbing my arms, I shivered. The gems had been mined from the northern ice sheet above the Territory of Ixia, a vast expanse of snow and ice almost as big as Ixia. Mr. Lune had lied about the mountains.

"...pay Elita and the two agents who brought you here, plus my workers, there'll be nothing left," Mr. Lune said.

"I know how much miners are paid. My offer is more than generous," Pazia countered.

The negotiations launched into another round. My thoughts shifted to Ulrick. He would be worried if we delayed too long. A deluge of emotions swirled in my chest. The thrill of holding his hand, the wonderment over his attraction to me, the annoyance about his protectiveness, and the worry we lacked a certain spark all churned. I shied away from the last thought. Since our brief touch in Zitora's office, I couldn't think of sparks without thinking of Kade.

"...five golds per carat, and if you can find me six more diamonds over ten carats from the same mine, I'll up it to six," Pazia said.

Mr. Lune blinked a few times. "Six more diamonds that big? They're hard to find. Their rarity increases the cost more than a gold. The other gems will cost you twelve golds a carat."

They haggled. A wild glint shone in Pazia's eyes. She enjoyed the verbal battle. She offered a flat rate of nine golds per carat if he could secure six more large gems.

"Deal." Mr. Lune shook Pazia's hand.

She counted out twenty golds as down payment for twelve diamonds. Mr. Lune would send her a message when he returned, and they would complete the exchange.

By the time we left Elita's shop, all the Citadel's stores had closed. The taverns remained opened. Bursts of laughter and measures of music formed pools of warmth in the cold night air. Pazia walked through them without notice. She reviewed the bargaining session with glee, detailing the finer moments.

Her enthusiasm was infectious, but I kept watch for strangers following us or worse—someone I recognized.

She ceased her chatter and placed a warning hand on my arm. "Around the corner...a man..." Pazia pressed her lips together.

My insides felt tight. I reached for my sais.

With an exasperated huff she relaxed. "Ulrick. Guess you forgot to tie his leash."

The instant vision of Ulrick chained to a post like a dog made me laugh out loud. To an outsider who didn't know about the various threats, Ulrick's behavior around me would appear guard doggish.

My laughter wasn't the reaction Pazia hoped for. She frowned, flashing me a cold stare from her olive-colored eyes.

"I haven't pushed him away, and you're jealous," I said.

"Of course. He's gorgeous, smart and caring. He deserves better than you."

"I was right. You *do* think you're better than me."

"No. You're still wrong. I said he deserved better. Not that he deserved me. In one small way, Opal, I'm just like you. I don't know who to trust." She strode on ahead and rounded the corner.

I stared at her back for a moment before rushing to catch up. Ulrick was berating her for leaving me alone. She met his tirade with a bored air, answered him with a flippant response and sauntered away.

"She only cares about one person," Ulrick said. "Herself."

But I wasn't so sure I agreed with him.

Once the kiln reached the proper temperature, the sand mixture was loaded into the inner cauldron. It would take another half day to melt into molten glass. In the meantime, we set a schedule for the three of us to keep the fire hot.

"We could use a few more people to help," Mara said. "Leif would—"

"You can't ask Leif to shovel coal," Ulrick said.

"Why not?" she asked.

"He's too important. It's like asking Master Cowan to mend socks."

Mara fixed him with a cold stare. "If Leif thought shoveling coal was too menial for him, I wouldn't be here."

"It's just—"

I touched his shoulder. "You really shouldn't say any more. You'll just dig yourself in deeper."

He threw his hands up in surrender and checked the temperature of the annealing oven. However, Mara was right, we did need more helpers. I wondered if I could send out a general request to the Keep's student body. Perhaps a few would be interested in learning how to work with the glass.

Zitora approved the idea and I wrote a message on the dining hall's announcement blackboard. In no time, a handful of students arrived at our glass shop, offering to lend a hand. Working with their class schedules, Mara added the five of them in when they had free time and promised glass lessons in exchange for shoveling coal.

I erased the request off the board. Five would be enough for now.

Finally the melt was ready. We had loaded the kiln with a sand recipe that was similar to the Stormdancers' mix. The three of us had decided to craft a few orbs for our first project to see if I could channel another's magic into glass as I had done when Tricky attacked me.

"It almost feels like home," Mara said as she gathered a slug for Ulrick on the end of a blowpipe.

"Do you miss home?" I asked.

"Yes, but it really was time for me to move on. If Mother mentioned grandchildren to me once more, I would have…"

"What?" I smiled.

"Threatened to remain childless!" Mara shaped the molten slug into a sphere then handed the pipe to Ulrick.

"My nieces and nephews were constantly underfoot," Ulrick said. He blew a bubble into the sphere.

Annoyance twinged at how easy he made it look, and I was sure by the end of the day even our new helpers could thumb a bubble. Swallowing my frustrations, I reflected on Ulrick's comment.

"Do you miss your family?" I asked him.

Mara lifted the pipe from his workbench, and reheated the glass in the glory hole.

"Not at all," he said.

My sister returned when the glass glowed yellow. Ulrick grabbed the jacks and, as he turned the pipe, Mara blew into one end as he narrowed the glass around the other end, forming an almost-complete ball. I hurried to get a small amount of glass on a pontil iron and formed a punty. Using the metal tweezers, Ulrick brought the punty to the end of the ball, then dripped water near the end of the blowpipe. One hit with the end of his tweezers, the orb cracked off the blowpipe and was now attached to the pontil rod.

The orb was inserted back into the glory hole to heat. When the tip was pliable, Ulrick worked to craft a lip for the orb. He used the orb I stole from Tricky as a guide to how to shape it. Since we didn't plan to trap energy inside, we didn't worry about finding a way to plug the opening.

We made four orbs and set them in the annealing oven to cool. It would be twelve hours before we could work with the orbs.

"I have twenty pounds of my special sand mix on order," Ulrick said. "When it arrives, I'll show you how I make those vases."

While Ulrick helped Mara make a bowl, I showed Piecov how to gather glass from the kiln. The first-year student had signed up to help with the glass shop. He had watched us work, and now it was his turn to try.

"Watch, it's very hot. You want to get in and out as fast as possible," I said. "And keep the rod turning all the time or the glass will drip to the floor."

He was quick to learn and asked all the right questions.

Overall, I was very pleased with the glass shop's first day of operation. Everyone worked together well, and the equipment ran without problems. It was a shame the harmony didn't last very long.

The next day we inspected the orbs. No cracks or flaws and the glass felt thick enough to withstand any jostling. Our creations matched the one containing the spiders.

"Do you think it'll work?" Ulrick asked.

"Only one way to find out."

We would have to wait for Stefan's morning classes to finish. He promised to stop by and attack me with a magical illusion during lunch.

When the door to the glass shop opened, I expected to see Stefan. Instead an aggrieved Pazia stood in the threshold.

"Stefan's not coming," she said. She scanned the shop with distaste.

"Why not?" I demanded.

"Master Bloodgood needs him." She joined us by the table of orbs. "Bain sent me to help." Her stiff demeanor revealed that she would rather be doing anything but aid us.

"No," Ulrick said. "We'll find someone else."

"As much as I would love to leave, there is no one better at illusions than me. If you're going to experiment with magic, you might as well do it right or not bother at all."

I considered. Master Bloodgood knew our plans. If he thought Pazia would be useful, then she would be. "All right. Do you know what we're trying to do?"

"Opal, may I have a word with you?" Ulrick grabbed my arm and propelled me outside. "I don't think it's a good idea."

"Why not? She's a very powerful magician and could be useful with our experiments."

"What if she tries to sabotage them? She's jealous of you."

"Then we'll ask her to leave. You have to keep an open mind."

"I just don't want her to hurt you." He pulled me into an embrace.

I melted against him, enjoying the moment. "Do you think I would let her?"

"Not intentionally. You're too nice, Opal. You always think the best of people so you're always going to get hurt."

I mulled over his comment. He was right in a way, but my interactions with people didn't always lead to pain. Interesting how Pazia said I didn't trust anyone and Ulrick claimed I trust too much. Who was right?

"Do you think she's up to something?" Ulrick asked.

"Like what?"

"Spying on you, seeing what you can do with your magic."

"For what purpose?"

"You have people after you. She could tell them how to neutralize your magic or where to find you."

"I haven't seen a sign of anyone in a while. Don't you think you're being a little paranoid?" I pulled away from him.

"I'm being smart. As time passes without any hint of danger, you'll begin to relax. Eventually you'll think the danger is past and then… Bam! Surprised and unprepared you're caught. That's what I would do if I were Tricky."

He had a point. My skin felt hot and tight as if I was trapped in a spotlight. Could I ever relax?

"You shouldn't trust anyone besides me and your sister," Ulrick said.

"What about Zitora or my parents or Kade?" The Stormdancer's name slipped out.

He frowned. "They all could be compromised. How do you know Kade wasn't the one who spiked the glass with Brittle Talc? He could be working with Tricky for his own reasons. Maybe for revenge over his sister's death. Maybe her death was really an accident and he wants to put a stop to all stormdancing."

I couldn't believe that scenario. "You can make up any story you want to fit, but it doesn't mean it's true. I could even come up with a reason for my sister and Leif to plot against me."

"But it *could* be true. Perhaps you should trust no one."

If my first four years at the Keep had been lonely, not being able to trust anyone would make my life worse. But then Pazia's words about trust drifted through my thoughts again. She was wrong. I trusted Ulrick with my life, Zitora with my education, my sister with my dreams, and Kade with... With what? I didn't have an answer.

Ulrick and I returned to the glass shop. Mara was giving Pazia a tour of the small shop. I explained to Pazia about the experiment, and showed her the glass orbs and spiders.

"We want to recreate the attack and see if I can defend myself again," I said.

As she considered my request, the annoyance faded and genuine interest glowed in her eyes, making Ulrick suspicious. I believed if she offered to fetch us a drink he would still be unhappy.

"Do you want me to conjure spiders?" she asked me.

"How about something a little less creepy?"

"Snakes?"

"No!" Mara and I said together in horror.

Pazia rolled her eyes. "Puppies?"

"Butterflies," I suggested.

"I'm good, but not powerful enough to make butter-flies menacing. Try again."

"Bees?"

"Better."

"What type of bee?" Ulrick asked.

"I'll decide. Opal wouldn't get to choose if a magician were really after her. Better if she's surprised. Ready?"

I picked one of our orbs, and held it between my hands. Pazia concentrated. The lines of her neck pulled taut as she gathered power.

A low hum sounded. I exchanged glances with Mara. She heard the sound, too. The steady drone increased in volume until the room vibrated with the noise.

"What the—" Ulrick batted at the air near his head.

At first, a few bees blazed by my head. I jumped back as another green-and-black bee flew by my ear. Mara cried out, swatting at her skirt.

A finger of ice brushed my spine when I recognized the Greenblade bees. All six inches of the hairy insect were striped with green and brown. Impossible to spot in their home forests, they attacked with relish and pumped lethal quantities of venom into their victims. Fortunately they lived deep in the Greenblade Clan's forest and only awoke to mate every three years.

"Anytime now, Opal," Ulrick said. He ducked to avoid a cloud of them. One landed on his shoulder and plunged its stinger into his upper arm. He grunted in pain.

Mara raced around the room, yelling. The air was thick with bees, many more than the spiders. A blanket of insects covered Ulrick. A twinge of doubt squeezed my stomach, but I concentrated on the orb. It waited as if interested in the commotion yet content to just watch. I rolled it between my palms, imagining it on the end of a blowpipe. Pulling the buzz closer to me, I channeled the magic into the glass sphere.

One ping, then another. Soon the ringing of glass dominated. The sound echoed in my heart and continued for a long time. Bees disappeared, and more were created. Because of the sheer numbers, it felt like years before Ulrick's body was uncovered and the swarm around Mara was gone. Finally, all grew quiet.

My muscles strained to hold the full orb. I placed it on a table and a handful of the contents spilled. Trapped inside glass, miniature Greenblade bees sparkled. A success, but at what cost? I glanced at the others.

Ulrick moved closer to see the glass bees. Sweat soaked his tunic, but no other sign of the attack was visible. Mara's disheveled hair stuck out in all directions, and she panted, winded from her exertions. Pazia had slumped to the ground.

Mara bent over her.

I joined her. "Is she okay?" I asked.

"I think she fainted."

Her skin lacked color.

Mara settled on the ground and gently placed the

magician's head in her lap. "Should we take her to the infirmary? Maybe we should send for a healer."

"Oh for sand's sake, just throw water on her." Ulrick picked up a bucket.

"Wait." I grabbed the pail from him. "She hasn't been overcome by the heat like in a glass factory. She might have exhausted her magic. Throwing water on her might just make her wet."

When Zitora had used all her energy, she'd slept until her energy was restored. I dipped my fingers into the cold water and rubbed it on Pazia's forehead. No reaction. "We should have a healer look at her just in case."

Mara, worried and upset, left her in my care while she fetched a healer. She returned with Healer Hayes and Zitora. We followed as they carried her to the infirmary on the first floor of the administration building.

"She used her magic to create an illusion," I told Zitora. The four of us stood around Pazia's bed. "I didn't think it would be such a big drain on her energy."

"It shouldn't. For a few younger students, they would be tired, but not Pazia. Something else must be wrong."

"If there is, I can't find it," Healer Hayes said. His hand pressed against Pazia's forehead. "She has all the classic signs of exhaustion. We should let her rest and she should be fine."

"I'll stay with her," Mara offered. "Go see if your experiment worked."

I returned to the shop with Ulrick, and examined one of the bees.

He put a hand on my arm. "Do you think they'll obey you like the spiders? I'd rather not get stung again. Besides the whole dying from the poison aspect, it hurt like hell."

"Only one—"

"Just do it."

I broke a glass bee. A whoosh, a huff and a flash followed. The same energy burst as the spiders. One Greenblade bee hovered over the table, buzzing.

Ulrick poked it with a rod. It moved away, but didn't attack him. "Feels real. Give it a command."

"Sting that orange." I pointed to a bowl of fruit. Mara always kept plenty of food around for the helpers who worked during mealtimes.

The bee flew straight toward the bowl, landed on the orange and stung it. After a few convulsions, the bee disappeared. Ulrick plucked the tainted fruit with care. He found a knife and cut the orange in half.

A rotten sour smell emanated. Brown mucuslike liquid oozed from the orange—the bee's venom.

"Remind me never to get you angry," Ulrick said.

Pazia didn't wake while we experimented with the glass bees. I had hoped that with the release of the bees, she would recover faster. But her unconscious state remained despite breaking over a hundred bees. It appeared once the magic was trapped and transformed, it was available for me to use and no one else.

Zitora wanted a full report on our experiments. Ulrick and I briefed her in her office.

"You've discovered a great defense against a magical attack," she said.

"Against illusions," I agreed. "I was going to try channeling other types of attacks, but since Pazia's collapse, I'm not so sure."

"It's best to wait until she recovers. I'm sure you have plenty to do in the meantime." Zitora moved a few papers on her desk. "The Masters could use a few more of your messengers, Opal."

Hint taken, I used my workshop time to craft a variety of animals for the Masters to use to communicate.

My worry for Pazia tipped toward panic as three days passed without any change in her condition. She had gone too far in sending so many bees against us, and conjuring Greenblade bees was just plain cruel. I could claim I acted in self-defense. Although I didn't like her, I hadn't wanted to cause her real harm.

During those three days, Ulrick's special sand arrived and we loaded the mix into the kiln to melt, planning for him to demonstrate his vase-making method the next day. Just as we were leaving the shop, one of Healer Hayes's assistants ran up to us.

"Pazia is awake. Master Cowan wants you to come. Now," he said, before running back to the infirmary.

Thank fate! Relief gave me a burst of energy and I kept pace with the assistant, slowing only when we reached the door to Pazia's room. Ulrick was right behind me.

A little color had returned to her cheeks, but exhaustion left dark circles under her eyes. She stared at me.

Horror and accusation pulsed from her. Healer Hayes propped her against the pillows and Zitora positioned a tray of food on her lap.

"Eat. And it's not a request," she said.

I glanced at Zitora. Her concern was evident, but before I could explain, she asked me, "Did you feel tired after your experiment with Pazia?"

Surprised by the odd question, I needed a moment to collect my thoughts. "No. Why?"

Zitora looked at Pazia. She moved her fork to her mouth as if it weighed a hundred pounds.

"You must have used Pazia's energy to channel her own magic."

"Is that why she collapsed?"

"Not the whole reason. Pazia?"

She finished chewing, then paused as if summoning the strength to speak. "You stole everything from me. Every bit of magic. I have none left."

23

"WHAT DO YOU mean none?" I asked.

Pazia dropped the fork onto the tray and fell back against her pillows. The effort of eating and talking was too much for her. I turned to Zitora. The Master Magician's worry alarmed me.

"Her magic will come back, won't it?" I asked.

"We don't know. Nothing like this has ever happened before. Don't do any more channeling until we know for sure."

Ulrick and I left Pazia's room. We returned to my quarters in the apprentice wing, but I had no memory of the trip. When Ulrick suggested we eat dinner, the thought of food soured my stomach. What if Pazia's magic never returned? The possibility frightened me to the core.

"If you can strip a person's magic with those orbs," Ulrick said, "we don't have to worry about Tricky anymore. I wonder if you could take Master Cowan's power."

"Ulrick, I don't want to talk about it. I may have destroyed Pazia's ability to use magic. There is no positive side." I entered my bedroom and shut the door.

I lay on top of the bed and stared at the ceiling. Unable to stop my thoughts, I watched as they replayed the series of events over and over and over in my mind. Filling the orb with Pazia's bees felt effortless and I had been fine when Tricky had attacked with the spiders.

What else had I done with the orbs? I had helped Kade with the storm. But then exhaustion claimed me as soon as we finished. In that case, Kade's energy was depleted—he struggled to control the bubble of calm keeping him from the storm's fury. I had given him my energy to use as he harvested the storm's essence. If he had tried to attack me with wind, could I channel it? I shied away from the answer.

I must have fallen asleep, because Ulrick woke me in the morning. I picked at my breakfast, letting the drone of conversation flow around me. Mara joined us and we headed for the glass shop.

Excitement and pride used to bloom whenever I saw the new shop, but not this time. Mara and I helped Ulrick create his vases. Beautiful long-necked pieces with swirls of color. He had purchased a number of different colored crystals to dip the molten glass into. The crystals melted when heated, coloring the glass.

I couldn't tell if he used magic while working with the

pieces. Only when the vases cooled and I could touch them would I know if he had trapped magic inside.

"Opal, you haven't said a word all day. You shouldn't worry so much. I'm sure Pazia will be fine," Mara said.

Cracking off Ulrick's last vase, I transferred it to the annealing oven.

"No sense moping about it until you know for certain," Ulrick said. "Come on." He gathered a ball of molten glass. "I saved you some of my mix to play with."

Outnumbered, I worked at the gaffer's bench. The glass moved as if made of silk. It was easy to shape and fun to manipulate. It didn't take long for my dark mood to lighten.

"Is the flexibility due to the Krystal Clan's gold sand?" I asked him.

"Nice try, but I'm not telling you the mix ingredients."

The next day the vases cooled down enough to handle. Popping in my hands, they held Ulrick's magic within them. But Mara couldn't "feel" the vibrations at all.

When Ulrick and I both held the vase, it sang a sad tune. Mara heard nothing when she tried holding it with him.

A few of our student helpers had arrived. We tested a vase on each of them. No one could feel the pops, but they heard a song with Ulrick's touch. The song was different for each person. We puzzled over the discrepancy. After a few more tries with different vases, we discovered a person would hear his unique song no matter which vase he touched.

"Piecov, how are you feeling?" Mara asked him.

The first-year student frowned in confusion. "I feel fine."

She shook her head. "Are you happy, sad, lonely?"

"Oh. I'm rather glad. I found out this morning I passed my history test."

"Touch the vase with Ulrick again," she instructed.

Piecov complied.

"Does the song you hear match your mood?"

He considered for a moment. "Yes."

She asked the others and they agreed. We strolled around the Keep's campus and tested the vases on the other students. Even going so far as to interrupt an argument. In each instance, the student's song reflected his or her mood. We also couldn't find any other magician who could feel the vase's vibrations. Not even Ulrick felt it—only me. Even when I held the vase with another, I couldn't hear a song and the vase remained inert. We returned to the shop.

"A mood indicator," Ulrick said in disgust. "And not even *my* moods, but others. A useless parlor trick!"

"I wouldn't say useless," I said. "You might be able to use the vases to interrogate criminals, find out if they feel guilty or are lying."

"Not the job I hoped for." He snatched a broom and swept the floor with hard strokes.

"We might still discover other uses for your pieces." I straightened the workbenches, replacing the tools.

He didn't comment as we finished cleaning up the

shop. I understood his disappointment. Four years in the Keep had been one letdown after another for me. But the Keep's instructors had been trying to teach me to use magic in the traditional ways. Only when I had been in dire situations did my other abilities manifest themselves. While I wouldn't recommend that method, perhaps Ulrick would have other opportunities to find out more.

Before dinner, Ulrick, Mara and I stopped at the infirmary to ask Healer Hayes about Pazia. She was only slightly better. In the hallway, we encountered Zitora. The magician sent Ulrick and Mara on to dinner and asked me to accompany her to her office. Usually Ulrick would fuss about leaving me alone, but he shuffled after Mara without saying a word.

"What's wrong with him?" Zitora asked as we climbed the stairs to the fourth floor.

"Difficult day." I explained about his power.

"When I first met him, I didn't think he had any. His magic may include only one trick, but it's better than nothing."

I kept quiet, remembering my own frustrations. Once you get a taste, sometimes it's hard not to crave more.

"How's Pazia's progress with magic?" I asked instead.

"She's regaining her strength little by little, but it'll be a good week before we know about her magic." Zitora stared at me with a pained expression. "Opal, if you have truly taken her ability to access the power source, the Sitian Council will view you as a threat."

Her words failed to sink in. I expected her to tell me the Council was livid, upset, horrified or all three. Pazia had the potential to become another Master Magician. "A threat?"

"Think about it. You can strip magicians of their powers. What if you decide Master Bloodgood should not be First Magician anymore? Or you don't want the Council to be in charge anymore. You can take everyone's powers and build an army of glass creatures."

It sounded like a fairy tale. "I wouldn't do that."

"Really? What if Bain Bloodgood attacks you and you suspect he is working with Sir?"

"That's ridiculous."

"No, it isn't. The most powerful magician in Sitia attacks you with his magic. Will you die or use your magic to save yourself? Or if he attacks Mara or Ulrick? Will you save them?"

"What's the reason?"

"Does it matter?"

"Yes."

"So now you get to decide if the reason is good or bad? What if he has a very good reason, but you don't know about it?"

"I..."

"See? With this new power, you could be a danger to Sitia."

I bristled. "I could be an asset, if anyone would trust me."

"Aha! But what have you done to earn this trust? You

already robbed Sitia of Pazia's considerable talent just by experimenting with your own."

"We don't know that for sure. Besides, she attacked me with an illusion. It might not work against another type of attack. And it was a genuine accident."

"Could you drain a person's power who isn't attacking you?" Zitora asked.

"I don't know."

"*That's* why the Council would consider you a threat."

And I wouldn't want to try another experiment and risk losing another magician. I had wished to do more with my magic, but this wasn't what I desired.

"Is this why you wanted me to come to your office? Another lesson?"

"Part of the reason. And not quite a lesson. I want you to be prepared for the ramifications if Pazia doesn't recover. The Council could incarcerate you in the Keep's cells while they decide what to do with you. You remember how long the Council needed before they trusted Yelena and she saved them from the Daviian Warpers."

I had thought I felt terrible *before* talking with Zitora. The air in the room pressed on my body, stuck in my throat and pounded in my ears, matching the tight compressions in my chest.

Locked in the Keep's cells would be horrible. The special magical barrier wasn't needed for me, unless someone wanted to rescue me. I imagined Kade trying to blow the door down and the loop of protective magic, channeling his energy to trap him.

All the Council needed to do was keep me away from glass orbs and Sitia should be safe. The thought of not being able to work with glass terrified me more than spending time in the Keep's prison.

"But what about my messengers? If I'm in a cell, I can't make them for the Council or for you."

"The Council would have to decide how important they are. The magicians are used to having them so we would be the most...inconvenienced." A slight smile touched her lips.

"Inconvenienced? So good to know how heartbroken you'd be."

"And the Council would have to disband the messenger committee. Another inconvenience," she teased.

"They put together a committee?"

"Yes."

I imagined the endless political wrangling and debate that would occur and was glad all I would have to do is supply the messengers. That I could do without hurting anyone. "Is there another reason you wanted to talk to me?"

"I've received a message from Kade via Yelena. He's made a few interesting discoveries in the Moon Clan lands and she would like you to join them."

"Me? Why?"

"I don't know the full details, but it has to do with the fake diamond merchant, Chun."

"What about Mr. Lune? Did your magician track him?"

"Yes, but lost him at the border of Ixia."

"At the Moon's border?"

"No. At the Krystal Clan's border." Zitora slouched in

her chair. "It seems the people selling the fakes and the real diamonds are not working together. I want you to follow the fake lead and I'll have another magician watch the border, see where Mr. Lune goes when he comes back." She rubbed her hands over her face. "I also think it's a good idea for you to get away from the Citadel for a while."

"Are you coming with me?"

"No. Irys and Yelena will both be there."

"What about Ulrick? He'll want to come."

"That's fine. Do you want me to assign a few soldiers to go with you?"

I hadn't seen a sign of Tricky or Sir in weeks, but Ulrick's warning about getting complacent echoed in my mind. I really didn't want to travel with an armed escort. "How about Leif?"

"I can check his schedule. What if he can't make it?"

"Then I guess we should have another guard along just in case."

"Only one?"

"I've been practicing with my sais. Besides…"

Zitora waited.

"I can bring a handful of my glass spiders and bees along. Keep them in my pocket in case we're ambushed."

"Now you're thinking." Zitora moved a few papers on her desk. "You should leave in the morning. I'll contact Leif."

"More secret magician stuff," Ulrick said.

"It's not…" I sighed, no sense arguing. "It's not—"

"Important because I'm allowed to go?" His joke was weak, and he couldn't maintain a light tone.

"We leave in the morning. You'll need a horse. This time you might want to *ask* Stable Master about borrowing one."

He rubbed his hands in anticipation. "If he won't let me, I can steal Moonlight again and then placate the Stable Master with Avibian honey. Mara told me he loves the stuff." He seemed determined to keep upbeat, but I knew by the tension in his body he still wasn't happy.

I didn't know how to make him feel better. No matter what I said, I knew it wouldn't be right and could upset him further. He needed time to adapt, and to be content with what he could do.

Funny. I almost huffed. Funny because I was never content with my one trick, but now with the spiders and with Pazia still recovering, I wished for simpler times.

We packed for the trip, securing supplies and food. Hardly a word was spoken between us. I debated over taking Kade's orb. It would be perfectly safe under my bed, but I had grown used to its humming presence at night, and the thought of leaving it behind caused my stomach to tighten.

It was late when I slipped into bed. I tossed and turned, unable to find a comfortable spot. Strange dreams filled my brief snatches of sleep. Images of Pazia and Tricky, staring at me with dead and accusing eyes. I woke from one nightmare convinced Tricky stood over my bed. But no one was there.

Unable to return to sleep, I crept past Ulrick's prone form on the couch and slipped outside. No sense waking him, I rationalized. My cloak's pockets were filled with glass spiders and bees. I clutched a spider in my palm as I walked through the silent campus.

The glass shop's welcoming hum greeted me. I entered into the dry warmth and relaxed. Piecov sat at the table, studying from a huge text. He jumped to his feet when he saw me.

"I just filled the kiln," he said.

"Then why aren't you back in bed?"

He shrugged and looked around. "I like it here. The first year's barracks are crowded and noisy."

I remembered the night sounds of so many people in one room. The snores, the homesick crying, the whispered conversations, giggles and sighs. The steady roar of the kiln would be considered peaceful in comparison.

"Maybe we should install a cot for those who have overnight shifts."

"Great idea." He peered at me for a moment. "Why are you here? The next feeding isn't until dawn."

"Feeding?"

He gave me a sheepish grin. "The kiln's like a baby. Instead of giving it milk, we feed it coal."

"Appropriate."

His eyes still held a question.

"I couldn't sleep," I said.

He nodded as if he understood completely. "This place

has a certain draw. Know what I mean?" Piecov gestured to the kiln.

"I do. There is such potential contained within the cauldron. A whole vat of melted glass just waiting to be gathered and spun into something...wonderful."

"Yes!" He looked surprised by his outburst then ducked his head in embarrassment. "Well...I only made a lumpy paperweight so far."

"I still have my very first paperweight."

"You do?"

"I had to stand on a box to reach in with the punty rod. But I did everything myself. It resembled a squashed apple, but my parents were so proud of my creation I thought it was the best paperweight in the world."

"I guess I'll keep mine."

"It'll be a good gauge of how much you improve. When you become frustrated when a piece cracks or turns out wrong, you can look back at that paperweight and see just how far you've come."

He brightened at the idea and I suggested we work the glass together. He made another paperweight and I helped him craft a swan. The items in the annealing oven had finished cooling. I removed them and put his new creations inside, marking the date and time on the door as I moved the oven next to the kiln.

Inspecting the finished pieces, I lined them along the table. Two of Ulrick's vases popped in my hands. One of Mara's bowls had cracked so I tossed it in the cullet barrel.

The contents of the barrel would be added to the cauldron and remelted. Four of my glass animals survived the cooling process.

Among the four was a little dog sitting on his haunches. His ears perked forward as if he hoped for a treat. He glowed with magic and promise, reminding me of Piecov.

At dawn, another student arrived to feed the kilns. Piecov and I left. I brought the animals with me. Zitora needed them and I planned to drop them at her office before going back to my rooms. On the way, I stopped at the infirmary.

Healer Hayes was just leaving Pazia's room.

"She's regaining strength. We won't know about her magic for a while," he said.

"Can I visit?"

"As long as you don't wake her."

A lantern burned on the night table in her room. Turned down to the lowest setting, the feeble flame cast a weak light. She didn't stir at the sound of my arrival. Nor when I sat in the chair beside her bed.

I remembered watching my brother, Ahir, sleep. Relaxed and innocent, masking the high energy, annoying and smart-assed boy underneath. Asleep, Pazia's smooth beauty held a regal quality. Easy for me to imagine her a queen of the Cloud Mist Clan, needing no gems to augment her loveliness.

Underneath was another story. While she plagued me over the years, working the diamond mission had given me another perspective. Perhaps she was right. Maybe I was the one with the attitude and big chip on my shoulder. Maybe I nursed it. Clung to it and refused to see the positive. Maybe I had kept everyone at a distance, afraid to make a new friend. Afraid to care about someone, because I might lose them the way I had lost my sister, Tula. I probably had acted as Kade does now. Cold and aloof.

The realization shot through me like a crack zigzagging through glass. My loneliness had been my own fault. The blame rested solely within me. I gazed at the sleeping girl, wishing I could help her.

I left the little dog by her bedside. His hopeful demeanor might brighten the room. Before I left, she said my name. I braced for her recriminations, determined to listen to her.

She held the statue, examining it in the dim light. "For me?" she asked.

"Yes. Can you see the glow inside?" I waited. If she couldn't then she had lost all her magic.

"Purple fire."

I knelt beside her bed with relief. "Pazia, I'm so—"

"Shut up," she said. "Don't apologize."

"But—"

"Didn't you hear me? Are you a simpleton as well as talentless?"

I clamped my lips together. Her anger and hatred were justifiable.

"Don't say another word. I had a lot of time to think

about this. Losing my powers was my fault. Opal," she
warned, correctly reading my desire to contradict her,
"I was sure I could beat you. I wanted to make your experiment a failure. You only stole what I offered. And I
offered you *everything*." She placed the dog on the nightstand. "My current state is the price for my conceit. Now
we're even."

A few moments passed as I tried to comprehend her
words. "Even?"

She closed her eyes. "Those accidents over the years
weren't due to your clumsiness or lack of magic. I
am...was...responsible for all of them. I did it to
torment you, and to prove to everyone that you didn't
deserve to be here."

I laughed long and hard.

Pazia stared at me in disbelief. "You're not upset?"

"This morning, I would have been. But I realized you
were right about me. I kept my distance from everyone
because I was afraid of getting too close. Plus I'm happy
I didn't cause all those accidents."

"I still think you don't belong here."

"Even now?"

"Yes."

"Guess I'll just have to prove you wrong."

Of course, Ulrick wasn't happy I left without him. He
thought my new abilities made me reckless. No sense
contradicting him. Maybe having the spiders and bees
with me added to my confidence.

We carried our saddlebags to the barn. Mara helped Leif saddle Rusalka.

"How's my favorite glass wizard today?" Leif asked.

"Better now that you're here."

"Wouldn't miss it. Besides, I haven't seen my sister in a while. I need my danger fix."

"You don't really think Yelena's in danger?" I asked.

"No. She'll just use me as bait and cast me aside." Leif sighed dramatically. "I'm so deprived of attention, I'll take any little bit."

"Leif, you're being melodramatic. You're very important," Mara said.

She continued to fawn over him. Mara would be staying behind to run the glass shop. Ulrick searched for the Stable Master.

After several minutes of listening to Mara's annoying praise, I said, "For sand's sake, we won't be gone long."

"Oh hush!" Mara said. "I've had to work with you and Ulrick as you make moon eyes at each other all day. You can handle a few minutes of goodbyes."

"Moon eyes! We kept a professional attitude in the shop at *all* times."

Mara's humor faded. "I know. Actually I would like to see more mooning with you two."

"Spare me the advice. Please."

But she wouldn't listen.

"He's gorgeous, Opal. Relax. Have fun. On your trip to the Moon lands take him into the woods one night and make him forget about all his troubles. Do you want a few pointers?"

"Mara!" I said.

Leif turned every shade of red. "Milk oats…ah…I'll see if I can get…" He disappeared in a hurry.

"What?" Mara asked. "If you don't need pointers, what's stopping you?" When I didn't answer she said, "It's that Stormdancer, isn't it?"

"His name is Kade, and it has nothing to do with him. We're taking it slow."

"Slow? I've seen turtles mate faster."

"Mara, what's gotten into you?"

She slid her foot forward. Just below the hem of her skirt, two red scabs still marked the snake's bite on her ankle. "I had seconds to live. You know how people will say their life flashed in front of their eyes?"

"Yes."

"Not for me. My future hopes and dreams played in my mind. All the things I would never experience, and I had only one regret. That I hadn't shown Leif how much I cared for him. After you saved me, I decided I would stop hoping and dreaming, and start acting. So when the snake finally catches up to me, I won't have any regrets." She stared at me as if seeking an answer. "You've been in a few bad situations. Who did you think of? What did you regret? Have you changed anything?"

There was no quick reply to her questions.

"Think about it."

Ulrick returned smiling. "Stable Master said I could take Moonlight."

"He's still here?" Leif asked. His hands were full of milk oats. Rusalka charged toward him. "Whoa, girl! These are for later." He danced back, trying to avoid the horse's determined lunge for the treats. "Now we can cut through the Avibian Plains and reach Fulgor faster. Although we're not going anywhere if you two don't get your horses saddled." Leif shooed us into motion.

Quartz nickered at me and Moonlight's head poked over his stall door. Ulrick and I brought the horses out and saddled them.

"Did I hear Leif right?" Ulrick asked. "Cut through the Avibian Plains?"

"Yes."

"Won't the Sandseed's protective magic confuse us?"

"Leif is a distant cousin of the Sandseeds so he's welcome in the plains. And..."

"And, what?"

I was reluctant to mention magic to Ulrick and destroy his good mood.

"Opal?"

"And Leif mentioned how fast the Sandseed horses can run in the plains, but I've never been there before even though the border abuts my family's glass factory. Have you?"

"Are you kidding? Growing up, going into the plains was *the dare* with my friends. The way to prove to everyone you're a man."

"Did you prove yourself?"

He laughed. "I guess I'll find out."

The three of us left the Citadel and headed east toward the Moon Clan lands. Farm fields spotted with houses and barns spread before us as we traveled though Featherstone country. The Citadel was located in the southwest corner of the Featherstone Clan at a point bordering the Krystal and Stormdance lands and the Avibian Plains.

It was a couple of weeks into the cold season. The air smelled damp. Dark clouds in the west threatened to dump the rain and sleet mix so common this time of year. I peered at the sky, hoping the weather would hold off a few days. Snow would even be welcome. Better than having the road turn into a mushy mess.

I wondered if Kade could turn rain into snow. My knowledge of Stormdancers' powers was limited to what I had learned in school. I had been surprised when Kade told me storms had moods. What else didn't I know about the storms or Kade? And why was I so curious?

Mara's encouragement to consider my regrets came to mind. In order for me to answer her questions, I would have to review difficult events. Not a pleasant task.

"It's four days to Fulgor, but if we cross into the northern hump of the plains, we can make it there in three," Leif said.

"Wouldn't that be a few miles out of the way?" Ulrick asked.

"Yep. We'll head straight east then turn north instead of going northeast."

"Then—"

"Don't worry." Leif grinned widely. "You'll find out soon enough."

We stopped for the night in a travelers' shelter, still within the Featherstone boundaries. No other travelers were inside. When Leif set a watch schedule, I asked for the last shift. My lack of sleep the previous night had caught up with me and I couldn't even follow the conversation at dinner. I headed straight for bed. Ulrick volunteered for the first shift and Leif brought me my pack.

"Ugh. What's in here? Rocks?" Leif asked.

"Glass."

He raised his thick eyebrows, prompting me to continue.

"A bunch of spiders and bees. An empty orb." It also contained Kade's orb, but I was reluctant to tell him.

"Empty?"

"For an emergency only."

"Scary."

"Believe me, I know." If attacked, would I use the orb to drain another's power? Maybe, if there was no other option. One thing I did know, if Tricky lost his power when I had channeled his magic, I would not regret that.

The night remained quiet. Leif woke me a few hours before dawn.

"Your turn. Try not to wake everyone this time," he said, yawning.

I swatted him and headed outside to check on the horses.

The darkness pressed down. Moist air blew through the trees, rattling the dead leaves. The wind had extinguished three of the lanterns. Flames clutched the other lamps in desperation, flapping in resistance with each gust. Clouds blocked the moon. Once my eyes adjusted, I checked the stable. Quartz dozed, leaning against Rusalka. Moonlight came over and nuzzled my hand, looking for a treat. The three horses shared one large stall.

Nothing out of the ordinary. Nothing to cause concern. So why did I feel watched? I circled the two buildings. An icy splat hit my forehead. I cried out in alarm and yanked my sais from my cloak. Another cold drop struck my cheek. Chagrined, I replaced my sais as the drizzle turned into a soaking rain fueled by the wind. I found a calm spot next to the shelter and pulled my hood over my head.

For the next two hours, I kept a diligent watch. The storm would be a great cover for anyone sneaking up. The wind swirled and diluted smells, moaning in sorrow. Why sorrow? The sound almost matched the keening emanating from Kade's orb. As the storm approached, the orb's song grew louder to me. No one else heard it, but Leif had remarked on sensing magic.

Kade told me the energy trapped inside the orb would get agitated when another storm came near. But the mournful sounds of the orb held no distress, just a lonely ache to be free.

My imagination no doubt. It tended to exaggerate emotions and see things that weren't there. Just like the black shape slinking between shadows. Or the brief movement to my left—pure imagination. Right? I gripped the handles of my sais.

The storm raged for a moment, blocking out all sense of my surroundings. A sudden blast of wind extinguished the remaining lantern light.

Something struck me behind my knees. I fell forward as pain flared. Arms wrapped around me and a hand clamped over my mouth. Lifted off the ground, I yanked my sais from my cloak and blindly struck out. I was rewarded by one yelp before my arms were pinned.

I struggled. There had to be three or four of them. A sharp point jabbed the skin below my left ear.

"Quit fighting or I'll shove my knife into your throat," a man's voice growled.

24

I STOPPED STRUGGLING.

"Smart choice," the man said.

I didn't recognize his voice, which gave me little comfort, considering my circumstances. The knife stayed against my throat, and the hand remained over my mouth. A wet dog smell emanated from him.

"I've got her. Go," he ordered.

The men who held me put me down. They headed for the shelter. Leif and Ulrick slept within and I couldn't warn them. Powerless, I counted five of them as they slipped inside. My own fear forgotten, I worried for my companions.

Although muted by the wind and rain, shouts, curses and the sounds of fighting reached me, I tensed. The knife dug deeper.

"Relax. It'll all be over soon," the man said.

The next few seconds moved as if we stood there for

days. Five against two, but Leif had learned to fight from Valek. I cursed the storm's wild winds. Otherwise the horses would have alerted us to the danger. And now the storm masked the noise of the attack, so the three horses huddled together without knowing the danger.

When one of the attackers signaled from the door, I knew Leif and Ulrick had lost.

"Told you. Let's go." He kept me with him as he guided me into the shelter.

Ulrick and Leif knelt by the hearth. Hands on their heads, various cuts bleeding on their arms and their spines stiff with anger.

Ulrick's concern turned to relief when he saw me. "Are you all right?"

"No talking!" One of the four men guarding them hit Ulrick with the flat of his sword.

Ulrick winced with pain, but kept quiet. His helpless situation was all my fault. Leif was used to trouble, but not Ulrick. Mara's comments replayed in my mind.

What if Ulrick died? her voice asked.

Guilt, of course, for bringing him along. Missing his smile and protective bearishness. Missing his company.

Regrets?

Wishing I hadn't snapped at him in annoyance and had been more considerate. Wishing I had been a better guard.

Unkempt and wearing tattered clothes, the men kept their weapons pointed at Leif and Ulrick. The rain left clean streaks on the men's dirty faces.

My captor released me, pushing me toward my friends. I stumbled.

"Take off your cloak." He gestured with his knife. A long thin blade with my blood on its tip.

Confused and alarmed, I shrugged off the sodden garment, letting it plop to the ground.

"Search her," the leader ordered.

The man who had signaled the all clear checked me for weapons. I recoiled at his rough touch, but he was fast. Declaring me clean, he pushed me down on my knees next to Leif. He didn't miss anything. Everything I could use in my defense was in my cloak. If I was ever given a second chance, I wouldn't be so stupid again.

"See what goodies you can find," the leader said.

While two men kept guard, the others searched through our belongings. It finally dawned on me they might be robbers, and I actually began to hope they would take what they wanted and leave.

Unfortunately, we didn't have much besides coins and weapons. Piling the goods in front of us, they puzzled over the glass orbs and spilled my glass spiders and bees on the floor. The glass tree leopard Leif used to communicate with other magicians drew laughs of derision over what they thought was a toy.

The leader picked up one of the bees and examined it in the firelight. "What's this?" he asked me.

"Don't tell him," Leif said.

I glanced at Leif. He looked worried. Too worried.

He wanted the leader to think they were significant. I caught on.

"It's gotta be important, boss. They don't have anything else with them," the Signal Man said.

The leader grabbed my hair, yanking me to my feet. He jabbed me with his knife's point in the exact same spot as before. Pain blazed. "What is it?"

"Glass...decorations...worthless." I held still.

"You want to die over a few trinkets?" He twisted the knife.

I cried out as fire ringed my throat.

"Stop," Ulrick yelled. "Tell him."

"Hurry up or I'm going to carve my initials deep into your smooth skin."

"There are jewels...hidden inside." I relaxed a bit as he pulled his knife away. Warm wetness flowed down my neck.

"The spiders?" he asked.

"Topaz," I said.

"The bees?"

"Emeralds and onyx."

"How do we get to them?"

"Don't—" Leif tried, but a guard kicked him in the stomach.

The leader dragged his blade along my cheek, leaving a trail of pain.

"Break it," I said as if he had forced it from me. I hoped this was what Leif wanted.

With greedy glints in their eyes, the leader and three of his men tried to snap the glass items in half.

"Only I can break them open," I said.

The leader thrust them in my hand. "Do it."

The resultant whoosh and flash distracted the men long enough for Leif and Ulrick to jump to their feet and snatch their weapons from the pile.

I broke all the glass. "Attack them," I yelled to the three spiders and one bee that had been released, keeping the image of our ambushers in my mind.

The leader backed away as the bee flew toward him. Cries and yells sounded as chaos descended. Ulrick fought with his sword and Leif hacked with his machete. I dived for my cloak and pulled more spiders from a pocket. Breaking them open, I sent each one into the fight to add to the robbers' confusion. A spider's bite hurts, but doesn't kill.

I pulled my sais, and checked where the leader had gone. Unfortunately, the Greenblade bee had stung him. His body convulsed on the floor as he died. I pushed the horrible image from my mind and engaged in the battle.

Swinging my sais, I knocked one man unconscious and trapped another's sword long enough for Ulrick to disarm him. Within minutes the fight was over. The attackers surrendered.

Ulrick, Leif and I stood and stared at each other for a long moment.

Then Leif laughed. "Damn. For just a second, I thought you weren't going to tell them about the spiders and had missed my hint. My heart actually ceased to beat."

"I'm sorry for letting them through," I said.

Leif waved the apology away. "You didn't stand a chance. It was six against one, during a storm. I must have been tired to sleep through the rain. If I had known, I would have joined you. Here, hold this." He handed me his machete. "Chop anyone that moves, I'll contact the authorities." Picking up his tree leopard, Leif stared into the glowing depths of the glass, sending out a message.

I moved closer to Ulrick. Two men had been knocked out, and three robbers huddled together and nursed the bleeding gashes and bite marks turning into red welts on their skin.

He glanced at me before returning his attention to the men. "Are you all right?"

I probed the wound on my neck with a finger. It throbbed. "I'll live, but I wish Leif had healing powers."

"Leif's magic—"

"Useless in this case," Leif said. "I could smell the foul things they've done, know they had no remorse for their actions, but couldn't do a damn thing about it." He rummaged in his saddlebags. "Ah, I do have one." Firelight glinted off a vial of liquid. Leif dipped metal darts into the substance.

"Curare?" I asked.

"Yep. The closest town is Owl's Hill. They're sending guards, but it'll be a while until they get here. I don't want these guys following us." He jabbed each one. "The town's been getting reports about a gang of men robbing travelers. Called them the Storm Thieves."

Leif checked the pulse on the leader and met my gaze. My guilt burned through my heart and I thought I should be arrested, too. He was dead because of me. The rationalization of kill or be killed was not a comfort—our situation hadn't seemed that dire. A life gone. My first. Now I had a true regret.

"You saved lives with his death," Leif said. "He reeks of blood. Killed many and captured women for his pleasure before leaving them to die. He was wanted for murder, a hanging offense."

"But that is for a judge to decide. Not me."

"And you decided he would die?"

"No, but—"

"It was my plan. Do you think I would have let you trick them into breaking open the bees, if I knew they would take what they wanted and go?"

"I—"

"Hadn't thought of it that way? I smelled their intentions. You were part of their spoils and Ulrick and I were soon to be dead." Leif returned to his bags and removed his water skin, a handful of leaves and a white roll. Pouring water into a pot, he crushed the leaves and sprinkled them in. "Sit," he ordered me. "Those guys aren't going anywhere and I want to clean your wound before it gets infected. Ulrick, heat the water."

Stirring the fire to roaring life, Ulrick boiled the water. Leif's ministrations caused my eyes to tear. The burning pain was worse than the knife as he rubbed an earthy-smelling goo into my cut. When Ulrick sat beside me, I clung to his hand.

"It's deep, but the poultice should keep it clean until we reach Yelena. The mark on your cheek is just a scratch." He wrapped a bandage around my neck.

"Why wait until we reach the Soulfinder?" Ulrick asked.

I explained about her healing abilities. "She could have saved my sister's life, if Ferde hadn't stolen Tula's soul."

"Only if she was there *before* Tula died," Leif said. "Once the body dies, she won't return the soul."

"Why not?" he asked.

"The two people she 'woke' from the dead came back with different personalities. They obsessed about death and eventually killed themselves." Leif finished tying the bandage. "Now, I'm depressed. Let's get out of here before I start to cry."

I checked on the horses as Leif and Ulrick gathered our supplies. The sky lightened, turning the darkness into a dreary gray fog. Rain and sleet continued to blow. Propelled by the wind, the chilly wetness soaked my cloak and reached my skin.

After a cold breakfast, we continued our journey east. As expected, the roads softened into muck that clung to the horses' legs and filled their hooves. The storm followed us into the plains.

We stopped just past the border to clean the mud from the horses' feet. The tall gold-brown stalks of the grass bowed under the weight of the rain. At least the ground remained firm. Spreading as far as I could see in the gloom, the plains' terrain undulated as if it were a frozen sea. But then the scene shifted. It looked foreign. Hostile.

"We're lost," Ulrick said. He pulled his sword, glancing around him as if searching for attackers. "We must go back."

I agreed. "We should leave. Now." I peered around as my panic increased. Which way had we come? Which way was safe?

"Relax," Leif said. "It's just the Sandseed protection. Let me…" He drew in a breath and closed his eyes.

The landscape returned to a more benign setting. My conviction of being lost dissipated. "What did you do?"

"Introduced you to the Sandseed's magic. Promised you would behave and not be a threat to them."

"What happens if they think we're a threat?" Ulrick asked.

"You don't want to know," Leif said.

"Bad?"

"Very bad."

"How does the protection know you're related?" I asked Leif.

"My blood. It can…smell it, and knows if I'm family or not." He squinted into the rain. "We better get moving. I want to be in Fulgor by tomorrow afternoon."

We mounted and Leif gave us a few instructions.

"Follow my lead. Let your horses have control. And hold on!" He spurred Rusalka into a gallop.

Quartz and Moonlight raced after them.

Leif shouted, "Gust-of-wind."

My world changed. The ground under Quartz's hooves transformed into a river of sand. Streaks of color flowed by me. I no longer felt I rode on a horse, but was propelled by a wave of air. Quartz sliced through the pouring rain. Exhilaration and terror pulsed in my veins, blocking out all other thoughts. A heady sensation.

My world returned to normal when Leif stopped Rusalka. Quartz snorted and huffed as if she'd had a good run. Sweat darkened her coat. My cloak felt dry and we had outrun the storm. Sunlight painted the plains with wide swatches of yellows, golds, browns and reds.

"Do you want to stop and eat, or ride farther?" Leif asked.

"Ride." I had no appetite. Memories of the Storm Thieves' attack rushed into my mind. While Leif's explanation had eased my heart-burning guilt over their leader's death, I couldn't shake the feeling that I should have ordered the bee not to sting. I hadn't fully realized the consequences of these glass weapons. Packing them with vague thoughts of defense, I had never considered exactly what I would use them for and what the results would be. As if I had given a child a sword and didn't tell him what would happen if he used it. It was irresponsible and dangerous.

After we rested and watered the horses, we resumed our journey. When the horses slowed again, we stopped for the night.

I helped collect a few sticks of wood for the fire from the stunted trees and sparse bushes growing in the plains. What I found wasn't enough to cook with, but Leif had come prepared.

"Mara gave me these." He unpacked a handful of white coals.

While he made dinner, I groomed the horses. We ate in near silence.

"What's the watch schedule?" I asked Leif.

"No need for one in the plains."

I lay down by the fire. The earth was still damp from the rain and I shivered.

"Oh, for sand's sake," Ulrick whispered next to me. "I know we're taking it slow, but this is ridiculous. Come here."

He lifted his blanket and I rolled to him, ending with my back to his chest. He covered us both and put his arm around my stomach, pulling me tight against him.

"It's been an awful day. I need to hold you," he said.

His warmth drove the chill from my body.

"I thought you were dead. Some protector. If it wasn't for you, we'd all be…" He swallowed. "You did what you had to. I would have done the same."

I agreed. "But I feel like I cheated."

"You played by their rules. They set the standard when they attacked without warning, creeping up while we slept."

His arm trembled and I wondered if he was angry or finally reacting to the fight.

"I landed a few blows, but couldn't reach my sword. Then being ordered to my knees and feeling so..."

"Powerless," I supplied.

"Yes. I didn't like it."

Having been in the same situation many times, I was about to commiserate. But with the morning's events still fresh in my mind, I made a realization. "We really weren't completely powerless. In this case, we had Leif's intelligence, tricking them. And there is always the power to choose. Cooperate or die—not a stellar choice, but a choice nonetheless."

"What about cooperate or someone you love dies?"

"You still have a choice."

"But when he jabbed his knife into your throat, the choice was no longer mine."

"Right. It was mine," I said.

"That's why I felt so helpless."

"You shouldn't. It's my choice. You need to trust me to make the right one." And I needed to trust myself. Recognizing the lack was one step in the right direction.

Sleep came in fits and my dreams hovered on the edge of nightmares. I dreamed about a cave of lights. The images were sharp and the air smelled of wet minerals. Dampness caressed my skin. A pleading voice scratched at my thoughts. It beckoned and begged from its hidden location. Whispered promises in exchange for freedom. Promises of power.

I woke with a cry and Ulrick's arm around my waist.

"A nightmare?" he asked.

"Not quite." I told him about the cave of lights.

I drifted through the rest of the night. The voice haunted my sleep and the morning sun was a relief. Leif already had a pot of water heating on the coals. "These are wonderful."

"They're expensive," I grumped.

"Rough night?" he asked.

"I've had better."

He poured three cups of tea. I sipped mine and savored my sour mood. I felt trapped and the feeling lasted for the rest of the day. By late afternoon, we arrived at the main road to Fulgor. By then, the insistent voice from my dreams echoed in my mind. I ignored it and focused on the world around me.

The crowded cobblestone streets of Fulgor buzzed with activity. As the capital of the Moon Clan lands, the large city hosted all the government offices and boasted the wealthiest market district. The proud citizens chose to ignore the fact no one wanted to travel all the way to the Emerald Mountains to purchase jewels from the Cloud Mist Clan. Far better to have the mine owners ship their goods to Fulgor for sale and trade.

Unfortunately, rich shoppers attracted thieves and beggars; so the city guards patrolled the streets and kept a close watch.

"Yelena and Irys are staying in Councillor Moon's guest quarters," Leif said, angling Rusalka through the late-day traffic. "She said there was enough room for us."

I scanned the goods in the windows of the closing shops. Fulgor was known for its variety of clay, and, sure enough, I spotted several bowls and plates fashioned from the clay. Why anyone would want to eat from a clunky, heavy piece of pottery when they could use glass was beyond my imagination. The earthenwares competed with the glasswares at the market stands. My father always sent his sturdiest cups when selling to the Fulgor merchants.

A few pottery pieces drew my attention. I would have liked to stop and examine them, but Leif was determined to reach the Councillor's Hall before it closed for the evening and the cooks left for their homes.

The white dome of the Hall rose above the other city buildings. All Sitian government buildings had been constructed from the white marble mined from the Moon lands. The green-veined slabs had been painstakingly chiseled from the ground and exported to the other capital cities.

When we arrived at the courtyard, our horses were taken to the stable and we were directed inside. Leif had been "communicating" with his sister through his glass messenger.

Yelena waited in the main lobby, which was a huge cavern with a black-and-white marble floor and was open all the way up to the dome ten stories above.

She rushed over and hugged Leif. "It's been so long. I'm beginning to think you're avoiding me," she said.

He smirked. "Then you'd be thinking right. Every time I visit, you get me into trouble."

"You have it all wrong. *Again.* Every time you visit me, *you* bring trouble."

Yelena winked at me. I introduced her to Ulrick. He stuttered through his greeting, seeming to be awed by her. I didn't blame him. Not only were her Soulfinding abilities legendary, but she radiated warmth and intelligence. And with those stunning green eyes and long black hair, she never lacked for admirers.

Of course, they wouldn't dream of competing for her attentions. Valek, a master swordsman, assassin and leader of the intelligence network for Ixia was her soul mate. Sitia's number one enemy. Despite her connection to Valek, she had become Ixia's and Sitia's liaison.

I glanced around the Hall's lobby, searching for Valek. Yelena laughed. "He's not here, Opal. If the Councillor heard even a whiff of a rumor about him, she'd have heart failure." She grew serious. "I'm glad you're here. We've had some...interesting developments."

Leif groaned. "That's Yelena-speak for life-threatening danger."

She shot him an annoyed look. I would have wilted under her stare, but Leif was nonplussed.

"Come up to my office. Irys and Kade are waiting for us." Yelena led the way to a sweeping staircase.

An elaborate chandelier hung above the first landing. I marveled at its intricate construction and brilliance.

"That's one of Gressa's pieces," Ulrick said in a neutral tone. Gressa was his talented younger sister. "She has a glass shop in Fulgor. She and Mother never worked well together. Gressa left as soon as she turned eighteen."

"Do you want to visit her while we're here?" I asked.

"I guess, if we have time."

We climbed three stories before walking down a long corridor. I marveled at the sculptures and paintings decorating the hallways. The Moon Councillor's Hall made Booruby's look dumpy in comparison.

Yelena escorted us to an impressive office with a reception room. Dark crimson couches and brown leather armchairs contrasted in a pleasing way against the white marble walls. Thick red-and-gold carpets covered the floor.

"Good thing I was traveling with Master Jewelrose," Yelena said. "Otherwise, they would have stuck me in the basement, using a barrel for a seat and an old packing crate as a desk."

Third Magician pished at Yelena. "She exaggerates."

Kade lounged in one of the armchairs. His dusty boots matched his disheveled appearance. One elbow was propped and he rested his head in his hand. He said nothing. Master Jewelrose waved at us to sit down and sent Yelena for tea.

Ulrick coughed. He was the only one bothered by sending a Soulfinder for refreshments. Leif plopped on the couch, kicked off his muddy boots and put his feet on the table.

"We've come to a standstill," Master Jewelrose said. "Councillor Moon's sister is organizing a coup, but the Councillor refuses to believe us. She insists the Commander of Ixia has sent Valek here to assassinate her." She leaned back in her chair. A few black strands of hair had escaped her tight bun. Dark smudges stood out under her emerald-colored eyes.

"Why is she convinced Ambrose is out to get her?" Leif asked.

"Ambrose?" Yelena raised a slender eyebrow. She carried a tray of tea and fruit. "You're on a first name basis with the Commander now?"

"I usually call him Amby, but not in mixed company. Hey!" Leif caught the apple his sister threw at him.

They looked chastised after Master Jewelrose gave them a stern stare. Yelena retrieved a black statue from a desk in the corner. She handed it to me.

"What's this?" I asked.

"You tell me."

Carved into the shape of a dagger, the smooth statue glinted. "It's not stone. Probably a type of high-quality glass. Just like those fake diamonds." I turned the piece in my hands.

"What's the significance?" Leif asked.

"It was found on Councillor Moon's pillow. Her advisers warned it was a calling card from Valek, and she had been targeted for assassination," Yelena said.

Before the Commander's takeover of Ixia, Valek had assassinated the entire royal family. To make the job more interesting and challenging, he would leave one of his carvings on his victim's bed to warn them.

"Valek doesn't leave warnings anymore and, truthfully, if the Commander wrote an order for Councillor Moon's assassination, she would be dead by now."

Ulrick gaped at Yelena's matter-of-fact tone.

"There has to be another reason the Councillor thinks the Commander is after her." Leif reached for the dagger.

"The Councillor recently sent a team of specialists to search the Moon lands for diamond deposits. She believes the Commander wants to stop her before she finds any," Yelena explained.

"Meanwhile, dear old sis is amassing arms and soldiers by selling fake diamonds?" Leif guessed.

"Right, but we had no proof. Until now." She smiled at me. "Opal and Kade found the link between the sister and the fakes. Chun. Kade followed him straight to the mine."

"It's in a cave," Kade said.

"What about the real diamonds? Any ideas on those?" Leif asked.

"Nothing substantial. Although…" I wondered if I should say more.

"Although?" Yelena prompted

"When I held the real diamonds, a vision entered my mind. It was cold with white all around."

"Like a marble quarry?" Master Jewelrose asked.

"Perhaps." I had assumed the white was snow, but it could be marble.

"So we still haven't connected the real diamonds with the sister," Yelena said.

"Does it matter?" Leif asked.

"Not for this case, but I would like to know where they're coming from. Perhaps if Opal accompanies me and Kade to the cave, she can sense where the real diamonds are."

Happy tones emanated from the dream voice in my mind. It had been quiet all day as if growing roots deep into my soul. An uneasy feeling rolled along my spine, and dread pulsed. Something waited for me in the cave.

25

"ARE YOU UP for a trip to the cave?" Yelena asked.

"Sure," I said.

"No," Ulrick said.

"Don't you think three magicians can keep her safe?" Yelena fixed Ulrick with her powerful stare. He blanched and quickly apologized.

"Three?" I asked her.

"Kade, Leif and me."

"Me?" Leif squeaked. "Why me?"

"I need someone to light the torches. And Kade knows where to go."

"What about Irys?" Leif asked.

"Someone needs to guard the Councillor at night. We don't trust her people," Master Jewelrose said.

"We'll go tonight. Around midnight."

"Tonight? We just arrived," Leif whined.

Yelena frowned, then brightened as if she had a sudden

idea. "Rest now and join us for a late dinner. I've made friends with the Councillor's cook and I'll ask him to make your favorite beef stew with garlic potatoes and apple cake for dessert."

Leif's petulance disappeared in an instant. "When's dinner? Maybe I should grab a piece of cake now to tide me over for later. Which way is the kitchen?"

Yelena shooed us out the door. "Guest quarters are behind the Hall, next to the stables."

As Leif, Kade and Ulrick headed out, I asked Yelena, "Friends with the cook?"

She gave me a conspiratorial smirk. "The Councillor is in danger. I don't want her poisoned on my watch."

"Leif, light the torch. There's no one around," Yelena said.

We crouched a few feet inside the mouth of a cave; inky blackness surrounded us as the wet smell of minerals filled my nose. The cave was located about an hour's ride north of Fulgor. Kade had seen Chun enter and then exit carrying a bulging bag.

"I had to make a decision," Kade had said during the ride north. "Either follow Chun or investigate the cave. I chose the cave, but didn't get far without a light."

"Any luck with the sand suppliers?" I asked.

"No. Although the Brubaker brothers offered me a discount on something called lightning strike?"

I laughed. "How much?"

"Twenty percent."

"I would have haggled for thirty."

"Excuse me, what is lightning strike?" Leif asked.

"When lightning strikes the sand, the heat melts the grains. When it cools, you can have a crude glass rod shaped like a lightning bolt. Its purpose is decorative. They must have guessed Kade was connected to the Stormdance Clan."

Two torches blazed to life, pushing the darkness back. Shadows danced on the uneven walls of the cave and pebbles crunched under our boots. Leif peered at a small hole toward the back of the chamber with a dubious expression.

"I'm *not* squeezing. If I don't fit, I'll just wait for you," he said.

"Relax. Once you go through that tunnel, the cave opens up," Yelena said.

"Have you been here before?" I asked. The prospect of getting lost was unappealing.

"No. My friend told me." A bat sat on her shoulder. "He agreed to scout for us."

"Wonderful," Leif muttered.

I really couldn't say anything about a scouting bat. I claimed glass and spiders spoke to me, and diamonds gave me visions. Each person's magic had their own quirks.

Yelena led the way with one torch. I followed. Leif held the other torch and Kade came last. We crawled through the narrow chute. As predicted, the tunnel widened until we could stand. I wiped the dirt from my hands as I looked around the small chamber.

My dream voice cut through my skull as if the person

stood next to me and shouted in my ears. He wanted me to save him. Promised me more magical powers and whatever else I wanted. I tried to block the voice with my hands. It didn't work.

Kade glanced at me with a question in his eyes. I waved his concern away. Nothing he or anyone could do about a voice in my head. If Yelena heard it, she would have said something. Ignoring it, I focused on the cavern. A few stalagmites ringed a pool of water. I couldn't see another opening.

"Here's where it gets…interesting," Yelena said.

Leif and I exchanged a horrified glance. My heart flipped as Yelena placed her torch in a sconce and removed her cloak.

"It's just a short swim to the bottom and there's a rope," she said.

My thoughts scattered as fear roiled the contents of my stomach.

"Are you insane?" Leif asked. "How do you know there's a rope? Are you going to tell me your bat can swim?"

"I sent him here to observe the workers after Kade told me the location. And I can see the rope." She pointed down.

In the surprisingly clear depths, the end of a rope had been tied to a metal rung. The rope followed the bottom of the pool and disappeared under a rock.

"I'll go first and see where it leads." She kicked off her boots and her bat hunched down, taking a firmer grip on her shirt.

"Do you want a bubble of air around you?" Kade asked her.

She considered. "I think it would make it difficult for me to get to the bottom. I'd be too buoyant. How about just around my nose?"

"Too hard to create for these conditions. If we were outside in the daylight, I probably could."

"I'll manage. If I get stuck, though—bubble me."

"How will we know you're stuck?" I asked.

Yelena stared at Kade.

"Yes, I hear you fine," the Stormdancer said.

I realized she had mentally communicated with him and I suppressed the pinch of longing. The dream voice flared to life. It promised me the power to read minds if I set him free. A strong compulsion to hunt for the voice pressed between my shoulder blades.

Find me. Find me. Set me free. The scratchy voice clung to my thoughts, and dominated my senses. No longer just a murmur in my mind, but almost a physical force.

I struggled to concentrate on Yelena, wondering if bats could swim as she jumped into the pool. Water splashed on us. Leif muttered oaths under his breath. He held his torch over the water. The silt on the bottom of the pool stirred into milky white clouds when she reached the rope. Soon she disappeared from our sight.

"You know what I'd like to know?" Leif asked.

Set me free.

"How to swim?" I guessed.

Powerful magic will be yours.

"Real funny. I'd like to know who was the crazy son of a bitch who reached this spot and said, 'Gee, I wonder where this pool goes?' Any other reasonable person would have looked around and declared this room a dead end."

Find me. Find me.

As we waited, I tried to push the voice away. Concentrated on the type of person who would dive into a pool just to see what was there. An adventurer? An explorer? If someone didn't take a chance or try an experiment, then certain discoveries would never have been made.

Find me. Set me free and I'll reward you with unlimited power.

I staggered, but steadied myself against the wall before Leif or Kade noticed.

"Finally," Leif said as Yelena broke the surface. "Well?"

"The water's cold."

"I knew I should have let Ulrick come along. He's serious. And with no sense of humor, he would counter your wisecracks perfectly."

"Leif, that's enough," Yelena said. "Don't listen to him, Opal. He tends to babble when he's nervous. I want you to follow me back over. Swim down to the rope and pull yourself through the tunnel to the next pool. When you get to the other rung, let go and float up to the surface. You do know how to swim. Right?"

Kade snorted.

I shot him a nasty look. "Yes. I do." I pulled my cloak off and hung it from a stalagmite, then tossed my boots next to Yelena's.

"Kade, stay here and keep watch. Leif, follow Opal," she said.

"Why can't I keep watch?" Leif pouted.

"Lighting torches, remember?"

"Oh, joy."

Hesitating on the edge, I braced myself for the cold. When I entered the water, the shock tore threw me, robbing my lungs of air for a moment. The voice in my mind was stunned into silence.

"Deep breath," Yelena said. She swam to the bottom.

Drawing in a shaky, clattery breath, I ducked under the surface and followed her. She had made it sound so easy, but the cloudy water obscured the rope. In a panic, I searched with my hands, making it worse. I would have given up, but my tingling fingers finally brushed the rough threads.

Hand over hand, I pulled. With each stroke, the light faded until I moved through liquid darkness. My lungs protested as air bubbled from my lips. I didn't know how much longer I could hold my breath. Just about to panic, I touched a knot of rope tied to another metal rung. I released my hold and floated to the surface, gasping for air.

"Here." Yelena grabbed my hand and pulled me from the water. "Once Leif gets here, we'll have light. I found a couple of torches."

I lay on the hard floor, sucking in breaths. Soon a loud splash and coughing sounded beside me.

"Next time," Leif puffed. "Next time…I'm staying… home…."

"And miss all the fun?" Yelena asked.

"Come here, so...I can strangle...you."

"You'll have to catch me first. Light these."

Wood thumped against wet skin.

"Ow!"

"Sorry."

Leif muttered about buying his sister flint before fire ignited on the torches. The light caused a chain reaction throughout the cavern. Leif never did strangle his sister, and I forgot all about the cold numbing my bones. We were too captivated by the spectacle around us.

Every surface in the room sparkled as if alive. The yellow firelight raced through and reflected from a million facets. Crystals of every shape and size lined the walls, grew on the rocks and hung from the ceiling. Gressa's glass chandelier was dull and ordinary in comparison. My dream images a poor copy at best.

"Worth the swim?" Yelena asked.

All I could manage was a thin squeak of assent. The voice consumed me. He was here, trapped in a glass prison, which I had made and helped Yelena to fill. I had been a conduit for the evil souls. Tainted—their black thoughts occupied my mind for a mere second but enough to...what? To reconnect with me? To claim me.

My chest tightened. The compulsion to go straight to the prison wrapped around me like a rope, pulling. I glanced at Yelena. Did she hear him? He was one of the Daviian Warpers. The seven prisons had disappeared soon after Yelena and I filled them. Hidden by Valek,

Yelena assured me in locations unknown to everyone but him, and she had made it clear she didn't want to know. And now me.

Free me. Crush the prison in your hand. Only you can do it.

"Oh, yes. Worth getting wet for. Did I ever tell you you're my favorite sister?"

Yelena rolled her eyes since she was his only sister. "Are these your fake diamonds, Opal?"

I closed my mouth and pushed to my feet, taking one of the torches with me. She didn't hear him. I tried to do my job, despite the ghost's increasing demands for freedom.

A path wound through the chamber. From what I could see by the torchlight, it appeared to be several stories high, a couple hundred feet wide, and about seventy feet deep. Toward the back, I spotted an area where the crystals had been chiseled. These crystals were brilliant and clear. I rubbed my fingertips along the surface, pieces cracked off in my wake.

"These are too brittle." I searched until I found black-colored crystals. "These, too. They wouldn't survive being shaped." So why come here?

Free me. You'll be stronger than the Soulfinder.

"Do you know what these are?" Yelena asked.

"A type of gypsum crystal, but I'm not an expert. Pazia or someone from the Cloud Mist Clan would know."

I can tell you. Everything and anything you want to know.

"What are they used for?" Leif asked.

"They could be added into a glass mixture. Perhaps they are needed in the recipe to make the fakes."

"We'll take a few samples to identify it. Leif, there's a table on the other side of the pool," Yelena called. "See if you can find a chisel."

Crush the prison in your hand. Release me.

After a few minutes of grumbling, Leif brought a chisel, hammer and a cloth bag. Trying not to make a noticeable break, I chipped off a finger-sized piece of the clear, then broke a similar-sized chuck of black and stuffed them into the bag.

The pressure in my mind bloomed into an unbearable torment. I sank to my knees and, without conscious thought, pried the prison from the corner where it had been wedged, one sparkle among thousands. Relief and power flowed through me as if I had drunk an elixir. I gazed at the glass, muddy-red light pulsed from its core.

Leif and Yelena didn't notice; they stared at her bat flying overhead.

I now knew Valek had been crazy enough to swim through the pool. He probably thought no one else would brave the cold water. He had been wrong.

The bat landed on Yelena's shoulder. She glanced at the rear wall. "There's another tunnel."

Leif groaned, but followed his sister. I shoved the prison deep into my pocket and hurried after them. After traversing two chutes and three caverns, we came to a dead end. None of the other chambers contained crystals, and there was no sign of real diamonds.

Through the thin fabric of my pants the prison's heat jabbed me as if searching for a weak spot. I should give it to Valek so he could find a better hiding place. A sudden possessiveness welled. The prison was mine.

"Can we go now? My feet are numb," Leif said.

We retraced our steps and once again stood in the crystal chamber.

"Let's hurry." Leif pointed to the pool.

I hesitated, fighting the desire to stay silent. This was too important. Yelena needed to know about the Warper. I tried to speak. A jolt of fire sliced up my body and stabbed into my head. I fell to my knees, pressing my fingertips into my temples. The man wouldn't let me talk.

Yelena's voice sounded. Her hand on my back. His desire burned my thoughts.

Break the glass and release the pain, he ordered. *Now!*

My hand closed on the glass. Normally so strong a material, I knew I could reduce it to powder in my fist. No one else could. The magic within the glass responded to me. Heady mix of power within my palm. To no longer be afraid. Exactly what I wanted.

Crush it. Be powerful. In control.

My fingers tightened. Yelena's presence reminded me of a time I had held a Curare-laced dart and jabbed it into her arm.

Do it. Together we will have more power than her.

I yanked the prison from my pocket. Energy sizzled along my skin. One hard squeeze of my hand, and the pain would disappear.

Obey me.

Those words cut through my fog of misery and confusion. Different voice. Same words. Words I would never forget. I thrust the prison into Yelena's hands. Unbroken.

The blazing pain remained; caused by shame over what I had almost done and knowledge that these glass prisons would haunt me until I died. I huddled on the floor, hot and miserable.

Yelena's touch on my forehead cooled the maelstrom. Her energy revived my spirit.

"What's going on?" Leif asked.

"It's better you don't know," Yelena said. "Go on through the pool, we'll be there in a minute."

"Oh that's right. I forgot I'm just here to light fires," Leif grumbled, but dived into the water.

Yelena held out the glass prison. "When did you know this was here?"

I told her about the dreams. "I have a general idea where the others are, too." I searched her expression. "Didn't you know?"

"I knew as soon as we entered the cave." She paused and chewed on her lower lip as if debating what she should tell me. "I've been hanging around Valek too long. I heard the Warper's pleas, but wanted to see what *you* would do."

"But...but I almost crushed the glass and released him."

"You didn't."

"But what if I did? He has Master-level powers."

"Then I would have another problem to deal with."

"That was a big risk."

"Actually, I wasn't worried. I trusted you, Opal."

If the Warper hadn't said those two words, I would have freed him. "You shouldn't. Because when you sent those evil souls to the glass, they traveled through me. I think a piece of them stayed with me. Sometimes I feel my thoughts and actions aren't mine."

Yelena placed her hand flat on my chest and closed her eyes. After a moment, she stepped back. "We all have thoughts we're not proud of. I've done a couple things I wish I hadn't. I can assure you there are no remnants of those souls within you."

"But they call to me."

"Your other glass animals call to you."

"That's different."

Yelena said nothing.

"I sense emotions from my animals. I hear voices and feel pain with the prisons."

"Have you been dealing with this for the past four years?" Yelena asked.

The answer surprised me. "No. I started having the vivid dreams..." After my trip to the Stormdance lands. After I had connected with Kade through the orb. "Around the middle of the cooling season. Around the time I discovered a few new...things I could do with my magic." I explained about the spiders, but not about Kade.

"The new abilities could have set off a chain reaction. Your magic is linked to glass and perhaps in increasing your powers you expanded your connection to your other creations."

I guessed it was possible.

"Or there could be another reason altogether. In this case, I would say dealing with the problem is more important right now than figuring it out. You must not tell anyone you know where the prisons are. This one will be hidden again. Stay away from the others lest you be tempted." She smiled. "The next trapped soul might offer you warmth and dry clothes. Then we'd be in trouble."

I released a shaky breath. "You're right. I'd do anything for a warm fire."

She cringed. "Not me. I tend to avoid fires." She shivered. "I'm more tempted by a piece of apple cake."

"You sound like Leif." But my stomach rumbled in agreement. We didn't waste any more time. The trip back through the chilly water wasn't as bad, perhaps because I knew a dry cloak waited on the other side.

Kade helped me out of the pool. His hand pulsed hot against my icy skin. Soothing warmth spread from where he had touched me. My body felt bruised and battered, and the sudden desire to wrap myself in his arms coursed through me. I pushed the notion away, knowing he would reject me.

What a night. I couldn't wait to leave the cave. Staying far away from the prisons was an excellent idea, but how do I avoid the nightmares? What if I encountered another stronger Warper? Would I be able to resist freeing him if Yelena wasn't by my side?

Yelena and Leif crawled through the tunnel toward the cave's exit. Kade and I waited for the all clear signal.

"Something's wrong," Kade said. He helped me wrap my cloak around my shoulders. "You hold yourself as if you've ingested Brittle Talc."

I smiled, remembering our conversation on The Cliffs. "Now you're using glassmaking analogies. If you hang around me too much, you'll be spouting glassmaking lingo like a gaffer."

He gasped dramatically, pressing a hand to his chest. "Then I'd better go."

Kade joked, but the thought of him leaving felt as if I had dived into the cave's pool again. Without thought, I stepped closer to him. He stiffened.

I moved away, letting my blood turn into ice.

"Did something happen in the cavern?" he asked.

"No. I'm just cold. You know what cold does to metal."

"You're not made of metal."

Right now, I wished I was.

We returned to Fulgor an hour before dawn. Kade had rented a room in the Good Inn near the center of the town. In the Councillor's guest quarters, Leif shared a room with Ulrick, and I had the other bedroom. A living area with a marble hearth separated the three rooms. Leif immediately roused the dying embers of the fire into a full blaze.

"Ahh... I'm sleeping here." He pulled the couch closer.

"Get changed first," I said. "Or you'll soak the cushions."

I entered my room. My still-damp shirt clung to my body and my hair had dried into a tangled knot. Clean, dry clothes felt like the finest silk against my skin. I wrestled with a comb, but put it down when a knock sounded.

Yelena stood at the door. "Do you have those samples from the cave? I want to show them to Irys."

I stepped back, opening the door wider. "I put them in my pocket."

As I dug for the crystals, Yelena wandered around my room.

"Opal?"

I grabbed the crystals and joined her. She had stopped by my saddlebags. One of the pouches gaped open.

Yelena pointed to the orb visible through the gap. "What is that?"

Her voice sounded odd and I guessed she heard the magic's song. I had grown so used to the melody, I no longer muffled it. "It's a Stormdancer orb. A storm's essence is inside. Kade wanted me to keep it safe." I shrugged. "I didn't feel right leaving it behind."

She turned to me in shock. I almost stepped back.

"Can you hear it?" I asked.

"Hear it? Can't you *see* her?"

I knew who Yelena meant. "No. I only hear her name.

She's Kade's sister. Kaya died while he harvested a storm."

"Her soul is trapped inside that orb. She must be freed."

26

Yelena moved toward the orb.

"No. Wait." I stepped in front of her. I stood about three inches taller than her, but I knew she possessed the power to move me aside.

"Why?" she asked.

"It's Kade's orb. He asked me to keep it safe."

"Does he know his sister is trapped inside?"

I thought back. "On an unconscious level he does. He's kept it with him since she died. But I doubt he knows her actual soul is there."

"She should be released so she can find joy in the sky."

"Is Kaya unhappy?"

"Let's ask her."

She grabbed my hand before I could say a word. The room swirled and spun as color drained, leaving gray in its wake. The furniture faded away. The walls curved around us and transformed into glass.

We stood inside the orb. My second trip, but this time Kaya didn't form from sand granules. She waited for us—a ghost with a sad smile, her resemblance to Kade unmistakable. Her short brown hair was streaked blond by the sun.

Yelena asked her if she wanted to go to the sky.

"I would love to go to the sky, but you can't set me free, Soulfinder," Kaya said. "Only my brother can."

Frowning, Yelena's forehead crinkled with effort as she reached toward Kaya.

"That's a first," Yelena said. "I guess I shouldn't be surprised, I've met a few...interesting souls in the past four years."

I remembered Leif's translation of Yelena-speak, and *interesting* meant *dangerous*. "I didn't know souls could be treacherous."

"The ones who belong in the fire world are. They always fight." She placed her hands on her hips. "We'll have a talk with your brother."

Kaya sighed. "I tried to tell him I was here, but he thinks I'm with the storms."

"What does he have to do to free her?" I asked Yelena.

"Pull out the stopper."

"Then why can't we do that now?"

The Soulfinder smiled. "I know you've discovered more uses for your power, but do you really think you can control the force of the storm? I know I can't."

"Point taken. How about another Stormdancer?"

"No," Kaya said. "Kade *needs* to free me."

* * *

Lost in a blizzard, I yelled Kade's name. My feet were frozen. I dragged them along as the wind whipped me with icy pellets.

"Opal, wake up." Ulrick's harsh voice woke me from another nightmare.

I shivered under my blankets.

His frown softened. He sat on the edge of the bed. "Another one?"

I nodded.

"The cave of lights?"

"No. I don't think I'll dream of that one again."

"Why not?" His eyes held an intensity. Yelena had told me to keep my knowledge of the prison's location a secret.

"Because we were there last night. And I found…"

"What?" He leaned closer to me.

"Gypsum crystals. A possible ingredient for the fake diamonds."

"Makes sense, but what about this new nightmare?"

"Being lost in the cold. You know how much I hate the cold." I shuddered.

But he wouldn't let the subject drop. "You called for that Stormdancer."

The real reason for his frown. "Kade's my friend, Ulrick. I have friends. I have family. They're all part of my life. Besides, dreams are strange. You can't get upset over them." Trying to listen to my own advice, I stretched and yawned. "What time is it?"

"Almost dinnertime, but we're having a meeting in Yelena's office. She wants everyone there."

"Leif won't be happy."

"He's bringing a snack."

I eyed Leif's slice of cake with envy as I listened to Yelena. Ulrick sat next to me on the couch, and Master Jewelrose lounged in the other armchair. Kade wasn't there. According to Yelena, he wasn't at the inn so the messenger left a note.

Yelena preferred to pace around the office as she talked. "We'll have to pick up Chun's trail again to see where he delivers the crystals. And we still don't know where the real diamonds are coming from."

"We'll set a watch at the cave," Master Jewelrose said. "Hopefully he'll come back for more supplies."

"Have you figured out what the crystals are?" I asked.

"Yes. You were right. They're gypsum crystals of high quality. The first ever found in Sitia." The Master Magician seemed pleased. "And I'm guessing Councillor Moon's team of surveyors found this cave and instead of reporting the find to the Councillor, told the Councillor's sister."

"So the question remains, what else have they discovered?" Leif asked between bites.

"What's the plan?" I asked.

"You and Ulrick go back to the Citadel. Mr. Lune may return with your real diamonds and you need to be there to purchase them," Yelena said. "Leif helps me with tracking down the surveyors and Irys stays here and babysits the Councillor."

"Why do I have to babysit?"

Yelena laughed. "Imagine you're the Councillor. Who would you rather have watching your back—a Master Magician or a scary Soulfinder with an Ixian boyfriend?"

With no way to dispute her, Master Jewelrose conceded the point, but she wasn't happy about it. She left the room to attend to her "babysitting" duties.

"What about Kade?" Yelena asked me. "Do you think he wants to help us?"

"He's tracking down a group of troublemakers," I said. "I'm guessing after we talk with him, he'll want to continue searching for them."

"You two aren't planning to gang up on him, are you?" Leif asked. "Because that's not fair."

I shook my head, glancing at Ulrick. He had remained quiet during the meeting and I wondered if he felt left out.

The rest of the time we made arrangements for our assigned tasks.

"If we discover any questionable gemstones, I'll send them to the Citadel with Leif," Yelena said to me.

"Yippee. I've been promoted from fire lighter to delivery boy. I'll write a letter home to Mother. She'll be so pleased." Leif ducked his sister's swing.

As we returned to our rooms, Ulrick's gloom continued. I thought about our trip back to the Keep.

Now that these nightmares invaded my sleep, Ulrick would be alarmed. I understood the need to keep certain secrets, but this one could ruin our relationship. By not confiding in him, I wasn't being honest with him. I pulled him into my bedroom and closed the door.

His shock was almost comical, until I realized I hadn't been alone with him in a long time.

"Sit down. I need to talk to you." I gestured to the only place to sit—the bed.

"What's wrong?" Ulrick held my hand in his. "You're not telling me everything." His gaze bored into me. "How can I trust you to make the right choices, if you don't trust me?"

"This is big. Telling you could make you a target."

He refused to back down. Just being with me endangered him, so I explained about finding the glass prison.

"What did you do with it?" he asked.

"Gave it to Yelena."

"Wow. It must have been difficult to turn down all that magic."

"It was painful. But an increase in power is an increase in responsibility." I thought of Zitora's warning about being considered a threat. "I already hurt Pazia, killed the storm thief leader and almost released a Warper. I don't need any more complications."

"At least the prison is no longer a problem."

When I didn't agree, he asked, "Or is it?"

"The trapped souls haunt my dreams. I think all I

need to do is get close to another prison and I'll be able to find it."

"We'll stay away from them and I'll ask Leif to brew you a sleeping potion." He pulled me down next to him. "And here I was afraid you were leaving me for that Stormdancer."

That Stormdancer had no desire to be with me. Mara's advice, *make him forget about his troubles* sounded in my mind.

I leaned forward and kissed him. His surprise didn't last long. He kissed me back with passion, wrapped his arms around me and pulled me close. For a while, I forgot all my problems.

When his hands tugged at my shirt, I pulled away. Another of Mara's comments floated in my mind, *I've seen turtles mate faster*. But I couldn't continue. I wasn't ready.

Ulrick said he understood, but the pain in his eyes haunted me for the rest of the day. Eventually, he would give up trying, and then how would I feel? The answer eluded me.

The next morning we visited Ulrick's sister.

"Seems silly not to," he said. "Besides, you should meet her."

"Maybe I can get her to tell me a few embarrassing stories about you. My family has an endless supply."

He grinned. "I will admit, the one your mother told about the sandpile—"

"Stop. I've heard it a million times, I don't need to hear it again."

The streets of Fulgor buzzed with activity. Wagons rumbled along the cobblestones, dogs barked and merchants called. With the blue sky above and not a hint of a breeze, the air warmed.

Whenever I contemplated the weather, my thoughts automatically turned to Kade. Yelena had received a message from him. He had left for the Cloud Mist Clan's main town of Ognap, hoping to interview lava flake suppliers. He would meet up with us back at the Citadel to get another list of sand merchants from me. The dry wording of the message made it quite clear to me that Kade viewed me as a colleague. I vowed to forget about his "spark" and focus on Ulrick by following Mara's advice.

Gressa's shop was on the end of a long row of stores. Displayed in the window was a variety of glasswares. Sunlight glinted off the exquisite vases and bowls.

"It's one thing to have a talented sister, another to have a glass genius," Ulrick said.

"Does she have any magic?" I asked.

"You'll have to tell me." He turned away to open the door.

Dressed in expensive silk tunics, saleswomen descended on Ulrick as soon as we entered the shop. I let him explain while I strolled around the display cases. A fruit bowl with rippled sides drew my attention. I ran a finger along the light purple glass. No magic, but the craftsmanship was superb.

"Please don't touch," a saleswoman said. She eyed

my cloak. "I doubt you have the gold to pay for it if you break it."

"Sina, that is no way to talk to a customer," another woman admonished.

I turned my head to see a tall beauty with long ebony hair and vibrant green eyes. Ulrick's sister. They could have been twins. I liked her immediately.

"She's with me," Ulrick said, untangling himself from a persistent salesgirl.

"Ulrick! What a surprise." They embraced briefly. She invited us to join her in the back. "My office is next to the workshop."

Four kilns roared and eight workers scurried about the workbenches. The place resembled more a factory than a shop.

"Production pieces." Gressa dismissed the activity. "It's the only way I can keep up with the demand." She chatted about her work, listing all the projects she'd been commissioned for in one speech.

We entered her office. Sheets of colored glass had been attached to the walls, floor and ceiling. Each pane a different color and when she closed the door to block the noise, I felt as if I stood in a glass box. Her desk and tables were made out of clear glass. Various glass items littered the tables and paper was piled on her desk.

She gestured to a round table made from brown-colored glass. The cushions on the four chairs surrounding the table were the only soft things in the entire office. We sat and stared at each other for a moment.

"Why are you here?" she asked.

Ulrick huffed with annoyance. "I wanted you to meet Opal. Do you remember her? She's one of Jaymes's daughters."

Her mouth twisted into a little frown. "You're obviously not the older one or the dead one." Recognition lit her eyes. "The youngest one!" She seemed pleased with herself for figuring it out.

Perhaps I had been too hasty in liking her. She prattled on about how she could have been friends with Tula at school, but her talent manifested early and working glass was more important than classes.

"I remember now. You're the glass magician." Gressa regarded me with more interest. "You have important friends. Why are *you* wasting time with my brother?"

I changed my mind. I didn't like her at all. "He's *important* to me. And he's a glass magician, too."

"Really?" She ignored my heated tone. "Everyone always says I work magic with glass. Do I have power, too?"

From the corner of my eye, I saw Ulrick roll his eyes. No wonder he hadn't wanted to visit her at first. I glanced at the wares on the table. "Are they yours?"

"Yes." She hopped to her feet. "Experiments, but I liked the way they catch the light."

"May I?" My hand hovered over a small glass rose.

"Go ahead. I'm working on a whole bouquet of flowers made of glass for Councillor Moon."

The rose was expertly wrought, but the glass remained

silent. None of her other items popped or glowed. I dug out my seashell and showed it to her.

"Ugh. What a horrid creation. Here, let me toss that into the cullet barrel for you."

"Gressa," Ulrick said with outrage.

"What?" She seemed genuinely confused. So focused on herself, she wasn't aware of how her words and actions affected others.

"It's all right." I explained about the magic trapped inside the piece. "It usually is a very good indicator of a person's magic ability, but Ulrick can't see it, either."

"Figures. Poor Ulrick always had just enough talent to make his life frustrating. Why would magic be any different?"

He jumped up. "I've had enough. Come on, Opal."

Gressa scrambled to apologize. "At least, let me show you my shop. I implemented the water system you designed."

Ulrick crossed his arms. "The system you laughed at and said wouldn't work?"

"I was wrong."

He dropped his arms in surprise. "Can you write that down for me?"

"Now don't make a big stink about it. Come see." She breezed out of the room, leaving us to either follow or stay.

"Interesting lady," I said.

"She's actually better than she used to be. I wonder if she even installed the system right. Let's go."

I was impressed with the shop. She had a number of helpful little gadgets. Eventually, though, the siblings discussed technical details and I wandered away bored.

As with most shops, the mixing room was separated from the factory to avoid having dust contaminate the glass. It was usually locked to keep ingredients and recipes a secret. Gressa's wasn't. She was either confident her workers wouldn't intrude, or careless. I poked around the room. Despite my curiosity, I wasn't going to pry open barrels or look in drawers. Standard mixing equipment and bowls were scattered on the counters. Powdered colors filled jars.

A sparkle from behind the scale drew my attention. Tiny diamonds covered the bottom of a tray. I moved closer and pinched a few between my fingertips, rolling them around. No flash. Not diamonds, but gypsum crystals.

27

"OPAL."

I jumped and turned around. Gressa stood in the doorway.

"Don't you know it's rude to snoop in other people's mixing rooms?" She studied me as if seeking a sign of guilt.

"Just looking for more innovations. Your factory is a wonder." I hoped appealing to her ego would throw her off the scent.

"It *is* the only factory of its kind." Sweeping in to hook her arm around mine, she drew me out. "Let me show you my new hopper bins for sand."

In a whirl, she finished the tour. Ulrick and I were dismissed without fanfare. We stood out on the street for a moment amazed by the speed of events.

"She didn't even offer us anything to drink," Ulrick said. "Not once did she ask any questions about you or me or our family. Sorry to put you through that. I don't think I'll visit her again." He looked at me. "Something's wrong. I can see it in your eyes."

How to word my discovery without sounding accusing?

Ulrick grabbed my arm with alarm. "It can't be that bad. Can it?"

I tried the straightforward method. "I found gypsum crystals in your sister's mixing room."

"Are you sure?"

"Yes."

"Damn." He pulled me along as he walked away from the factory. "Maybe it's not hers? No. She would never share her space."

"Maybe she viewed it as a challenge to create a glass resembling diamonds. Perhaps she doesn't know what they're being used for." I tried to apply logic.

"I'd agree with the challenge, but I'm not so sure about the ignorance." He remained quiet during the trip back to the guest quarters.

He stopped outside the building. A gamut of emotions washed over his face before he looked at me with a painful determination. "We need to know how involved she is."

"Should we tell Yelena and Master Jewelrose?"

"Not yet. Opal, she's family. Let me talk to her first."

"Sounds fair. What if she's part of the Councillor's sister's plot?"

"Then we see if she'll help collect evidence against the sister in exchange for a lighter sentence."

"Will she agree to that?"

"Only one way to find out."

"That's my father's line." I didn't know what else to say. Ulrick faced a difficult task.

"Smart man, your father."

Ulrick returned to Gressa's shop while I finished gathering supplies. I worried when the sun set and Ulrick hadn't returned. As time elapsed, my imagination created a series of horrible scenarios, from being robbed in the city to murdered by Gressa. I convinced myself Ulrick was in dire straits.

Mara's comments once again nagged me as I paced the room. *What do you regret?* Yes, Mara, I regret letting Ulrick go alone. I regret dragging him into trouble. I regret being distracted by Kade and taking Ulrick for granted. Are you happy now, Mara?

I couldn't wait any longer. Shoving my sais in my cloak, I grabbed a handful of bees, raced from my room and collided with a messenger. We landed in a heap. So much for the appearance of a heroic rescue. I helped him to his feet, apologizing.

"Isn't the first time and won't be the last," the messenger said. "I've been run over by much worse." The man peered around the hallway. "Can you tell me where Opal Cowan's rooms are?"

"I'm Opal."

The messenger looked pleased. "Good timing, then. I love it when that happens. Tracking people down is no fun." He handed me an envelope and was on his way.

I recognized Ulrick's tight writing. Taking the message back inside, I opened the note. He wrote his sister was very upset and wanted him to spend the night. He thought by morning she would agree to help Master Jewelrose and Yelena.

Relief melted my fears. I sagged on the couch and decided not to take Ulrick for granted anymore.

Ulrick woke me early the next morning. His hair was disheveled and his clothes were wrinkled. He frowned.

"What happened?" Alarmed, I sat up.

"She escaped. Fed me a sleeping draft and was gone by morning. I'm such an idiot. I fell for the whole baby sister routine." His voice held a rough edge as if he tried to suppress his emotions.

My brother, Ahir, used to do the same thing, pretending to be fine after getting hurt. "What do you want to do?"

"Master Jewelrose and Yelena will have to be informed. Can you tell them for me? I really don't want to repeat all this."

"Sure, I understand. I have a sister, too."

He brooded for a while, sitting on the edge of my bed.

"Was Gressa part of the plot?" I asked.

"What plot?" Ulrick seemed confused.

"With Councillor Moon's sister."

"Sorry. I'm still groggy." He ran a hand through his

hair. "Gressa told me she had bragged during a government party that her crystal glass could pass for diamonds, and the Councillor's sister challenged her to prove it. She did. The sister paid her for more fakes and when Gressa found out they were passing them off for real diamonds, she demanded more money. Typical."

An odd huskiness still tainted his voice. Perhaps it was a side effect of the sleeping draft or it could be because he had been tricked and betrayed by Gressa.

"Why did she run?"

"I don't know. Maybe to tip off the sister? Perhaps she supports her." He turned to me with a sudden intensity blazing in his eyes. "You know what? I don't care anymore. We solved who's making the fake diamonds, let the authorities deal with the whys. Besides, Gressa's self-absorbed behavior made me realize just how self-centered and mopey I've been acting. No more. I'm not going to wish my life away. I'm going to enjoy life. Consider me a new man."

He gazed at me as if seeing me for the first time. A slow smile spread. "With a beautiful girl by my side, I have better things to do than mope."

"Eating breakfast?"

He tugged my covers down.

"Packing your bags?"

He pushed me back onto the pillow.

"Saddling Moonlight?"

He stretched out beside me and ran a hand along my arm.

"Catching up on your sleep?"

His arm encircled my waist and he pressed his body against me.

Before I made another guess, his mouth sought mine. As we kissed, I turned off my logical mind, and stopped worrying about the lack of a spark between us. After all, a steady flame could get just as hot.

His deft fingers unbuttoned my shirt. A shiver brushed my skin as he pulled the fabric free. Ulrick sensed my desire and didn't hesitate. Instead of making him forget his troubles, he made me forget mine. Either way, I knew Mara would be happy.

Later in the day, I reported Gressa's involvement with the fake diamonds to Yelena and Master Jewelrose while Ulrick packed our bags. When we mounted our horses for the trip back to the Citadel, Leif handed me a message for my sister.

"Tell her I'd rather be home than traipsing around Moon lands, searching for more caves," he said. Then he grew serious. "Be careful."

We had discussed taking a couple of soldiers with us, but decided Ulrick and I could handle any attacks. Plus we would stick to the main roads and overnight at town inns instead of in travel shelters.

"And keep hold of those bees, they're handy in a fight," Leif said.

"You watch yourself, too, or Yelena might promote you to scout." I smiled at his mock horror.

We mounted our horses and headed out of town. Bright sunshine lit the landscape. The air felt crisp. Townspeople bustled about and I realized their sense of expectation was due to the upcoming half-moon festival. Each of the eleven clans held a festival to celebrate the middle of the cold season, which was thirteen days away. The Keep hosted a dance every year. For the first time in four years, I'd have a date.

Sitting on Moonlight, Ulrick scanned the crowded streets probably looking for any signs of trouble. My thoughts turned to when we had been ambushed by the Storm Thieves, but I decided not to dwell on the past.

We stopped for the night in a small town just over the western border of Moon lands. Renting a room at the Fireside Inn, we ate dinner in the cozy common room. A huge fire roared in a stone hearth.

"You've been quiet all day," I said to him.

"A lot has happened." He stirred his tea. "Did you have another nightmare last night?"

My newest dream, being trapped in ice. "Yes, but..." I waved it away. No sense rehashing it.

In a flicker of firelight, his eyes changed color. I blinked and they returned to normal. My imagination no doubt.

He covered my hand with his. "How bad are they?"

"I think one of the glass prisons is calling to me."

He nodded as if expecting this answer. "The one you found in the cave?"

"No," I said in surprise. "I haven't felt that one since I handed it to Yelena."

"Do you know where this new one is?"

"All I know is it's in the snow. An area that could include the northern ice sheet, northern Ixia, or on top of the mountains. Too big an area to search." Ixia and Sitia shared a mountain chain. Called the Soul Mountains in Ixia, they were connected to the Emerald Mountains, which stretched all the way south to the Daviian Plateau in Sitia.

"Your dreams get more specific the closer you get. We should travel north and see what happens. Once you find the prison, it may leave your dreams alone."

"Into Ixia? Without permission? You're crazy."

He stared at me a moment, then smiled. "You're right. Bad idea. A good idea is to increase the amount of sleeping potion Leif gave us. He told me it wouldn't hurt you to drink more."

We finished dinner and climbed the stairs to our room. The icy dreams returned. I caught flashes of buildings while the snow blew, but I couldn't move.

I woke feeling as if my body had frozen solid. Rubbing my hands over my arms, I tried to work out the stiffness. With slow movements, I managed to sit up without waking Ulrick, sleeping beside me. I didn't want to disturb him so I quietly changed into less-wrinkled pants, thinking about the fire downstairs and a cup of hot tea.

I wrote him a note so he wouldn't get upset, but when I laid it on my pillow, I paused. His sleep-tousled hair covered his eyes and he slept without a shirt. His chest and arms were muscular with only a few burn scars marring them.

Since his run-in with his sister he'd been more... More what? Affectionate? Bold? He had always hesitated before, waiting for me to initiate. Then again, I had shown him I wasn't afraid of his touch after he returned from his sister's. Heat flushed my skin, remembering that morning and the hours we had spent entwined together.

Leaning over, I gently brushed the hair from his eyes. In a blur of motion, he seized my wrist.

"Where are you going?" Ulrick demanded.

Surprised by his quickness, I gaped at him.

"I didn't mean to wake you," I said. "Even with taking a double dose, Leif's sleeping potion isn't working. It tastes like a rusty nail. Did you tell Leif what we needed it for?"

"Not specifically. Just to help you sleep."

"I can't sleep and I'm freezing. I'm going to fetch a cup of tea."

With a playful smile, he yanked me down next to him. "You don't need one. I'll warm you up."

Definitely more bold.

We returned to the Citadel without incident. It had taken us five days instead of four. Without Leif, neither one of us wanted to brave the plains to cut our trip by a day. Besides, we enjoyed the time together. Ulrick was full of questions, and I marveled at his changed attitude. I should thank his sister for making him realize how withdrawn he had become since discovering his limited magical abilities.

Mara greeted our arrival with mixed emotions. Glad to see us and disappointed Leif hadn't also returned. She turned all dreamy after reading his note.

Later that day, Mara and I worked in the shop. My hands itched for a punty iron with a slug of molten glass. When we had finished, she pulled me aside. "You took my advice, didn't you?"

"I'm not admitting to it unless you agree *not* to gloat about it."

"Not gloat? No way." She smirked. "I can tell by your expression anyway. You're blushing."

"Am not."

"Are, too."

"Am..." I stopped. It was a no-win argument. "We're *supposed* to be taking inventory so I can order more supplies for the shop."

She pouted for only a second before helping me. A few students arrived and I was glad to see Piecov. He showed me his new pieces and I made appreciative noises over them. "Look how much you improved."

"But I have a long way to go," Piecov said.

As he talked about his plans for his next project, I could see the avid gleam in his eyes. He was hooked.

Unfortunately, Ulrick had lost his passion for glass, and avoided the shop. When I asked him about it the next morning, he mentioned his sister.

"She's talented, but look what she has done. My mother put so much pressure on all of us to do great things with glass, since I've been away I realized there are other things in life. I need a break. Besides—" he pulled me into a tight embrace "—I'm enjoying being the fetch boy."

I wiggled away. "I think you've been enjoying it too much. Remember there are other things in life."

Ulrick sobered. "I know. In time."

Time. Enough time had passed and yet Pazia hadn't regained her magical powers. All she could do was see the glow in my glass, but nothing else. We had been back at the Citadel for a couple of days and she finally recovered enough energy to be discharged from the infirmary.

I arrived in her room to help her carry all the items she had collected during her stay. She wasn't happy to see me, but I was determined.

"I can't wait to get out of here," she said. "Then I won't have to see Healer Hayes or you again."

"Don't count on it."

The table beside her bed was heaped with books, and a variety of warped glass vases lined a shelf.

Pazia stopped near me. "I have many admirers who help at your shop. Too bad they can't make anything decent."

I ignored her harsh tone, and pulled the vases down, carefully wrapping them in towels. "There is a special pride in first efforts."

Pazia stared at me in pain. "I want to…" She wrapped her arms around her body. "I need something…" Frustration choked off her words.

I opened my mouth to apologize again, but she shot me a warning look. Instead, I packed the vases into a carrying basket. My thoughts remained on her as I tried to figure out what she needed.

"Can you help at the glass shop?" I kept my voice casual. "You have an artistic flair." I pointed to her ring. The ruby and diamond starburst design was created by her. "And we might still discover a way to reverse what I did and…" I avoided mentioning her magic.

She bustled about the room, piling books into another basket. We worked for a while in silence.

"Have you ever decorated glass with jewels?" Pazia asked as she finished folding her clothes. "I can imagine a tall and skinny white vase with a ring of sapphires around the middle. You know, where it narrows before flaring out?" She demonstrated with her hands.

It was her way of accepting the invitation. "Sounds exquisite, but very expensive."

She shrugged. "My father's friends would snap them up. People love to display jewels and you can only wear so many rings and necklaces."

A handful of students arrived to help carry the baskets to her room in the apprentice wing. I recognized Piecov and a few others from the glass shop. They fawned and fretted over her. She basked in their attention.

They trooped out with Pazia in the lead, leaving me behind. Healer Hayes poked his head into the room.

"That was fast," he said.

"I think she was anxious to go."

"An understatement." He moved back, but I called his name. "Yes?" He hovered in the doorway.

"I'm…" I suddenly felt silly. "I've been having…nightmares. Bad ones and the potion Leif gave me isn't working. Do you…?"

Stepping into the room, he said, "I'm not surprised Leif's potion isn't working. Those jungle recipes are effective, but lose their potency fast." He pressed his cool hands on my forehead.

"My dear child, you're near exhaustion. I'll get you a sleeping draft. Unless you want me to admit you to the infirmary?"

"Admit me? I don't feel that bad."

"You're not. It's just if you're here, you won't be bothered by teachers or friends and can rest."

I suppressed a smile. Ulrick would probably demand to stay in the infirmary with me. "I only need a couple of peaceful nights."

Nights without the snowy images plaguing my sleep. The dreams had become more specific, but I hadn't told anyone. I dreamed of wooden buildings leaning together as if bracing against a strong wind. A sign hung above a doorway, the letters burned into the splintered wood, dancing in my mind. I struggled to read them. Icefaren Station. Nearby, a deep pit gaped.

A Warper called to me from a vast northern distance. Imprisoned in glass on the Ixian ice sheet, he pleaded and promised. But I couldn't find him. He could be anywhere on the ice sheet. It covered miles and miles of territory. And if the cold season's blizzards didn't kill me, the snow cats would.

Healer Hayes returned with a vial full of liquid. "Two swallows before bed. If it doesn't work, take three, but no more."

Before bed that evening, I braced myself and swigged the potion.

Ulrick studied me. "How bad?"

"Tastes like sweet lemons. Much better than Leif's. His potion must have spoiled." I gulped another mouthful.

He didn't comment. Soon a heaviness flowed through my limbs as if my blood thickened inside my veins. The night was free of horrors and I woke feeling refreshed.

"That Stormdancer is here," Ulrick said when he entered the glass shop.

His scowl was back and I realized I hadn't missed it at all.

"He's waiting in Zitora's office and wants to talk to you."

"Are you coming?" I asked.

"I'm not invited."

The reason for the scowl, or so I thought until he said, "Just don't run off with him."

"Ulrick, don't be silly. Why would I do that?"

"He's a Stormdancer. He's powerful."

"He's my friend and too busy tracking down the men who killed Indra and Nodin. An important effort that we should support." Another thing I hadn't missed, any signs of Sir, Tricky or Devlen.

I hurried to Zitora's office. It had been a week since I'd seen Kade and I promised myself I would stick to business and remain distant. Knocking on her door, I pushed it open.

"...can't find the Councillor's sister or Gressa and rumors are circulating about an army forming in the foothills of the Emerald Mountains," Kade said.

He perched in a chair in front of Zitora's desk, and, despite the promise to myself, I felt a tug deep down. His lean build, wind-tossed hair and gold-flecked eyes melted my resolve.

Zitora gestured for me to come in. "Moon Clan troubles. The Sitian Council is still debating whether to intervene. Coups are part of life, and if the Moon citizens want a new Councillor and the current one won't step down we shouldn't interfere in the takeover. But if she's using illegal means and methods, then we should. Problem is, we have no proof." She drummed her knuckles on her desk. "Thanks for the update, Kade. Did you have any luck with the suppliers?"

"No. One of the reasons I stopped here, I need a list of sand merchants for the western and southern clans from Opal."

"Of course." I wrote down the names and locations of

the suppliers I knew. "There may be more, you'll want to ask the merchants themselves. And I received a message from my father. No one has ordered that particular combination of sand."

Kade examined the list.

"There is another matter I need to talk to you about," I said. When he glanced up, the tug jerked. The streaks of gold and red in his hair shone in the sunlight. A desire to touch him flared to life. So distracted by the feeling, I missed his question, but sensed the gist of it. "It's a private matter."

He followed me from the office and through the campus to my rooms. The orb's joyful song pierced the silence, yet Kade seemed in no hurry to broach the subject.

"Where's your watchdog?" he asked, looking around the room.

"At the glass shop, helping Mara."

"Impressive. He's learned to trust you."

But he shouldn't. The unexpected thought popped in my head.

I retrieved the orb from under my bed before I could say anything I would regret. Unwrapped, the orb's song vibrated through the room as the energy tingled up my arms.

"I'm not done searching for Varun," he said when I carried it out.

"Have you talked with Yelena since our expedition to the cave?"

"No. I talked with Master Jewelrose before coming here. Why?" His demeanor seemed guarded as if I was going to accuse him of a misdeed.

I couldn't formulate a way to soften the information, so I didn't. "Kaya's soul is trapped inside the orb."

"How do you...oh, the Soulfinder." He sank down onto the couch. A brief struggle of emotions creased his brow. "I don't possess the power to capture souls. Are you sure?"

"Positive." Hard to forget having a conversation with Kaya and Yelena inside the orb. "Her essence must have been in the storm long enough for you to harvest it." I stepped closer to him, holding the orb out. "*You* need to free her so she can find peace in the sky."

When he touched the orb, pure fire raced along my skin, sucking the breath from me. My thoughts and emotions mixed with his and Kaya's as the storm's energy sizzled and popped. Through them I could harness the energy and redirect it, controlling the wind and water and lightning. I felt Kade's torment and Kaya's longing.

The sensation stopped with such abruptness, I fell to my hands and knees as tremors ran rampant through my body. I gasped for breath.

Once I regained my composure I sat on the floor and looked at Kade. The orb rested in his lap with his head bowed over it.

He didn't move. "I can't. She's all I have left."

"What about Raiden and the other Stormdancers?"

No answer.

"Friends?"

"Not the same. We had a special bond. You wouldn't understand."

Frustration boiled. "You're as thick as a fog bank. I *do* understand. Tula wasn't my twin, but we did everything together, shared everything. I fought her demons with her after she had been attacked by Ferde. And I was so mad at her for dying when I needed her the most. Two weeks I suffered for her and she didn't wait for me. I returned and there was no one I could talk to, confide in, cry with." The words flew from my mouth. Unexpected. Unintentional. But there all the same.

Kade stared at me as if I had grown antennae. And perhaps I had. I felt like a different person.

"Then you understand why I don't want to get close to another again. What happens when she dies, too? I couldn't bear it."

"Then you miss out on life."

"What do you mean?"

"You'll be alone, trusting no one because of fear. I know. I have four years of experience of pushing people away, missing out on life. Four years spent by myself, living in my glass cage. Four years of self-doubt, worries, fears."

"And now?" he asked. His voice rough with emotion.

"I still have my fears, doubts and worries, but I also have Mara, Leif, Zitora and Ulrick."

"The watchdog?"

"No. A person to confide in and share with. A person

willing to take a risk and *be with me* despite my track record."

"And if he dies?"

"I'll have Mara, Leif and Zitora."

"So the more people you invite in, the easier it is to lose one?"

"No. I'll still feel as if my heart is being torn into strips, but I'll have support and love to hold the fragments together until they heal."

"Then you're braver than I am." Kade stood. He dropped the orb into my lap. "Keep it safe. Please."

I stared at the swirling colors on the surface of the orb. Muted, sad colors. No song. The door clicked shut. Kade was gone.

Routine. Routine felt safe and warm. Routine was waking in the morning next to Ulrick and spending a day in the glass shop with my sister. Routine was riding Quartz through figure eights and jumping her over fences. Routine was discussing politics with Zitora and making plans for the midseason festival. Routine was weapons training and letting Pazia take her frustrations out on me.

Just when I settled into a routine, Ulrick informed me about another mission.

"Illegal diamonds were discovered hidden in a merchant's wagon. He was stopped and searched after he crossed the border from Ixia," he said.

We were in the Keep's dining hall, decorating for the

midseason dance. Each of the glass helpers had made a centerpiece for the tables. Pazia's was the best, but I would never say so out loud. Ulrick refused to make one, but he seemed content to assist the others.

"Zitora wants us to go to Mica, where you can test the diamonds to see if they're the same as Mr. Lune's." Ulrick positioned a vase with a sunflower made of pale yellow glass.

"Now?" I had been anticipating the dance for the last week. Leif had even returned from the Moon lands just to attend.

Ulrick's expression was hard to read. He acted as if the trip was bad news. "We'll leave tomorrow morning. Tonight is for dancing and fun only. No business talk. Promise?"

"That's an easy promise to make."

It was an easy promise to keep. Everyone dressed in their finest clothes. I wore a simple and elegant gown made with purple silk. Fisk had found the material on sale, and introduced me to a little-known dressmaker who had designed the formfitting gown for me.

Ulrick's openmouthed gape said it all.

The dining hall had been transformed into a ballroom. The music enticed us onto the dance floor. The divine smell of roasting meat and sweet pastries pulled us to the buffet table. Mara and Leif looked splendid together. Ulrick charmed. Conversation remained on light and frothy topics. A perfect evening.

* * *

I wrapped the memories of the evening around myself
as I lugged my saddlebags through the cold air and to the
stable the next morning. Humming a tune from the dance,
I saddled Quartz and helped Ulrick with Moonlight.

The trip to Mica would take three days. We traveled
on main roads and stayed overnight at inns. Late on the
second night, I woke feeling uneasy. I stared into the
darkness and listened for a moment. Nothing. A wedge
of light reflected off the window and I slid out of bed to
investigate the source. It emanated from my saddlebags
beneath the flap.

Apprehension churned as I moved the flap. Kaya's
orb glowed. I brushed the orb with my fingertips. An
intense wave of energy shot through my hand. My sight
blurred as Kaya's voice filled my head.

Kade's in trouble, she said with urgency.

A vision of Sir, Tal and Tricky wrestling with the
Stormdancer formed in my mind. Snow-laced wind
swirled around the fighters. They wore heavy cloaks. I
watched him, powerless to help. Debris flew around the
men and for a moment it appeared as if Kade had the
upper hand.

Tricky reached behind a wagon and threw a net over
Kade. The scene disappeared in an instant.

What happened? I asked Kaya.

The net...has a null shield intertwined with the ropes.

A null shield blocks magic. The Sandseeds used it and
Leif could create one, but I've never heard of it being

tied into a net. It didn't matter how. All I cared about was Kade. Would they kill him?

Kaya interrupted my growing panic. *Help him,* she said.

How?

You're smart, Opal. You'll figure it out.

Where is he?

Northern Ixia. Kaya severed our connection.

Urgency grew in my heart. I *had* to rescue him. Because if I didn't help him then... What? This time I didn't shy away from the answer. If I didn't find him, I would regret it for the rest of my life. There, I admitted it to myself, but I knew not to hold any romantic notions of us riding off into the sunset.

I shook Ulrick awake. He sat up in alarm, grabbing his sword. "What happened?"

"Kade's in trouble. We have to help him."

Annoyed, he asked, "How do you know? Another dream?"

"No. From Kade's orb. I told you I was keeping it safe."

"But you didn't tell me you were bringing it along."

"Doesn't matter. Kade's in trouble."

"Send a message to his clan, I'm sure they can send another dancer."

"No time. We're in the Krystal lands and can interview sand suppliers. He must have gotten a lead on where Sir and Tal are—"

"Opal, we're not helping him." Ulrick stood. "He's a grown man and a Stormdancer. He can take care of himself. We're expected in Mica."

"You don't have to come, but I'm going to try and find out where he is. I can't just send a message."

"Are you serious?"

"Yes."

"You don't want to be with me anymore?" His tone was flat and curious.

"That's not it. I enjoy being with you, it's just he's in trouble."

"Enjoy? How about love, Opal? Do you love me?"

"This has nothing to do with us. You don't understand. I won't let them hurt him."

Ulrick laughed. Not the reaction I expected.

"What a useless statement, 'I won't let them hurt him.' They'll do whatever they please to him whether you let them or not. Frankly, I hope they kill him."

My outrage froze on my lips. This was all wrong. When he lit the lantern, I stared at his shadow. It matched.

"You have no clue, but you're really not in a position to rescue anybody, including yourself." He stepped toward me.

His eyes blazed with blue fire.

"Now do you understand?"

"No." The truth. I didn't understand. His shadow matched his body. He lived in the Keep for weeks. Led me around the dance floor. Shared my bed.

"You will. Because you're my little glass finder, who's going to help me find my imprisoned mentor so I can complete the Kirakawa ritual."

Logic shattered into fragments. My mind reduced to admiring the pretty pieces floating around my head. No matter how hard I tried, I couldn't put them together into a reasonable picture.

"Do you submit?"

Realization crushed my confusion. Familiar words from the wrong face. Blue-eyed Devlen had disguised himself as Ulrick.

28

"HOW...WHAT...WHY..." I stared at Ulrick—Devlen. His eye color returned to the vibrant green of Ulrick's. He looked the same. I touched his arm—the one not holding the sword. It felt the same. He even smelled the same.

Laughing at my confusion, he said, "Blood magic with a twist."

"But you don't have any tattoos." The Daviian Warpers had gained their power by using blood magic and the Kirakawa ritual. By injecting the blood of their victims into their skin, they increased their magical power. As a Warper ascended through the levels of the ritual, he would be able to trap the victim's soul and inject it into himself. At that point, he would have enough power to equal a Master Magician.

However, Yelena stopped the Warpers, pulling the trapped souls from them and reducing their powers. The Warpers who knew the final steps of the Kirakawa ritual were imprisoned in glass to keep them from communicating with anyone else.

"But all the Warpers were caught and executed by the Council." My mind still couldn't accept his claims.

"Not *all* the Warpers died. I hid and waited, biding my time. I learned how to use blood magic. Learned it so well, I was able to exchange my blood with another and switch souls." Devlen pointed to his…Ulrick's body. "For such a complete exchange there is no magic to detect. I can live in the Keep. And as long as I avoid the Soulfinder, I don't need to worry."

I had to close my eyes to understand. Devlen's soul was in Ulrick's body and vice versa. "Where is Ulrick?"

"He is a…guest of mine. Safe and sound. For now."

I opened my eyes. For now! Fury replaced numbed shock and I reached for his neck, intent on strangling him. But he grabbed my wrists and yanked me close.

"Now, now. You weren't this feisty before."

Before? I had fought him with my sais in the alley, and protected Zitora from him during the ambush with Sir.

He peered at me. "Maybe this will remind you." He adjusted his grip on my right wrist, and pressed his finger into the soft part of my forearm.

Unbearable pain shot up my arm and into my head. He released me and the agony ceased.

I staggered, panting in panic. This would be a good time to faint. To hide in the black comfort of unconsciousness. To not have to deal with or think about any of this. But he was an expert on bringing me to the edge of oblivion then yanking me back. Knew exactly how much I could take, what I would do to make him stop.

"Remember me now?"

The man who had come to the tent when Alea had captured me. The one who guaranteed I would obey Alea and jab Yelena with the Curare. He had worn a mask and dark glasses then, and now he wore Ulrick's face, but there was no denying his touch.

My sais rested beside the bed. Too far.

I dived for his sword. I wanted to kill him or myself. At this point it didn't matter. My hand closed on the handle, but he was quick. His hands around my neck, thumbs digging into my collarbone. My muscles turned to liquid. The sword clattered to the floor. The world faded and this time he let me slide into the blackness.

I woke, but resisted opening my eyes. The dreams of snow and ice preferable to the reality on the other side of my eyelids. If I kept my thoughts rooted in my dreamworld, could I ignore my situation? Only for a while.

The physical world intruded with muscle cramps along my arms and legs. Aches radiated up my back and soreness pulsed from where my body rested on the hard surface. All from being in one position for too long.

I cracked an eye open, peeking out. A wall built from wood loomed inches from my nose. Growing braver, I scanned my surroundings. I lay on my right side on the floor of an empty room. It was about four feet wide by six feet long. One closed door. Four metal clasps attached to the wall—two high and two low.

Staring at the clasps, I tried not to imagine what they were for, but as I moved to relieve the cramps in my arms, an unwelcome image came to mind. My wrists were hooked together behind my back, but my legs were free. The metal cuffs around my ankles sported bright silver clips which would be easy to attach to the clasps on the wall.

Don't panic. Don't panic. I repeated the phrase, but my heart had its own agenda, slamming in my chest as if I ran for my life. I struggled into a sitting position and tried to organize my thoughts, examine the situation.

I should check the door. It might be unlocked, but I might make noise. I didn't want *him* to know I was awake. Not yet. I needed time to sort things out.

Pushing through the confusion and my fear on learning about Ulrick's capture, I concentrated on Devlen's words. He needed my help, called me his glass finder and mentioned his mentor. A Warper in hiding, he wanted to complete the Kirakawa ritual and the only people who knew the final steps were imprisoned in my glass.

Since I confided everything to him, he knew the glass called to me. I wondered when Devlen switched souls with Ulrick. Had there been a change in Ulrick's behavior? I thought back. It was so obvious I felt a fool for not questioning his actions. Devlen must have captured him the night he had confronted his sister,

Gressa. Ulrick had been alone. And since he had been my constant companion, Devlen had targeted him. I hadn't even warned Ulrick about Devlen because I didn't want to hear another lecture about being careful.

Horror and guilt swelled, but I squashed the emotions. Devlen would have found another person to switch souls with. Besides, it had happened, there was nothing I could do to change the past.

Right now I needed to focus on the present. I had two goals. Rescue Kade and Ulrick without helping Devlen. The thought of going against Devlen turned my resolve to mush. And how could I help anyone when I was so easily fooled? His voice had sounded different, he had been bolder, and he'd refused to work with glass. All glaring signs, and I had rationalized each one away.

My emotions once again threatened to overwhelm me. I needed an image to hold to help me concentrate. I needed glass. So I imagined my heart encased in glass. Strong, unbreakable glass to lock away the doubts, worries, fears and to protect myself from further damage. The image helped cool my molten emotions and hardened my determination.

I staggered to my feet and tried the door. Locked.

Of course, my resolve threatened to crack as soon as the lock snapped and the door swung open. Glass heart, glass heart, I repeated to myself. It still jolted me to see a calculating coldness in Ulrick's eyes. The lips that had smiled at me and kissed me... No—glass heart. Devlen, not Ulrick stood in front of me.

"Figured it out yet?"

"Some. You want me to find your mentor's prison and release him so you can finish the Kirakawa ritual."

"You're smarter than you were five years ago."

"I've learned a lot."

"So have I." He stepped into the room.

Instinct made me move back. Glass heart, I thought. I peered past his shoulder and into a living room. "Where are we?"

"In a cabin deep in the woods. No one around for miles so you can scream all you want." His flat tone lacked emotion.

My hands hit the wall, but I didn't remember moving away. "Krystal lands?"

Devlen placed his hands on my shoulders. I cringed, but stayed still.

"Now you know what I want. The question remains. Are you going to help me?"

I kneed him in the groin. He hunched forward and I rammed my knee into his nose. But as he fell, he kept hold of me. His hands slid to my waist and he pressed his thumbs into my hip bones.

The pain sucked my breath from my lungs and everything from the waist down numbed. Seconds, minutes, years passed before he relaxed his grip. He had regained his breath. Blood dripped from his nose.

"I take that as a no." Devlen reached for my collarbone.

My situation hadn't improved. Not surprising, but I could hope. When I woke for the second time in my room, I was attached to the wall. Once I managed to get my weight on my feet—rather difficult with ankles hooked to the wall clasps, I glanced up. My wrists sported the same metal cuffs. I tugged both arms and legs to no avail. The clasps had been securely fastened to the wood.

I was completely vulnerable. Memories from being in this same spread-eagle position boiled up from the depths. Then I had been staked to the ground. The number and location of all the pain spots on my body scrolled through my mind. What had he called them...? Pressure points. He had also used metal C-shaped clamps wide enough to fit over various parts of my body, leaving them there so his hands wouldn't tire.

Panic simmered. I wanted him to stop even before he started. But I couldn't agree to help him. Or could I? He knew my dreams led to the glass prisons. I've been dreaming about snow and ice. Kaya said Kade was in northern Ixia. If I told Devlen the prison was near Icefaren Station, we would go there. He would have to figure out how to cross the border and travel through Ixia without being caught. During that time, I might get an opportunity to escape, or send a message to Zitora or anyone at this point. If not, when we reached northern Ixia, I could trick Devlen into searching for Kade instead of the prison.

A nasty little worry that Kade might already be dead tried to speak up. I slapped it down and continued plotting. Once I found and freed Kade, we could search for Ulrick.

There were so many ifs and unknowns, but I didn't have any other options and now I had a plan to focus on. I rolled my shoulders, easing the pain. The worst part would be convincing Devlen I had given in. He would be suspicious if I agreed too soon. I had to endure his torture longer than before. But this time, I had a goal in mind. I had a measure of control. A tiny one, but it was enough.

When the door swung wide, I centered my thoughts on my goals. He held two clamps. Save Kade. Save Ulrick. The words echoed in my mind.

"Will you help me?" he asked.

Save Kade. "No." Save Ulrick.

His mouth pressed into a grim line as if the prospect of torturing me was unappealing. "I need to hurry things along this time." He waved both clamps in front of me. "Something new for you. Two." He ran his hand along my right leg. "Let's see, where was that spot you particularly hated."

My leg jerked when his finger found the location on my upper thigh. He positioned the clamp and twisted the screw. Every muscle in my body spasmed, but there was no preparing for the waves of burning pain that would not stop. I writhed and bucked, but no position eased the torment.

Distantly, he mentioned the second, and as he pushed against me with his body an additional center of stabbing pain exploded from my left shoulder. My stomach heaved, trying to expel the agony. Too much, I couldn't draw breath and I hovered at the edge of passing out.

"Oops." He fiddled with one of the clamps.

I sucked in great gasps of air, quite conscious. He left. Save Kade, I thought as each wave of agony slammed through my body. Save Ulrick. Save Kade. But eventually the words just buzzed in a haze of unrelenting pain. I rocked and moaned, wishing for it to stop.

When it did stop, I sagged in my restraints. Joy was in the relief. And gratitude.

Devlen nodded. "Two gets the job done faster. Before you lasted three days." He frowned. "I wasn't planning to do this. If you had kept taking Leif's potion, I'd still be trying to romance the location from you."

I shoved the romance comment into my glass heart and focused on the details. "Leif's potion?"

"It wasn't Leif's. It was more blood magic. I mixed my mentor's blood with a sleeping potion to help your dreams become more specific as to where his prison is located. It was working until you switched potions. Then I had to go to Plan B."

Did I even want to know? Better to keep him talking than the alternative. "Plan B?"

"Lure you away from the Keep and…" He waved a hand at me.

"So the diamond merchant they stopped at the border?"

"I made it up."

"But Zitora—"

"Believes you're going to help that Stormdancer with his sand search. Why do you think I arranged everything? And wouldn't let you mention business at the dance?"

"Because I'm an idiot."

"No. You're not an idiot at all. I've been watching you since we had the fight in Thunder Valley, waiting for you to trust someone other than Master Cowan and that Stormdancer. Both too powerful for me to trick. Ulrick, however, was easy to convince. He wanted magical power more than he wanted you. I made him an offer he couldn't refuse. He has taken the first step to becoming a Warper."

"I don't believe you."

"Or is it you don't *want* to believe me? How much did you care for Ulrick *before* I came along?" He stroked my face.

Jerking back from his touch, I banged my head.

"Ulrick's thoughts and emotions were easy to read. Frustrated, disappointed, craving more from you, but feeling he received more warmth from a glass statue. His memories showed me everything. A couple of kisses, was it? All you gave him before cooling in his arms. Not nearly enough from you for him to refuse my offer." He leaned into me. "You certainly gave me *much more* than a kiss."

I tried to bite him, but he stayed just out of reach. He lied about Ulrick. I held on to that thought, because to think he told the truth would make me sick.

"I wouldn't have given you anything, if I'd known it was you," I said.

"If it makes you feel better, you can lie to yourself, but we both know the truth. Ulrick would have waited for you like a dog ordered to stay. *I'm* the one who showed initiative. Such a shame you had to be so stubborn about that Stormdancer. I was enjoying myself, playing the boyfriend." He leered.

I stifled my desire to scream at him, preferring to keep him talking. "How did you get to Ulrick?"

"I trailed him back to his sister's factory and listened to their little family squabble. She was proud her work passed for diamonds and supports Councillor Moon's sister. He tried to convince her to switch sides and join Master Jewelrose and Yelena. She hit him on the head with a glass plate and ran." Devlen stared into the past. "He was dazed and I led him to a small inn just outside of town, pretending to take him to a healer." He rubbed a spot on his temple. "I did heal the gash on his forehead. Then I showed him what he could do with blood magic. He was hooked."

I shook my head. "I still don't believe you."

He shrugged. "You asked." His mouth twisted as if he tasted something bad. "Are you going to help me find my mentor? I would like to put all this unpleasantness behind us."

"No." It was easy to say. My muscles pulsed with a desire to pound him into a bloody pulp.

He nodded, not surprised by my answer, and positioned the clamps in two new spots, twisting them tight. I lost track of time, of my sanity and my reasons for living.

After the third session, I didn't need to pretend to give in. At that point I would have done anything. I clung to the fact that it wasn't a complete submission, because I had planned to tell him all along.

"Icefaren Station." The words puffed out between my cracked and bleeding lips. My raw throat burned and I longed for a drink. "In Ixia on the ice sheet, but I don't know where."

"How interesting. I know where it is. Before the Commander's takeover, Ixia was divided into provinces. Icefaren province was renamed Military District 1." His forehead creased as he considered. "I knew we'd have to go into Ixia eventually. Good thing I have a few contacts in the area. Hang out here for a while, I need to fetch some supplies." He shut and locked the door.

Too exhausted to care, I leaned against the wall. Anything was better than that pain. Anything.

I even fell asleep. Cold air whipped through my clothes, freezing the sweat on my skin. Kade was trapped in a block of ice and I couldn't get to him. My legs refused to move. I drowned in a snowdrift.

The door banged open, waking me.

Devlen threw a bundle onto the floor and set down a bucket of water and soap. "Clean up and change your clothes." He unhooked my wrists from the wall. "No trouble. You will do *exactly* what I tell you. Any deviations and you'll be punished. I'm bringing a gag and my clamps. Understand?"

I nodded.

"I'm leaving your cuffs on. They fit together. See?" He demonstrated, securing and freeing my wrists.

When he left, I removed my soiled and stained clothes. There was no dignity with pain. I tossed the ruined garments. They landed with a muted clunk.

A bubble of hope pushed up my throat as I dug through my clothes. I had learned my lesson with the robbers and hid weapons on my person. Ulrick...Devlen knew about it and probably searched me. But I found a little nugget of glass inside my pants. Even though it was a spider, it was the most precious item. I didn't know how I would use it or when. What mattered was I had it.

I washed the grime from my body and dressed in the clean clothes. The black pants sagged around my waist. I used the sash to tighten them, hiding my spider in the folds of the material. Down the long sleeves of the white tunic was a column of black diamond shapes connected end to end. A row of three black diamonds decorated the breast pocket. I wore an Ixian uniform.

The door was unlocked. I joined Devlen in the other room. He stood with my saddlebags and my sais at his feet. Wearing another black and white Ixian uniform, he examined the empty orb.

"Planning to steal magic?" he asked.

"Yes. Give it to me." I held out a hand.

"Okay. Catch." He flung the empty sphere across the room.

It shattered against the wall. The sound from the impact cut through me.

454 Maria V. Snyder

"Now, what should I do with this one?" Devlen removed Kade's orb. Iridescent colors swirled in agitation under his touch.

"Smash it," I said. The storm's trapped energy would kill us both.

"Nice try, but I'm not stupid." He packed it into a large backpack. Another pack rested on the floor next to it. "I'll sell it. I know a group of Krystal Clan members who are looking for full orbs."

"Sir's gang?" When he nodded, I asked, "Why were you with them? What's their goal?"

"Don't know. Don't care. I was just the hired help. They needed a swordsman for a job and I needed money. Hiding out from the Sitian authorities is expensive. If I had known our target was a Master Magician, I wouldn't have taken the job, but it led me to you so it worked out nicely. Don't you think?"

"No. I would rather you were still locked up in the Thunder Valley jail."

"Watch it. Your attitude is not helpful. Do you need a reminder in how to be helpful?"

"No."

"Good. I think we'll leave the rest of your stuff here." He closed my bags and pushed them along with my sais into a corner of the room. "Don't want any of your little creatures to get in my way."

Devlen handed me the smaller backpack, a cloak and a sheet of parchment. Three white diamonds decorated the black cloak.

"Just in case you're seen and approached by the Ixians. You'll tell them you're a kitchen attendant returning home from visiting relatives in MD-7. You live in MD-1, General Kitvivan is the general in charge and the uniform colors for MD-1 are black and white. If you're asked for papers, you are to give them that sheet without question."

Permission to visit MD-7 was printed on the parchment. My first name was written in the bearer's space. At least I didn't have to remember a fake name.

"Don't lose that paper. It cost a small fortune. Also don't try to alert any Ixians about your situation. I will confess, telling them you're a magician. And you know what they do to magicians in Ixia."

Killed on sight. Depending on my circumstances, I might give myself up. Better than the alternative. I shuddered and Devlen seemed satisfied with my reaction.

"Horses?" I asked, wondering if Quartz was nearby.

"I stabled them. Only high-ranking officers travel with horses in Ixia. We'll go on foot."

"How do you plan to cross the border?"

"The Daviians set up a number of smuggling routes. Valek and the Ixian border patrol have discovered a few, but there is always a way through." Strapping his sword around his waist, he shouldered a short cape and the large backpack. "Come on. We're wasting time."

I glanced at my sais four feet away. Could I reach them before he grabbed me? Devlen noticed my hesitation and hooked his arm in mine.

"Helpful, remember." He dug his fingers into my wrist.

Spikes of pain shot up to my elbow. He kept the pressure until we were well away from the cabin. With his hand still around my arm, we walked through the woods, heading north.

Doubts about my tenuous plan nagged at me. My best chance to escape would be while in Sitia. One little spider wouldn't save me. What if Kade was already dead? Muted by Devlen's backpack, Kaya's orb hummed an urgent tone. I guessed if Kade died, the tune would change.

Each step closer to Ixia brought more worries to my mind. By the evening, I had convinced myself it would be best to escape and return to the Keep to recruit help for Kade. Interesting how the memory of pain fades with time.

Unfortunately, he gave me no opportunity. As soon as we stopped, he hooked my wrists behind a tree trunk while he set up camp in a tight clearing. He released me only to eat then forced me to take a swig of his blood potion before securing me again. Knowing the ingredients made me gag, I slept sitting down, leaning my head against the trunk.

Cold nightmares invaded my dreams.

The next day we met up with a caravan of merchants with five wagons. One wagon was filled with sand, another with lime, but I couldn't see what was beneath the canvas tarps of the other three. They had been expecting us.

One of the merchants, a heavyset man with thick eyebrows, approached Devlen. "Is this the cargo?"

"Yes."

The merchant eyed the cuffs on my wrists. "An unusual request. We're used to smuggling goods in and Ixians out. If she makes a sound—"

"She won't."

Hitching his pants over his ample stomach, the man chewed on his lip. "Gonna cost you extra."

"How much?"

"Three golds, but I'll give you a discount if me and my boys can play, too." He gestured to the four men waiting by the horses.

Devlen turned to me. "Care to play with the gentlemen?"

Breathing became difficult as I guessed they weren't referring to a game of tag. "No, thank you." My voice quavered just a bit.

"How about two golds and, if she causes any trouble at any time, you can play for one night?" Devlen offered.

"Deal. Load her up." The merchant returned to his caravan.

Devlen led me to the middle wagon. "Now you have extra incentive to behave."

A small rectangular hole was at the bottom of the mound of white sand. There was a hinged door attached and I realized the sand covered a long box.

Devlen grabbed my arms and secured my wrists behind me.

"What—"

He shoved a hard rubber bar between my teeth and pulled the straps behind my head.

"It's too important to trust you when we cross into Ixia. I guess you could pound with your feet, but the sand should muffle it. However, our merchant friend would feel the vibrations and get his night of fun." He stepped back. "Put her in."

Two of the boys picked me up and shoved me feet first into the hole under the sand. A thud and a few clicks followed. It was dark, coffin-like and I puffed in alarm, convinced the sand or the gag would smother me.

My panic increased with the drumming sound of sand being poured to cover the box's door. After a few terrifying moments, my eyes adjusted to the darkness. I rolled to my side to take my weight off my arms. Small holes had been drilled into the floor of the box, allowing light and air to seep in.

The wagon lurched forward. Through my peepholes, the ground slid past and my hope of escaping drained drop by drop with each passing mile.

Voices woke me from a light doze. The wagons had stopped and the shuffling sounds of footsteps reached me. I debated taking the risk and making noise, but the image of being given to five men for the night caused me to hesitate too long. The wagon moved. The opportunity gone. Coward.

Ixia passed under my wagon, but I didn't see much of

it. Taken out of my box only at night to eat, I caught a few glimpses of pine trees and frozen farmland. The ground was rock hard and after a few days of travel, muddy snow rolled under the wagon.

The men complained of the weather and stared at me with hungry eyes. After another three days, the air became too cold for the merchants to sleep outside at night. They stopped at a travel shelter. We sat by the fire, finishing our dinner.

"She'll have to stay in here. The cold could kill her," Rutz said. "You don't want to deliver a corpse."

After being with the men for a total of six days, I knew all their names.

Namir, their large leader said, "The Ixian patrols target the shelters, especially this far north."

"Opal has papers," Devlen said.

"But will she cooperate?" Namir asked.

"She has so far."

"But she hasn't had the chance to misbehave. With Ixian soldiers here, she could get us all arrested." Namir frowned.

"Put the gag back on her and I'll watch her," Rutz offered.

"No way. She's more likely to behave with me," Shen said.

The other two men watched the exchange with interest. Yannis, the man who wore his woolen cap all the time, seemed tense, as if ready to fight. Something about him nagged at me as if I had seen him before. I checked his shadow, but it matched his shape. Owin's dark brown eyes sparkled with anticipation as his gaze swept my body.

"*I'll* ensure she cooperates." Devlen laid a possessive hand on my shoulder, bringing me closer to him.

From the placement of his fingertips, I understood his warning. All he had to do was squeeze and I would be in agony.

When it was time to sleep, Devlen lay on the cot with me. I flinched away.

"Would you rather share with one of the boys?" he asked, whispering in my ear.

I relented and he pulled me close. His chest against my back and his arm around my waist.

"Just like the good old days. Perhaps?" His hand moved downward.

I grabbed it and lifted his arm off me. "No."

He put it back around my waist. "You're causing trouble," he said with a gruff tone. "The boys are getting antsy."

"Do we have to travel with them?" I asked.

He remained quiet for a moment. "It's the safest way to get you north, but in a few days they will turn west. Unless you'll volunteer to play—"

"No."

"Then we'll strike out on our own tomorrow."

I listened as Devlen's breathing slowed and his arm around my waist relaxed. My thoughts whirled. He could have given me to the boys—I was defenseless—but he didn't. Why not? He was a murdering, power-hungry

Warper, who enjoyed torturing people. I thought back to the room in the cabin and realized he didn't enjoy the torture. In fact, his whole posture radiated his distaste. I hadn't noticed before when I was writhing in pain—a hard time to be objective. The same could be said about the time I had spent in the tent. Looking back at his actions, I sensed he performed his job without emotion, and without touching me in any inappropriate place. Odd.

My thoughts turned to his comments about Ulrick. However much I resisted the notion, he had been right about my feelings toward Ulrick. I had kept my distance even when I knew Ulrick desired me.

I tried to justify my actions with Devlen. But in my heart, I couldn't say for sure if I would have stuck to my decision the previous night and made love to the real Ulrick. I had to acknowledge the fact that it was Devlen I had been drawn to—not Ulrick. I hoped Ulrick was really safe from harm. And I hoped I would live through this ordeal, so I could explain everything to him, and apologize.

Various plans to escape, to fight and to trick formed in my mind, but all of them led nowhere because I didn't have enough information. I would have to wait and see what developed, but the tightness around my chest eased a bit. At least I had a few reactions planned, so if a particular situation arose, I wouldn't hesitate.

Eventually I drifted into sleep. Snow-filled dreams swirled. I didn't need the potion as we drew closer to the ice sheet. Details of Icefaren Station sharpened and I could see the scratches on the rocky sides of the pit. A snow cat crouched at the edge, its white coat invisible against the snow. The predator moved away. Its sleek muscles capable of incredible power and speed. Snow cats were almost impossible to hunt. All their senses were heightened to such a degree a hunter couldn't even get within bow-and-arrow range. The Commander of Ixia was the only known person to kill one.

My dream followed the creature. About four feet long and three feet high, the snow cat circled the buildings of the station before heading west. The landscape seemed vast and flat until I viewed it through the snow cat's eyes. Then ridges of ice and mounds of snow were visible. And a den, filled with six other cats. The heat from their bodies welcoming. Farther inside the white walls turned to gray. A small cave with a pool of water. The cat stopped to drink. At the bottom of the pool rested one of my glass animals, pulsing with a muddy red light. Gede's prison. The Story Weaver turned Warper. Devlen's teacher.

I jerked awake.

"What did you see?" Devlen asked. His splayed hand rested on my stomach. Fingertips near pain spots.

"A pit. Buildings." I could tell him where the prison was. Seven snow cats, more than adequate guards.

"The glass prison?"

"Near the pit. That's why it called to me. If they dig any wider, they will find it."

"Who is there?"

"Nobody now, but something is being mined from the pit. Probably during the warmer seasons." The truth.

He moved his hand away. I remembered to breathe. Weak sunlight lit the shelter. I stood and stretched my stiff muscles while Devlen stirred the fire to life. Two of Namir's men woke, but Namir and the others came in from outside, bringing a cold blast of air with them.

"Everything's covered with ice," Namir said. "We're going to need a chisel to break up the sand covering her hidey-hole. It's gonna be hard smoothing it out."

"Since you're so worried about being caught with her," Devlen said, "we'll travel on our own a few days earlier than planned, and you can make your delivery without trouble."

Rutz and Shen glanced at each other, then at Namir.

"Well…me and the boys been talking." Namir hooked his thumb in his belt near a sword.

I couldn't remember if he always wore a sword or not.

"We're a little concerned about your girl," Rutz said.

Owin and Yannis joined them. Knives and swords that I hadn't noticed before hung from belts.

"And we've grown fond of the little girl. Don't want to see her hurt," Shen said. "Looks to us like she doesn't want to be with you."

"I assure you, gentlemen, she's quite content with my company." Devlen stood with his sword in hand.

"We think she would be safer with us." Namir drew his weapon.

"Since we disagree. Let's ask her. Opal, who would you rather be with?" Devlen kept his tone neutral.

I had a choice. Stay with the Warper or go with the men. Devlen's pain was horrible. Rape was horrible. A choice of two horrors. As Leif would say, "Yippee for me." But with five against one, would I really have a choice?

"Thank you for your concern. I—"

The shelter's door banged open. An Ixian soldier entered. In a heartbeat, the weapons returned to their holders. Devlen yanked my sleeves down to cover the cuffs.

The big soldier wore black and orange—Military District 8's colors. Three more men followed him inside. He eyed us with suspicion. "Something wrong?" he asked.

"Perhaps you know the answer, Lieutenant," Devlen said. "I said General Rasmussen has three daughters, but my friend insists he has two. Who's right?"

"Neither. The General has one daughter and twin boys." The Lieutenant's concern disappeared as Namir's men laughed.

"My wife was right after all." Devlen draped an arm around my shoulder.

Another soldier entered. "The wagons are clean," he said to the Lieutenant.

"Of course they are," Namir said, sounding offended, "special delivery for MD-1."

"Papers, please." The Lieutenant inspected each one with care. "Why are you traveling with these merchants?"

he asked me. His eyes were a light blue and small white curls poked out from under his wool cap.

I stared at the soldier. He seemed familiar, and he presented me with a chance to cause trouble and escape from Devlen. A chance to get everyone arrested and hope they didn't kill me right away. Should I take the chance?

"We're not with these merchants, sir," Devlen said. "Just sharing the shelter. My wife and I are on our way home from visiting relatives."

"I didn't ask you. Ma'am?"

29

IF I TOLD the Ixian soldier I was a hostage, we would be arrested and two scenarios could happen from there. Devlen would claim I was a magician and I would be executed without hesitation. Or they would listen to my story and confirm my connection with Liaison Yelena through one of Valek's corps.

Valek's corps. Of course.

"We met these men last night, sir. My husband and I are returning home from my parents' house," I said. The tension in Devlen's arm eased.

The Lieutenant handed my papers back to me. "You'll want to hurry. A big blizzard is coming. I can feel it. You have three, maybe four days at most. Perhaps these merchants can take you north with them?"

"It would be our pleasure," Namir said.

Right back where we started. I would have laughed at the ironic twist if the Ixians hadn't been with us. The soldiers weren't in any hurry to part ways, either. They traveled with us to the border of MD-1. The Lieutenant guided his horse alongside the lead wagon, talking with Namir and Devlen as if killing time.

I sat on the second wagon as far away from Rutz as possible. His extra-wide smile when he had patted the seat next to him made my insides feel queasy. Glancing behind me, I counted the three other wagons. Shen leered and waved. Bile pushed up my throat, but I focused on the man driving the last wagon.

Now I knew why Yannis wore his woolen cap all the time. Most people knew Janco, one of Valek's second-in-commands, was missing the lower half of his right ear. And it wouldn't be wise for these merchants or Devlen to suspect that Yannis was really Janco in disguise. I had put it together when I recognized the Lieutenant as Janco's partner, Ari.

They both had been at the Warper battle when Yelena defeated the Fire Warper. I had met them briefly after crafting the prisons for the souls. Janco had joked and called me the glass warden.

I swung my attention forward. Ari and Janco were obviously part of an undercover operation, and I hadn't wanted to jeopardize it. Janco knew about my predicament, yet he kept quiet when his partner showed up. I would just have to sit tight.

A wave of relief passed through the men when the Ixian soldiers headed west. We crossed into MD-1 without any trouble. Namir took the Lieutenant's warning about the coming storm to heart. He pushed the caravan farther than usual, stopping late into the night.

At least there was one person on my side. Five against two seemed better odds than six against one. Plus Janco's skills with the sword were legendary. He wouldn't be Valek's second unless he could fight.

I worried about when Janco needed to follow Namir, leaving me and Devlen alone again. Once we arrived at Icefaren Station, how would I find Kade? Pangs of nervousness echoed in my chest. I suppressed my turmoil back into my glass heart.

The storm also proved to be a good distraction, especially since Namir promised to wake everyone well before dawn. The men collapsed into bed without a word about my situation. Although Devlen insisted on sharing my cot again, I was able to endure his touch by noting Yannis's proximity.

The next night Devlen and Namir held an intense discussion out of earshot. Devlen's amused smile and hearty laugh stabbed through me. The chumminess couldn't be to my benefit. Devlen confirmed my unease when he joined me, sliding under the covers.

"I have a surprise for you," he whispered.

I tensed. "What is it?"

"Namir's delivery is to Icefaren Station. He can take us there."

"But I didn't see anyone." Mixed emotions rolled through me. Glad Yannis would be close, but scared about the other boys.

"Did you see inside the buildings?"

"No." And that would also explain about the blood-stained snow. If it had happened during the hot or cooling season, the snow would have covered the stain by now.

"Well then," he said. Discussion over.

As I considered this new information, a bit of hope bloomed. Miners at the station meant more people and potential allies.

The next two days followed without incident. We reached the ice sheet as fat snowflakes drifted down. A blanket of dark gray clouds sealed the sky, allowing a pale half-light through. Full darkness would descend by early afternoon.

According to Namir, it could snow for a full day before the killing winds came. The men hurried to switch the wagons' wheels for wooden skids, making sleds. Dogs were exchanged for the horses.

"No stops until we reach the station," Namir said.

"How long?" Devlen asked.

"Four hours if we don't hit any surprises."

I asked, "Surprises?"

"Snow cats, crevasses, ridges, or if the winds start early." Namir stared off to the west. "Bad timing."

I couldn't agree more.

The trip to the station turned into an ordeal. Big snowflakes soaked into our cloaks, and getting a sled full of sand over ridges involved a lot of muscle from everyone, including me. Each hour of effort meant I drew closer to the station, and I remained the only person not to be too excited by the sight of a cluster of wooden buildings in the distance.

When we arrived, no one braved the weather to come out and greet us. By the time we stored the supplies in the shed and fed the dogs, the wind had increased. Those fluffy flakes became projectiles, stinging exposed skin. Rolling waves of snow encompassed us like a fog and visibility shrank. For once, I was glad of Devlen's guiding hand on my elbow. Snow blindness took on a whole new meaning.

We tumbled into the main building like an invading army—shouts and curses and stamping feet, surprising the occupants.

I guess I should have known. Should have learned not to be shocked by anything and anyone. But no. My mouth gaped and my thoughts scattered.

Sir and Tal argued with Namir. By Sir's tone, I guessed our arrival was unexpected.

"You're not due for another week. And the last time you came, you led the Stormdancer right to us," Sir said to Namir in anger. "Who did you bring this time?"

They both looked at Devlen with expectation. An explanation was in order.

A rush of movement to my left and I was slammed into the wall. Fists bunched in my cloak and my feet no longer touched the floor.

Tricky. Pure fury burned in his eyes, and I feared for my life. He pulled me toward him and then shoved me back against the wall. My head banged hard enough to blur my vision as pain ringed my neck.

More shouts. Yannis and Devlen yanking on Tricky's shoulders. He dropped me and I huddled on the floor, thinking about my stupidity. How could I save Kade and Ulrick when I couldn't even save myself?

Then I began to understand Tricky's hoarse yells.

"Bitch…has…to…die." He struggled against four other men. "Nothing…nothing left. She stole all my…magic… let me go."

Devlen's fingers dug into Tricky's collarbone. In moments, the big man slumped to the floor, unconscious.

For a few heartbeats, the men panted and regained their breaths. I counted them. Namir and his three men, Devlen, Sir, Tricky, Tal—the traitor—and Crafty. Yannis hung near me. No Kade or Varun. Ten against two. No way.

"Who the hell are you?" Sir demanded of Devlen.

"Devlen, and I can prove it."

"An illusion?" Crafty asked. She was the only other magician in the room.

"Blood magic." Devlen explained about switching souls with Ulrick. "And I brought you a present."

Grabbing me by the arm, he yanked me to my feet.

"We already know the sand recipe," Tal said in a dismissive tone. "Ash has been making orbs for weeks and shipping them to us." He gestured to Namir.

"But she's the only other person who knows it. Right

now the Stormdancers don't have anyone with that knowledge." Devlen smiled. "I need her to help me, after that, she's *all* yours."

Sir's eyes gleamed with sudden understanding as cold calculation caused him to dance with glee. "And she'll be very useful with a certain stubborn Stormdancer. Especially with this blizzard. He can fill all the orbs for us."

"It's too soon," Tal said. "The full energy of the storm won't be on us until tomorrow."

"Then there's plenty of time to convince him," Sir said.

"I can help with that," Devlen said. "I'll only need a few hours."

Horror swept through me, crushing my bones into powder. Kade was here. And they planned to use me to make Kade help them.

"Take her in the back," Sir said. "Next to the Stormdancer. Let them get reacquainted."

Tal carried a torch and led the way as Devlen pulled me along. I exchanged a glance with Yannis. Wait, I mouthed to him, hoping there would be an opportunity to use him later.

The back ended up being a storeroom. New locks gleamed on the thick door. Inside the room, barrels littered the floor and piles of burlap sacks rested against the walls. A few empty orbs rested on a table. No windows and no fireplace, yet the one stone wall might be the backside of a hearth. I felt a bit of heat when I passed it. The torchlight swung over a net-covered bundle.

"Over here," Tal said. He pointed to a pair of manacles dangling from long chains attached to the ceiling.

My metal cuffs wouldn't fit inside, so Devlen removed them. I had a second of relief before my raw wrists were snapped into the manacles. He pocketed the small silver key and surveyed my new predicament. My feet didn't touch the floor so Devlen moved a few sacks under me until I could stand.

"No sense making you suffer yet," he said. "Perhaps your friend will be reasonable and you won't suffer at all."

Tal had gone over to the bundle and kicked it. "Wake up. We have a surprise for you."

The net-covered bundle groaned and rolled over. Kade appeared between the netting. I bit my lip to keep from crying out. He had been beaten. Bloody welts and huge purple bruises marked his jaw. His hands and feet were hog-tied behind him.

Tal gestured to me. Kade turned his head and met my gaze. He closed his eyes for a moment as if enduring a wave of pain.

The traitor watched him with a gloating satisfaction. "She's special to you, isn't she? You won't let her get eaten by a snow cat like you did Varun. Will you?"

Kade said nothing. He switched his attention to Devlen—he saw only Ulrick, though. Disappointment and chagrin touched his eyes before he stared at the men with determination.

His stubborn resolve gave me an idea. Why not have him dance for these men? He would be allowed out of the null shield net. Given access to his powers. But I had to make it seem as if I didn't want him to do it.

I said, "Don't give in. They won't kill me."

Tal moved toward me, raising his fist. Devlen intercepted him. "Your crude methods won't work." He rummaged in his pack until he found one of his clamps.

I couldn't stop my cry of alarm.

"Hold her still." Devlen instructed Tal where to hold me to immobilize my right leg.

I struggled, not about to make it easy. "Don't give in," I yelped when he found the horrid spot and positioned the clamp. "They won't kill me."

"There are worse things than death," Devlen said as he tightened the screw. "We'll give him a few hours to think it over."

Once the clamp pressed into my leg, my ability to form coherent words dissolved as my world shrank to a single intolerable sensation—worse than death.

When the pain stopped, I reconnected to the world.

Devlen stood before me. "Good news. Your Stormdancer decided to cooperate. But you'll have to hang out here for a while. At least until the storm blows over."

He moved aside to let Shen and Rutz build up a pile of sacks under me. Enough so I could lie down and still be attached to the ceiling.

"The boys are very concerned about your welfare,"

Devlen said. "I think they're hoping you'll show your gratitude."

Rutz rubbed against me as he positioned another bag. I jerked away.

"They even offered to help convince the Storm-dancer, because they thought my methods too harsh." Devlen swept his arm out, pointing toward Kade.

Kade had risen to his knees. He was pressed against the net as far as he could go. If it hadn't been attached to the wall, I guessed he would have been next to me.

"Perhaps they are harsh, but they are effective. No one expected him to give in so easily," Devlen said. "I have not failed yet."

The three men left, taking the light with them. After the locking sounds ceased, I lay there and tried to put my thoughts into words. The wind howled through the rafters. My sweat-dampened clothes turned icy on my skin.

"I never did like him," Kade said in the darkness.

"He's not Ulrick. He's a Warper." I explained about the blood magic.

"I trusted you to stay safe. Did Ul—Devlen trick you into coming here?" Kade asked.

"I actually led him here."

No response except shuffling sounds as Kade moved into a more comfortable position.

"Why?" he asked.

"So I could rescue you."

He laughed, but it was a strained, incredulous sound.

"I know what you're thinking," I said. "It looks bad—"

"Bad? Watching you tortured for hours was the worst thing I've endured in my entire life. My sister's death... was quick. She didn't suffer."

"What about Varun?" Tal had mentioned him being eaten.

"I agreed to work for them as soon as they threatened to hurt him. When Varun heard about his brother's and sister's death, he flew into a rage and attacked Sir. He even managed to escape, but they found the bloodstained snow and evidence a snow cat had gotten to him before he left the compound." Kade's voice cracked. "Once he was gone, I was free to refuse them. But now... You said not to give in. They wouldn't kill you, but I couldn't stand..."

"You did the right thing, Kade. I was counting on you to give in."

"Then why didn't you ask me to, like Varun did?"

"Because I wanted you to see that death is better than Devlen's torture. So you won't hesitate to do the right thing."

"What do you want me to do?" Kade asked in alarm.

I drew in a deep breath. "When you go out into the storm, I want you to use the storm's energy to rip apart the buildings, scatter everyone to the four winds, and—" I steeled myself for his reaction "—to kill me."

"Absolutely not. I could use the storm's force to help us escape."

"No. They'll have me close so if even an errant wind comes, they'll hurt me."

A pause. "You said they won't kill you. Why not?"

Time for a confession. "Devlen needs me. I can find his mentor's prison, which he desires. And the truth is...I'll tell him. I can't...I'm too weak to resist. A few sessions of his torture and I'll do anything. *Anything.* I'm not proud about it. It's just a fact."

"Opal, you're not—"

"Let me finish." The howling of the wind turned shrill as the storm approached. They would come for him soon. I lay on the sacks, and, for once, I knew my course of action was the right choice.

"With me...dead..." Despite my decision, the word was difficult to say. "...there is only one person left who knows the locations of the prisons. I'm no longer a liability. No other Warper can use me to find them."

"A noble sacrifice, but you'll have to figure out another plan. I'm not going to kill you."

"You want Devlen to torture me? Get what he wants and become a powerful Warper?" Anger fueled my words. "That's all I am. Someone to use. Alea used me, Yelena used me, and now Devlen. And they do it because I let them. I want it to stop. I won't be useful to anyone when I'm dead." I screamed with the wind, releasing all my pent-up fury and frustrations.

"Feel better now?"

"A little."

"Good. I don't want anyone to use you, Opal. I don't want to see you hurt. I would love to tear them apart with the storm's force. But I'm too weak." His voice trailed off.

"Once the net's off you should have enough energy."

"I didn't mean…" He huffed. "Time for a weather analogy. I don't have the strength to be more creative. Opal, you arrived in my life like an unwelcome hot-season squall. After my sister died, I just wanted to languish in the sun and be left alone. But no, you wouldn't let me. You blocked the sun and pelted me with your raindrops of curiosity and empathy and intelligence. And you blew out of my life as fast as you arrived—"

"But you told—"

"Quiet until I'm finished." He paused. "I should have been glad you were gone, but I found myself missing the turbulence. When I saw you at the Keep with Ulrick, I convinced myself you were better off with him, and I didn't need the heartache of losing someone I loved again. I managed to hold on to that conviction until today.

"No. I won't do anything to endanger you, because I'm being selfish this time. There will be an opportunity for you to escape, and I'll hold out hope. Because without you in my life, I might as well let the storm take me, too."

"I thought… You made it clear…" Logic dribbled from my mind. Deep cracks snaked through my glass heart. It broke apart.

I had known what to do. It had made sense. I wouldn't have left any regrets behind. But now… "Kade, I can't—"

"I know I hurt you and I understand if you no longer feel the same toward me. But I'm not changing my mind."

Chained to a ceiling, recovering from torture, staring at a bleak future and yet I managed to find an instant of joy. Kade had been my choice from the moment on the beach when he handed me Kaya's orb. I wished I had trusted myself, held on to hope and waited for him.

"Opal?"

"My feelings for you haven't changed. I just lied to myself for a while. But now... Damn it, Kade, you've given me a reason to live."

"How is that bad?"

"My plans worked so much better when I thought you didn't want me. I don't have any other ideas on how to get us out of this."

"You're smart, Opal. You'll figure it out."

Kade's words matched his sister's exactly. They both had such confidence in me. Perhaps it was time I proved myself worthy and had confidence in myself. Time to stop moping over Devlen's trick. He romanced me. Plain and simple. I fell for him and probably would still be with him if he hadn't revealed his true self. Another fact I wasn't proud of, but I can't change the past. My thoughts reviewed all the dumb and tragic mistakes I had made.

Yelena's words, *You can't let the past ruin your future,* had just been words to repeat before. The past shouldn't be forgotten. It should be used as a guide for future situations and not used as a reason to avoid making difficult decisions. There was always a choice.

I focused on my abilities. So far, I tricked Devlen

into coming here. I had discovered who made the fake diamonds. Tricky could no longer access the power source because of me.

My goals were simple. Save Kade, save myself and rescue Ulrick. I hoped Devlen hadn't lied about him being safe and sound. With the possibility of Kade in my future, I had a reward. Now all I needed was a plan.

"If I manage to figure something out, you have to promise me one thing?"

"I promise." His content tone made me smile.

"Don't you want to know what the promise is?"

"Tell me later."

30

DEVLEN WOKE ME from a light doze. He held a clamp in one hand and a knife in the other. He had changed his clothes and smelled of soap. "The fun begins," he said as Sir and Tal came for Kade.

They untied his hands and feet, but left the netting draped around him until Crafty entered the storeroom. She pulled the net off him. Sir and Tal drew their weapons and stepped back as the Stormdancer stood.

Crafty said, "I have a null shield around him."

Kade rubbed the blood back into his arms and legs. His focus never left Devlen. The Warper positioned a clamp on my left arm, twisting the screw until the device was secured enough to stay put without causing me pain.

"Crafty will escort you outside. As soon as the null shield is dropped, you're to fill the orbs, and teach her how to dance," Sir said.

"How many orbs?" Kade asked.

"I'm sure the great and wonderful Kade can fill at least five," Tal said. He picked up five empty ones from the table, leaving two behind.

"*If* Crafty can dance, five will be fine," Kade said. "*If* she can't, I can only do three." His tone remained flat.

I eyed the extra orbs. Potential weapons? Not if no one attacked me with magic. Besides, I couldn't reach them.

I cried out as Devlen dug his thumb into my hip. "Deviate from your job in any way and—"

"Save the threat. I said I would cooperate. Let's go." Kade led the way from the room with a sense of purpose in his stride as if he were the one in charge. Crafty, Sir and Tal hurried after him.

After a few uncomfortable moments alone with Devlen, Tricky brought in Devlen's pack. The day turned from bad to worse. Kaya's orb sounded agitated and upset, emitting a high-pitched keening louder than the blizzard's winds.

"We are going to try an experiment," Devlen said, digging into his bag. "I know how much you like them." He withdrew a knife.

"Let me see…somewhere her boyfriend won't notice." Devlen pushed my sleeve up, exposing my elbow. "Sit up. I want your arm bent."

I struggled into a sitting position. My wrists ached from being manacled.

"Find the bowl," Devlen ordered Tricky.

The storm winds shook the rafters. Tricky glanced up

before searching in Devlen's pack. "Your Stormdancer better hurry," he said as he removed a wooden bowl from the bag.

"Hold it under her elbow." Devlen rested the knife's blade against my forearm.

The inside of the bowl was stained dark brown. Unease twisted around my heart.

Once the bowl was in position, Devlen cut a long gash in my arm. I gasped as fire raced along my skin. Blood welled and flowed, splattering the bowl with crimson drops.

When the bleeding stopped, Tricky asked Devlen, "More?"

"No. We'll start small. I don't want to waste blood if it doesn't work."

"It better work." Tricky stared at me with murder in his eyes.

"Even though her powers are weak, blood magic is very powerful. I will inject her blood into your skin and we'll see if that helps you reclaim any of your magic. There are bandages in my pack. Cover her wound and join me when you're done. I need a fire to complete the ritual."

"What about her? Sir said to stay—"

"She isn't going anywhere. Let her alone. Besides—" Devlen cocked his head as if listening to the storm "—the winds are dying down. I suspect you will have plenty of orbs to appease your General friend." He left the room, taking my blood with him.

Tricky dug through the pack, removing items as he rummaged. He laid Kaya's orb and a pair of Devlen's pants on the ground, scattering a few other things. Finding the bandages, he quickly stuffed most of the items back in.

He delighted in causing me pain as he cleaned and wrapped my cut and pulled my sleeve down.

"If this blood magic works, then I get to siphon the Stormdancer's power. Once he teaches Crafty, we won't need him anymore." He laughed at my dismay. "I don't trust you in here by yourself." Tricky put his hand on the screw.

"Don't—"

He tightened the clamp. Pain dominated all my senses, but I clung to the knowledge that, in his haste, Tricky missed the little silver key.

My world returned the moment the pressure abated. Devlen held the clamp. His mouth twisted in displeasure as he scanned the others in the storeroom. Sir and Tal carried Kade. Exhaustion pulled on him and he offered no resistance as they bound his hands and wrapped him in the null shield net. He appeared to fall asleep the moment he was pushed to the floor.

"Can you dance the storms?" Sir asked Crafty.

"Yes. But with two of us, we get more orbs."

"He'll eventually cause trouble." Sir turned to Devlen. "What about this blood magic Tricky's so excited about? He has regained some power. Does that mean if you transferred the Stormdancer's powers to Tricky, he could dance in the storms?"

Devlen's blood magic experiment had worked. However, this bit of news didn't spark a brilliant plan for escape.

"He should have the magic. He will need to learn how to use it. But Tricky must follow my orders or else I'll keep the Stormdancer's power for myself." Annoyance colored the last few words.

"Oh, come on." Sir gestured to me. "It was a measure of revenge for what she did to him."

"What if she had a connection with the Stormdancer and he felt her distress while harnessing the storm's energy? All deals would have been off and he would have ripped this place to shreds."

"You cut her on the arm," Sir shot back.

"A moment of pain."

"Didn't matter anyway. He danced and we've cornered the market!" Sir's eyes lit up. "We'll send the full orbs back with Namir and his crew after the next storm. He can sell them in Sitia. Factories outside the Stormdance lands will be willing to pay lots of gold for them. Since the Stormdancer Clan can't make their own orbs, we can sell our empty ones to their clan. The blizzard died before reaching MD-1, so the General has his proof we've done the job and we'll have even more gold."

Sir left in good spirits to make his plans. Devlen turned to me.

"Why don't *you* want Kade's power?" I asked.

"If I didn't help Tricky, he would have found a way to kill you. I need you alive for now. One more storm and then you *will* keep your promise and find the prison."

"One more?"

"These northern blizzards come in pairs about a day apart. I waited almost five years to find my mentor. I can wait a little more." When Devlen turned to leave, he stopped. "What's this?" He bent over and picked up the key. "Where did this come from?"

All plans for using the key vanished. I'd admit the plans were vague and dependent on many factors, but still it could have been useful. No reason to lie, I told him about Tricky's mess.

"Must have been frustrating, knowing it was there and unable to get to it."

"You want me to admit it so you can feel a perverse pleasure from my aggravation?"

His gaze flattened. "I take *no* pleasure in this. I wanted to be Ulrick the entire time, tricking you into finding the prison." He stepped closer, lowering his voice. "Stay with *me* after we free my mentor. I lied to Sir. I intended you to be my Kirakawa sacrifice. Instead, I'll teach you blood magic. We'll increase your limited powers, and you won't have to worry about being at anyone's mercy again."

I stared at him, seeking deceit. He seemed sincere in his offer and I was unable to match the man before me and the man who frequently tortured me. The thought of not being at anyone's mercy, especially his, was tempting. "I don't trust you. You have no qualms with lying. Even if I agree to stay with you, you'll probably use me for the ritual anyway."

"Everyone lies when it suits their needs, and everybody uses people, too. It's in our nature."

I looked at Kade's inert form. "Kade and Ulrick didn't."

He flicked his hand in anger. "Does it make you feel better to lie to yourself?"

I didn't answer.

"It must. Because Kade used you when he gave you his orb to keep safe. It's a dangerous object to have lying around."

"He *asked* me. Big difference."

"If the orb scared you, would you have said no?" He didn't wait for my reply. "Of course not. Ulrick was right, you're a nice accommodating doormat."

"He didn't say that."

"Not to you. You claim Ulrick never used you. His connection to the Keep and the Master Magicians was through you. Why do you think he pretended to care and to act as your bodyguard? He worried he would be sent home if something happened to you."

Devlen tortured me without even touching my body. But I remained stubborn. "You're lying again."

He pointed to his temple. "I've seen his memories and I've felt his emotions. He had no regrets when he swapped you for magic."

My reaction must have betrayed the turmoil in my mind. A smug half smile quirked his lips. "I'll let you think over my offer."

An automatic refusal pushed from my chest, but I

clamped down on the impulse. Instead, I asked, "Since you consider me an accommodating doormat who lies to herself, why would you offer me more power?"

A rush of emotions, too fast for me to decipher, crossed his face. "You've endured more than anyone else. Usually I only need one session and the person is mine, yet you suffered a long time before giving in to me. I admire your inner strength and your courage." A wistful lilt stole into his voice. "I enjoyed our time together, and I know you did, too. Think about what I'm willing to do for you, and, this time, don't lie to yourself." He strode from the room.

I already had finished deluding myself. I knew who I desired, and it wasn't Devlen. But I wouldn't tell him. Not yet. Pretending to go with him might be the only chance I would have to escape.

Once I was sure Devlen wouldn't return to the storeroom for a while, I wiggled up on my knees then gained my feet on the pile of sacks. I remained attached to the ceiling, but now my hands could reach my waistband. It was a relief having my arms down. The breaks Devlen gave me for eating and such were never long enough.

My fingers sought the glass spider and after a panicked moment, I pulled it from where I had wedged it. But what to do with it? Kade lay in an exhausted sleep and another blizzard was on its way. Sir would want him to dance in the next storm and he should be rested by then. The best time to attempt an escape was right as the next storm hit. Kade would have the storm's full power at his disposal.

I mulled over my logic. Unfortunately that was when Sir and the others were extra careful and on guard. Tucking the spider back into its hiding space, I sat. Ideas formed and dissipated when exposed to reason.

Eventually, I lay down, drifting off to sleep. A muted click woke me. The door swung open, revealing a wedge of firelight and the outline of a man before shutting without a sound. I drew in a breath and prepared to scream if it was one of Namir's men looking for fun. My eyes strained in the darkness, but I lost sight of the silent intruder.

A hand clamped over my mouth, muffling my outcry.

"Shhhh. It's me, Yannis...er...Janco," he whispered in my ear.

I quit struggling and he removed his hand.

"I don't have much time. Even though it's the middle of the night, Devlen watches us closely. The man doesn't blink an eye over torture, but he's very protective of you," he huffed. "So what's the plan?"

"Isn't the Ixian army coming to our rescue? Your partner?"

"This was a discovery mission. Top secret. Ari can't get here until a day after the blizzards anyway, but by then Sir and Devlen planned to bleed your Stormdancer dry." He shuddered. "All this magic gives me the creeps."

No choice but to figure it out on my own. I thought fast. What did I do best? Looking at the solution as a series of glassmaking steps, I created a list of needs. Need a storm, need an orb and need the freedom to move.

"Janco, can you bring the orb from Devlen's pack in here when they come for Kade tomorrow?"

"The swirly green one he just sold to Sir?"

"Yes. Toss it to Kade when I give the signal. Do they have more orbs for the storms?"

"Yeah. There were a ton of glass balls hidden under the tarps in the wagons, that's what Namir has been delivering. The sand and lime are just decoys."

"What's the pit for?"

"General Kitvivan's started a mining operation up here in the hot season. That's one of the reasons why I'm here. To see what he's been mining."

I knew the answer. "Diamonds. To pay Sir for this operation in taming the blizzards."

"Makes sense. The Commander's not going to be happy about all this." He paused. "What else?"

"Can you get me a key for these cuffs?"

"No, but I can unlock them for you." He pulled a few picks from his pocket, reached up and the manacles popped open in seconds.

"Handy skill."

"Since you have the same propensity for getting into trouble, you should ask Yelena to teach you."

"Assuming I live through this." I touched my raw wrists.

"Think positive. Anything else?"

"When and if things begin to happen, don't kill Devlen."

"Why not?"

"I need his body," I said, thinking about Ulrick stuck in Devlen's real body. I didn't know if there was even a way to switch them back. I'd worry about it later.

"Magic." Janco spat the word out. "Twisted."

"I need a knife. Do you have one?"

"Always." He handed me his switchblade. "Yours."

I triggered the blade.

"You do know how to use it, right?" A hint of worry laced his voice.

"Think positive."

He laughed and slipped from the room without another sound.

I waited for a few minutes before sliding off my sack pile. The thin line of firelight from underneath the door gave off just enough light to illuminate black shapes. I wove my way through them and almost tripped over Kade's net-covered form.

"Kade?" I whispered. A sleepy mumble. I cut the ropes around his wrists and ankles. Then sawed through the net.

Without warning, his hands seized my shoulders. He rolled over me, pinning me to the ground.

"It's me," I said.

"Opal?"

"Don't sound so surprised."

"Sorry." He released me.

I finished cutting the net, and peeled it away from his body.

"Ah. Better." Kade stretched.

"Don't get used to it." I explained my plan.

"What happens if Crafty tries to trap you in a null shield? Can you siphon that?"

"Don't know, but if she's focused on me, you should be free."

"Should be. Opal, no offense, but this plan has a lot of holes in it."

I challenged him. "You have any better ideas?"

He sucked in a breath then released it all at once. "No."

I rearranged the net around Kade and he pretended his hands and feet were still tied. Tal had left two empty orbs in the storeroom so I moved them closer to me. I hid the knife in my pocket and palmed my glass spider. Then it was my turn to pretend to be manacled.

The wait was excruciating. Doubts chased worries. Fears followed hope. Impatience warred with the need to conserve energy. The increased keening of the wind didn't help at all. The noise sawed through my body with its icy teeth.

When the door opened, I jumped. But settled my nerves. Hunched on the sack pile, I assumed a dejected and wary posture. Sir, Tal and Crafty entered first, then Devlen and Tricky. I noticed Tricky looked to Devlen as if waiting for permission. Janco hovered in the doorway.

"Time to dance," Sir said. He and Tal bent over Kade. Crafty raised her arms.

"Now," I yelled. I yanked my wrists from the cuffs and broke the glass spider in half. Kade leaped to his feet and tossed the net over Crafty. She yelped in surprise.

Bite Tricky, I ordered the spider.

Jumping from the pile, I grabbed one of the empty orbs. From the doorway Janco threw Kaya's orb at Kade. He caught it in midair.

Janco spun and the clangs of a sword fight rang from the hallway as he blocked the entrance to the room. A snippet of a rhyme, "Five against one is so much fun," hopefully meant Janco kept Namir and his men occupied. He wouldn't last long.

An angry breeze stirred to life. And died.

Devlen smirked. "Now what?" He pointed to Tal and Sir, both had swords mere inches from Kade. His fingers grasping the stopper to Kaya's orb, Kade grimaced with pain.

The spider had disappeared, leaving behind a nasty red welt and a livid man. Crafty found the hole in the net and shrugged it off of her. It landed in a heap.

"Crafty isn't the only one who knows how to work a null shield," Devlen said, breaking the silence. "It was one of the first skills I learned." He considered Kade. "Now if the Stormdancer releases the energy inside his orb while he's caught in a null shield, I'm assuming we'll all die. But I really don't think he wants you to die." He turned to me. "And what are you planning? Unless one of us attacks you with magic, the empty orb is nothing but glass in your hands."

I had miscalculated and underestimated Devlen. Failed. The rings of steel and grunts from the hallway ceased with a curse. Janco came into the room with his hands behind his head. Rutz and Shen following with swords aimed at his back.

"Did I miss the party?" Janco asked.

"Oh no. We're just beginning," Devlen said.

I still held the orb.

Devlen stepped toward me unconcerned.

I could smash it on his head or use a broken shard to cut my throat.

"Back into your chains like a good girl." His manner confident. He expected me to obey without hesitation.

Being an accommodating doormat, I had always listened to him. Not this time. Glass was in my hands. It throbbed with potential.

I reached. Reached toward Devlen and siphoned his magic. The clinks of glass sounded like hail on the windows. He struggled in panic, but to no avail. I pulled until he had nothing left.

Crafty started to move her null shield to encompass me, but I reached for her power before it touched me. Crafty's magic rained into the orb for many minutes until I drained her dry. I turned to Tricky and plucked at his small power. It refused to budge. He grinned with triumph until a gust of wind slammed him into the wall, knocking him unconscious.

I staggered back as Kade used the air to disarm the rest of the men. The realization of what I had done knocked me to my knees.

I didn't channel Devlen's and Crafty's magic.

I stole it. Using my own powers.

Dizziness and exhaustion swirled. Pressing my forehead on the floor, I closed my eyes.

31

I WOKE TO bright sunshine reflecting off the snow. In bed and able to move freely, my day started better than the previous ten. Twenty? Exhaustion weighed on me like a heavy blanket. And from the way his body slumped, I guessed Kade was tired, too. Or it could just be from sleeping in a chair. His head rested on the back, his elbows propped on the arms, hands laced on his stomach and his legs were spread out in front.

"Kade," I said.

He woke. The cuts on his face had scabbed over, and the bruises faded to a grayish-yellow. He shot me a sheepish grin. "I'm not much of a guard, sleeping on the job."

"Guard? What's going on?" I struggled into a sitting position.

"Relax." He pushed me back onto the pillows. "I'm here to guard that you don't get out of bed and to fetch things for you. Are you thirsty?"

"Very."

He poured a glass of water from the pitcher on the night table and handed it to me. I downed it, stopping only when a dagger of ice knifed my forehead.

"Easy. There's plenty of cold water around here."

I glanced around the room. One bed, night table, chair and fireplace. Spartan and warm considering we were on the northern ice sheet.

No longer able to delay the question, I asked, "What happened?"

Kade sobered. "After you…harvested the magic from the magicians, I had to fill three orbs with the energy from the blizzard or risk having the station blown over and buried by snow. When I returned, Janco had secured the others."

"Tell Janco to keep a close eye on Tricky. He still has a small bit of magic." My magic.

Kade said nothing. He refused to meet my gaze, and I sensed he wasn't telling me the whole story. "Spill," I ordered.

"Your orb…" He paused as if trying to find the right words. "Your orb is filled with…with diamonds."

This time I managed to sit up without a struggle. "Diamonds? Are you sure? They could be high-quality glass." Glass made sense.

He didn't respond. Instead he pulled a clear sparkle from his pocket and handed it to me. The diamond burned ice-cold then a vision of Devlen formed in my mind's eye. He wore his own face. I dropped the gem onto the table. Flabbergasted, I couldn't begin to contemplate the ramifications. Why diamonds? I remembered a vague connection between magic and diamonds, but failed to grasp it. Bain Bloodgood would know.

"My suggestion would be to not tell anyone you have this new ability," he said. "Only I know you harvested their powers *without* them attacking you."

Kade rubbed his hands on his legs, then jumped to his feet. "If the Sitian Council finds out…"

"I'm arrested and locked in the Keep's cells until the Council decides what to do with me, which, according to Yelena, would be a long time."

"You've already thought about this."

"Yes. Zitora mentioned the possibility as an exercise in logic. I can't lie about it, Kade. I'll tell Zitora and the other Master Magicians and let them choose how to handle it."

Kade slumped on the edge of my bed. "The right decision."

"You don't look happy about it."

"I'm thinking selfish thoughts. If you're locked up in the Keep's cells, I will have no one again."

"What about Kaya?"

"I've thought about what you said back at the Keep."

"When I called you as thick as a fog bank?"

"Funny, I had forgotten *that* part. But I had plenty of time to consider your words, and your actions these last couple days have taught me much. I'm going to say goodbye to Kaya."

"The right decision."

Before Kade could respond, Janco poked his head into the room.

"Ah, the glass warden's awake. Good! Ari's coming with backup. Should I pretend we barely survived without his help or gloat that we didn't need him at all?"

"Tough decision," I said.

"You can't go wrong with either one," Kade said.

"You guys are *no* fun. I have to go with the gloating. But no mention of that magic stuff. It ruins the effect." Janco rushed off.

Ari arrived with a handful of men. He ignored Janco's smug boasts and proceeded right to the heart of the matter. "What do we do with them?" he asked.

He referred to Sir, Tricky and the others.

"Arrest them. They're here illegally. They used magic. Smuggled goods," Janco said.

"Can they still use their magic?" Ari asked me.

"Only one. The rest have been…neutralized."

"One?"

"Sleeping," Janco said. "Until we figure out what to do with him."

"Tricky's powers are weak, and I don't know what he can do with them," I explained.

"We'll arrest them all and let the Commander decide their fates," Ari said.

"We need to take one with us," I said.

"Which one?"

"Devlen."

"Why?"

"His body and soul don't match." I explained about the blood magic.

"I know I hated magic for a reason," Janco said.

"Congratulations. This is the first time you've had a *valid* reason to hate something," Ari countered. "Remember your campaign against sand?"

"Sand! Horrid little stuff. Gets everywhere. I had a perfectly good argue—"

"Janco." Ari's voice rumbled deep in his throat.

In a heartbeat, Janco switched gears. "Well, this blood magic sounds worse than sand."

"Do you know how to switch them back?" Kade asked. He had been following the conversation with an amused smile.

"I'm not sure." I shuddered, thinking I would need to learn more about blood magic.

"It's easy," Janco said.

We all stared at him, waiting.

"Holy snow cats! You don't know?" His incredulous tone transformed into a huge smirk. He danced a little jig.

As he gloated, I made the connection. His knowledge of magic was limited to his contact with Yelena. "The Soulfinder," I said.

"Righto! Souls switched while you wait." Janco twirled.

Then I would need to rescue Ulrick. I figured Devlen wouldn't help me find him. And what about my feelings for Ulrick? When I had thought he had been injured by his sister, I had realized how much I cared for him.

Even though I know I loved Kade, I owed it to Ulrick and myself to explore our relationship without Devlen's taint. Would Kade help me? As my father would say, only one way to find out.

Kade watched me and I wondered what he thought. I didn't have a chance to ask him until the next day.

We carried Kaya's orb far away from the building and onto the ice pack. Janco warned us to keep an eye out for snow cats. I held an empty orb. Once Kade released the storm's energy and Kaya, he would recapture the storm, but let Kaya go.

"Don't want another blizzard to blow down on MD-1," Kade had said.

Our boots crunched on the new snow and I shivered in my cloak, thinking about hot kilns.

"I understand why General Kitvivan would want to tame the blizzards. They're nasty." Kade's eyes glowed with admiration for the storms. "I would be willing to come here every cold season to help him. Those extra full orbs would be useful, and I'm sure other Storm-dancers would be happy to come along."

"Not me," I said. "Too cold." His words reminded me of my new mission. "Would you be willing to come along with me to rescue Ulrick?"

"Shouldn't you let the authorities deal with Devlen and Ulrick?" Kade asked instead of answering me.

"No. I'm responsible. My relationship with Ulrick put him in jeopardy. I need to find him and talk with him—figure out how I feel."

"Then I would only complicate matters." Kade reached for my free hand. "*You* know my feelings for you and *you* know where I'll be waiting. While I would love to fight for your love in a dramatic duel with lightning bolts flashing, I trust you, Opal. Always have. Always will."

His faith warmed me to my core. "You don't have to fight for my love. You already *have* it. I just need to discover what Ulrick has."

He smiled with confidence, squeezing my hand. "You're a problem solver, Opal. I've no doubt you'll solve this one, as well."

His comment about solving problems reminded me of our first encounter. I had to chuckle. "If you *always* trusted me, then what about when you first met me and stormed off in a huff?"

He laughed. "All right, maybe not *always,* but very, very close. In my defense, you looked twelve years old, and we were desperate for help."

When Kade felt we were far enough from the station, he stopped. I moved away as he cradled Kaya's orb. My thoughts turned to my sister Tula and how I wished I had a chance to say goodbye to her.

Cold air blasted, sending snow into the air to swirl around us. Kaya's joy filled the air. She spun around me for a moment. Her gratitude pulsed in my heart before she vanished. When the snow settled, Kade crouched in the drifts. Remembering my lecture to him about having others to help hold you together as you heal, I embraced him.

He clung to me for a while. Snow thawed under us and soaked into my pants, but I felt warm in his arms.

"You could always try to bribe the Council," Kade said.

"What are you talking about?"

"Give your diamonds to them and maybe they won't lock you in the Keep's cells."

"Being selfish again?"

He nodded.

"They're not my diamonds," I said.

"Really? Then whose are they?"

I didn't have an answer for him. We remained silent for a moment.

He was inches from me. My desire to kiss him pushed away all other thoughts, so I pressed my lips to his. He pulled me closer and heat spread throughout my body. More snow melted underneath us, but I didn't care.

Eventually an icy wind intruded. I broke away from his embrace.

"Shall we continue our *conversation* inside?" Kade asked with a wide grin.

We trudged through the snow, holding hands. "I wish we could just freeze this time together, and all the—" I waved, indicating the future problems that waited for me "—would disappear." It was quite a list, finding Ulrick, switching his soul, convincing the Council *not* to arrest me, discovering how my new powers would affect Sitia.

Kade kept quiet for a while. "This calls for a glass analogy."

I groaned, but he ignored me.

"Life is like molten glass. It flows, it's flexible, it can be molded and shaped and...what do you say? Ah, yes. It holds vast potential. You have a number of uncertainties in your melt right now. But they will always be there in one form or another. Always. Unlike molten glass, life can't be fixed or frozen into a pretty vase and placed on a shelf to gather dust."

"I wouldn't mind a little coating of dust instead of facing the Master Magicians and the Council. What if they just lock me away?"

He stopped and drew me into a tight hug. "They won't. Because you're smart, Opal. You'll figure it out."

"You said the same thing in the storeroom and I almost killed us."

"But you didn't. And that reminds me. What exactly did I promise you?"

I thought back to his description of me, arriving like an unwelcome squall when all he desired was to be left alone. "You promised me that the next time you decide to languish in the sun, you'll take me with you. I'm in desperate need of a vacation and I'm sure you know the best beach for languishing."

He laughed. "There is this beautiful little cove along Bloodgood's coast. White sands, crystal-clear water, but it can get hot during the day."

"Perfect. I hate the cold."

* * * * *

ACKNOWLEDGEMENTS

Thanks go to my husband, Rodney, and my children, Luke and Jenna. For being patient when I need to finish a book, and for not complaining (too much) when I travel to book signings and conventions. Without you three, there would be no books to write.

A special thank-you goes out to my critique partner, Kimberley J. Howe. She rose to the challenge when I hit a dead end and dumped three hundred pages of this book on her, crying for help. Your encouragement, phone calls and comments helped pull this book together.

Huge thanks go to all the hardworking people at MIRA Books. Your enthusiasm and love of books has made working with you a joy. Special kudos to my editor, Mary-Theresa Hussey, whose expert comments greatly improve my stories.

Thanks to my agent, Robert Mecoy, whose help has been invaluable, and to his daughter, Dash, for her wonderful support.

For this book I once again enrolled in a variety of glass classes at the Goggle Works. I would like to thank a quartet of teachers and artists who helped me: Helen Tegeler, Sandra Kaye, Karen Lesniak and Louise Mehaffey. I think I'm addicted to glass.

And a continuing heartfelt thanks to my army of Book Commandos! Your efforts in the field are deeply appreciated! Special mention to those who have gone well above and beyond the call of duty: Suzanne Ledford, Alethea Allarey, Patrice de Avila, Elizabeth Darrach, Jeff Young, Heather Tebbs, Megan Knight, Jamie Perry and Jen Runkle. The Commander would be proud.

AN UNDERCOVER MISSION LEADS TO DANGER, ADVENTURE AND AN IMPOSSIBLE CHOICE...

After siphoning her own blood magic, Opal Cowan has lost her powers and is immune to magic. Now Opal spies through the glass on those with power.

Until spying through the glass *becomes* her new power. Suddenly, her glass pieces flash in the presence of magic. And then she learns of her stolen blood – now she may regain her powers for good...

The third part in the unmissable Glass series

www.miraink.co.uk

THE APPRENTICESHIP IS OVER—NOW THE REAL TEST HAS BEGUN

When word spreads that Yelena is a Soulfinder—able to capture and release souls—people grow uneasy. Then she receives news of a plot rising against her homeland, led by a murderous sorcerer she has defeated before.

Honour sets Yelena on a path that will test the limits of her skills, and the hope of reuniting with her beloved spurs her onward. Yelena will have but one chance to prove herself—and save the land she holds dear.

www.miraink.co.uk

BL_292_FS

THEY DESTROYED HER WORLD. BUT SHE'S THEIR ONLY HOPE...

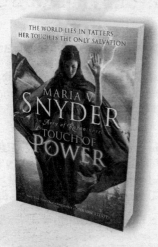

Avry's power to heal the sick should earn her respect in the plague-torn land of Kazan. Instead she is feared and blamed for spreading the plague.

When Avry uses her forbidden magic, she faces the guillotine. Until a dark, mysterious man rescues her from her prison cell. His people need Avry's magic to save their dying prince.

Saving the prince is certain to kill Avry. Now she must choose—use her healing touch to show the ultimate mercy or die a martyr to a lost cause?

HARLEQUIN®MIRA®
www.mirabooks.co.uk

M292_TOP

Read Me. Love Me. Share Me.

Did you love this book? Want to read other amazing teen books for free online and have your voice heard as a reviewer, trend-spotter and all-round expert?

Then join us at **facebook.com/MIRAink** and chat with authors, watch trailers, WIN books, share reviews and help us to create the kind of books that you'll want to carry on reading forever!

Romance. Horror. Paranormal. Dystopia. Fantasy.

Whatever you're in the mood for, we've got it covered.

Don't miss a single word

 twitter.com/MIRAink

let's be friends

 facebook.com/MIRAink

Scan me with your smart phone

 to go straight to our facebook page